THE GOOD, THE BAD AND THE GRINGO

Kae Bahar is a writer and filmmaker. He grew up in Kurdistan under the regime of Saddam Hussein and was arrested and tortured by the secret police at the age of fourteen. With his family's help, he managed to escape to Italy to avoid a second arrest and possible death. Once in Europe, he worked as an actor and produced films for major broadcasters. What kept Kae's hope alive was storytelling and watching films. Most of his films have won multiple awards. *The Good, the Bad, and the Gringo* is his first novel.

For more information: www.jokafilms.com/English/

'*The Good, the Bad, and the Gringo* is a brilliant, touching and eye-opening, beautifully written novel. I was immersed in Merywan's struggle for survival in the harsh realities of 1980s Iraqi Kurdistan from start to end – a must-read for all.'

—**Nahro Zagros**, Editor-in-Chief of *Kurdistan Chronicle*

'It makes me laugh out loud and gasp in horror, too. I think it's really, really special and I feel very excited about it and honoured to read it.'

—**Barbara Marsh**, writer, poet and musician, author of *To the Boneyard* and *Mr Ferndean Takes Stock*

'This is an incredibly difficult and affecting book that will help you understand much about modern-day Iraq and its troubles from the perspective of a normal human who becomes drawn into a pervasive conflict. It's a work of fiction that illuminates the many real horrors faced by brave and resolute people over the years. This is the type of people's history that must be read and understood to have a meaningful perspective when talking or thinking critically about politics and how they affect humanity.'

—**Jon Michael Anzalone**, photographer and author

'The ongoing struggle of the Kurdish people, unknown to many, is adroitly brought into focus through the story of Mery Rashaba. Simultaneously broad in scope, harrowing, and insightful, I found Kae Bahar's novel an unputdownable, exciting read that both moved me and broadened my horizons. An important book and not to be missed.'

—**Katherine Hahn Halbheer**, translator and proofreader

'Kae Bahar tells the story of a 'boygirl' searching for his/her own place in life, and describes the darkness that Iraq and Kurdistan went through during the Saddam era with a luminous language. *The Good, the Bad, and the Gringo* presents the story of individuals in dilemmas, who try to shape their own destiny, despite the harsh realities that surround them. The story flows with fluent and enthusiastic language, reflecting the mood of the protagonist. Each page is more intriguing than the previous one and moves with an increasingly intense pace. Kae Bahar has a unique pen to picture the suffering and the hopes of people.'

—**Burhan Sönmez**, novelist, President of PEN International, author of *Istanbul Istanbul* and *Labyrinth*

The Good, the Bad and the Gringo

Kae Bahar

Afsana Press
London

This new edition first published in 2024
by Afsana Press Ltd, London
www.afsana-press.com

First published under the title *Letters From a Kurd*
in 2014 by Yolk Publishing

All rights reserved
Copyright © Kae Bahar, 2014
Kae Bahar has asserted his right under the Copyright, Designs
and Patents Act, 1988, to be identified as Author of this work.

The Good, the Bad and the Gringo is a work of fiction. All names, characters and events are the products of the author's imagination, and while certain organisations and institutions are mentioned, the characters involved are wholly imaginary. Any resemblance to actual persons, living or dead, is purely coincidental, except for the well-known persons. Places and times may have been rearranged to suit the purposes of the book. The opinions expressed are those of the characters, and should not be confused with the author's.

Typeset by Afsana Press Ltd
Printed and bound in Great Britain by Clays Ltd, Elcograf S.p.A.

A CIP catalogue record for this book is available from the British Library

ISBN paperback: 978-1-7385552-3-9
ISBN e-book: 978-1-7385552-4-6

MIX
Paper | Supporting
responsible forestry
FSC® C018072

To Daya Badri and Bawa Salih, my mother and father,
neither of whom ever read a book

My special thanks go to:

Claudio Von Planta, Brie Burkeman, Isobel Creed, Trudy Gardner, Jeff Gulvin, Deb Wright, Katherine Hahn Halbheer, James Attlee, Truska Sheri, Dave, Steve and Audrey Swindells, Suzanne Ruggi, Miran Dizayee, Andrea Beades, James Godden, Neil Ferguson, Rachel Giaccone, Courttia Newland, Barbara Marsh, Madelene Boberg, Carla Greco, James Hobbs, Phil Dines, Afsana Press and my publishers Aleksandra Markovic and Goran Baba Ali, my wonderful wife Josie Bahar and our children Tashan, Leon and Taro.

I feel very lucky and am grateful to you all. Without you, your kind help and generous support I could not have brought *The Good, the Bad and the Gringo* to life.

Love you all and thank you with all my heart, Kae Bahar.

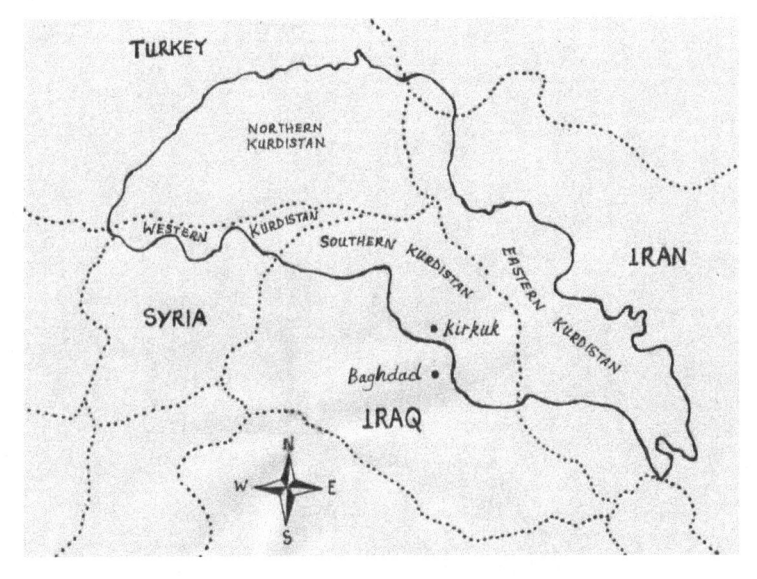

A suggestive map of Kurdistan, drawn by Josie Bahar

Kurdistan, the land of the Kurds, was divided by the British and the French colonial powers shortly after WWI. Ever since, the Kurds have struggled to regain their freedom and self-determination.

I miss my long hair

Somewhere in Iraq, July 1987

I don't exist. Officially I am dead. I was hanged a month ago. There was no court case, no judge, no defence. The decision to end my life was taken by a man I nicknamed the Ugly Arab, He's the head of Saddam's secret police, in my hometown, Kirkuk. My name, Merywan Rashaba, must be filed alongside thousands of others who have been executed in this country, although I would have been given a false age because, even by the twisted standards of Iraq's dictatorship, as a sixteen-year-old boy I am still too young to be hanged. Yet somehow, hanging would have seemed like a blessing, a relief from suffering, an escape from the man who had the power to end my life but then kept me alive only to gratify his disgusting desires.

He is the one person who knows that I am not dead. I have no idea where I am, and since he has locked me in, I have seen nobody else. The only window in this room is blocked, so there are no more days and nights in my life, and the bulb hanging from the ceiling goes out whenever there's a power cut, which is as often as not. I live in the company of a rusty military bed, a smelly blanket, a mattress stained with blood and semen, a bucket from which I drink water, another one that I use instead of a toilet, and a broken wooden chair.

As soon as he brought me here, the Ugly Arab beat me, stripped me of my clothes, sat on the chair watching me, touched himself and then rubbed himself over my shaking body and pushed his filth into me. When he'd satisfied his lust, he dressed and left, taking my clothes.

I was naked, trapped inside my wretched body, humiliated and more alone than I had ever been. Driven by sheer desperation, I pressed the pillow onto my face in a hopeless effort to arrest my breathing, struggling for the courage to kill myself.

'Don't live to die, die to live,' I remembered the sentence, which had been tattooed on the arm of my uncle Hercules. I had seen it so often that I no longer even noticed it, but now it came back to me. I pushed the pillow away, gasping for air.

The Ugly Arab keeps coming back. He lashes me harder with his leather belt and while I cry silently, he jumps on top of me, bites my neck and snarls, 'I will finish you off rat boy and replace you with another bastard Kurd.' I know he will, he has almost succeeded in defeating me, but in this darkest moment of my life I still hope to survive and escape to see you, Gringo, in America.

After his last visit, I kept staring at a couple of cockroaches scavenging around my toilet bucket. Then I laid eyes on the broken chair. On my hands and knees I crawled from the bed. I pulled off one of the chair legs that was already split and whittled it away with my teeth until I had turned one end into a sharp point. I tried it out on the mattress where it stuck like a knife. When he next comes for me, I will wait until he is distracted by his loathsome orgasm and then I will stick the spear into his hairy chest.

Heavy footsteps echo on the concrete floor. The Ugly Arab is back, opening the locks to my prison. Soon I must kill him. If I fail he will kill me, but if I succeed and somehow manage to escape, I will finally leave this doomed country and come to see you in America.

My first letter to Gringo

Kirkuk, March 1981

Dear Mr Clint Eastwood,

I hope you don't mind me calling you Gringo; it's my favourite nickname for you. I am sitting opposite your portrait taken from the film, *A Fistful of Dollars*. I often talk to you and have decided to write you a letter. I like your poncho, the cigar in your mouth and the way you hold the pistol. I don't like guns, except for yours. You only use it in films and to defend your freedom. I wish you could come here and help me with my freedom too.

My name is Mery, short for Merywan, and I am nicknamed kurakchani, boygirl. You may wonder why? I will soon come to that. I am ten years old and I live in Iraq, amongst people of different races and faiths: Kurds, Sunni and Shiite Arabs, Turkmen and Christians, who are full of hate and want to kill each other. I am not sure who is going to win, if anyone, but I don't want to take part.

You are a big secret in my life. My father says it is forbidden by our religion, Islam, to have pictures on our walls. But I keep you safe in my treasure box with all my photos. Whenever Father is out, I open my silver box like Aladdin's lamp, and have long chats with you. I want to go to America and I want you to help me. I want to become an actor like you and to work in films. People would laugh at me here if I said I wish to act, sing and dance. Not that I care about their opinions, but you have to understand that in Kirkuk we have no theatre, radio stations, TV or film studios.

There is another worry. My father wants me to follow his path and become a dervish, a devout Muslim belonging to a sect in Islam. He does not even know what the word actor means and he has never been to the cinema. So I have to keep this a secret. I have many more secrets, which I may tell you about in my letters. If my father learns of my desire to go on stage or in front of a camera, he will brand the top of my hand, just as you marked the cows in *Rawhide*. The closest to a performance that my father could understand is singing; unfortunately he cannot abide it.

'Singing is an act of evil that brings God's hatred upon us,' he says. This is why we have no radio, no cassette player or television at home.

Even though I am faithful to Allah, my religious duty requires that I must always obey my father, but I can never become a dervish because I have a problem: I don't know exactly what I am. To some people I am a boy, but others see me as a girl. Why does it matter so much to be either one or the other? Why can't I be both? I can't because I'm a neuter. I am neither a boy nor a girl. My nickname, boygirl, was not given to me because I am a neuter, but due to my looks. I have long black hair, large blue eyes, also my mother always wished for a girl. I love my mum and feel sorry to have disappointed her right from my birth. I have not told anyone about being a neuter. My parents must have some doubts but they would not utter them, the consequences would be too terrible. I am so dreading the day when my father becomes convinced I am sexually ambiguous. He will consider me a cursed child and cut my throat.

I feel that I don't belong to this world of absolute rules. But I have found another secret life full of colour and fantasy, the magic world of cinema, and it is that which keeps me going. I could not live without the hope of one day becoming an actor, and you are my only hope.

My fears about the future also come from the fact that I am a Kurd living in Iraq. Well, I live in Kurdistan, but I am not allowed to say my country's name. The Arabs in power hate us, and would happily wipe us out. My uncle Hercules explained to me that we Kurds are the largest ethnic group in the world who don't have a nation state. More than forty million of us live in Kurdistan, a land that is occupied by Iran, Iraq, Turkey and Syria. But, as Hercules says, 'We are determined to get our freedom back!'

Hercules is not his real name, but I am writing you letters, Gringo, and to protect my family and friends from our enemy. I need to disguise the identity of the people involved in my life, and I think it best if I refer to them by their nicknames.

I worry I will end up like many around me, working for the

government, becoming a spy, then a killer, or being eaten by Qayshbaldar, the monster, which has thousands of heads. I cannot tell you the real name of the beast in case someone else reads this before it gets to you – I would be killed. But one day I will. I also keep the monster's picture in my box; each time I look at it, I spit on its horrid faces. I often have nightmares about it.

So, please Gringo, my best friend and my hope. My life is in danger. Please don't leave it too long to come and take me with you to America. I promise I am a good child and will not be any trouble to you. In America I know I could be operated on, to become a girl, or a boy. I could work as an actor and feel free to sing and dance with my hair uncovered.

Thank you, with all my heart,

Mery Rashaba

P.S. Please don't send your answer to my home but to my school. My father will kill me if he learns that I am writing you letters.

This is the address:

Merywan Rashaba
Year Four, Class C
Al Quds Primary School, Qala,
Kirkuk, Iraq

The war is far away

Kirkuk, March 1981

The haluk flew up between the buildings of Qala, Kirkuk's ancient citadel, and into the blue sky of a late winter's day. I put one hand on my hat and ran backwards while watching its movement. I had to catch it in the air or else I would lose the game, Haluken, a Kurdish version of baseball.

Apart from going to the cinema to see films, this was my favourite pastime. I had spent my month's pocket money buying a metre-long piece of chestnut wood as thick as a chicken's egg. I soaked it for a few days, to make it stronger, leaving it in the water tank on the roof of our house, a place my father would never look. He didn't want me to play. For him games were synonymous with gambling and following the path of the devil. After letting the stick dry out, I cut an arm's length to make the bat, and a palm's length to make the haluk, which was used instead of the ball.

We divided into two teams to play Haluken, boys only, as girls were not allowed to take part. Most of us wore *sharwal*, Kurdish baggy trousers which were generally hand-me-downs. A couple of the boys wore tracksuits, a sign of wealth because the old sharwal made you look like a peasant. If you wore *dishdasha*, the long dress, it meant you were an Arab, but there were none amongst us. We looked grubby and poor, not that we cared.

My friend, Popcorn, was marking the score with chalk on the wall behind him. He was sitting on the side of the pitch singing a melancholy song. Popcorn was a popcorn seller and was at least twice my age. He was Yezidi by religion and was considered a devil worshipper by us Muslims. The boys called him crazy and teased him because of his calm, passive nature, and his strange love of singing in the open. When they couldn't snatch free popcorn, the boys threw stones at him. He never fought back. He just picked up his rattan basket and disappeared. If I was around, I defended him. I felt sad to see him humiliated.

I stopped running, feeling well-positioned to catch the haluk. I spat into my hands and rubbed them together because they were sweaty, not from the heat but out of fear of losing the game on my tenth birthday. I loved having Popcorn there singing, it made my birthday feel more special.

'Go for it, Mery!' Popcorn called. 'Catch it!'

I dried my hands. The sun shone into my eyes but I could see the haluk against the clear sky. The other four boys in my team were also shouting excitedly. I was their captain. I glanced quickly at Kojak's tense face. He was captain of the opposing team and stood at the base, hoping I would miss the haluk. The haluk came down like a rocket and I prayed, 'God, with your help.' I moved slightly to my left. I held my breath. It fell beautifully into my hands, but then slipped from between my fingers and fell to the ground. My teammates groaned and I felt the terrible sense of having let them down. Kojak jumped for joy. I picked up the haluk and said, 'It's not finished yet, put it down!'

He laid the bat on the ground. All eyes were on me, because everyone knew that my one chance to win was to throw the haluk and hit the bat. *If I miss I will not sleep for the rest of the week. I would hate to lose to Kojak, and on my birthday too.* I kissed the haluk, cleaned the dust from my eyes, aimed and threw. Like Robin Hood's arrow it whizzed through the air, straight at the target and bang! A hit!

'Yes!' I exclaimed.

My team cheered, 'We won...' running towards me.

'Well done, Mery,' Popcorn said.

Kojak blew a raspberry, a pointed insult at me. We all turned to him. 'It did not hit,' he yelled. 'The bat didn't move. I swear on the Qur'an. I swear on Allah, on Prophet Muhammad, and in the name of the angels...'

'You're lying,' Popcorn said.

'Shut up, you idiot.' Kojak ran towards Popcorn to smash him with the bat. I got hold of his wrist just in time and saved Popcorn's head.

'It did not, Mery, I swear on my life.'

'Swear on your father's life,' I challenged him.

His real name was Ali but I called him 'Kojak' because of his bald head. I did not like him. He enjoyed fighting and was always looking for any weakness to nail me. He didn't belong to our gang, but ever since I met him at the start of the new school year, he came to play with us. The minute he appeared, he shouted, 'Either I play, or I will mess it up for you!' It was no surprise that he was so nasty. His father, Shawes, who we secretly called 'Shawes Dog', was a devious and dangerous bully.

'My father goes around with a dagger,' Kojak said. 'He will slice open the belly of anyone who dares to stand up to him.' There was constant rivalry between us because I wouldn't let him boss me about. He was two years older, had a bigger build and a squeaky baby-dog voice. We often had verbal clashes but never physical. Not yet, anyway.

'I swear on my, on my...' Kojak bit his lips. We laughed. He knew too well that if he swore on his father's life, and he was lying, his father would cut out his tongue.

'I won! I won!' Kojak said, and freed his wrist.

'Give back my bat,' I said, facing him. 'I did hit it and you have won nothing.'

He banged the bat on a boulder to break it. 'No! Kojak, don't. That's my best bat.' I grabbed it from him, and after a struggle he gave up. But he was as hard to get rid of as a leech. As he let go of my bat, he pulled off my hat, revealing my long black hair.

'You lost, boygirl!' he bellowed.

My hair reached down to the middle of my back. This was unusual for my age and was not normally tolerated, but I was different because my father wanted me to be a dervish, and as such, I could have long hair. Although the real significance of this was never explained to me, I loved my hair as much as Samson, and believed that it held all my strength, desire and hope. But I was not allowed to show my hair in public except in Takya, the religious house. That is why I always had to wear a hat.

Kojak spat at my hat, threw it to the ground and trampled on it. I punched him. He retaliated, or tried to, but I was all over him. *Certain people choose to learn the hard way.* He called for help, but when his team saw how furious I was, they stayed back.

'Cry louder, you sack of shit,' I said, punching him one last time on his camel face. 'You got what you deserve.' I pulled myself away, shook the dust from my hat and put it back on my head hiding my hair again. I went to the haluk and picked it up. 'OK, the game is over,' I called.

At first the boys cheered but suddenly they stopped and stared at me. *Why is everyone looking at me with such fear?*

Through his tears Kojak's face lit up with a smile. Popcorn waved, pointing at someone behind me, but before I could turn, a hand grabbed my right ear. When I caught a glimpse of him, I saw the anger in his eyes, even though his face was half-covered with his turban.

My father's stony hands

He slapped me hard and turned the bright day into a dark abyss. I fell down as a couple of kicks drummed into my empty stomach. Full-strength football kicks like those could only have come from my own father.

Darwesh Rashaba was a tall, thin man with a heart darkened by fear and ignorance. Despite his constant gloomy mood, he wore a false smile because of his three over-sized gold teeth. He blamed the world's misfortunes on science. 'Science,' he would say, 'is the greatest enemy of God.' I was convinced he didn't understand anything about science, not even the fact that rain was a result of vapour rising from the seas and trees. 'God orders his angels to whip the clouds and make rain,' was his interpretation.

Father was born at the end of the Second World War in Grdi Ashqan, the village of Lover's Hill, on the outskirts of Kirkuk. In 1961, at the age of sixteen, he became a Peshmerga, a guerrilla fighter, and fought the Iraqi army for the rights of our people. Two years later, Saddam Hussein's Ba'ath political party took power in Iraq, with the help of the American CIA. The Ba'ath party's henchmen destroyed many Kurdish villages, among them Lover's Hill, and killed my father's entire family. I learned this tragic story from my mother, since I wasn't allowed to speak to Darwesh Rashaba about it. She also told me that once, during a battle, after an explosion, a piece of rock hit Rashaba in the face, breaking his three front teeth, two on the top and one at the bottom. He spent a lot of money replacing them with gold ones, but was always afraid of being robbed of the precious replacements.

In 1966, five years after the Kurds had taken up arms in the mountains and began their fight for freedom against Iraq's central government, the resistance faced a major blow. The Kurdish leaders could no longer share power, and the Kurds also split into opposing factions. My father, like many other Peshmerga, laid down his gun in protest. 'The leaders' greed for power was an act of betrayal to us Kurds that I can never forgive,' he said later to my mother. 'I left, and I never looked back at our beautiful mountains which I defended with my gun for years, for fear of crying.'

One night, in a town centre during a sudden summer storm, he climbed up on to the back of a parked truck and slept under a tarpaulin sheet. The next thing he knew, he was woken at gunpoint at a checkpoint.

'Who are you? Who are you?' shouted the soldiers, poking him with their guns. It was like a foreign language, as Rashaba didn't speak a word of Arabic. The truck driver answered for him, 'He is my assistant.' The Iraqi soldiers let them go and Rashaba became doggedly loyal to King Sherzad, the driver, for saving him from the soldiers. He became his assistant and respected him to the point of worship. This admirable man was my grandfather. A year later Rashaba married his boss's only daughter, Drawshan, or Shining, who became my mother.

Rashaba never again talked politics and on his orders no one in the family was allowed to discuss this subject, either at home or anywhere else, and particularly not with strangers.

'The monster has ears everywhere in this country and, he can eat you in one bite,' Rashaba warned me. 'I cannot protect you, nor can anyone else. Do you understand, Merywan?' I had as much understanding of politics as any naïve boy of five, yet I dutifully replied, 'I do, Father. I will never talk politics.'

'Swear?'

'I swear on my life.'

'No. On mine!' He took hold of my hand and placed it on his chest.

'Please, Father, I don't want to swear for anything on your life.'

'I want you to.'

I did and kissed his hands. He kissed me back on my forehead. This was one of the rare times I remember him kissing me. I was not happy to swear on his life, but was pleased about this important secret we shared. At my young age I didn't even understand what 'politics' meant, so it wouldn't be that hard to keep my promise. Of course, I knew that we were Kurds and were hated by the Arabs in the government, especially Saddam's invisible men, and I knew that I was not supposed to say this to anyone, or the monster would eat me. I was also not permitted to ever question my father's decisions, and I had to accept them even when I could clearly see that he was wrong. I longed for the freedom to ask so many questions, and one of the first would have been why I was not allowed to play Haluken. What did this have to do with politics or science or religion?

Lying on my chest in the dust, to Kojak's delight, Rashaba gave me another kick in the belly. He then pulled me up, grabbing me by my ear again, and with it, the collar of my shirt. I could not take my eyes away from the haluk and the bat in his other hand. Popcorn begged him to stop hitting me, his voice full of anguish. I was leaning over onto my left side and could see Popcorn's face from a strange angle. I was bending like this to reduce the agony of my pinched ear. *I must look like a shirt and a pair of sharwal hanging from a washing line.*

A father beating his son was not considered bad in my world. No matter how innocent you were, you had to obey him, second only to God. But I could not help disliking my father for ridiculing me in front of Kojak. The son of the Dog, full of himself, seeing me reduced to a quivering ball. Rashaba ignored Popcorn's plea and dragged me away by my ear. 'How many times have I told you not to play this game? And now you fight over it.'

I was trying to hold back my tears because most of all, I did not want to cry in front of Kojak.

'Loser!' Kojak shouted, flapping his arms in the air like a beheaded turkey. 'Look everyone, the loser is crying.'

'You will see a camel going through the eye of a needle before you see me crying,' I responded, despite being in the grasp of my unmerciful father. Out of frustration, Kojak grabbed Popcorn's basket and ran around throwing fistfuls of popcorn to the boys.

How I wish I didn't have my ear trapped between Rashaba's scorpion-like claws and could help Popcorn.

'You fight Ali?' Rashaba said incredulously, as we turned the corner onto our street. 'You want troubles for me? You fight the son of Shawes Dog…'

I realised that in his heart my father agreed Kojak was the bad one and the son of a savage bully, and it assuaged my pain.

Qala, where I lived, was a man-made mound of mud raised like a giant mushroom overlooking the Khasa River to the west. I knew little about its history, but having seen a few films set during the time of the Roman Empire, I had no doubt that our citadel was once an important settlement for prosperous powers like the Assyrians, and was the old centre from where modern-day Kirkuk grew. Most of the buildings were three storeys high with flat rooftops, but a few lower ones were distinct because of their cupolas, marble floors and columns, with different shaped arches, balconies and gardens. I loved Qala because it was like a fairy-tale city. Apart from the two main streets, which linked the gates at the east and west, the other roads were very narrow. It was a labyrinth laden with history. We had no government buildings or offices and no hospital, but there was a school where I studied. The inhabitants were mainly Kurds and Turkmans. In the last few years we also had Arabs coming from the south of Iraq to settle there, as they came to work for Saddam. Because of his fear of the Arabs, and those who spied for them, Father did not have any friends. He didn't visit anyone and had no visitors, except for when there was a birth or a death. He did not acknowledge people on the street, not even those who lived next door. But Old Zorab insisted on exchanging a few words. With his white beard, white cape, white jacket and white hat, Zorab was the image of Omar Al Mukhtar in the film *Lion of the Desert*, except that he always carried a leather-cased radio.

'Hello, Darwesh Rashaba,' Zorab said, keeping his radio to his left ear. 'Answer, my son, saluting is from God and keeps us friends.'

Rashaba did not, and kept going. I was looking at Zorab in the hope he might see me hanging by my ear from Rashaba's hand. Zorab cut across his way. 'I am listening to news of the war.' Zorab said, and followed us. 'Who do you think is going to win?' he asked and then he whispered as if to reveal a secret, 'Saddam Hussein or we Kurds?'

'Put your hands on your hat so that the wind won't blow it away,' Rashaba uttered. I had to run to keep up with Rashaba's long strides, and save my ear. 'I know the answer,' Zorab called behind us, standing alone and annoyed. 'I know who it will be, but will not tell you. Darwesh Rashaba, get yourself a radio, listen to the news and let the children free, let them play.'

Play? I thought to myself. Today I'm turning ten and I'm about to have my ear torn. What a great way to celebrate my birthday.

Mum, please help me

My mother was right. I must be made of rubber, if my ear was still attached to my head. Rashaba pushed through the rusty metal door to our house, which was never locked because we had nothing worth stealing. He stopped in the middle of the courtyard. I hoped my uncles would be at home, but they were not. We rented a room in a two-storey house, it was on the first floor, and it had a covered veranda from which we looked down through an Islamic arch into the stone-paved courtyard. This was where we had an open kitchen, a water tap and two wooden doors, one to my uncles' rooms and the other to Hercules' sports room, which he grandly called his gymnasium. A large jar kept in the shade under the veranda provided us with cold water, as we had no fridge, and there was a clay oven that my mother used for making bread. We had no garden, yet we kept a couple of chickens as best we could. The house had electricity but Rashaba had cut off the power to our room, and we were not allowed to turn on the light in the bathroom, so that he would not have to pay his share of the bills.

He let go of my ear, although I didn't notice at first as I couldn't feel it any longer. 'Stay there and don't move,' he said. 'You!' he turned to his wife, 'Do not say a word.' She was in the kitchen when we entered. She saw the haluk and bat in his hand, and remained silent.

Father did not greet her. No 'Good morning' or 'Good night' or 'Have a nice day' like the husbands and wives do in American films. I had never seen him give Mother a hug or a kiss. I often wondered how they managed to produce us children.

'Can I go and pray?' I asked, trying my luck. 'Shut up!' he said, as he walked to the tap with my game set. He took off his turban, revealing his long black hair. He washed his unshaven face, his gold teeth shining in the sunlight. He took off his rubber shoes, which he wore without socks. He rolled up his dusty sharwal and his shirt sleeves. Washing was part of the Islamic ritual for his afternoon prayers. Like most of the Kurds my parents did not speak Arabic and therefore could not understand the Qur'an. They prayed five times a day, spending more than two hours every day reciting words that were totally alien to them.

Mother looked at me again, standing there like a dead tree ready to be chopped. She scooped up a pot of water from the jar and walked in my direction. I noticed her slow movements, her tired and pale face. She held up the pot. I was thirsty, but I shook my head. She placed it by my feet. 'Mum, you brought me into this world ten years ago today,' I said, and managed to give her a smile. She forced a dry smile through cracked lips, then lowered her head and went up to our room, sparing herself the pain of seeing her youngest son beaten.

Mother was short in stature and had a round, benign expression. As always, she wore her long dress and a scarf on her head. She was born in Qala and had had a happy childhood. In her time the monster was not around. 'There were parties and weddings going on until late in the night, children like you had lots of fun,' she told me. She often described my grandfather's three-storey house with its six double bedrooms, the courtyard with its own well and a garden full of flowers, all carefully looked after by my grandfather himself. 'He favoured roses the most because he loved his wife, and she was called Gulbahar, Spring Rose.' My grandfather was a renowned storyteller. He named the big house 'The Castle' and himself 'King'. He told my mother how his family were descendents of the Kurdish Kings of Garmekan. He sent Mother and my two uncles to sleep by telling them fairy tales and ancient legends of Nawroz, Mam and Zin, Brader… Later, Mother told my brother and me the same stories. These were not from books, since we had none, but were instead passed down from generation to generation. *I have my grandfather to thank for planting the seed of my love of stories.*

Mother was three years younger than Father. She had married him at nineteen, which was late for a woman in our culture, but she had had to look after her two brothers and my grandfather from the age of ten, the year her mother died from some unknown illness. 'Every year when the roses blossomed,' Mother said, 'your grandfather would cut a bunch and place it on your grandmother's grave.' Tragedy struck Mother like a tornado a year after her marriage to Rashaba. My grandfather was taken away exactly two months after she gave birth to her first child, my elder brother, Ardalan. It happened in 1968, when Saddam's men arrested Grandfather for political reasons, which were never properly explained to me, and hanged him without trial. The government confiscated their house and belongings. Soldiers forced my parents out onto the street at gunpoint, and the house was given to Arab settlers. My parents stayed for a while with friends, until Father found a job as a labourer on a building site and they could afford to rent an empty room. My mother told me these things gradually, over many years, and each time it brought tears to her eyes. She was deeply scarred. She wore only black, and she said that she cried every day and every night. She swore not to smile or to make love to Rashaba again until the Kurds avenged her father's blood. She longed to have her two brothers with her, but they were in the mountains. They had become Peshmerga, fighting the Iraqi government. Two years after Grandfather's death, the Peshmerga, under the leadership of General Barzani, were winning the war. This put enough pressure on the government to sign the historic peace agreement of 11 March 1970 that brought an end to a decade of devastating war between the Kurds and the Arab Iraqi government. This agreement had given autonomy to the Kurdistan region of Iraq. Mother felt avenged and slept with Rashaba soon after, allowing me to be conceived. This is why there was a gap of three years between Ardalan and I. My grandfather's house, only a few minutes' walk away from where we lived, was still occupied by the Arab family. I saw how Mother always avoided walking past it on her way to work. In her spare time, she made bread for the rich people in Qala, which brought in some extra cash. She had to give most of her wages to Rashaba. She often told us that my father was the sweetest man on earth until my grandfather's death, but sadly I never saw that side of him.

Rashaba finished praying. He walked down the stone steps into the courtyard. He kicked the pot of water but he did not hit me. Instead, he picked up a tin of naphthalene and poured it onto my haluk and bat. I ran to him, begging him not to burn my favourite toy. He grabbed me by the same ear and pulled a knife out from the kitchen. He raised the knife to my face. *Is he going to cut off my ear?* 'No! Don't cut my ear! Mum, please help me.'

Mother came out onto the veranda. I knew she could not help.

She couldn't have been more different from Father, and I often wondered if she had accepted her marriage out of love, or because of the love she had for my grandfather.

Rashaba crouched down, pulling me to his side. He let go of my ear and took out a lighter from his pocket, lit the wet haluk and bat, which caught fire in no time. He placed the knife on the fire.

'Which hand do you use for writing?' he asked.

Typical. After four years, he still doesn't know. I lifted my left hand. He gripped my wrist tightly. 'I will burn you on this hand so that they can see it at school. They can see you are a bad boy.'

Rashaba raised the knife, with its steel burning red, so close to my hand that I felt roasted already. 'Playing games is not for Darwesh Rashaba's son. Will you repent?' he yelled at me.

'Yes, Father, I repent, and I swear I will not play again. Please, Father, don't burn me.' He kept staring into my eyes until, after a while, he put down the knife. 'Good,' he said, and pushed me away.

I sighed with relief for escaping the branding, yet my heartbeat still raced as I watched my Haluken set burning. I did not cry, but I knew I would not play my favourite game for a long time.

Possessed by the devil

In March 1976, a couple of weeks before I turned five, Rashaba slapped me across the face for the first time. I was playing with Shaady, Happiness, who was five like me, my best friend, and lived next door. We sat by the main door of her house on the rough ground of our street in the warmth of the morning sun. We giggled as we examined our funny faces reflected in a piece of a broken mirror that Happiness had found. Like a dark shadow suddenly descending, Rashaba appeared out of nowhere and stormed over. He grabbed me by my ear and dragged me away. Happiness put her thumb into her mouth and stood there watching me as I was taken home. Once in the courtyard of our house, Rashaba began his lecture with a warning to wear my hat at all times. 'You are a boy. You are not a girl, you don't show your hair in public,' he said, and then he squeezed my ear more and banned me from looking at myself. 'The devil will steal your soul if you stare into mirrors.' He pointed his finger at me, and then slapped my cheek hard.

This is how I learned another of my father's rules. We were not allowed a mirror in our home. When he went out to work, I crouched down opposite Mother's wedding box. It was the only piece of furniture Rashaba had bought her after renting their first room. Inside, she kept our modest collection of clothes and I hid my treasure in there, along with my photos. The box was waist-high and had three doors. Every day, after making our beds, Mother laid the pillows, mattresses and duvets on top of it. The middle door had a glass panel painted with Boraq, a fantastical creature that combined a young woman's head and the body of a horse with two outstretched wings. Rashaba tolerated Boraq as the only painting in the house because she was considered to be the Prophet Muhammad's horse. At times, when I was in trouble with Father, I wished I could ride Boraq and fly all the way to Gringo, in America. At the same time I asked God to forgive me, because it was wrong for me to ride the Prophet's special horse.

What I most liked about Boraq was her long hair reaching down to her knees. In Rashaba's absence, I spent many hours looking at her, but also beyond her at myself, reflected in her glass panel, combing my hair. I lifted up my long hair and held it in different styles, looking in amazement at myself, for I could have been a girl.

'Mum, am I a boy or a girl?' I asked, when she dressed me up again in one of her sparkly dresses. 'You are a girl,' Mother answered, 'a lovely girl like Princess Boraq,' and she combed my hair.

'Father wants me to be a boy and you want me to be a girl. Can I be both?'

'You are a boy when your father is home, but my girl when he is out. That makes you a boygirl.' That's how she gave me my nickname. Before I was born Mother was convinced she would give birth to a girl, and was disappointed to have a boy. During my childhood I was her sweet one. I did not want to be a boy because I was not allowed to play in the presence of Rashaba. He only wanted me to pray and dance in the House of God. I preferred to think of myself as a girl, to make Mother happy, and mostly so I could play skipping, hop scotch, and other girly games with Happiness. But I had to be careful not to be caught by Rashaba. So being a boy-girl was a playful pastime, an innocent disguise that I could share with Mother until the day Happiness was circumcised. I was not allowed into her house or to see her but her awful news soon became the gossip among the children and the women in our street and, finally, my brother Ardalan told me the truth. Happiness was living in agony because something had gone badly wrong with the circumcision.

The day after my fifth birthday Mother faced me. 'Happiness is dead,' she said, pulling me to herself to hug me. This unexpected tragedy took the life of my dear friend, and her death changed my life, too. I cried and cried for her. I missed her spirit and kind friendship. For several months, I waited every day outside our house in the hope that by some miracle she might appear again, hopping on one leg, as she always did. It took me a long time before I accepted that she was really gone.

Then came the time to think about school, when, at the age of five, my parents were supposed to enrol me. But Rashaba did not. He considered school the devil's house, where they teach you how to become an infidel. 'School is where women wear trousers and skirts and teach you science,' he said. 'Teaching you that the earth is round and that man has landed on the moon. School is not a place for Darwesh Rashaba's son,' he concluded. He took me to Madrasa, a religious school. 'Here you will learn how to read the Qur'an,' he said, 'and when you grow up, you will become a dervish like your father.'

I loved to read the Qur'an, but I didn't like to do it in Arabic, the language of the same people who had hanged my grandfather. The Madrasa had just one room, with no daylight because the Mullah, Zao'Adin, whose name meant 'religion's light', had covered the window with cardboard. I did not trust him at all: he was the one who had circumcised Happiness and had sent her to her grave.

Zao'Adin seemed older than Father. He was married with no children. He had a trimmed white goatee beard and was short and round. He rarely smiled and went around holding a cane, always staring at the ceiling and muttering prayers. He wore a grey cape that was slightly too long for him. He often tripped on it and one or two boys could not help but snigger. Despite looking upwards, he always knew the culprits and hit them on their heads with his cane. He also practised Falaqa, the religious punishment. He would make a boy lie on his back and hit the soles of his feet with his cane. This made the boy scream, and it terrified me. I did not giggle and only talked after I had held up my hand. I soon became his apprentice, holding onto the feet of the boys while he hit them. They cried out to be forgiven, but were not. I learned the Arabic alphabet from a brown book with some twenty pages – my first ever book. A month later, I could recite a few prayers, which I used in my five daily sessions. According to our Mullah, the more I prayed, the more souls I saved, including those of my parents. Zao'Adin taught us how we would burn forever if we did not obey our parents, and of course Allah and his messenger, Prophet Muhammad, by reading a prayer from Surat Al Nisa'a in our holy book:

Those who reject
Our Signs.
We shall soon
Cast into the Fire;
As often as their skins

Are roasted through.
We shall change them
For fresh skins,
That they may taste
The Chastisement:
For Allah
Is Exalted in Power,
Wise.

We also needed to obey Zao'Adin himself, so that Allah would recompense us with eternal heaven, with bountiful gardens through which rivers flowed, where we could eat delicious food and drink, even wine, and be surrounded by many young virgins whom we could choose to sleep with. As a five-year-old, I did not understand wine and virgins, but it all sounded so incredible. I wished I was already living in the Hereafter, and not under the same roof as Rashaba.

'Mum, what are virgins and wine?' I asked her later that day.

'Virgins are God's daughters, the purest, they are in heaven and are given to faithful Muslims in compensation for their being obedient to Allah.'

'Would you get a virgin, Mum? You pray all the time.'

Mother laughed and explained the virgins were only given to male Muslims, and I thought, *God must be a man.*

Two weeks before term began in September, I was enrolled for my first year at school. This would not have happened without the intervention of my uncles, who fervently believed in the importance of education. I went to the same primary school as my mother, in Qala. It was no longer called Freedom, its Kurdish name, but Al Quds, which was the Arabic name for Jerusalem.

The opening ceremony started early in the morning with the teachers standing to attention, like soldiers, next to a life-size portrait of Saddam, in the school courtyard. We watched a group of ten older boys who were in the Juvenile Brigade, who had been recruited by members of the Student Union, another organ of Saddam's Ba'ath Party. They marched behind their commander to the flagpole in the centre of the courtyard. Teachers and pupils saluted the Iraqi flag, by singing obediently:

Dear Rais Saddam
We praise you for your bravery
We offer you our blood
We offer you our Souls
Oh dear Rais Saddam
We salute you and your flag.

As much as I loved singing and knew that this presented a rare opportunity to do so without being punished by Father, I loathed that song and the ceremony. I knew the words because they were heard everywhere; on radio, on television and through loudspeakers hanging on the street corners, but I only hummed along while the commander untied the rope and slowly pulled up the Iraqi flag.

I was very glad to step inside a classroom, and was so eager to learn, to ask many questions of our teachers that I couldn't ask of Rashaba, although I hated the first page of our books, each with its portrait of the monster. The boy sitting next to me tore the portrait in his reading book slightly, and the teacher beat him. We were warned we would get the same treatment if we didn't look after the picture of our 'great leader'.

Father was right to say, 'The monster has eyes and ears everywhere.' We had them in the walls of our school too. *The teacher is a Kurd, but he must be a spy, otherwise he could have easily ignored such a slight tear.*

The pupils, the teachers and the caretaker were all Kurds, yet we had to study in Arabic, a language that hardly anyone spoke, except in the new schools, which had been opened for Arab settlers. We had to memorise many pages of books, and repeat them parrot-fashion on the day of exams. We suffered because we struggled to understand subjects like history and geography, and I particularly hated Arabic. Every year, moving on, I felt that I hadn't learnt a thing, and this was, in fact, true.

For the first three years, whenever I was not at school, I went to the Madrasa for the remainder of the day. One afternoon Zao'Adin asked me to stay behind to assist him in performing a circumcision. I was horrified. I could hardly comprehend that it could be God's will to remove a boy's skin from his penis, and wanted to ask why God created boys with this skin in the first place, except that this came from God himself, and to question it meant committing blasphemy. Even so, I was curious about girls. What did they have to cut off, and why? Zao'Adin explained that girls were also circumcised and said that it was for their own good, taking the devil out of them and keeping them pure. This did not help, as I immediately thought about Happiness. The horrible way her life was ended had traumatised me. I had a deep fear of circumcision. Whenever I heard the word, I instantly put my hand over my willie and prayed that they would never cut me.

'You come with me,' Zao'Adin said, as he handed me his black leather bag containing his tools.

'I would like to help, but I really don't know much about circumcision,' I said. 'Can I go home now?'

'No.'

'I need to go to the toilet.' I asked, and I wished I had never gone to Madrasa. But this was also owing to the deep resentment I felt about Happiness's death.

Zao'Adin explained that Happiness's death was God's will and he could have done nothing to save her.

If this was God's will, then I must accept it, and not blame Mullah Zao'Adin for the death of Happiness.

The child was a girl. I was not allowed to look when he took out his sharp knife, for it was a sin for me to see her private parts. The helpless child, tightly held by her mother, cried and pleaded and screamed her heart out when Zao'Adin cut her. I felt sick and wanted to run away. I kept thinking about Happiness and how much she too must have suffered. From then on, Zao'Adin asked me to assist with more circumcisions, though these were generally of boys. It took a long time before I could watch. Most of them were younger than me and yet they had much bigger penises. One day while we were on our way to perform another circumcision, he stopped outside my grandfather's house. He walked to the large carved wooden gate and rang the bell. I stayed where I was holding his bag.

'What's wrong?' he asked.

'I can't enter this house. My parents will not agree,' I said, and I held up the bag for him. But just then the door opened. A big-bellied man with bushy moustache and sunglasses, and an AK-47 in his hand, appeared. 'Mullah Zao'Adin, welcome,' he said. Fear of the armed man consumed me and I hurried to stand next to Zao'Adin and hold his hand in mine. The guard gestured with his gun in a form of an order and guided us into the courtyard of the house that I had heard so much about. The garden, the well, the arches and the marble steps leading up to the hallway were all just as Mother had described time and time again. But not the people who occupied the house, they were different. They were Arabs from the south and were there to haunt us. The family were in a party mood, all elegantly dressed, and surrounded by gunmen who stared at us suspiciously, making me feel more uneasy than ever. I was worried that they might find out who I was. I knew they would not ask questions of a young boy like me, but I was so pent up that I barely trusted myself not to blurt out that it should be me playing on the swing, it should be my party, celebrated by my mother and King Sherzad who were born here, surrounded by all my family.

Distracted by these thoughts, I bumped into one of the guards, who just grinned broadly and patted my head. I flinched and jumped back, pretending that I'd been scared by his gun. The gunmen suddenly became more serious when a stocky, swarthy man appeared. He wore a khaki suit and hat and looked like Rod Steiger in Al Capone, which was surely what he intended. *He must be their boss.* I could only think that he was the new landlord, and he was one of the monster's men. He greeted Zao'Adin and we were ushered inside the house and offered cake and Pepsi. They would have been offended if I refused for no reason, so I thanked them and said that I had a stomach ache, which was true, I was sweating and felt like I would throw up. Despite all my love for Grandfather's house, at that instant, in the company of those men, I felt terrified, as if I had been put in the captivity of a dark ugly cell in the scary Abu Ghraib prison that was known to us all as The Termination Palace. But it was not the house, no, it was the fear of being so close to the monster's men. I was so relieved when we finally left. I did not tell my parents about this episode and from then on, like Mother, I avoided walking near Grandfather's house.

I slowly grew fond of Zao'Adin. He was always kind to me, gave me sweets and encouraged my reading. I was grateful. He brought a new light to my life, the light of religion.

'Are you ready to read the holy book?', Zao'Adin asked one day, in the Madrasa. I nodded. 'Bismiallah, in the name of God,' I had to say before picking it up. I had to kiss the Qur'an three times and hold it against my eyes. I did all this with a blissful feeling of lightness. I was about to read the unequivocal words of God. I sat down and placed it on the small wooden table and started to read Surat Al Baqara. I did this with much love for my Allah. Zao'Adin stopped. I could also feel the eyes of the other boys fixed on me.

'Masha Allah,' Zao'Adin said, when I finished. 'What a holy voice, a mesmerising gift from God. You could read in the mosque one day soon and make your father proud.' The boys also seemed to like my voice. They might have wanted to give me a round of applause, but applause is not allowed in Islam.

Zao'Adin asked me to stay behind again. 'I need to teach you more about reading the Qur'an,' he said, and waited until the last boy had walked out. 'Amina,' he called to his wife across the courtyard, 'I don't want to be disturbed for another hour.' He closed the door. 'God's blessing! What a voice...' He sat on the rug, crossed-legged. 'Come and sit,' he asked, with a smile. 'Sit on my lap.'

I was alone with him in the room and it felt strange to sit on his lap. After all, he was not a member of my family. 'It is fine, I will sit here,' I said. But he held on to me and sat me on his lap. He opened his hand. 'Take it my son,' he offered. I felt comforted by the word son. 'You can buy yourself an ice-lolly on your way home,' he suggested. I hesitated. 'I will not tell your father. Don't worry, this is our secret,' and he placed a coin in my palm.

Twenty-five cents! That is as much as I would get in one week from Mother. My father didn't give me pocket money.

'My gift for your loving voice and for being my assistant.' He kissed me on my cheek. I don't know why, but I disliked feeling his wet lips on me. I did not buy an ice-lolly, but added the twenty-five cents to my pocket money that I was saving to buy a wooden stick and make a new set of haluk and bat.

In September 1980, when I was nine years old, I started my fourth year at school. Two-by-two we walked towards our new classroom.

Unfortunately, I had Kojak by my side and he was to sit next to me. During his six years of school, he had failed twice, and for this reason, he was in the same class as me. I studied intensively. I was looking forward to Year Five and starting English lessons. I already knew some of my ABCs but did not mention this to Zao'Adin, or to Rashaba. They considered English the language of the infidels. In the cinema, the films were screened in their original language, and were subtitled in Arabic and English. I always tried to read the English subtitles. When Kojak insisted on playing Haluken with me, or on messing it up, I confided in Zao'Adin and asked his advice.

'I know Ali's father. I will talk to him,' Zao'Adin told me. I kissed his hands. He locked the door, something that he had never done before. He pulled off my hat. 'I am not allowed,' I said.

'You are in my house.'

'It will go into my eyes, I can't read.'

'I will hold it for you,' and he did. 'I love your hair. I hope you don't mind me touching it?' I did not. He was like a caring father to me. He pulled out a dishdasha. 'Wear this. It's more appropriate for reading the Qur'an.'

The Arab dress!

He took off my shirt and helped me out of my sharwal. He looked at me wearing nothing but my underpants. He laid my hair on my shoulders. 'Take off your pants.'

'Can I put the dishdasha on first?'

'You don't need to feel ashamed. I have seen many naked boys.'

'I am not circumcised,' and I put my hands over my private parts. He removed my hands, lowered my underpants and crouched down. He looked up baffled. He touched my penis. I turned red.

'I always doubted you being a boy,' he said. 'Your tender voice, your delicate skin, your hair and your big blue eyes, none are those of a normal boy.'

'I don't understand.'

'The devil in you wants to possess your soul, to stop you from becoming a dervish.'

'Can I cover myself?' I was scared.

'I could save you. I would need to circumcise you, but first I have to get rid of the devil.'

'What do you mean?'

'Do you know what purgatory is?'

'No.'

'People who are neither in hell nor in heaven. You are neither a boy nor a girl but possessed by the devil.'

I sat still and cried.

'Does anyone else know?'

I shook my head. 'My mother sometimes thinks of me more a girl than a boy.'

'I will turn you into a healthy boy. Unless you want to be a girl?'

'I want to be a dervish to make my father proud.'

'Once I destroy the devil and take away the curse, I will circumcise you and make you into a strong boy with a big cock.' We looked at each other, we laughed, though mine was forced because I was frightened of being cut. I held on to his hands and kissed them again, and I promised to pay him.

'Don't worry about payment, but could you keep it a secret?'

'I will do anything for you. I swear on the Qur'an,' and I put my hands on the holy book. 'Well then, we shall waste no time,' he said, dressing me in the dishdasha, which brought on the urgent need to pee.

When I came back in from the toilet, he locked the door again.

'Please don't mention my problem to Shawes. Ali mustn't learn I am a cursed child, he will tell everyone and ruin me.'

'I won't, I swear.' He lit some incense and had me sit on his lap. He read a prayer over my head and then gave me a drink of water.

'This is holy Zamzam water from Mecca to poison the devil.'

I drank, closing my eyes and prayed to God to forgive me for whatever sin I had committed to deserve this. He circled his finger around my head, shouting at the devil to get out. His wife called from the courtyard, he had visitors. 'We'll continue tomorrow,' he said. 'Soon you will become a man. It is not as bad as I thought,' and he walked out, leaving me alone in the room.

This treatment went on for a while, but I noticed no difference. He started to touch my face, kiss my cheeks and move me about on his lap, rubbing me over his hard cock. 'My cock is holy,' he said, putting my hand on it. 'Feel it, it will make yours grow like mine.'

Oh, it is very big. Yes, I would be a real man if I could ever have one like his. He poured oil into his hands out of a small green bottle, warmed them by the candlelight and rubbed it over my shoulders, my back and thighs. When he reached my bottom, I stopped his hand. 'But it is necessary,' and he pushed me forwards, positioning me on my hands and knees. 'Don't move,' he said, feeling for my anus with his finger. 'I need to put my holy cock in your possessed bottom and take out the devil.'

He warned me that if I refused, all his good work might be in vain and I would be doomed forever. I nodded but slightly straightened myself. A voice inside was calling, *Don't Mery, don't give yourself to Zao'Adin.*

I turned to him. He was completely naked. 'Let me make you into a boy, a great dervish,' he said. 'You don't want your father to get to know. What would Ali do if he learns your secret? Come Mery, come into my arms and let's free you.'

I hated him for mentioning Kojak. I lost all my faith in him. I put on my clothes. 'If you are tired, we can continue tomorrow, you are nearly there,' he said, and opened his arms wide. 'Come to me.'

I spat into his face and ran to the door, but tripped on the rug and fell over. He held on to me, his cane in his hand. His wife called from the courtyard.

'Let me go or I will scream. Wouldn't your wife like to know what you want to do to me?' He was still naked, and after the second call from his wife, he let go.

'I will never be alone in a room with a strange man again,' I repeated to myself like a mantra, as I ran away from the Madrasa. 'I will never trust anyone again.'

No one was at home. I picked up the kitchen knife. I strode onto the rooftop. Out of the water tank, I took the latest wooden stick that I had bought. To forget Zao'Adin and to fight the tears pouring down my cheeks, I sat down to peel off the bark and make my haluk and bat, the same set that I would use to play against Kojak, defeating him every time, until, a couple of months later, on my tenth birthday, my father caught me fighting with Kojak and turned my bat to smoke, along with the one pastime that brought me some ephemeral happiness.

Facing the enemy in the mist

One Thursday afternoon, nearly a week after my tenth birthday and the day I had my fight with Kojak over the Haluken game, Rashaba and I went to the men's Turkish baths. This was a family routine, observed each week, which Father called "our treat" to acknowledge the pleasure and privilege of washing with hot water. Rashaba wore a piece of cloth to cover himself, and as always, I kept my underpants on. Fortunately he did not ask me to take them off. He had not seen my private parts since I had had my first doubts about my penis five years earlier. From an early age, we had to cover ourselves, and I had never seen Father naked. It was another forbidden thing to do, even within the family, but I was curious. In the baths, under the haze, I looked at him and at the other men, to see if I could sneak a quick look at their penises. If you could afford to pay, you could call the assistant to give you a massage and wash you. But not for me, not after what I had been through with Zao'Adin. Father washed my back and I would wash his.

After a good sweat in the steam, we moved to sit on the concrete floor each side of a small tub where hot and cold water poured in from two taps. In no time Rashaba covered his head with soap and started to scratch the skin on his round skull, digging for the whole week's accumulated dirt out of his long hair. I had to wait for my turn because we shared just one bar of soap. He tapped about searching for the copper pot that I was using to pour water over my head.

'Give me the pot,' he said, spitting foam. I passed it to him. I was thinking about my treat. After each bath, we would rest in the foyer and have lemon tea. 'Father, could I have a Pepsi instead of lemon tea?' I asked. 'No,' he answered with a tut, as he always did whenever I asked him for a treat. After such a warm bath, I longed to have a cold Pepsi, but Rashaba would not buy me one.

'Wash my back,' he ordered.

I started to soap him. The large wooden door was pushed roughly to one side, letting out clouds of steam, and introducing the sound of clogs. Kojak and his father strode in, and the world seemed to turn on me. Since our fight over the Haluken, I knew that sooner or later he would seek his revenge. Unlike his fat son, Shawes Dog was tall and robust. He was thirty years old, covered in a field of hair, with rough skin matching that of a beaten donkey. A long moustache drooped down his pointed chin like two snakes, and he walked with his arms swinging wide, swaggering, like the bully he was. His son, Baby Dog, followed him. I ducked behind Rashaba. Shawes Dog walked straight to us. 'Your father's bath, is it?' he said, and kicked Rashaba's legs. 'Move your legs out of my way, idiot.'

Rashaba briskly stopped pouring water over his head. He wiped the soap from his face and looked up. He slowed down when he saw the man who was looming over him, pulling up his legs.

'Sorry,' he mumbled. I wished he hadn't, because I could see the smile on Kojak's face.

They sat opposite, to prove that they didn't even need to walk by our side and kick my father. They kept staring at me as the water was swishing down into their tub. Rashaba started to wash my back in a hurry. Kojak pointed his finger. 'He hit me,' he said with a victim's cry. 'She hit you?' Shawes yelled, bashing his son's head with the pot. Kojak let out a shriek. 'You let a girl hit you?'

How dare he bully a ten-year-old and call me a girl? Yet he seemed to know something, calling me a girl so confidently. What if Zao'Adin had told him?

'Why are you bringing your daughter here?' the Dog called to Rashaba. 'Don't you know this is the men's bath and seeing a naked girl could raise desires?'

'He is not a girl. He is my son, a dervish like myself, that is why he has long hair.'

'Is he also wearing his underpants because he is a dervish? Or because he is hiding his hairless pussy?' Shawes said, sneering.

I could feel the rage steaming out of Rashaba at this insult, but it didn't matter how much he wanted to avoid Shawes, he was trapped. To my horror, he made it even worse. 'Merywan, son! Pull down your underpants, show him your big cock.'

Hearing him saying such a ridiculous thing, I realised he had completely forgotten I was not circumcised. This is the moment I had feared, I would quite literally be naked and finally give Kojak what he sought – my weakness. 'I want to go home, Father,' and I stood up half covered in soap. 'Your daughter wants to run away,' Shawes goaded with the utmost sarcasm.

'Merywan, take off your underpants at once. I said take them off!'

'Please, Father, can we go?'

The Dog asked his son to drop his sarong. Kojak stood up and proudly exposed his penis, dangling it in my face. 'Do you have one of these, Dervish Mery?' Kojak asked, grinning broadly. He filled up his pot with waste water and threw it over me, soaking me from top to toe. 'Take them off and show us your pussy! Don't be shy, girl,' he squeaked, throwing another pot over me.

If only Rashaba and the Dog had not been present, I would have held Kojak's head under the hot water and made Pacha, a sheep head soup. But I was powerless, and my father wouldn't walk away, even to prevent the poisonous scorpions from stinging me.

'She doesn't want to show us what she hides down there, does she?' the Dog barked. 'Take them off, I said!' Rashaba shouted, and banged the empty pot so hard on the floor that the sound sped to the cupola's broad belly, bouncing back and echoing around the walls. The other men stopped washing and turned towards us. Rashaba lost his patience now, grabbing at my underpants. Before he could pull them down, I freed myself and ducked away. All I could hear behind me was the Dog and his bald son's awful laughter, echoing around the cupola and pursuing me as I ran.

For fear of Rashaba chasing after me, I did not stop but grabbed my clothes from the foyer of the baths and ran out onto the street. Half naked as I was, I prayed I would not come across someone familiar from the neighbourhood. I made it home and ran through the door, soaked to the skin and wearing only my underpants. Mother saw me coming in alone holding on to my clothes, panicking, running around in my half-naked state, looking for a safe place to hide. She realised that I was in trouble again with Father, but before she could ask anything, I jumped into the tandoor, a large vase-shaped oven made of clay that she used for making bread. Somehow, I quickly managed to put on my clothes in that narrow space. *Rashaba will cut my throat from shock and shame if he takes off my underpants.*

Mother sat down by the oven and started flattening the dough to make thin circular bread. She didn't talk to me, and fortunately did not light the oven, or I might have been roasted alive. She was obviously doing this to protect me from Rashaba.

'Please, Mum, move away.' She pretended not to hear. 'I don't want to get you into trouble…'

'Shush,' she said.

Rashaba rushed in and threw the fabric bag containing his bath stuff on the floor. 'Merywan…' he was shouting. He searched the bathroom and hurried up to our room. A second later he was out again and on the veranda. 'Merywan Rashaba, come out, before I find you.' Mother kept at her bread making. 'Where is he? Where is your son? Or should I say your daughter?' He came and stood right by her. I could see his irate face through the gap in the metal tray covering the mouth of the oven. 'Woman, where is Merywan?' He pushed Mother violently, but she ignored his provocation. 'I have never hit you before, don't make me do it now.'

I dreaded my own reaction if he should hit my mother. *Please God, don't let the devil inside me stand up to him.* He took the wooden stick from her hands and raised it threateningly, just as the front door slammed and my brother, Ardalan, walked in.

Ardalan was his given name, but Father called him Katinkar, Trouble, because of his rebellious attitude. He was born two months before my grandfather's execution. Ever since, Rashaba had considered him a cursed child, and often repeated that Trouble's birth was the cause of our grandfather's fate. It was a common superstition to pin the blame on a child if a family member died around the time of the birth.

Trouble was wearing the oil-spattered blue overalls of an apprentice car mechanic. According to Mother, he had inherited my grandfather's deep blue eyes and his tall stature. He was sturdy, and already behaved like an independent man. He often hit me, but I did not hit him back because, whenever I had enough money for my ticket, he would take me to the cinema. He was very different to me, and was a natural-born liar. If I protested and cried he called me "cry-boygirl". When I threatened him with our father, his retort would be, 'I will cut your hair while you are asleep.' Even so, I missed him sometimes, for he no longer played with me. He did not go to the Madrasa, or to school. From the age of five Father had sent him out to work, and for all those years, at the end of each week, on Thursday afternoon, he took Trouble's wages. Despite this, Father never seemed to like him. Trouble too was a dervish. He had clearly done this to satisfy Rashaba, but unlike us, he had very short hair.

'Where are your wages?' Rashaba asked. Trouble reluctantly handed over his money. Rashaba counted. 'Where's the tip?' he asked.

'We didn't have much work this week.'

'Liar, let me see your pockets.' Rashaba searched him and found nothing.

'My friends are going out on a picnic tomorrow, Friday, and I have the day off. I was thinking of going with them.'

'Don't go,' Rashaba answered, pocketing the money.

'I work six days a week, surely you could let me have part of my wages?' Trouble opened his hand.

'To go gambling and drink Arak?'

'No, Father.'

'What else do you need money for? You eat at home, sleep at home and pay no rent. What happens if I get ill and am out of work for weeks, or months? What if I have an accident? Who would pay the rent and where would you go to live?'

When Father first started working on building sites for a living, he was paid around ten dinars a week, but over the years his wages had doubled. When it rained, he got depressed because it meant staying at home and not earning. He would spend most of his time praying to God to give him good health until he managed to buy us a house and secure our future. He was terrified about the future: he did not have a pension and was convinced that Trouble would not look after him. Like many other Kurdish fathers, he had no interests other than to work and make money. I respected Rashaba because that was my Muslim duty, but we were not close, like friends. He never asked me about my school work, and the most he would say was, 'Merywan, read me a prayer from the Qur'an, and pray that we will have our own house one day.' When Rashaba stayed at home I was not allowed out except to go to school and the Madrasa. Trouble was different, he could go anytime because he was working. If it weren't for my ambition to become an actor and my desire to learn English so that I could go to America, I would have gone to work like Trouble, just to stay away from him.

'If I don't get any money,' Trouble said. 'I will no longer go to work.'

'Are you kidding me?' Rashaba said, and grabbed him by his ear. Trouble shook his head. 'I would never permit myself to disrespect you,' and he kissed Rashaba's hands, 'but please, let me have some of my wages?'

'We must save until we have our own house...'

Mother suddenly jumped up, screaming 'Mouse!' several times as she ran to hide behind Rashaba. It always surprised me how frightened she was of such small creatures. Rashaba took off one of his shoes and chased after the mouse. He threw it but I instantly knew that he must have missed when I heard him explode angrily: 'Motherfucker!' The mice lived between the flour sacks, making holes, eating and leaving behind their tiny faeces. After Mother's many complaints Rashaba had bought a wooden trap, but it was proving useless, and there were still many mice around.

'I will get some poison and wipe out those pests,' Mother decided.

'Trouble, go and get ready,' Rashaba said, as he picked up his shoe. 'We need to go to Takya.'

Trouble, defeated, walked up towards our room. 'Merywan,' Rashaba called one last time. 'I know you can hear me. I am off to the House of God, but if I don't find you there before I arrive, I will cut off your ear. I swear on my father's soul.'

Dancing with the enemy

I knew from experience that if I made it before him, he would be pleased to the point of forgetting about the day's events. At least he was not going to chop off my ear. I took all the short cuts. I came across Popcorn sitting in a corner, singing one of his songs in the light of a henna-and-saffron sunset. 'I have to make it to Takya before my father,' I said as I ran by. He held up a fistful of popcorn, which I grabbed gratefully, munching it on my way.

The Takya had a spacious guesthouse and a wide courtyard. I hit the single drum with two wooden sticks, playing the starting rhythm, tum ttum tum tum... Four drummers accompanied me. Circling the courtyard, some twenty dervishes were dancing around a crackling wood fire. They swung their long hair left and right with their heads bent forward, calling, 'God be praised.' Dervishism is not hereditary and to earn the title, you must turn up regularly on Thursday nights at your local Takya and make a monthly contribution towards the running costs of the house, until the day the Sheikh could fully trust you and officially recognise you as one of his followers. Although I had been going there for more than five years, I still had to wait for that day. There is no training as such, as dervishes are not judged upon learned techniques but by the actions they perform to demonstrate their faith. The long hair is optional, but Rashaba believed a true dervish would not have it short. He was ordained a dervish and received his spiritual licence from Sheikh Baba, our sacred master and a descendent of the Prophet. This always puzzled me, but I wasn't foolish enough to question it publicly. Our Sheikh was a Kurd and Prophet Muhammad was an Arab, so how could Sheikh Baba be his descendant? Unless our Prophet had had a Kurdish wife, but that did not seem to have been recorded. Mother could have been a dervish as well, but could not take part in the dance. That puzzled me, too. Muslim women were also created by God, but I had to accept that God had given them an inferior status and left them at the mercy of their husbands. The one good thing about all this was that if the men let me play drum and dance, they must have seen me as a boy, so at least on Thursday nights I didn't have to worry about my gender.

Sheikh Baba, in his late fifties, wearing a green silk cape and a turban, stood by the door of the guesthouse with a few men around him. He twisted a black stone rosary in his hand, praying silently. Every now and then he called out, 'The master of the world, the Prophet be praised.'

A dozen men standing by the main entrance admired the spectacular dancing. Women and children were perched on the flat rooftops that overlooked the courtyard. The worshipping ritual was warming up as Rashaba and Trouble entered. I felt better now, for this was the one place where Father showed pride in me and I could be proud of him. He often repeated to the Sheikh that I was going to become a great dervish one day, which is how I thought of him. I had seen him perform so many incredibly risky acts within these walls, always emerging unscathed due to his immense faith in Allah. Trouble came to join me playing drum.

'Will you take me to the cinema tomorrow?' I said.

'I don't have money, and you shouldn't mention the cinema here.'

'I'll go by myself. I am ten now and grown up. Last Friday was my birthday.'

Trouble had to look down to hold back his giggles. I also had to turn away to avoid seeing his face and laughing myself, which would have been a shameful embarrassment for Darwesh Rashaba.

'Do you have money?' he asked.

'No, but you have.'

'I don't, and I will cut off your legs if you go to the cinema alone.'

'Please? They are showing Zorro with Alain Delon.'

'Shall I tell Father?' He knew that would be the end of our conversation. Rashaba had his hair down now, and he was chanting.

'If you tell me where Father hides his savings,' Trouble whispered, 'then I will take you to the cinema tomorrow and every week for many years to come.'

He is not nicknamed Trouble for nothing. I was so intrigued by this that I had to concentrate on my hands to stop myself from messing up the drumming. I could see in his eyes that if he found out where the money was hidden, he would steal it at once. 'I will not tell you,' I said. 'Then I will never take you to the cinema again,' he answered, hitting his drum hard. 'I don't care.' I was lying, obviously, and he knew it, but there was no way I would tell him where Father kept his life savings.

'One of these nights, while you are asleep, I will cut your hair if I don't get his money.' This time he really meant it. I almost hit him with the drumsticks. 'I will kill you if you cut my hair,' I said, hitting my drum harder than his for extra emphasis. After a while though, I had to surrender, muttering, 'Mother says he keeps his money safe with Sheikh Baba.' Trouble turned towards the Sheikh, then he shook his head. 'Where else could he keep it?' I asked.

'You tell me.'

'I don't know, I swear on Mother's life.' I felt really nervous when Trouble was like this, as he so often was when trying to dominate me. Sure, he too did not have it easy and suffered under Rashaba's rules, but it was not right for my brother to take out his frustration on me whenever he had a chance. Now he was even asking me to spy for him. *I am sad because I cannot trust Trouble and I don't really like him when he behaves like this.*

Fortunately, at a sign from the Sheikh, I had to change the rhythm to a more frenetic one: tum tt tum tt tum... The dervishes went wild; they took out their swords, waved skewers and daggers as they started the ritual of inflicting pain on themselves to demonstrate the power and depth of their faith. I had seen it so often by now and each time I doubted whether my faith could be strong enough that I could leave my body behind and not feel the pain, just as my father had described. But looking around as I drummed, it still astounded me how the dervishes placed their bare bellies onto the sharp edge of swords or pushed skewers through their cheeks and tongues. Right in front of me, one dervish was even crunching a fluorescent light tube in his mouth, chewing the glass like he was eating chocolate!

I still wondered how they could cut and stab like this with no blood, and without killing themselves. Despite all my faith, I never lost control and was conscious of everything. I was glad that I was a drummer and didn't have to cut myself. The Sheikh poured some more petrol on the fire. Then he held up a stone and used it to hammer a dagger into the skull of a crouching dervish. The others spun and jumped around, losing all sense of time, while the Sheikh prayed for the safety of his followers. Rashaba was charging like a bull repeatedly headbutting the wall to demonstrate his faith. He didn't even seem dazed by the impact of these crazy manoeuvres.

This was all familiar to me, but when Shawes Dog and Kojak appeared, I thought I must be imagining it, like a vision conjured up in the smoke rising from the fire. Everyone was mystified: Shawes, the number one bully, had no place in Takya. I tried not to lose control of the rhythm, but I could not help it. I stopped playing, and the dancing ceased. Shawes smiled beneath his moustache, went to our master, kissed his hands and called, 'Allah u Akbar.' The Sheikh placed a hand on his head – a sign of welcome and forgiveness and praised Allah. I began to drum again and everyone tried to behave just as they had been moments before. Shawes seemed to have become one of us, but I did not trust him. Kojak started to sway next to him. Slowly, the Dog approached Rashaba, who was close by Trouble and myself, but barely moving at all.

'Sorry,' Shawes said, and asked Kojak to kiss Rashaba's hands.

'Let's put a stone on the past and dance for Allah,' the Dog declared with the air of a gentleman, and held out his hand. *What is Shawes playing at?* Rashaba believed him and shook his hand. Before Shawes began gyrating again, he patted me on the head in a gesture of affection, but the menacing look in his eyes told me what I had feared as soon as he walked in, he was after me. I was not safe anywhere now, not even in the House of God.

Kojak asked me to teach him how to dance. I left the drumming to another dervish. As he was such an idiot, I knew Kojak was sure to reveal the real reason for their presence. He moved his head left and right, imitating me, and calling, 'Hey Allah...'

I could sense the Dog's sharp eyes pursuing me. I went ahead and entered the tranquil, candle-lit guesthouse. I took off my rubber shoes, walked to the far end of the room. I thanked God for allowing me to make peace with my enemy, and begged forgiveness for wrongly doubting Shawes. Kojak came in, declaring proudly, 'I am to become the Sheikh's coffee-making assistant.'

'Then you must start by taking your shoes off when you come in here,' I suggested.

He smiled as he did so. I smiled back, and we stood there silently for a while, staring at each other and exchanging false smiles. I felt increasingly nervous, asking myself whether he knew my secret. *No, of course he doesn't. If he did know, Kojak would have already told everyone he could, from our schoolmates to the Sheikh himself. And worst of all, he would have told Rashaba.* Finally, though, he let out the truth. 'My father wants you to go to the Turkish baths with him,' he said. If he had plunged a dagger into my heart he could not have caused me more pain than he did with those words. 'You know what I mean?' he asked casually. The implication was only too clear. *Forgive me God, for I stand on a prayer carpet facing You, but I feel like punching Kojak's camel face right here. Better still, I could take one of the swords hanging on the wall and chop off his head.* I struggled with my temper, and was quite pleased with myself for appearing calm.

'Thanks for the invitation, but I don't think I will,' I said, which was as polite as I could manage, before I turned and left.

The spying game

Rashaba asked Mother to turn off the oil-lamp. It was still early but tonight was special. Despite our fear of the monster, every year at this time, which we knew as 'Nawroz' and celebrated as our New Year, the light of hope sparked in our hearts. I slipped into my bed and lied my head on the hard round pillow in our dark room. We slept on the floor, my parents on one side and the children towards the door. Darkness scared me. The light of the full moon shining on my face through the window was comforting.

Since my experience with Zao'Adin and his discovery that I was neither a boy nor a girl, I found it hard to sleep as I had before. I often pretended to sleep without making the slightest movement. I did not wish to disturb my parents, in case they were having sex. I had not seen them doing it and was very curious about it. With Father at work almost every day and us children around in the evening, my parents had no privacy, so it must have happened secretly during the night when we were asleep. *What is wrong with me? No one that I know of my age ever talks about spying on their parents while they make love. Father will never excuse me and I will be severely punished for my spying if he finds out, but I can't close my eyes.*

'Why did you allow Ardalan to stay out on this night?' Mother said.

'Damn his eyes and I hope he will break his neck.' That was just how Rashaba was, so it did not seem unusual. I was used to his dislike for my brother.

After a while Mother asked, 'Have you spoken to Zao'Adin?'

What about? What did she mean?

'Not yet,' Rashaba answered wearily.

'Mery is getting too old. It is about time we paid to have him circumcised.'

How could she bring this up on Nawroz Eve? I felt the urgent need to pee and had to squeeze my legs together.

Rashaba did not answer as we heard patriotic slogans being

shouted in Kurdish on the street, followed by police sirens, dogs barking, a few gunshots, and much yelling in Arabic. The monster's men were trying to catch the few brave Kurds who dared to break the curfew, and light the fire of our New Year. I was petrified, not because of the men outside, but *what if Father calls Zao'Adin?* I wet myself.

Before leaving for work at around four, Rashaba looked at me in bed but said nothing. After he had left, I got up and went down to the courtyard. I washed myself in the burning-cold water, recited my morning prayer and listened to the birds welcoming the dawn on the first day of spring, 21 March. It was Nawroz, which literally means 'new day'. The story of a blacksmith who crushed the head of a tyrant king with his hammer, and then lit a victory fire on top of his palace, this went back thousands of years. Ever since then, Nawroz had been celebrated all over Kurdistan. But now, we Kurds were not allowed to build fires in the squares and on the rooftops, let alone sing or dance around the symbolic flames to celebrate our freedom. Nawroz was no longer a public holiday. The very mention of the word was forbidden. Lighting a fire, or even a candle, was deemed a sufficient crime to have you gobbled up.

I was having yoghurt and bread for breakfast when Rashaba came back and faced Mother. 'I've spoken to Zao'Adin,' he said in his familiar gloomy mood. I gripped the cup in my hand so tightly I nearly spilled my tea. He turned to me. 'You should have a bath today because you will not have one for a couple of weeks. You will be circumcised this afternoon. I have to go back to work. You will go with your mother.'

I managed to put down my cup but I couldn't chew, and kept my eyes on Rashaba. He went to the door. I had to say something to prevent this, so I blurted out, 'I don't want to be cut by Mullah Zao'Adin.' Immediately I regretted it, as Rashaba stopped. He pulled his turban off his face and came for me so swiftly that I thought he was about to cut my throat! He held up my face and squeezed my jaws. 'He is one of the best and cheapest. Why don't you want him?'

I had to search for words. 'He doesn't use anaesthetic.'

'No Mullah uses anaesthetic,' he said, as he let go of my face and walked out, and with him the shadow of fear left the room, but not my heart. I held Mother's hands. 'Can we tell no one, not even the neighbours, about my circumcision?'

'Mery, we need to celebrate.'

'At least until after it is done?' She nodded. I think she understood my concerns very well. 'Thank you, Mum.'

I held the holy book to my heart. *Allah, I am Your slave and You are the Almighty, Your decision will not be questioned or altered, but please, keep Kojak away from me, just for today.*

I had no fears of meeting the Dog and his son in the women's baths, but from the minute we entered I searched around. Five years of age was the usual limit for boys to enter with their mothers, but I wasn't a boy, was I? With my long hair and smooth skin, I could have easily been a girl, as some of the women complimented my mother. 'Oh, look at her, what a pretty daughter you have. She has your eyes. Where are her little pomegranates?' Referring to my flat breasts.

The last time I was in the women's baths was five years earlier. I used to like going there and loved all the games the women played and the jokes they told. Inside the wet steamy hall, they were like noisy children, with no men around to control their joy. These naked women, whose bodies were of all shapes and sizes, had fun. They threw water over each other, they combed each other's hair, made jokes and sang songs. They did all that women were not allowed to do anywhere else. In there, I wished I really was a girl.

I had never seen Mother so content and radiant as in the baths, and I would never see her like that again, because this was to be my last time there. Although I was certainly happy to be back, I was sad too, seeing all the girls of my age, who were running freely around without underwear, proudly bouncing their newly grown pomegranate breasts. But I did not have any, did I?

The big day

The day that I feared the most, when my secret would be revealed. I fervently wished Rashaba would stay away, but he had left work and come home early for the special occasion. Through the window I saw Zao'Adin walk into the courtyard holding his bag. As he climbed up the stairs, followed by Rashaba, my heart wanted to burst out of my chest. 'The child is too grown up,' Zao'Adin said. 'It will be embarrassing to have his parents present.' He clearly had his own plan, and it worked, as Rashaba went back downstairs.

I had taken off my sharwal. Tradition had it that on the day of circumcision the dishdasha was worn, as it was comfortable and easy to keep away from your sore penis. I resented the Arab dress, and would not wear it. Earlier, I had asked if I could have one of my mum's. It wasn't that I wanted to wear a woman's dress, but anything was better than the dishdasha. I had no secrets with Zao'Adin and I was sitting on a mattress with my hair down. At first sight, he pretended to be taken aback. 'I was told I was meeting a boy.'

I hated his sarcasm. I put my back to the wall, raised my knees and opened my legs, exposing myself to the man I most detested. *It's a disgrace to have people like him amongst Muslims, but he will not alter my faith in Allah in the slightest.* He pulled out his knives, cotton and alcohol, as if he was about to perform another of his routine circumcisions. 'Look up to the sky.' He pointed to the window. 'There is a flying camel, and don't look down until I tell you to.'

I had heard him saying this too often to fall for his line about the flying camel, but I preferred to look skywards rather than watch him touching me again. 'I am only examining you,' he said, and I felt his dirty hands on my thighs.

I closed my eyes. *God! Are You watching Your faithful dervish? Am I to be freed today, or am I to be shamed for the rest of my life? God, I am not a bad person. I don't lie or steal and I don't want to harm anyone, not even animals. I promise I will become one of the best dervishes in Kirkuk. I will proudly do my Jihad as a good Muslim, if only You allow this circumcision to be successful. It is a trivial thing to ask, almost nothing given all your powers, Almighty. I beg You to show me mercy, have Zao'Adin cut me and save me from my shame.*

'I can't do it,' he said. I opened my eyes to find his face close to mine. 'Are you going to cry?' He knew I wanted to. 'Come back to the Madrasa. It is the only way to keep your secret safe.'

'Have you told Shawes?'

'No, but you must come back to me.'

'I would rather die than be fucked by a Mullah in the name of Islam.' I had never spoken such words, even in my worst moments with Kojak, but the fear and hatred stirred up a level of courage in me that took me by surprise.

'Watch your tongue!' he rasped. 'I was only trying to help you,' he said, his tone softening. 'I am not a paedophile. I was possessed by your devil, it was entirely your fault. You're making me dirty too, you cursed child.'

'How many boys have you taken the devil out of like that?'

'Shut your filthy mouth, you shameless brat. One more word and I will tell Shawes everything.'

'Then I will tell my uncles what you tried to do to me. And you will burn in hell forever.'

'Nobody will believe you. I am a respected man. I pray ahead of hundreds in the mosque. Come back to me. I will...'

'Go away. I don't want to see you ever again.'

'In that case your father will be the first one to know.' He stood up to go.

'What will you tell him?'

'That you are a... a...'

'A what?'

He spat into my face and walked out. Rashaba ran up to him on the veranda. 'That was quick,' he said. Zao'Adin turned, and stood beyond the window where he could see me too. 'I didn't cut it. I am shocked at his unusually small willy. It's so small that I can't do it.' *Liar. You've seen my willy many times before.* Rashaba was shattered. 'I can pay more. How much? Please, save me this shame.' He kissed Zao'Adin's hands.

'You should have done it when he was still a child,' Zao'Adin said.

'He is my best boy. I want him to become the greatest dervish.'

'Then pray for him to grow, if he ever will, because he may be...'

Zao'Adin did not finish and walked down the stairs. 'He may be what?' Rashaba asked.

I had tears in my eyes but did not cry. Since the day I ran away from Zao'Adin and cried my heart out on the roof, I had promised myself never again to bemoan my fate. This was God's decision, and therefore I should not question it. But I wanted to shout out *Why me? What have I done to deserve all this?*

'There is still hope,' Mother's uncertain voice preceded her into the room. 'My sweet boygirl, there is still hope, Mullah Zao'Adin's last words.' She dried the tears on my cheeks and cuddled me.

'Mum, I am very lucky to have you. I love you.'

There is no hope for me here, Mum. You don't really know the last words Zao'Adin said before he left because he did not finish...

But he had told my father.

Yes, my master

It was a cold spring night. I couldn't sleep. After what had happened that day, how could I? Lying in bed, staring at the window, I was distracted for a short while. I had discovered a great secret, the hiding place of Father's life savings. All along, he and Mother had lied about keeping the money with the Sheikh. Perhaps Rashaba allowed Trouble to sleep away from home so that they could safely count his hidden fortune. '…forty-five, forty-six, forty-seven…' Mother recited quietly by the light of the oil lamp. It must have been a couple of hours past midnight. In the silence I could hear the flowing sound of the Iraqi dinars, slipping from her hands, one at a time, to Rashaba. 'Forty-seven,' Rashaba echoed.

'Stop repeating,' Mother complained. 'You distract me and I make mistakes. It will be morning before I finish.'

'Fine, lower your voice, woman.'

It was moments like these when I really learned to act, because I had to pretend to know nothing. If I were caught spying on them he would bury me alive. It thrilled me to know the whereabouts of his hidden treasure, but when I remembered Trouble's demands I was overcome by a sudden panic. He really would chop off my hair if he learned that I knew where Rashaba hid his money.

'Forty-nine, fifty,' Mother concluded.

'Fifty? How much does that make in total?'

'Six thousand dinars.'

Six thousand dinars! The most I ever had was one hundred and fifty cents. Six thousand dinars – six million cents – enough to buy sixty thousand cinema tickets!

'We need at least four thousand more to buy us a house, InshaAllah, wife!'

'God willing,' she repeated.

'Put them back in my pillow,' Rashaba said. 'Let me lay my head on them. I have sweated blood earning them, working in the extreme heat of summer and in the bitter winters.'

After helping Mother stuff the dinars back into his pillow, Rashaba, lying down, in his half-asleep voice, whispered, 'Mery is a neuter. That was Zao'Adin's last word.'

'God forbid it!' Mother almost choked, but then rose from her bed and leaned towards me. I closed my eyes. She put a hand on my forehead. 'God curse the devil and spit on him.' She then spat several times, pulled the blanket over me and quietly lay next to Rashaba. They kept talking, but I was deaf to their words.

I will be a laughing stock and, even worse, I will be responsible for my mother's suffering because she will be blamed for giving birth to a sexless child. A stabbing pain cut through my chest. I was gripped by fear and despair. I had to bite my hand to stop crying out. I felt the warmth of a tear falling onto my hand. If it wasn't for the doubts I had about Zao'Adin and the hope of escaping to America, I think I could have stopped breathing and ended my life that night.

Nightmarish visions of Kojak and Shawes Dog disturbed me even before I slept, to be replaced by more monstrous figures – my classmates, teachers, the Sheikh and dervishes, looming out of the darkness to chant, 'the boygirl is a neuter...' and laughing mirthlessly.

I needed to speak to someone, but whom? I could hardly trust my parents and fretted whether they actually knew what was wrong, or how to put it right. Instead of helping me, Rashaba would probably take me to the Sheikh and make things even worse. I stayed put, imprisoned by my thoughts. I wanted to ask my parents if, as a neuter, they would keep me at home because I could never have a family of my own. *Is there a future for me? Would I feel Rashaba's knife on my throat?* I knew for sure that there was nothing worse than being a neuter, apart from being a Hiz, the name given to young boys who were sexually abused by paedophiles, exactly what Zao'Adin wanted to do to me. There were many of these ruthless paedophiles in Kirkuk, and one of them was Shawes Dog himself.

I was five when I first learnt about such men, who sought out vulnerable young boys. It was in the cinema. Trouble and I went to see Haci Murat. We bought the cheapest tickets and were standing only a few steps away from the screen, so that it felt like we were part of the action. I was totally absorbed, watching the warrior galloping on his horse, shooting left and right. I thought it was Trouble grabbing my hand, but when I felt something hard, like a cucumber, I looked up and saw the silhouette of a man next to me. I hurried away to stand in front of Trouble, holding both of his hands in mine. I could no longer concentrate and didn't enjoy the rest of the film.

On our way home, on the old bridge, I told Trouble about the man's cucumber in my hand. He was furious. 'You should have told me immediately.' He wanted to go back and kill him. 'They are paedophiles,' Trouble explained. 'They are very dangerous because they fuck little boys and turn them into Hiz.' He grabbed my face. 'You must not let them touch you ever again, because if you become a Hiz, you are finished. Do you get it?' I nodded. He took hold of my hand and dragged me home. He had planted the fear in me, yet he was right, sexually abused boys were ruined forever. They could live in hiding, but once their secret was revealed, their families often killed them because of the shame. Such honour killings, which usually applied to women, were also used against young boys identified as Hiz, or, even worse, who were merely suspected of being Hiz. Without witnesses it was almost impossible to prove someone was a paedophile. I mean, they were adults, who often held important positions in society. It was common for the family and friends of such men to cover for them and accuse the abused boy of lying. That was why I did not tell Trouble or my father about Zao'Adin.

Kojak would relish the chance to spread rumours about me being a Hiz, and then what could I do?

With no one to talk to, I turned to Gringo, and I secretly wrote him my first letter, crying for his help to come and take me away to America. It was a sparkling spring morning with the sun already burning, though it had barely risen above the minaret, and I had just rushed to school from the post office. I was still shattered by the revelation of the night before.

During assembly, I was chosen as the best pupil of the week from Year Four. The head teacher called out my name and I stood in the centre of the courtyard alongside the best pupils from the other year groups, as hundreds of schoolmates applauded. I was given a box of pencil crayons as a prize, and I wished Rashaba could see me. Instead I felt Kojak's sharp eyes on me, full of envy. He glared defiantly, refusing to clap.

After school we ran out and gathered around the stalls selling boiled chickpeas, sunflower seeds, sesame cakes, sweets and sherbet drinks. I spent my five cents' pocket money on hot beetroot juice, which I relished. I was eager to get home and show my prize to Mother. The sky was darkening and high gusts of wind raced each other down the street. I held my hat tightly to my head and knew I must hurry, spring storms came suddenly. The beetroot juice was so delicious I drank it in one gulp, almost scalding my tongue. I cleaned my mouth with my wrist and ran, holding onto my prize and my hat, feeling the warmth and fierce strength of the wind buffeting my face.

I was only one street away from home when I came upon Kojak, who was waiting for me, standing directly in my path, holding on to his school bag. He had a wedge of watermelon in his other hand and was biting into it as though it was his enemy's neck. The street was deserted, but nearby doors and shutters crashed and clattered. The dust swirled around our feet, skittish, like a cat, threatening to get in our eyes any moment. I shielded my face with my hat and slowed down. We confronted each other as if preparing for a duel, though one in which we were drawn magnetically towards each other, each of us inching slowly forward. He held what little was left of the fruit before my eyes. There were no greetings or pretence now.

'My father wants you to go to the Turkish baths with him,' he said. That stopped me. I shook my head, preparing to pass him.

'I want to go home.'

'Yes, go home. But first take off your underpants. He wants to see your willy.' I followed his glance. Shawes Dog was standing behind a door, which swung wildly in the wind, revealing him leaning against a wall, combing his moustache with his dagger. 'Show us you are not a girl.'

'OK.' I put my hand next to my belt, encouraging Kojak to come closer, until I knew he was in range for the swift kick I delivered to his testicles. I tried to dart away before the squeal had left his lips, but I was not fast, nor far, enough. The Dog had gotten hold of my neck and mercilessly wrenched me up from behind. He hoisted me easily and carried me aside, gripping my arms behind my back as Kojak kicked and punched me. It was brutal, but not so painful as what was to follow. 'Take off his sharwal,' Shawes Dog said. 'I want to cut off his cock, if he has one!' I tried to resist, but he put the knife to my throat. 'It is fine, Dervish Mery. Don't worry, if we find out you are a girl you're free to go home. We only want to know, don't we?'

'Yes, Father,' Kojak answered, as he pulled down my sharwal and underpants in one go. I tried not to cry, not in front of Kojak, but could not help a few tears sliding down my face.

Above the sound of the storm and gust-battered shutters I could hear Zao'Adin's voice over the mosque's loudspeakers, starting the call for late afternoon prayers.

'Is that a willy, Father?' Kojak asked. 'It doesn't look like one, does it?' the Dog said with distaste. 'Dervish Mery, you are a neuter.'

He crushed my soul with that word. 'Don't tell anyone, please?' I could not have asked for mercy from anyone less likely to give it. My school prize dropped from my hand. Kojak was quick to pick it up.

'How would you like to become my pigeon?' Shawes Dog said, caressing my cheek. The name "pigeon" was used by paedophiles for the young Hiz boys they took under their wings as their exclusive property. 'I will kill myself if you rape me,' I spat, with the conviction of the damned.

'He is yours.' He tapped on Kojak's head with his dagger. 'It is down to my son if he wants to turn you into a Hiz.' He pointed his dagger into my face. 'He decides whether to let everyone know about your shame, or keep it a secret.' He faced Kojak. 'This is your game and it's your best chance to prove that you are as brave as your father, Great Shawes. He is now your slave, do whatever you want with him.' He finished preaching, put his weapon under his shirt and left with a satisfied smile of victory.

I stood before Kojak, with my trousers and underwear tangled around my ankles. I would have given everything that I owned not to be there. I glanced around, praying that my shame would not be witnessed, or that a saviour like my powerful uncle Hercules would appear. But we really were alone now.

'What is my name?'

'Ali.'

'What about Kojak?'

'I will not call you that... ever again.'

'Cry! I want to see you crying. I said cry.' He slapped my cheek.

'I can't,' I said holding back tears.

'You are my slave from now on, yes?' I nodded. 'Say, Yes, my master.'

'Yes, my master.'

He spat into my face and left with my prize. I leant back against the wall, barely able to hear Zao'Adin's chants now as thunder exploded across the city. I pulled up my clothes, wondering why I should ever heed the calls to prayer when all my ardent, faithful prayers had brought me was this.

I cannot let myself be Shawes Dog's Hiz, and I have to find some way to fight Kojak, because if I let him win I might as well be dead. With your help, Gringo, I will go to America, and I will never come back.

Don't live to die, die to live

The word 'Hiz' rang in my head. Pushing against the strong wind I felt a long way away from home. 'Don't walk with your head down. Always look up,' Old Zorab called. He was walking in the opposite direction, listening to his radio. 'Tell your father, it's useless to put your hand on your hat, you will see, one day the wind will blow it away and whoosh… Willing or not, we are all part of the game. So, it's better to fight back, die as a hero, with your head held high rather than stooped like a coward.'

Perhaps he had witnessed what happened to me? But he is a slow mover, so could he have stumbled upon what happened? Old Zorab was always generous with his advice either way.

Two bulky red Mercedes-Benz trucks were parked in the open space opposite our house, which could only mean one thing, that my uncles were home!

My uncle, Arsalan, named after Prince Arsalan in the fairy tale, was two years younger than Mother, but much more robust and chubby. He was nicknamed 'Flathead Drunk', because of the shape of his head and his drinking habit. Rashaba also considered him an infidel because whenever he was drunk, he told jokes. Flathead was one of the nicest men I knew, and I loved his sense of humour as any child would have.

Baban was six years younger than Mother. My grandfather had named him after the princes of the Baban Kingdom. But I nicknamed him 'Hercules' because of his muscles and his sculpted physique. When he was at home, he spent most of his time bodybuilding. Like Flathead, he worked as a truck driver and was not married. They rented three rooms on the ground floor. Hercules slept in their living room and had his gymnasium next door.

It was only due to their persistence that Rashaba had agreed to register me at school. Flathead and Hercules chuckled at his ignorance regarding science, and warned me that if I did not do well at school, they would no longer take me to the cinema. 'They are showing Gringo again,' Hercules said, at the time. 'Would you like to see it, Mery?' Flathead had asked, his eyes twinkling. I accepted at once. The film was actually *The Good, the Bad and the Ugly*, Sergio Leone's great spaghetti western with Gringo as the hero, the 'Good' guy. Over the years I would see it again and again, and each time I loved it more, though it never failed to make me wish that my uncles were there to see it with me.

When Grandfather was hanged, my uncles became Peshmerga in the mountains, and with the vital support of money and weapons provided by the Americans to the Kurdish resistance, my uncles and thousands of Peshmerga dutifully fought the Iraqi army for many years. But in 1975, US policy dramatically shifted in favour of the Iraqi government, and this betrayal left the Kurdish army to continue their struggle alone. Abandoned to our fate, the Kurdish people faced one of the worst disasters in our history, and the memories of this time brought tears of disappointment to my uncles' eyes. They had had to surrender their guns to the Iraqis and make their way home, defeated, and all that they had to show for their brave struggle were two books that Hercules had managed to smuggle out with him from the mountains.

These books, by our Kurdish poets, Piramerd and Goran, were forbidden, which made Hercules love them all the more. 'I was determined not to leave them behind, like my rifle,' he would say every time he read another poem.

A few months before I went to school, Hercules began teaching me to read and write in Kurdish. We sat on the sofa in my uncles' living room, which we knew Rashaba never entered. 'You need to learn your own language and protect it,' he said passionately.

'Without it, we Kurds would have been wiped out, like many people have been in our part of the world. Education is the best weapon for winning your freedom, not guns. And remember, never talk to anyone about the things I'm teaching you.'

I enjoyed having a small role to play in my people's history, but my uncles were ready to die for it. 'Would you and uncle Arsalan become Peshmerga again?' I had once asked Hercules during one of our Kurdish lessons. 'Absolutely! As soon as the Kurds in the mountains stop killing each other and unite their forces to face our enemy, we are ready to pick up our guns and fight for our freedom again. When we win, we will come back with our heads held high and live in the King's Castle.'

Hercules also told me that on 11 March 1971, the day I was born, my uncle Flathead wanted to burn down the King's Castle to free it from the Arab settlers. When my mother pleaded and succeeded in changing his mind, out of total frustration, Flathead swore he would never get married unless he lived in the big house. But for now, like Mother and me, my uncles avoided going near their old home that was still occupied by the Arab family.

I heard unusual noises in the courtyard and, as I walked through the door, I saw women moving about and climbing the stairs to our room. Rashaba was reciting the Qur'an on the veranda. The general atmosphere was one of mourning, until, out of the corner of my eye, I spotted Flathead making a barbecue. Trouble was holding a sandwich in one hand, and fanning the skewed lamb with the other. Flathead had rolled his sharwal up to his knees, as he always did.

'Mery,' he called with a wide grin. 'How about a nice juicy kebab?' Despite all the suffering Flathead had gone through, he never lost his sweet smile and his joyful humour. He always dressed casually and combed lots of gel through his hair. 'Mery, what's up?' Flathead asked when he noticed my agitated state.

'Nothing, Uncle. Welcome home.' I kissed his hands. 'I would like a kebab. Where is my mum?'

'She is not well. You may have to sleep in my room tonight.'

'Well, tell him what is going on,' Hercules said, as he stepped out of their room. He had on a white T-shirt with a red towel over his shoulder and was wearing a black sharwal. He too noticed my uneasiness but said nothing.

Instead, it was Flathead who broke the silence with an announcement that threw me completely off guard. 'Your mother is bringing you a brother, or maybe a sister any minute now.' I had not even realised that Mother was pregnant! But on reflection, under the baggy Kurdish dress, it was easy to hide a belly big enough to be bearing twins.

'Don't take it to heart, Mery. Whatever it is, just say, "up Kissinger's bum".' Hercules always made me laugh when he said that.

'Do you want to tell me something?'

'Only if you tell me what "up Kissinger's bum" means!'

'OK! First let's have one round together, ready?' He bent down to my height and looked me directly in the eyes. 'Up Kissinger's bum,' we said in unison, laughing spontaneously.

'Now tell me what it means.'

Hercules put his finger on his mouth. He looked around the courtyard at the women neighbours, as if they had a spy amongst them, and gestured with his head for me to follow.

In the gymnasium I sat on the edge of the window watching Hercules. He took off his sharwal. Underneath he was wearing black shorts. He did a couple of press-ups and started his bodybuilding. I admired his muscles and surged with pride, for he looked as strong as a mountain. He had a tattoo on his right arm – a heart with an arrow cutting through it. Flathead brought in a sandwich and a bottle of Pepsi. 'We need to celebrate with my sister and wish her an easy birth,' he said, tapping his Pepsi bottle against mine, as though we were toasting Mother with beer.

'Uncle, don't. You know clicking drinks is forbidden in Islam.' Flathead smiled at me, punched Hercules' muscles and gave him a kiss on his cheek. With their bright blue eyes and weatherworn skin my uncles often reminded me of Terence Hill and Bud Spencer in *They Call Me Trinity*, one of the first films I went to see with them.

Flathead went out. I tried to eat the kebab, but tears streamed from my eyes. *I am so lucky to have my kind uncles. If it were not for the monster and Kojak, I could have such a nice life.* Hercules noticed. 'Someone has hurt you?'

'First you tell me about "up Kissinger's bum"?'

'You promise not to tell anyone?' I nodded. 'Henry Kissinger was the American Secretary of State under President Gerald Ford Jr., who betrayed the Kurds in 1975 in our war against Saddam, bringing disaster to our people. He betrayed other people too and ignored his allies when, with his support, they attacked democracies and murdered thousands of people in South America, Africa and Asia. I consider him a criminal and one day wish to see him tried for crimes against humanity, like the leaders of the Nazis who ordered the killing of the Jews. But for now, all we can say is "up Kissinger's bum".'

I knew virtually nothing about Nazis, Jews, democracy and crimes against humanity. But I was truly disappointed to learn that Kissinger was American. Until then, I believed the Americans were all great people.

'Now tell me who hit you so that I can bring them to your feet.' Hercules was right, he could have stood up to anyone. He was not only strong, but as brave as anyone I knew. I pushed the kebab into my mouth to gain time to think. He started to oil his body. Observing him and his muscles, I felt jealous of how confidently he could expose himself. Something I thought I would never be able to do. I also felt ashamed at the thought of my uncles learning about my misfortune. That would shame them too, because their sister had given birth to me.

'Is it to do with Rashaba burning your haluk and bat?'

'Who told you this?'

'Ardalan. Don't tell him, OK?'

Trouble! He of course, would like to see my uncle's hands around Father's neck. 'No,' I said, and bit into my sandwich again. Hercules looked at me inquisitively. *If I tell him the truth, I will be free from Kojak and the Dog because Hercules will kill them after what they have done to me. This is a matter of family honour, so there could be no compromise. But then Hercules might go to prison and could even be hanged because of his Peshmerga past. That would still not solve my problem because it is not only to do with Kojak and his father, but also about my abnormality. Should I tell him this? No, never, not before I can prove that I am not a neuter, but how can I do that?*

'I cheated during the monthly maths exam,' I said. 'My teacher made me stand in a corner. When I came out of school, I had a fight with the boy who told on me. There were a few of them and I was on my own and now I just want to forget about it.'

'Do you want me to talk to the boy's family?'

'No, I will avenge myself.'

'Well, in that case, you need to build up your muscles like Steve Reeves in Hercules, to become the strongest man in the world and stand up to all your enemies. C'mon now.'

At that moment loud cries filled the courtyard from our room. Astera, Star, my baby sister, had been born, and finally the rains began to fall.

The Mongolian warrior

The oil lamp lit our room. Rashaba was sitting in a corner, staring blankly ahead. My uncles, Trouble and myself gathered around Mother. She was breastfeeding the baby. We may have been sitting there for hours, but even now, Trouble and I were not allowed to stretch our legs in the presence of Rashaba and had to keep them crossed. I envied the freedom my uncles enjoyed, leaning back comfortably on the pillows.

'A Kurd was standing by the old bridge,' Flathead started telling a joke. 'He had his left arm stretched out, his hand closed nearly into a fist but slightly open to make a tunnel. He held his right hand adjacent to the tunnel. An Englishman came by, and was amazed by the curious position in which the Kurd arranged his hands. He thought him a magician or perhaps a religious figure, meditating. Like the Arab man standing to the left of the Kurd, the Englishman stayed, watched and asked, 'What are you doing young man?' 'Catching birds, sir!' the Kurd answers, without moving. 'How so?' the Englishman asks. 'I have no knowledge of this technique.' The Kurd explains, 'See this tunnel in my hand? That is a trap. I wait motionless until a bird goes through and, vooom, I catch it with my right hand.' The Englishman shakes his head, 'Puhhh!' he snorts like a camel, 'No wonder the Arabs,' pointing to the man next to the Kurd, 'consider you Kurds ignorant mountain folk.' The Kurd jeers at him, 'You are wrong, sir,' he says. 'This is an easy job and I am paid excellent money for it, by this Arab gentleman.'

We all laughed, except for Rashaba. He clenched his teeth like those of an irritated lion to remind Trouble and myself that we were not allowed to laugh in his presence.

When I was born in this room ten years ago, Rashaba wanted to call me Muhammad, after our Prophet. Apart from it being the most sacred name of all, it was also easier for a Kurd to have an Arabic name. Flathead insisted on choosing Merywan, like the legendary hero in 'The Twelve Riders of Merywan', another of my grandfather's mythical stories. 'The children must all have Kurdish names,' Flathead had said. 'If we lose our identity, we will be lost forever.' I was glad I had a Kurdish name, for I was not an Arab. It would have been a terrible sin to have a neuter like me named Muhammad.

Rashaba wanted to call my sister Khadija after our Prophet's first wife. 'Astera, Star!' Flathead said. 'A Kurdish name for the little princess who will shine as much as her mother and bring light into our lives.' Rashaba moaned but did not protest. If it were not for the torrential rain, he would have preferred to be at the Takya. He resented losing his power over the family when my uncles were around.

'I am going to sleep on the veranda,' Rashaba said. 'Trouble, bring my mattress and my pillow.' He suddenly changed his mind and picked up his pillow himself, clutching it to his chest.

My uncles wished us good night and went down to their rooms. I looked at Star. I was glad to have a girl in our family. I never understood why men liked to have boys so much; they caused them trouble. The women cooked food, washed clothes, made beds and spent their lives looking after the family and treating their husbands like kings. *How can they prefer sons to daughters?* I held Star in my arms and in my heart made a wish, *I hope you will bring light to my life too.* She opened her blue eyes, lighting up her unblemished sweet face. She had blonde hair. Many of our children were born blond and around the age of five their hair turned black like mine. I was thankful to have to stay awake. I couldn't sleep for fear of Kojak appearing in my nightmares.

'Mother, I will not go to sleep for the first seven nights. I will look after Star and make sure Shawa won't kidnap her.'

Shawa was a princess. Her father, the King, prevented her from marrying the prince she loved. She was never to be a bride nor to have the children that she craved so much. For the first seven nights after a child's birth, she could come at any time and was invisible. She would only appear for an instant when she first touched the baby. At that moment, you had to put a pin on her glittery wedding dress and thus turn her into your slave. Mother's great-great-grandfather had once caught her, and she had had to serve him. He had fallen in love with Shawa and married her. They had had a happy life and many children together. Shawa did not take away the children she had with the men, her masters. My great-great-grandfather aged into an old man, yet Shawa always remained a youthful and graceful princess. 'I will free you, if you promise me not to take the children of my descendants away,' was the last thing he asked of her before dying. 'I promise I will not touch children of yours for the next five generations,' she replied. He gave her one final kiss and, by taking off the pin from her wedding dress, freed her.

This should have meant that Star was perfectly safe. The only problem was that Mother was not sure where in the family tree my great-great-grandfather stood, and therefore we had to watch out for Shawa.

'I wish I had been taken away by Shawa when I was born. I wish Zao'Adin had cut me and that I would die from the infection, just as my dear friend Happiness did.'

'Mery, my darling,' Mother said. 'You have a lot to live for. One day you will be holding your own children in your arms.'

'Do you think I will be a good father, or one like Rashaba?'

'He is not a bad man. Wait until you become a father yourself, you will learn why he does certain things.' I couldn't understand this. 'I think you will be a gentle father, and your children will love you dearly.' She must have known that this was not true, but I suppose she was trying to reassure me, while also defending her husband. Star screamed in my arms. I handed her over to Mother. She lay down next to Star and sang her a lullaby. Trouble came back and slipped into his bed next to me. He saw a red bead necklace in my hand. 'What's that?' he asked.

'A necklace! Happiness gave it to me before she died, on the day of my first bicycle ride. Do you remember?'

'Yes, and you still have to pay me back for what you did to me.'

'Rubbish! That was five years ago.'

As soon as Mother finished her lullaby and fell asleep next to Star, Trouble came closer. I did not like his approach. I knew what he was after. I asked if he knew why uncle Flathead didn't want to get married, but he refused to be distracted and continued staring intently at me. 'Have you found where Father hides his money?' he asked quietly.

'Ardalan, you should be looking after me, but you bully me and threaten me all the time. I would never do this to you if I was your older brother.'

'How about this?' he said, pulling out a photo of Gringo. 'Am I looking after you or not? You can only have this if you find Rashaba's money.

'I will, if you let me have Gringo.'

'Really? You will?'

'I will.' I kissed Gringo, and put his photo in my pocket next to my heart.

It kept raining throughout the night. Trouble was already asleep. I stayed awake to watch out for Princess Shawa. I put my head down on the round pillow thinking about Happiness, the day I had had my best time with her, soon after I turned five years old, and shortly before she died. It was Nawroz and I took her on a bicycle ride.

The mobile bicycle hire shop was made of a large cart pulled by two sturdy horses. We knew the rules: the new bicycles were expensive, and you had to already know how to ride to get a two-wheeled one.

As soon as the cycle cart arrived, boys crowded around and started to choose their bicycles. I spotted a brand-new, small blue two-wheeler. I only had twenty-five cents. The bicycle hire man was a real character. He came from the north and had a wide Mongolian face and long hair like mine. He also had a goatee beard, and with his sword and crown-like hat he looked like Kikuchiyo, the great warrior in The Seven Samurai. Kikuchiyo seemed as tall as a giant when I stood in front of him. His long sword was made of a palm tree branch. He was not allowed a real one unless he was a dervish. He used his to hit the children who cheated him.

'How old are you?' he asked. 'Five,' I answered. 'Good. Do you have money?' he roared. I quickly opened my hand. 'Good. Do you know how to ride two-wheel bicycles?' He did not let me answer, but I must have nodded. 'Good. You know how to read time?' I shook my head. 'Bad,' he said and lifted me up with one hand, my feet dangling in the air, and took me to his cart. 'See this hand?' He pointed to a large round clock with gold frame. He had a big silver ring on his finger with a skull on it and his dirty nails were as long as my middle finger, 'when this has moved to this point you bring back the bicycle.

That makes twenty-five minutes. Twenty-five cents for twenty-five minutes, understand?'

Of course I will bring it back on time.

He handed me the bicycle. 'Enjoy your ride,' Kikuchiyo bellowed, and chuckled for some reason that only he knew.

I spent half of my time working out how to stay on the saddle and keep my feet on the pedals without falling. Fortunately, Kikuchiyo was too busy to notice me falling again and again. Someone grabbed my saddle to keep me balanced. It was Popcorn. 'Try now, Mery,' he said. Gradually, I began to master it. All at once, I took off, hearing Popcorn's receding yells, 'Keep your weight to the right, but not too much! Don't look down…' I went straight ahead all the way to our street. I knew my ride was coming to an end, so I stopped, got off, turned the bicycle and was about to ride back, when Happiness came hopping over on one leg.

'Mery, can I have a ride?' she asked.

'You are a girl, you are not allowed.'

'You are a girl too.'

'But I'm not wearing girl's clothes, am I?' She sucked her thumb.

'Do you have money? I could buy some more time.' She shook her head.

'Nothing?'

She shook her head more.

'Not even five cents?'

'Not even five cents. But I have this,' she said, and she gave me her necklace.

We were close friends and I could not refuse her a ride. It felt good, because I wanted to behave like my film heroes did. I knew I had to get the bicycle back to avoid the sword on my head, but I did not. Instead, I got off the bicycle and turned it in the opposite direction to Kikuchiyo. Happiness started her ride, falling over and over again. When she got tired of it, she sat on the bar in the front and asked me to ride. I could not tell her I had only just learned myself. I jumped on the saddle, and like Manoj Kumar riding with Jaya Bhaduri on his bicycle in Shor, we cycled around in the open space not far from Top Qapi, the main gate of Qala. I completely forgot about taking the bicycle back.

It was an hour later, when Trouble appeared, that I finally remembered. 'Where did you get this from?' he asked. I stopped. Happiness got scared and ran away. 'I hired it. Would you like to have a ride?'

'How long do you have left?' and he jumped on the bicycle.

'Another ten minutes.'

'OK, you go home, I will take it back,' and he zoomed off. 'Enjoy the ride,' I called. Concerned about what Kikuchiyo might do to Trouble, I followed him. Trouble was riding joyfully, whistling as he whizzed along. After a couple of loops around, he took the bicycle back, thinking he was in good time. Kikuchiyo went for him with his sword.

Oh, shit!

He did not even give Trouble a chance to get off the bicycle. He just whacked him hard with the sword. I could not hear what they said but saw Trouble fleeing, chased by the Mongolian. Fortunately Kikuchiyo was too heavy to keep up with him. Once clear, Trouble slowed down and looked up, and seeing me watching from around the corner, he started running furiously... He was coming straight for me. I ran.

He followed me inside and found me on the veranda, praying next to Father. He stood in the middle of the courtyard and strode around puffing out his cheeks like a turkey, pulling up his shoulders, making faces, swearing silently, intimidating me by punching his right fist into the palm of his left hand... I was supposed to be praying but could not concentrate, and was also supposed to be scared, but he looked so funny and had fallen into my trap so easily, it made me laugh. Rashaba banged my head. 'Allah u Akbar,' he called, without interrupting his prayer. This was worse, because now Trouble and I both laughed.

We were punished, not allowed dinner and had to stay out on the veranda all night, it was freezing out there. Trouble never forgave me for this, and over the years he often reminded me that I owed him for tricking him.

'You can't see Happiness,' my mother said the next morning. 'Not for a few days. She's not well.'

I was worried that it had something to do with our bicycle ride. I was not allowed into her house and did not see her for a whole two weeks. 'Something is wrong with her,' Mother said, but she didn't say what it was. 'She will play with you again as soon as she recovers.' That night, after dancing, Trouble said Happiness was brought in to see Sheikh Baba. She was in a lot of pain. The Sheikh had prayed for her. I too prayed for my friend. Early in the morning we heard wailing coming from her house and Mother gave me the news. Happiness was dead. Trouble explained that she died because she was cut and she never healed. She had been losing blood, but her family did not take her to see a doctor. 'What do you mean, cut?' I asked.

'Circumcision,' Trouble answered.

'Girls too?'

'Yes. It is terribly painful for boys and must be unbearable for girls,' he said and involuntarily put his hand on his penis, as if he remembered the pain of his own experience. 'When were you cut?' I asked, and felt shivers going through my body at the thought that I still had to face this. 'About your age,' Trouble said.

'Did it hurt?'

'Like being hung up by your penis with a hook.' He formed the hook with his middle finger. 'I don't want to be cut,' I said and I wet myself.

I will miss Flathead and Hercules

At dawn, after my morning prayers, I went to sleep, because Shawa could not come for my sister in daylight. Rashaba and Trouble had gone back to work, the day after Star's birth.

Two hours later, when I woke up, I served breakfast, black tea and yoghurt, while Mother breastfed. I asked if I could stay home from school to spend time with Star. The truth was, I did not want to see Kojak.

Flathead arrived, and in a good mood. 'You have lost lots of blood, Sister,' he said. 'You need to eat lamb's liver to regain your energy.' He placed the takeaway food in front of Mother. Hercules left his shoes outside the door. He came in carrying a wooden cot and, grinning broadly, asked if I had caught Shawa?

'You would like me to catch her so that you could marry her. You want a princess, don't you?' I said, giggling.

'That could make Baban lose his virginity,' Flathead said, laughing.

'First you need to lose yours,' Mother said, reminding Flathead of his fiancé.

She was the daughter of a man who had tended Grandfather's garden. At her birth, she refused to come out at the hands of traditional midwives. The desperate gardener asked for my grandfather to help to save his wife and child. The King paid for the best doctor he knew to cut the wife's belly and to bring out the rebel child. The gardener kissed his hand and offered him to accept his newly born daughter as a gesture of thanks, to be engaged to Flathead, fifteen years older than her. Grandfather accepted, but on the condition that the final decision should be Flathead's.

'They are showing a Bruce Lee at the Atlas Cinema,' Flathead said, ignoring Mother's teasing about his fiancé. 'Would you like to see it?'

'Yes,' Hercules answered. 'After the film, we could go for a game of dominoes.'

On hearing Bruce Lee's name, my ears pricked up like those of a rabbit. My uncles knew how much I adored the cinema. Flathead asked Mother if I could go with them. She consented.

Sitting between my uncles watching Bruce Lee leaping around and kicking everyone left and right, I just felt depressed. I couldn't enjoy my treat, a doner kebab sandwich and a Pepsi. Bruce Lee, fighting his enemies so courageously, only reminded me that I could not stand up for myself. Then, I remembered talking with Hercules about the Kurdish infighting. I felt ashamed, as my number-one enemy, Kojak, was also a Kurd.

A couple of days later, it was time for my uncles to leave again. They kissed Mother's head and Star's rosy cheeks. They put five dinars each under the Qur'an which Star's head rested upon in the cot. Hercules held a carrier bag in his hand. I prayed for their safety as Mother kissed them. She always cried when they had to leave again to work. To hide her feelings, she sat next to the cot to breastfeed Star. 'You shouldn't let that poor girl wait for you much longer,' Mother said.

'She will have my answer next time I am back from Baghdad,' Flathead answered. Hercules lifted me onto his shoulders and took me out. I asked him what kind of things they transported to Baghdad.

'Rice, cement, barley and sometimes military equipment.'

'Guns too?'

'Yes, but not without heavily armed guards.' Hercules put me down by his truck and handed me the carrier bag. 'Keep up with your exercise and don't forget: up Kissinger's bum!'

'I will miss you very much. I hope you will be back soon.'

'You are asking too many questions for your age. Be careful,' he said, and pulled my cheek. Flathead kissed me too and put a coin in my hand, before climbing up into his truck and driving off first. Hercules didn't go so quietly; I thought the bellow of his horn might be heard in Baghdad. He beeped twice, put his foot down and they roared away, with me waving at them all the while. I looked into my hand, Flathead had given me fifty cents. Inside the bag was a new set of haluk and bat.

'Mery!' Kojak shouted, as he ran up to me. 'I haven't seen you at school for a few days.'

'I have a new sister.'

'Another girl?' he said sarcastically.

Kojak, with his fat belly and round wobbly face, and I, with my hat on, could have been a younger version of Stan Laurel and Oliver Hardy. We could have had lots of fun together, if only we were friends. But of course we were not, and I believed nothing in the world could have ever brought us together.

'Don't worry, your secret is safe with me. But you have to pay,' Kojak said.

'What do you want?'

'To start with, I want...' He put a hand on my new Haluken set. 'I want these.' Then he held up his homework book. 'From now on, I want you to do my homework.'

'Promise you will never tell anyone?'

'As long as you do everything I ask.'

'I will.'

'I promise.' Kojak put his hand on his head. I did not trust him, but I needed time to think this over, hoping I could find a way to save myself. I let my haluk and bat slip away into his hands and took his homework book. I was about to go. 'Wait!' He opened my other hand and snatched the fifty cents. His eyes widened.

At midday Kojak was waiting for me outside our school. I handed over his book. He looked at it and was pleased. 'Now give me your homework book,' he demanded.

'Why?' I asked.

He grabbed my hat in a firm grip, pulling my hair in his fist. 'Never ask why again. Just give it to me.' As I did he let go of my hat. He pulled out three pages. 'No more homework for you.' He began to walk away, tearing out pages as he went. I followed him, helplessly, trying not to cry. 'When you're in class you don't raise your hand. And when the teacher asks, you give incorrect answers. You no longer offer to go to the blackboard...' He went on piling on more rules. I was about to protest, but he slapped me, lightly, to discourage any dissent. 'Now give me your pocket money.'

Aras, our maths teacher was surprised that I had not done my homework. 'I wasn't feeling well.' The lie only worked for the first couple of days. Then, I was beaten with a cane. I became the lazy pupil, with red palms burning from the beatings while Kojak was complimented for his homework. I no longer had the joy of eating beetroot juice after school. Instead, I had to wait for Kojak while he ate it. Soon I had to do homework for his friends too. He charged them ten cents each for the entire week and I would spend hours every day to accomplish my task. In the last assembly of the year Kojak was called out for his cleverness while I was told off. My life at school became one torment after another, but Kojak did not stop there. He asked me to sit on the side of the Haluken pitch. 'You can't play at the beginning,' he said. 'Half way through the game I will let you join in.' But he never did. Time after time I had to sit and watch him play the only game I had ever dreamt about. None of the other boys ever protested. When Kojak was looking elsewhere they sometimes sheepishly looked over to me, throwing sympathetic glances followed by helpless shrugs or headshakes. Not one of them dared to object. *Selfish*, I thought, as I watched them playing freely and with my set of haluk and bat. *I would stand up for them. I did it in the past, and would fight for their freedom right now, if one of them were in my shoes.* But of course they were not me, and cared less. I was so pleased to see Popcorn, whenever he passed by, he always offered me free popcorn and tried his best to console me.

Aras, the maths teacher, knowing that Rashaba did not care, called my mother in. Mother could not understand because she saw me doing homework all the time. She wanted to know what was wrong, but I could not tell her that I was being bullied by one of the worst creatures in the world. Kojak was standing nearby, pretending to be a good friend of mine. *I would love to tell her the truth, but how could I?*

On the way home though, Mother soon forgot about my school problems. She was anxious. My uncles were a week late in coming home. 'Maybe they had an accident, or they have been sent to the front line,' she said, thinking aloud. 'As soon as your father is home, I'll ask him to go to my brothers' boss to ask for news.'

We heard Rashaba before we walked into the courtyard. He was shouting and kicking the door of the gymnasium, brandishing a large kitchen knife in his right hand. 'I will break the door down if you don't open it at once. Trouble, open up!' Rashaba shouted. Mother shut the main door with a bang, making sure Rashaba heard. 'Trouble has left his work and is not going back again,' he said, turning to Mother. 'Where have you been?' He walked over to take out his temper on us. 'I had to deliver some bread,' she said. 'Mery came to help me.' I wanted to kiss her hands for not telling him about my school difficulties. Not that he cared, but he would have loved to find any excuse to hit me instead of Trouble, since he couldn't get to him.

'Get your son out before I break that door and cut his throat,' Rashaba threatened. Trouble was staring from behind the bars in the window. 'I will, and I'll ask him to go back to his work,' Mother said. 'My brothers have been away for more than five weeks, and their boss might have some news.'

'Fine,' Rashaba's mood softened. 'I will go to the office tomorrow, but I don't want Trouble in my house if he doesn't go back to work,' he concluded, tapping the knife on the bars. Mother said she'd make dinner. 'I am not eating,' Rashaba grunted as he went towards the door. 'And you,' he pointed at me. 'Have some food and get to Takya.'

'Yes, Father.'

'You didn't leave your job, did you? You were sacked,' Mother said through the bars, as Trouble waited until he was certain Rashaba would not return.

'Well done, Mum. You got it. I can't go back to work.'

I left them and went up to our room to say hello to Star, who was tucked up in the cot alone. Trouble walked in behind me, making me nervous. 'Where is Father's money?' he hissed.

'With Sheikh Baba,' I said, bending down to kiss Star. He grabbed my hair and slapped me hard. Star was watching us, giggling.

'Mum!' I yelled, twisting aside as Trouble aimed a clumsy kick to my belly. He ran away before Mother reached our room. I knew I would not see him again for a long time.

What is your address?

Kirkuk, May 1981

Dear Gringo,
This is my third letter to you. I don't have your address, but on the envelope, as usual, I will write:

> To: Mr Clint Eastwood
> Great Actor and my Hero
> United States of America

I post my letters at the central and only post office in Kirkuk. This is on the western side of the river, a long walk from Qala. When I first went there I handed in the letter so the postman behind the desk could stick the stamp on. He read the address on the envelope and, with a nasty expression, said, 'America?' I nodded, paid the twenty-five cents for the stamp, and left quickly. I didn't know what was wrong, but I felt uncomfortable, as if sending you letters was forbidden. Fortunately he no longer looks at me suspiciously. In fact, now he even smiles and he chooses the most attractive stamps to stick on my letters. His name is Purtuqal, which means Orange, like the fruit, and he looks like one with his chubby, round face. He told me that he also sends letters to America, as he has a son over there studying to become a pilot.

'A civil pilot,' Purtuqal had told me, to be precise. Last time I was on my way to the post office, though, there was a group of armed men on the bridge. They were asking for identity cards and searched peoples' bags roughly. I was worried about being stopped because I was hiding your letter under my shirt. On my way back the checkpoint was clear, and I came across Popcorn. He taught me a new song, which I want to share with you:

> Oh moon! You and I share the same fate
> Both are feeling the same pain

Your pale face lost in the skies
And I lost in the earth's solitude.

At the moment Rashaba is keeping quiet about my sex, but it is only a matter of time. This is why I beg you again. It is urgent for you to come to take me away to America. My Gringo, you may sense how scared I am from my words, but I want you to know that while writing them, I am not crying. My family's life has twisted, and is going downhill by the day, in spite of the birth of my baby sister. I must be the doomed child, not Trouble, as Rashaba thinks. My bad luck is spreading amongst the rest of my family. My uncles have disappeared. Their boss says we just have to hope for the best. So we wait, but Mother cries constantly. She believes a shell might have killed her brothers while transporting soldiers to the front line. Trouble has left home and we don't know where he is now. He is not spoken of in the house. The only one of us with a bit of a smile is baby Star. She is now eight weeks old. She has just learned to roll on to her tummy and she can lift her head up.

Because of the unbearable heat, we have moved to sleep on the rooftop. Before closing my eyes, I look at the millions of twinkling stars and I pray for my uncles and my brother to be safe and I beg God to forgive whatever sins I have committed and free me from my slavery. Soon our school will be closed for three months, from June until the end of August. I have spoken to the caretaker, and he has kindly agreed to give me your letter, if it arrives, even during the summer holidays.

Since I sent you my first letter, I've gone to school every day hoping to get an answer from you. Perhaps it is taking you a long time because you can't read Kurdish. I could find someone here to help me write in English, but I can't trust anyone to share my secrets with. As soon as I start Year Five and learn English, I will write to you in your own language.

I have no friends left. They are all with Kojak now. I have a plan to hoodwink Kojak. I shall let you know the outcome in my next letter, if I am able to write to you again.

Gringo, my friend and my hope, I salute you. And as always, I thank you from my heart.

Mery Rashaba

Baghdad, here I come

I did a headstand against the courtyard wall. I was thinking about Happiness. I missed playing with her, and her friendship. She used to be much better than me at standing on her head. 'See the world upside down, Mery,' she would say, 'and nothing looks the same.' Her mother did not like Happiness to have her legs up like this, so she pulled her dress to cover them. If she was in a bad mood, she would hit her. 'Why can't I play?' Happiness protested.

'It is a boy's game,' her mother answered. I was obliged to play girly games and Happiness was not allowed to play boy's games. It was very confusing.

I liked seeing the world upside down. It looked funny to watch Mother washing her beloved Star in a bowl by pouring water over her head. Suddenly, Mother screamed and ran up the stairs, leaving Star alone in the water. 'Mery!' she called. 'There is a mouse. Come Mery, come and kill the vermin.'

'It is only a mouse. They won't bite you.'

'We must poison them before they take over the house. Dry your sister and put some clothes on her. I won't be long,' and she put on her black cape.

'Where are you going?'

'To buy some poison and wipe out the damn mice.'

I walked over to smiling Star and splashed some water over her face. She hated it and cried. I dried and dressed her. I tied two sticks together and covered them with some fabric to make a doll, which I named King Kong. I acted out the story of the giant ape that was in love with her and was coming to take her away to his remote island. In the game, Star was Jessica Lange, and I was Jeff Bridges. Star enjoyed seeing me banging on my chest and imitating the roaring sound of King Kong, and stopped crying.

Mother spread the mouse powder all around the kitchen and warned me not to touch it because the poison could kill me. After dinner, she waited for Rashaba to finish her delicious Dolma, vegetables stuffed with rice and minced meat, before announcing, 'If you can't make up your mind whether to go and search for my brothers then I will go myself.'

'No you won't,' Rashaba said, in a measured tone. 'You will not go to Arab land. You are far too afraid of them. All for your drunken brothers!' Mother heard his bitter remark even though he mumbled it. Star was crying. I swung her in my arms. Mother was too upset to look after her daughter. 'They may be dead in the war, for all we know, but my brothers are not infidels!' she shouted bitterly through tears of her own.

'I have asked for a few days off work,' Rashaba said. 'I will go to Baghdad early next week if your brothers don't show up by then.' Here was the opportunity I had dreamt of and planned for.

'Father, take me to Baghdad with you, to see a doctor?' My request surprised Rashaba. He fixed his eyes on mine, but carried on eating. 'I will stop eating and drinking until I die. I won't go to Takya ever again and will not become a dervish, if you don't take me.' That was the first time I had ever spoken so directly to him. This made him almost choke. 'Why not see one in Kirkuk? We have doctors here,' he spluttered, coughing out food.

'No, I don't want anyone to know about my problem here, in case we find out that I am a...' I could not finish.

'If they find out what?'

'I am ten, and I am not circumcised yet, and I can no longer be circumcised.' *Does he believe me? He must do, as he began to eat again.*

'It will cost more, but I don't mind. Not for Merywan, the son I so much want to become one of Kirkuk's finest dervishes.' Pride coloured his voice, and suddenly, grabbing me by my collar across the plates of food, he pulled me on to the mat. 'Never let me hear you say you don't want to be a dervish again in your life!' He gave me a pair of new trousers. 'Going to the Arab land, it is wiser to wear these and not Kurdish sharwal.' He asked me to try them on. They were slightly short and too tight, but I didn't care, I was finally wearing trousers like the children in America, and I was going to Baghdad.

When I return from Baghdad, I will crush Kojak. I will put a rope around his neck and ride on him like a donkey, kicking his arse all the way to school. I will have his dogface father beaten by Hercules and Flathead and have his long moustache publicly shaved off with his own dagger. Such fantasies kept my spirits up, but first we needed to find my uncles. Perhaps I was daydreaming, although the sun had barely risen at the time. It was just dawn as Rashaba and I made our way to Kirkuk's central bus station on foot. We arrived to find a dusty, noisy square packed with cars, with a couple of restaurants, handcarts from which sherbet drinks were sold, and a few boys of my age, running around with trays on their heads selling seeds, biscuits, and other snacks for hungry travellers.

Drivers called out, 'Baghdad! Mosul! Basra! Tikrit! Baghdad…' rounding up passengers and stuffing ever more sweaty bodies into their already overcrowded vehicles. My stomach was rumbling and my eyes lit upon a juicy kebab, but I knew better than to ask Rashaba for it. We got into a Koster, a sixteen-seat Japanese minibus. The greedy driver took twenty-two passengers for a journey of four and a half hours, and in the summer heat too, which would reach 45 degrees by the time we were halfway there. None of this mattered to me in the least. I was excited about my first journey to Baghdad, Iraq's capital city, where I could be operated upon and freed from my nightmares.

About five kilometres south of Kirkuk we pulled up at the main checkpoint. An Arab Special Forces soldier approached the middle door of the bus, and all conversation stopped at once. Three conscript soldiers, sitting next to the middle door, facing Rashaba and me, quickly put their military berets back on their heads, while everyone else, except for us, took their hats off. The soldier called for IDs. There was a hurried rustling as hands searched inside pockets, but no one spoke. Rashaba held up his and my identity cards. The soldier checked them carefully, one at a time, staring suspiciously for a while before handing them back. He came to the last regular soldier. 'Straighten your beret,' he scolded. 'Yes, sir,' the youth answered, with a military salute.

Unlike the conscript, the Special Forces were loyal to their leader. I had never been so close to one of the monster's men before. I must not panic. 'Take off your turban,' he pointed to Rashaba.

'And you, take off your hat,' he snapped at me. Rashaba had never learnt Arabic. The driver translated. We revealed our long hair.

'What is this?' he forced a smile. 'You are women?' Rashaba explained, and the driver translated into Arabic.

'Move on!' the soldier barked, banging hard on the door before he jumped off. Nobody spoke, and we avoided each other's gaze. After forty minutes we crossed the last hills and on into the ochre sand of the Iraqi desert. I knew from my uncles that this chain of the Hamrin Mountains marked the natural border between Kurdistan and Iraq, and might become the political border if we were ever to be free and have our own country. The vastness of this sea of sand fascinated me, and in the middle of it all we bounced along a highway so narrow that barely two cars could pass each other. The driver switched on the radio and we heard The Voice of Baghdad reading news of the war, but it was soon interrupted by the frantic shouts of 'Allah u Akbar', as the passengers at the front of the bus desperately invoked God's protection at the sight of a car speeding directly at us.

A taxi was overtaking a truck, but not quickly enough. There were shouts as our driver braked and swerved on the sandy road, our packed bus rocked crazily on straining axles, and then, metres away from a headlong collision, the taxi scraped narrowly by. I saw a coffin on its roof, which was covered with an Iraqi flag, and as it passed us I looked back, seeing the taxi lurching like a wild horse. The coffin fell and crashed onto the tarmac, throwing the dead man into the air and onto the roadside where his body rolled over and settled in the dust. The truck following them had to swerve off the road to avoid crushing the taxi, and only just avoided rolling on to its side. Our driver yelled profanities even as the Prophet was praised for saving our souls. When the hubbub faded an old man called for Al Fatiha, the prayer for the dead.

'Does he know the dead man?' I whispered to Rashaba. 'The dead man is a soldier killed in the war,' Rashaba said. 'Because he has honoured our president with his own life, he is a martyr and is covered by the Iraqi flag when he is taken back from the frontline to his family.'

Our president! Saddam is not my president and never would be. But of course I could understand that Rashaba had to be very careful in public. We drove further south into Arab land. Most of the passengers fell asleep in the stifling heat, but I stayed awake. I opened the window; there was not a breath of air. We came across a line of camels, ridden by Bedouins, heading towards a distant oasis. Despite not liking the animal because I associated it with Arabs and Kojak's face, I could not help feeling impressed by the scenery, which reminded me of *Lawrence of Arabia,* with Peter O'Toole and Omar Sharif forever riding on their camels, fighting epic battles to create Arabia.

My excitement didn't last. Rather, the journey to Baghdad became a nightmare for me, and it was entirely Rashaba's fault. He woke up with a jump from his sleep, banging his head on the window. 'Ya Allah...' he murmured.

'Are you all right, Father?'

'I had a dream,' he said. 'Your uncles with us two alone in the bus came across Shawes Dog. He was standing on the highway, holding an RPG on his shoulder. He fired it and blew up the bus, killing us all.'

I was shocked, but I managed to mumble, 'It's just a dream, Father.'

'Yesterday,' he continued, 'I came across Shawes in Qala. I don't know why, but I told him I was going to Baghdad and I was taking you with me.'

This astonished me. Rashaba had already decided to take me to Baghdad! So that was why he had bought me new trousers. But why, then, had we had an argument about it?

'Pray God we find your uncles safely,' Rashaba said, as he held up his hands. 'And I pray to God the doctor will not declare you a neuter.'

I thought about their meeting and what might have been said. Perhaps Shawes had asked 'Are you going to Baghdad to have your neuter son operated on?'

'I need to pee,' I said. 'Could you ask the driver to pull over?' Rashaba shook his head. I knew there were no toilets around, but peeing along the roadside, even in cities, was absolutely normal. So why couldn't I pee in this desert? 'I can't hold it in. Please, ask him to stop?'

'There will be a stop soon,' he said, and closed his eyes again. I could feel a few drops escaping and I shouted to the driver. He would only stop at the designated station, which was another half an hour away. 'Shut your mouth,' Rashaba said, but I couldn't. 'I need to pee and must do it now!' I called out, waking up most of the passengers.

'Hold on, we won't be long,' the driver answered carelessly. A hubbub started amongst the passengers. To my horror, it sounded more hostile than sympathetic. I could wait no longer, it was beyond my control. *I wish I was wearing my sharwal because they would hide the wet patch better than these tight trousers.* Rashaba looked shocked at the pee pouring down my legs.

'Dirty dog has pissed on himself!' the man next to me blurted out in Arabic and that much I understood. The driver slammed on the brakes, almost turning the bus over. 'I will throw you out if you have peed in my bus,' he growled, jumping down and marching towards the central door, towards me. Rashaba was embarrassed. The other passengers complained and gestured with their hands in all directions. The driver, seeing the pee on the floor of his bus, grabbed my arm. 'Get off my bus, you filthy orphan,' he said. Rashaba held my other arm tightly and pulled to keep me on. I hung suspended between the two. 'We paid our fares to get to Baghdad, and will not get off until we reach the city,' Rashaba said. I was calling to the driver to let my arm go. He pulled harder and I kicked him in his chest. I had to. He recovered and slapped me. I yelled. Rashaba let go of me and struck the driver with punches and kicks, arguing that his son was not an orphan. He finished by brutally headbutting the man. I was amazed. *He is strong, and how bravely he fights!*

The other passengers were much less impressed. They stood up for the driver and after more than half an hour, much longer than it would have taken me to pee, he got back to the wheel. Rashaba and I were left on the side of the highway as the bus drove away. He turned towards me and I saw his fierce look. I ran, but he chased after me. There were no cars, no people, no birds, no animals. There was nothing, nothing but a road and endless miles of sand, with Rashaba and me running in circles.

'No, Father! Don't...' I begged, as he got hold of my ear.

Heat haze shimmered in almost every direction, but especially above the tarmac, which became sticky and treacherous in this cauldron. A yellow desert scorpion scampered across the sand, leaving its tell-tale trail behind. In no time, my trousers were dry and felt hot enough to burn my skin.

'Don't worry, Father, we will make it to Baghdad,' I was repeating to myself. My battered body was shaking from pain. I was standing away from him, with my arm raised, ready to wave at any cars coming our way, in the hope of getting a lift. A couple of cars zoomed by, followed by a minibus. Rashaba was crouching like a frog, his turban opened over his head and shoulders. I went to sit next to him.

'Sorry, Father,' I said.

I spotted the silhouette of a truck going in the direction of Kirkuk. I let my arm drop because I was still hoping we would make it to Baghdad. As it approached us, the truck's horn blew deafeningly.

'Uncle Arsalan!' I called, jumping to my feet. He parked across the road. 'Are you lost?' Flathead asked, leaning out of his window. 'We went to Baghdad to search for you.'

'I am here now. C'mon, get in! I have good news.'

I ran across the road. I was so excited to see him, but also worried about Hercules. I got in the passenger's door and kissed Flathead's hands. 'Where is Uncle Baban?'

'He will be here soon.'

Rashaba was reluctant, but did not mind a free lift. He took the passenger's seat and I sat in between. Flathead opened the cool box and offered a bottle of cold water to Rashaba, which he refused because it had been cooled alongside the Arak. So Flathead handed it to me. I drank a lot of water. We heard the deep roar of a horn behind us. 'Your Uncle Baban,' Flathead said. I pushed myself across him, stuck my head out of the window and waved to Hercules. He waved back, surprised to see me in Flathead's truck. Rashaba pulled me back to my seat.

Flathead turned to me. 'Shall we go home now?' he said. That marked the end of my dream trip to the capital. Flathead pulled away first, followed by Hercules. They always travelled together like this, they were inseparable.

'Mum is so worried about you. She thought you were killed in the war. Where were you, Uncle?'

Flathead took off my hat and ruffled my hair. 'She wasn't far wrong. We were held up near the front line and I was almost killed by a shell.'

Rashaba, irritated, grabbed my hat and put it back on my head.

'You were in the war? Who do you think is going to win?' I asked.

'No politics,' Rashaba reminded me.

'Listen to this, Mery,' Flathead said, and his smile told me he was about to tell another joke. 'This is new. I heard it from the soldiers. A Kurd goes to the funeral of an Arab soldier killed in the war. You know, he is a Kurd, and the family of the dead are Arabs. It is very sensitive, so he tries his best to be sympathetic. "How did your son die?" he asks. "He was shot in the head," the father of the dead soldier answers. The Kurd nods a couple of times. "Good!" he says. "I mean, I am glad he was not hit in the heart, that would have been terrible."

I giggled, but Rashaba pinched me. Flathead laughed at his own joke. He took out a bottle of Arak. Rashaba looked away. Flathead switched on the radio and spun the dial to find a station that wasn't broadcasting war news. He stopped when he heard Um-Kalsum singing. 'She is an Arab but I love her poetic voice,' he said as he drank, to Rashaba's total disgust. 'Sorry, Darwesh Rashaba, but I need to finish it before we get to the checkpoint.' He gulped it down, opened his window and threw the bottle into the hot sand.

'Guess what, Mery? Your mother is right, I could do with a wife, and I am going to get married.'

'Really? But you said you will only get married in Grandfather's house?'

'Never mind, I will go there for my honeymoon.' He laughed.

'OK, "up Kissinger's bum",' I said, and laughed along.

'What was that you said?'

'It is just a joke, Father.'

'OK! You said OK! Where did you learn to say OK?'

'From Uncle Baban.'

'You are not allowed to talk in the infidel's language.'

'Fine, Father, I will not say OK again,' I said and turned to Flathead, who laughed louder.

'Mother is going to be very happy.'

'Me too. Soon I will be cuddling and kissing a gorgeous woman in my bed,' Flathead said, imitating a few kisses.

'God forgive us!' Rashaba repulsed, pulled me closer to his side.

'Good news for you too!' Flathead continued, 'Uncle Baban has something special for our little nephew.'

'What?'

'It's a surprise,' he said, looking at Rashaba as if to say 'and your father will not like it.'

'You will tell me what it is,' Rashaba muttered. Apart from his shushes, that was the only thing he said throughout the rest of the homeward journey.

Mother's new-moon smile

Our mother glowed. Her smile today made her look more beautiful than I had ever seen her before. She ululated loudly with joy. She was going to give the good news to Flathead's fiancé, and immediately start the preparations for the wedding day.

Hercules gave me a folded poster, and I felt like ululating too. It was of *The Good, the Bad and the Ugly* and it was in colour, one of my best-ever presents. I asked if I could hide the poster in his room. Hercules agreed, but called it Flathead's living room. 'I'm moving to sleep in the gymnasium. Uncle Arsalan needs to have some space and privacy while he cuddles his wife,' he said. Flathead's living room had three doors. The first led directly to a side road, the second opened on to the courtyard and the third connected the living room to his bedroom, which also had a window overlooking the courtyard.

Rashaba paced up and down the veranda, eventually signalling for me to come to him. 'What did Baban give you?' he asked. I took a shirt out of the plastic bag. It was Hercules who had thought of this trick. 'Shall I give it back, Father?'

'No.'

I put on the shirt; it was light blue, my favourite colour.

'Go and ask your brother if he might consider a Maulud for his wedding,' Rashaba told Mother. She was reluctant because she knew Flathead would never agree to Maulud, a Muslim ceremony. 'A Maulud, for the sake of your father, the King,' Rashaba said, with a sigh. I was about to pray when Rashaba sat down next to me. I couldn't work out if I should be pleased or worried, but I remembered it as a rare moment of intimacy between us.

'You miss my grandfather very much, don't you?' I said.

'He was one of the most honourable men I have ever known. I wish I had...' Rashaba could not finish the sentence, for that would have meant talking politics. But I guessed that he wanted to say, 'I wish I had been hanged in his place,' because Mother had also said it often, even though it was forbidden to mention his hanging in our family. 'I agree with you, Father. I think Uncle Arsalan should have Maulud for his wedding in Grandfather's honour.' Rashaba smiled, and ruffled my hair. I held his hand and kissed it.

He pulled me to him. 'Why is Trouble not as good a son as you are?' Then, for the first time, he began to tell me about his childhood.

'When I was your age, we lived in Lover's Hill village. I was the youngest and had three sisters and four brothers. I was the family's shepherd. I took the flock out to pasture and sometimes I would stay away for days. I had a donkey. I called him Zarazar because he brayed like the steam engine that travelled between Kirkuk and Erbil. I also had Bobby, a trustworthy dog, a name that came from the English people who used to work in the oilfields for the Iraqi government. I had to make sure thieves or wolves did not get to the sheep. I only ever lost two, and I was very upset about it. What I most loved was my 'duzala', a bamboo flute made by my father. I spent many hours on the hills playing it. Those where peaceful days.'

It was unbelievable to hear such things! To think that Rashaba had owned a dog named Bobby by the English, the infidels! And he played music every day? *What made him become such a miserable person?*

'Why are you called Rashaba, Darkstorm?'

'One day there was a heavy, violent storm and I got lost in the hills with the flock. I slipped in the floodwater and fell over a rock, breaking my leg. I managed to hobble around, leaning on my staff, but my family was worried that I had been killed and the flock was lost. Bobby and I worked hard through the fierce wind and managed to keep the flock together, except for the two sheep I mentioned earlier, which got lost. The moment I sat down, once the storm had abated, I fell into a deep sleep. It must have been two days later when, like Antar, my father appeared on his black stallion. He embraced me and kissed me. He nicknamed me Rashaba, strong like the Darkstorm, the proud son of his father.' *Did he really mention Antar? He has never read a book, been to the cinema or even watched television, so how does he know of Antar?* All of a sudden, I realised that he was not referring to Niazi Mostafa's film, but to the Arabian hero, whose fame rests on his story having been told countless times. I had many more questions to ask. Why didn't Rashaba play with me? Why did we have so many rules? Yet my curiosity about my father's parents, my uncles and aunties, his sisters and brothers that I had never met, was even stronger.

'I wish I had been able to meet your father and your family,' I said. Rashaba nodded thoughtfully. 'I can't forgive the Arab Iraqis for killing them so unjustly, can you, Father?' I thought he would agree, or perhaps tell me that this was God's will, but my question turned out to be one too many. Rashaba went quiet and could not stop the tears from streaming down his face. 'I am sorry, Father, if I caused you pain.'

Rashaba didn't speak to me about his childhood or his family again.

'Arsalan says no to Maulud,' Mother said, as she came back. Rashaba was despondent. 'He wants a traditional wedding, and says we could do the Maulud another time for my father.'

The next morning I walked to school. The gate was shut, but I knocked anyway, knowing I would find the caretaker inside. He took no holidays and kept himself busy with the small garden on the side of the school courtyard. 'No letters,' he said, when he saw me, gently shaking his head. I decided then not to send another letter to Gringo, until I had started Year Five and learned to write in his language.

I would have gladly stayed at home playing King Kong and enacting other stories to keep Star entertained, but that wasn't to be. I found Kojak waiting at our door when I returned. I pretended to be pleased to see him.

'Why did you go to Baghdad with your father?' he asked.

I longed to be able to say that I had seen a doctor there, and been operated upon! Kojak would have immediately demanded that I show him the evidence. Instead I said simply, 'My uncles were missing and we went to search for them.'

'Did you ask my permission to go away?'

'Sorry, Master. I should have.'

He raised his arm but did not slap me. 'I need some money.' He opened his hand.

'Uncle Arsalan is getting married soon. I will have a lot, but now I don't have any.'

'Get me four eggs.'

'Eggs?'

'Yes, be quick.'

Hercules was moving his bed into the gymnasium with Flathead's help. I tried to make myself invisible. I went into the kitchen and luckily, when I pulled up a cover, I found five eggs in a pot. I put two in each pocket of my sharwal and walked slowly towards the main door.

Mother rushed in, making me jump. She was very excited. 'Arsalan!' she called. I felt for my pockets, I hadn't broken the eggs. Mother had good news. Flathead's fiancé's mother was delighted about the wedding. She only wished that her husband, the gardener, had lived to see this long-awaited day. Flathead agreed that the wedding should take place when he returned from his next trip, and added that he wanted to take a two-week holiday for the occasion. I was stuck there, smiling between them. 'Ali is waiting for you outside,' Mother said.

Great! I was about to go.

'Mery!' she called. I stopped. 'Don't be late, I need you to look after Star, I have to bake some bread.'

Kojak took the eggs but warned me to turn up at his door with money soon. I nodded obediently. I couldn't fathom what Kojak wanted the money for, apart from his love of sweets. He never went to the cinema and did not wear nice clothes. Perhaps he gambled or had to give it to his father. It never occurred to me that he was demanding it simply because he could. As for eggs, that was an even deeper mystery! The thought of him making an omelette nearly made me laugh.

On the way home, I heard a deafening noise coming from a loudspeaker. It was mounted on a military Jeep with four armed Special Forces sitting in the back. The one holding the loudhailer called out in Arabic, 'Those who want to enrol voluntarily in the army will get a reward and an honourable medal from the president, and if they become a martyr for our beloved country, their families will be compensated for their deaths with nothing less than a brand-new Japanese Toyota Super worth ten thousand dinars! As for the traitors, they will be severely punished. Anybody who hides deserters from the army will be executed with the deserter on the spot…'

Old Zorab, with his ear clamped to his radio, cut across me.

'This is the Voice of Kurdistan,' he called, imitating the familiar deep voice of the Kurdish radio announcer who broadcast secretly from the mountains.

'Mr Zorab, they will put the rope around your neck if they hear you say Kurdistan.'

'They will do it anyway, I might as well get it off my chest. This is the Voice of Kurdistan...' he called again, moving down the middle of our street to stand directly in the path of the jeep. The Special Forces driver advanced the vehicle slowly forward until the front bumper was touching Zorab's white cape, but still he did not move. The officer in the passenger's seat, a handsome young captain with the battle-worn demeanour of a veteran, who like the others sported a Saddam-style moustache, leaned out. 'Move away, you old bastard, before I have you run over.'

Zorab did not. The captain got out of the car and pushed Zorab, knocking him to the ground. Zorab rolled over awkwardly as he tried to protect his precious radio, holding it aloft. Seeing this, the captain grabbed the radio and smashed it against the wall. As Zorab picked himself up off the ground he reached for a stone, hid it behind his back and stepped in front of the Jeep again. A few passers-by had stopped to watch. I stood by the wall to our house, only a few steps away from him. 'Mr Zorab!' I said, trying to get his attention, but he did not seem to hear me.

'Lieutenant Akbar!' the captain yelled to one of his men. 'Yes, sir!' Akbar responded, saluting automatically. 'Count to three,' the captain ordered, 'If he doesn't move away, shoot him.'

Akbar picked up his AK-47, aimed at Zorab and began counting slowly, 'One...'

'Please Mr Zorab,' I said.

'Two...' Akbar charged his gun.

'Mr Zorab, they will kill you.'

'Merywan, keep out of this!' Zorab smiled at me and looked strangely happy, exultant, as he turned back and threw the hidden stone, smashing the Jeep's windscreen.

'Three.' Akbar opened fire.

The bullets shook Zorab. His body rocked in a grotesque dance before he finally dropped to the ground. There was panic. People scattered. I ran around the corner and back home, and stood with my back against the door, pinning it shut, as my uncles hurried towards me. 'No,' I said. 'You can't go out. The monster's men are here.'

'Mery, come away from the door,' Flathead asked. 'Mum,' I shouted, 'don't let my uncles go.' But Flathead pushed me, and rushed out, arriving in time to see the Jeep bumping over the crumpled body of the old man, and driving away down the deserted street.

My body felt numb from the shock. 'I tried to help Mr Zorab,' I said to my mum, who clung tightly to me. 'I wanted to warn him, but Zorab didn't listen, and now he is dead.' I collapsed into Mother's arms as my uncles returned, and each of them reassured me time and again that it wasn't my fault, that I had been very brave and Old Zorab would be proud of me.

He had faced the monster's men with his head held high, defiant, but I was still shaking from the shock when I lay in bed that night, knowing that I would never see dear Old Zorab on our streets again, and trying not to remember how he had died.

I must kill Kojak

I was right to think Flathead would be generous with pocket money. He gave me an extra fifty cents before leaving again for work. I knocked on Kojak's door. His mother opened it with a crying child in her arms. She had a bruised face which she tried to hide from me. The sound of arguing echoed around the house, and when I asked for Ali I could hear him sobbing inside. I was already regretting coming here, when Shawes Dog saw me and pushed his wife aside. 'Ali,' he barked. 'Come, your pigeon is here.' He slammed the door into my face. I was shaken, but thanked Allah for giving me Rashaba as a father. The door opened once more, and Kojak tried to pretend everything was fine, but I could see his red cheeks were still wet with tears. Even so, he recovered rapidly. 'One of your fucking eggs was rotten,' he said. I opened my hand, giving him Flathead's money and everything I had saved. 'One hundred and fifty cents for you, Master.'

He took the money. 'This is not enough, you shitty neuter. I could tell your secret to Sheikh Baba and the dervishes, that will make your father's golden teeth shine a lot more, wouldn't it?'

'Do you want more eggs?'

'Fuck the eggs and the chickens, follow me.'

It was midday on Friday and Zao'Adin's mosque was crowded for prayer. Several beggars were gathered at the entrance. Kojak had set me a new challenge. He wanted me to steal from them. *Rashaba is working and Trouble is not likely to be anywhere near the mosque, but still, what if one of my teachers, or the caretaker, is here for the prayer, and sees me stealing from the beggars?*

Kojak stood to the side and watched. I started with one of the women covered in a black cloak and veil. I sat next to her and pretended to beg. I held up one hand and with the other, I slyly took the few cents from her handkerchief. Then, on my master's instruction, I moved to the next, a blind man who had plenty of coins in his pot. He was shaking his head left and right as if he was trying to bite the flies that were striking his face. Apart from the words, 'God's mercy on this poor blind man,' the rest of his murmuring was unintelligible.

I reached towards his money. Just as I touched the coins, he rapped me on my hand with his walking stick. I let out a shriek. *How did he realise what I was doing and be so precise in hitting me?* He lifted his stick to my face and I leapt up and ran away. I handed Kojak the coins I had stolen from the poor woman. I felt sick because this was not only wrong but also really dangerous. *Sooner or later I will find myself with one hand chopped off, and perhaps locked up behind bars.*

I was determined to free myself from Kojak, but how? *Maybe I could shove him under a speeding car, or push him into one of the wells, or fake an accident at the Takya so that one of the swords cuts his throat? But I would never get away with it. Imagine if I was caught, red-handed, with Kojak half-dead at my side...* Over dinner on the veranda, I was thinking all this when Mother screamed, 'Mouse!' She was clutching her shoe.

A mouse in the courtyard stood on its back legs in front of me, as if committing suicide, and blaming me for it, shook its little body and fell sideways. It was dead.

'The poison will wipe them out,' Mother said, satisfied. *The poison...* I smiled to myself for the first time in weeks.

A few days later Mother received the double bed she had ordered for Flathead and reorganised his room, cleaning it spotlessly. I helped with the invitation cards. Rashaba killed two sheep. He took on the job to make sure they would be served as halal meat. Mother sorted out the deliveries and more women helped with the preparations for the ever-popular meal.

I planned to poison Kojak on the wedding day, Friday, the day of the feast and the arrival of the bride. But Flathead wanted the celebration to start three days before. Or rather, three nights, because the dancing mostly took place during the evening, which was why the first thing Hercules did was to borrow an extension lead and hang cheerful lights above the open space outside our house.

Soon after sunset, half a dozen men and women, Flathead's closest friends, gathered under Hercules' lights. They held hands in a line, wearing their colourful clothes, and began to dance. More people joined in, even passers-by, since the party was open to everyone. The dance formation expanded into a broad circle and the musicians, Salah and Fayk Dawda, who were the best in town, had got hundreds to dance to the rhythm of their Daul, a large drum and Zurna, the pipe. Every now and then, Salah called, 'Long live...,' as they were given tips.

I handed out glasses of iced water from a bucket to the sweaty dancers. I came to Mother, and felt so pleased seeing her dancing between Hercules and Flathead, beaming. She ululated again and my female relatives joined in. Rashaba did not dance but looked after those who only wanted to sit and enjoy drinking sherbet, cups of tea and coffee, and admire the dancing. He did not condone mixed dancing, but this tradition dated back to long before Islam had reached Kurdistan, and although the majority of those present were Muslims, they preserved the dancing because they adored it. It was the only time that men and women could be so physically close together, which was another reason why weddings were popular, apart from the feast. Dancing was liberating in other ways too, as some of the frustrations that simmered and boiled under the heavy lid of the monster's regime could be released when we danced together. People often talked about letting off steam – no wonder it usually got sweaty.

I put my bucket down on the ground, lifted Star, who was now almost six months old, onto my shoulders, and began to 'shake it' with my uncles and my mother. I felt liberated too: this was one occasion where I could dance freely without being punished by Rashaba. Flathead whispered to the drummer and slipped him some coins. 'Long live Mery!' the musician called. I smiled at Flathead in gratitude for his caring so much about me. The drummer twisted his drum, and pummelled it with renewed vigour, which delighted the dancers. Even the crowd of watchers began to dance, and I saw Rashaba, unconsciously moving his head to the rhythm of the music, while serving coffee.

As they whirled about, with their feet, hips and shoulders moving in unison, Mother, while ululating, left the line and changed her dance to a mix of disco and belly dancing, directly opposite Trouble, who had just arrived. Flathead joined in. He picked up the bucket of water and put it on top of his flat head. The drummer played for him. Flathead bent backwards holding up his head. The crowd stopped dancing and clapped and Flathead arched his back more and more. I clicked the joints in my fingers as I squeezed my hands. I did not want Flathead to fail. He leaned back ever further, until he was dancing with the bucket still on his head all the way to the ground. Everyone was cheering, and there was a special drum-roll from Salah as Flathead jumped up, grinning triumphantly, and bowed extravagantly to all sides.

After three such nights of exhilarating dancing it was time to become serious. Well, serious about food anyway. From early Friday morning, in a corner of the open space, three large pots of basmati rice, and another four – two of bean stew and two of apricots, were cooking on a wood fire for the wedding feast. The dancing was now continuing all day. Sheikh Baba and many dervishes, Aras, the maths teacher and even Kamil Effendi, our landlord, arrived for the wedding lunch, along with hundreds of others. Zao'Adin and I exchanged a look as I served him his food and, for a moment, I thought about poisoning him too.

The male guests lined up in groups of twenty around a table in the courtyard, and, in less than five minutes, they stuffed down the food, drank tea, congratulated Flathead and his sister, and left. Within minutes the table was cleaned ready for another twenty. The women were fed inside Flathead's living room. There was also a line of beggars sitting on the dust outside the main door. I served them food. I recognised the one who had hit me with the stick outside the mosque. He searched with his hand. 'Could you help pass me the spoon?' he said, shaking his head. The spoon was next to his plate, clearly visible.

'There is no spoon,' I said. 'You have to eat with your hands.'

'What is that, then?' he replied irritably, pointing a finger.

'If you can see it, why can't you pick it up yourself, Mr Blindy?' He lowered his sunglasses and looked into my eyes. 'What is your name?' he asked.

'Merywan Rashaba.'

'Merywan, you are the first to trick me and I have been in this profession for five years, so well done.' He put his sunglasses back on and I handed him the spoon. 'Enjoy your meal,' I said. Kojak was dancing happily. *Why shouldn't he? He has a slave to give him money, to steal for him and serve him with a plateful fit for a king. He may as well enjoy it for this is going to be his last dance before his last supper.*

'Are you hungry, Master?' I asked, with a bow. 'Starving,' he said, touching his fat belly. 'I could eat a whole lamb on my own.'

'Go and sit on the veranda, and be my honoured guest. Master Ali, would you like bean stew or apricot?'

'Both. Bring both, big portions.'

I took a tray with two plates, one with stew and the other with rice. I covered the rice with roasted lamb and then crouched down so I was hidden behind the pots of steaming food. I took the whole packet of poison which Mother had bought for the mice, and stirred it into the stew with a stick that I found by the fire. I spat in his food. On my way to serve him I prayed to God to forgive me, even though Kojak was a bad person and it made much more sense for him to die rather than ruin my life. Hercules stopped me. He had a white suit on and had gelled his hair to look like Elvis Presley. 'That is special,' he said, and extended his hand towards the tray. I prayed again, this time so that he would not touch the stew! He picked up a piece of lamb from the rice plate and put it into his mouth. 'You will ride with me,' he said. 'We will be leaving soon.'

'This is the last plate I need to serve, and it is for my best friend, Ali,' I said.

Flathead was dressed elegantly, in a brand new Kurdish suit. A lively crowd was gathered outside and the musicians were playing enthusiastically around two Mercedes cars. The black one, with red roses arranged in the shape of a heart across the bonnet, was for the groom, while the bride's was white and decorated with brightly coloured balloons and streamers. When a pickup truck full of Arab policemen drove up, the music abruptly stopped and the noise died down. The crowd split into two halves to make way for the police. The officer asked for the groom. Mother's face went deathly pale. Flathead faced him, with Hercules standing behind him like a bodyguard.

'Are you the groom?' the officer asked. 'Yes, are there any problems?' Flathead answered in perfect Arabic. *Surely they hadn't come because of me. Could they possibly know that I am poisoning Kojak at this very moment?* Through the main door, I looked back to where Kojak, alone on the veranda, was busy eating.

'No,' the officer forced back a smile. 'I wondered if you might welcome Arab guests?'

Only Flathead's eyes revealed the truth. He would never welcome Arabs, given what they had done to his father. 'We are just leaving to pick up the bride, but you are welcome to stay,' Flathead replied. 'Darwesh Rashaba,' he turned to him, 'since you are staying, could you tend to our dear Arab guests?'

'I don't speak Arabic,' Rashaba protested. 'Just feed them and nod,' Flathead said quietly in Kurdish, 'that is what they expect us to do.' Rashaba waved the guests in. Mother embraced Flathead.

'For a moment I...' her voice was choked. 'I thought they were here for you.' My uncle reassured her with a smile. The music started again. I felt a tug on my shirt, and turned to see Kojak.

'Did you eat well, Master?' I asked.

'Yes, very tasty.'

Now I could look forward to seeing him drop dead like the mice. I just hope it wouldn't spoil the wedding. 'Are you ready for the ride?' I asked casually, so that he would not suspect anything.

'I don't know anyone with a car.'

'Don't worry, you can ride on the pickup with the musicians and Ardalan.' Trouble was already up there, dancing with a couple of his friends. 'Go,' I said. 'They know about it, I have arranged a place for you, Master.' As he left I ran back inside to look at his plate. The camel had left nothing, it was wiped clean.

Ten other cars were ready to follow in procession. Flathead wanted me to have a privileged place in the passenger's seat of the bride's car. Hercules was our driver. Mother sat in the back, and we lined up behind the groom's car, which in turn followed the pickup. We left with car horns beeping and blaring, drowning out the sound of the drum and pipe that played throughout the journey. We drove to the Priadi district, where another crowd awaited us. Naturally there was more dancing as the bride was brought out in a Western-style white wedding dress, her face hidden by a diaphanous pink veil. Mother held one of her arms. Flathead lifted the veil slightly, kissed her forehead and handed her a red rose. I could not see her face, so I jumped on top of our car, but I was not quick enough, her veil was back down.

We drove around town. It was customary to take the bride on her final parade before becoming a wife. I was eager to see her face and to discover what my new auntie looked like. Because of the heat, Mother suggested that she lifted the veil for a few seconds to freshen up her face. She nodded gracefully. As a bride, she was not allowed to talk on her wedding day and had to look miserable. Otherwise, people would have suggested that she was happy to leave her family, and aching so much to have a man on top of her that she smiled all the way to her new bedroom.

Hercules adjusted the rear-view mirror. He too was curious to see his new sister-in-law. She was sixteen, half Flathead's age, yet she looked even younger. Her face was powdered white with rouge on her cheeks and heavy crimson lipstick. She looked perfect to me, like a porcelain doll, but so delicate that I thought she might break when Flathead touched her. She had large green eyes and a narrow pointed nose. Hercules considerately wound down his window to let fresh air blow into the bride's face. She was good at looking miserable. She wore a grumpy expression, but seeing me staring at her so curiously, she relaxed slightly and gave me a sweet, mysterious smile which transformed her appearance. It was a smile that was full of mischief, one that reminded me of Scarlett O'Hara in *Gone with the Wind*.

I took off my hat and bowed, saluting her like Oliver Twist might have done. I am not sure why I did this, but for a few moments I felt like I was in a film and had known her for a long time.

'Hey, are you a girl?' she asked, when she saw my long hair. I bowed again, and she giggled. Mother shushed her. 'You know you're not supposed to talk today, and don't laugh.' Before she put the veil back on, the bride stuck her tongue out at me. Hercules noticed this too, because he smiled at my reaction. I liked my new auntie and felt we were going to become good friends. I turned around to look at Kojak on the pickup truck, and saw that he was hardly dancing. Hercules had his hand on the horn all the way back to Qala.

At Flathead's request, the cars stopped. Flathead courteously offered the bride his arm and they walked in fine style, followed by Mother and other young women, who were dancing to the rhythm of the music. Hundreds more guests converged and, to the chagrin of the Arab guards and family within, we paraded outside Grandfather's house and all the way home.

Flathead had not been able to marry in the King's Castle as he intended, but parading outside like this showed his true warrior spirit, and his sense of humour, too. When we reached our house I asked around for Kojak, until Trouble explained that he had a stomach ache and had gone home.

I will get you, Mery

Kojak did not die, although he did end up spending two days in hospital. On my visit to him he asked for more money, far more than I would ever receive as gifts or pocket money. He wanted five dinars, five thousand cents! He did not care how or where I got it from, but he warned me that if I did not have it on the first day of school, he would shout out my secret in the classroom, before telling Rashaba, Trouble and everyone in Takya.

I can think of no alternative but stealing from my father and giving Kojak large sums to keep him happy. It is a dreadful plan, but what else can I do? Rashaba and Mother didn't count their savings regularly, but simply added their newly earned dinars. *It would be a while before they realise that some are missing. Would this solve my problem? Not entirely, although it could keep Kojak off my back for a little longer. It is an unforgivable act to steal from my parents. I am crossing every boundary, and perhaps there will be no way back for me and I will follow this path down through one crime after another, but I have no intention of letting Kojak and his Dog-father win the battle. Old Zorab was wrong. I am not in their dirty game. I am different and I am going to save myself and go to America.*

Rashaba was at work when I got home and so was Trouble, having started a new job as an assistant gardener. Hercules was doing bodybuilding in his room. Flathead had left to buy a kebab for his wife. Mother had taken Star with her to bake bread for a rich family, but still, I was scared stiff when I touched Father's pillow. His words were echoing in the room, 'Let me lay my head on my money. I have sweated blood earning this working on the hottest days of summer…' Rashaba might burn my hand, or even cut my throat, but I had to take the risk. I looked out onto the courtyard from our window, it was quiet. I asked God for forgiveness and picked up the pillow, untying the cotton string knots at one end. As I had imagined, there were two layers. A thick layer of feathers came first, and inside that was a second pillow, hiding Father's fortune. I opened it. My hands were shaking, and I was sweating. The main door banged. 'Mery!' Mother called.

Shit! She was on her way up and I had no time to put the pillow back properly. 'Mery!' She must have been on the last step. 'Yes, Mum,' I called back. She found me sitting in front of Boraq's mirror, wearing one of her long dresses, combing my hair. *Don't ask me to stand up.* The pillow was missing from the bedding, but fortunately she barely walked in. 'Star just won't let me make the bread,' she said. 'Could you look after her?'

'I think I have lice in my hair,' I said, to distract her. 'I don't have time now,' she answered. She put Star down on the carpet and left. The pillow was still hidden between my legs under her dress. I rapidly counted the money I needed and put everything back as it had been. I must have examined the pillow dozens of times to make sure everything was placed back perfectly, and each time I did so I promised that I would pay back my father. But this did not assuage my guilt about my terrible crime.

As I arrived at school, I asked the caretaker about Gringo's letter, but again he shook his head.

'Where's the money?' Kojak said, facing me like a beast when he saw me. He raised his hands and counted five using his fingers. 'I will tell everyone, you are Hiz, fucked by my father many times, and of your own choice.'

Kojak calling me Hiz! I wanted to flatten his face. 'Master Ali, you better not,' I said. 'I will give you sixty dinars, that's sixty thousand cents.'

Kojak's face brightened. 'How much did you say?'

'Sixty dinars.'

'Say it again.' He made me repeat it twice more. He pulled up his hands and counted using his fingers. 'Sixty dinars?'

'Yes, sixty. But I will not go stealing ever again, and you promise you will forget about my being a neuter, and your father must not ask me ever to go to the Turkish baths with him again.'

'Where would you get sixty dinars from?'

'I have them already.' I put my hand in my pocket and took out the twelve five dinar notes. 'You can have five dinars now,' I pulled out a note. He snatched it from my hand. 'I will give you the rest over the year, five dinars at the start of each month.'

'Mery!' he said, with a smile. 'Of course I will let you be, I swear on my father's life. We are good friends now, aren't we?'

After the salute to the flag, our head teacher welcomed everyone back and presented a new teacher, Master Shamal, to us. He would be teaching English in Year Five. With a nod from the head, Shamal started to read the names. Due to all the homework I had had to do for Kojak and his friends, I knew I had done well in the final Year Four exams, so I had no worries about the outcome. Kojak's eyes were on me, and I just hoped that he would leave me in peace this time. 'Merywan Rashaba!' Shamal called and looked around. I put my hand up. 'Well done, Merywan, ten out of ten in all your subjects except in Arabic, which you passed with six out of ten. Welcome to Year Five.'

'Yes!' Kojak said. I was given a round of applause. Kojak clapped so excitedly, he did not realise the others had stopped.

'When will I get the next five dinars?' Kojak asked, as we walked to our class.

'In a month's time.'

'You must sit next to me,' he said, 'that is, if you wish to,' he corrected himself. 'Shhh,' Shamal said. 'No talking while you walk to your classroom.'

Shamal looked young in his black suit and red tie, though I later learned he was thirty-five. His skin was paler and pinker than our usual olive colour. He had no moustache and combed his short, curly, fair hair to the side. He was also wearing glasses, just like Michael Caine in *The Italian Job*. The first thing Shamal did was to shuffle the pupils around. I ended up sitting next to someone I didn't know, but I liked his friendly eyes. Shamal wanted to learn our names and asked each of us what we wanted to be when we grew up. One pupil said doctor, another chose engineer, followed by would-be lawyers, army generals and civil servants. Nobody wanted to be a painter or a musician, a writer, poet or actor. Then it came to Kojak.

'Road sweeper,' he said. The boys laughed. Not the one sitting next to me though. 'Donkey,' he said, referring to Kojak. Shamal waited calmly. A few pupils noticed his relaxed, almost indulgent attitude and stopped laughing, leaving Kojak chuckling on his own. I wished Shamal would slap him in the face, but he patiently told Kojak that he respected road sweepers as much as doctors and engineers. 'They keep our society clean. Good luck... what is your name?'

'Ali Shawes.'

'Good luck, Ali Shawes. I hope you become the best road sweeper in Kirkuk.'

Kojak squirmed and lowered his head.

'Merywan?' Shamal called.

'I can't tell you, sir.'

'Why is that?'

'My father would not allow me.'

'Your father is not present.'

'There are spies everywhere, sir.'

'School matters stay within the school. Do you all hear me?'

'Yes, sir,' everyone chorused, with the exception of Kojak.

'Would you spy on Merywan or anyone else?'

'No, sir,' they sang in unison, except for Kojak again.

'So, Merywan, please tell us?'

'I would like to do two jobs, sir.'

'Good! The first one?'

'Teacher.'

Shamal was surprised, and asked which subject I would like to teach.

'Films and cinema,' I said.

'Films?' Shamal repeated.

'Yes, sir, I would like to teach how to appreciate films and how to make them.'

There was silence.

'And your second job?'

'I want to become an actor.'

'Shirrr,' Kojak made a farting sound. The others laughed again, even more raucously this time. The new pupil alongside me promptly stood up. 'I fart on your father,' he said to Kojak. 'Enough!' he shouted, at which they all became silent at once. *Who is this boy who is so brave to stand up to Kojak?* I pitied him, because he couldn't have known that Kojak's Dog father would make his life a misery for defending me.

'Thank you, Hiwa!' Shamal said. 'You can sit down now.'

Oh, he is called Hiwa, Hope!

'Art,' Shamal announced, and he sat on the middle bench facing us. 'For those who do not know and, most importantly, do not appreciate art's essential value for building a civilised society, I would like to say a few words. Perhaps you think art is not necessary to life in the same way as doctors are. Well, do you enjoy it when you are sick and you go to see a doctor and are given medicine which tastes disgusting? You don't. What about when you go to the mechanic to repair your car, and the greasy-faced man makes you pay triple? Do you enjoy telling a lawyer that your brother has forcefully stolen your house, or your father-in-law wants you to divorce his daughter when you are getting on perfectly well? Is it enjoyable being a policeman, an army officer or a bank manager? Maybe not, but they are necessary to keep order in society. Art is different. Technically speaking it is not necessary. You don't listen to music from Mozart or Rachmaninov because you have to, you don't read books by James Joyce, Tolstoy, or Goran or Lorca's poems, admire Vincent van Gogh and Gauguin's paintings, or see plays by Shakespeare or Chekhov because you have to. You don't love art because you have to, but because you want to. Even with the best doctors, engineers, lawyers and police, you can only lead a dull, meaningless life without the many masterpieces of art to bring you joy, tickle your brain and keep your soul fresh. Art is the magic potion that pacifies broken hearts and motivates us to love life. Without art we will only have hate, intolerance, dictators and wars. The most powerful army will never be able to build a healthy society without art. Art is the freshest breath of life, it is the soul of life. So we should not tease Merywan if he wants to become an artist. We genuinely need people like him to change our way of life. Understand?'

'Yes, sir,' a few answered, but most had been lost long before Shamal finished.

'Merywan, do you know how to sing?'

'Yes, sir.'

'Would you be so kind as to sing us a song, preferably in Kurdish?'

'I can't, sir; singing in front of other people is a sin and my father would not allow me to.'

'I will take the sin and, once again, remind you all that classroom matters stay in here. I will severely punish spies. Let me be clear. I do not like spies,' Shamal said, and turned to me.

> Under the blue sky,
> On the side of the snowy mountains,
> I searched all over Kurdistan,
> Valley after valley,
> Neither in the villages nor in the towns,
> Did I meet anyone as beautiful as you.

I sang this for Shamal because he was truly the nicest teacher I had ever encountered. The class gave me a round of applause. Shamal too. Kojak seemed gloomy. Shamal went to the blackboard. 'OK!' he said in English, making me shiver with joy. 'Let's start with the alphabet. ABC... do any of you know how it goes?' I raised my hand. 'OK, Merywan.' I stood up and recited the English alphabet loud and proud. I didn't know exactly why it was, but I felt liberated in the presence of Shamal, and his beliefs about art. Although I had not recognised most of the names of the great masters that he had mentioned, they sang to my heart.

At the break, I stuck to the new pupil like glue. 'I'm glad Master Shamal did not punish you for coming to my defence,' I said.

'He is my father,' Hiwa answered.

'You will have serious problems with Kojak.'

'Who?'

'The class bully, his name is Ali but I call him Kojak, like the character in...'

'I know who Kojak is. I love his films too.'

Never before had I heard any of the boys say they loved films.

'Teaching about films, that could be very nice,' Hiwa said. 'Who knows, maybe one day we could make a film together? I could play the baddy.'

'No, that is Kojak's role,' I grinned.

'Then I will play the ugly,' Hiwa said and contorted his face, which made me laugh.

'Please, don't tell Ali I called him Kojak?' I looked over towards Kojak, who was standing with some of his friends.

From the back pocket of his trousers, Hiwa took out his comb and started to flatten down his fluffy hair. He had two unusually big ears, rather like those of Dr Spock in the *Star Trek* TV series. 'I like my ears. They make me look like a Karweshk, Rabbit,' he said casually, and smiled. I was surprised at how relaxed he seemed to be about everything, and it had a profound effect on me. I had never been so relaxed in my life. He offered me his comb. I shook my head because I had my hat on as usual.

'You are not a baldy, are you?'

'No. I am a dervish.'

'A dervish?'

'Yes. I have long hair. I am not allowed to show it in public.'

'Why? What is worse to show publicly, your hair or my ears?'

I nicknamed him 'Rabbit' and never again called him Hiwa. He was slightly shorter than I and had pockmarks and acne scars on his face. What was most noticeably different was our hair; his was fluffy candyfloss hair that made him look like he had had an electric shock. He spent hours combing it to flatten it down. At times, even in the classroom, he would spit in his hand, wet his hair and comb it again and again. Later, I found out he was also a Haqa, very ticklish. When touched on the side of his belly, he would start shouting 'Motherfucker' and then laugh out loud.

'How old are you?' I asked.

'Twelve,' Rabbit answered.

'And you are in Year Five?'

'Can I trust you?' he said, quietly.

'Yes. I swear on my heart,' and I put my hand on my heart.

'I missed two years because my father was a freedom fighter in the mountains. That was until he got sick of all the infighting between Kurds, laid down his gun and came back to teaching.'

I was not allowed to talk about this subject and did not know how far I could trust Rabbit.

'It was brave of you to sing about Kurdistan,' Rabbit said.

'I did not. It was a love song.'

'Yes, but you mentioned Kurdistan. Don't worry, I love Kurdistan and want my country free. It is the truth, I am not cheating you. I am not a spy, and I never will be one. I would rather die.'

'I am scared. I prefer not to talk about politics,' I said, even though I was sorry to build a barrier between us. 'I want to go to America.'

'America! Is that a dream?'

'No, it's real.'

'You want to escape, don't you? Who are you scared of?'

'I am sorry, it is a secret.'

'No secrets, Mery! Real Braders, friends?' he said, holding out his hand. This was an impossible pact for me to enter into with someone I hardly knew, yet I didn't think twice. 'No secrets and true Braders,' I repeated, and I shook his hand. 'I am scared of the monster,' I said, which he understood. 'True Braders keep no secrets,' Rabbit said, looking into my eyes. 'They never betray each other and never break their friendship, not for anything in the world.'

Kojak waved to me. Rabbit noticed. 'Why are you so afraid of this bastard?' he asked. This made me nervous. *If Rabbit gets to know I am a neuter, I am sure he will no longer be my friend.* I was about to go to Kojak but the bell rang.

I was hoping to go home with Rabbit but he had to stay with Master Shamal, who had some paperwork to do. I spent my pocket money on a pot of hot beetroot juice. I looked out for Kojak around the busy market. *He must have run all the way home out of joy, because he has five dinars.* I thanked God for letting me be rid of the son of the Dog. I skipped away, but before turning the corner, I came face to face with Kojak and a couple of his mates. The two joked about me wanting to teach filmmaking. Kojak shut them up. 'No one teases my friend, Merywan.' Then he whispered, 'I want the rest of the sixty dinars, now.'

'That was not our deal,' I answered. He pointed out his father watching us from across the street. Shawes Dog waved. 'Ali, you swore on your father's head to…'

'Hey guys, do you want to know what this piece of shit is made of?'

'Ali, no.'

'Give me the money or I will call it out. Last chance.' There was no deal to be made with the son of the Dog. 'Do you want to know if he is a boy or a girl or…'

'No, please, Ali?'

'Give me the money, now.'

'I will, just wait for the end of the month, and I will give you another five dinars.'

'My father says you lie to me, you bastard. Well, everyone this piece of shit is not a boy or a girl, but a neuter.'

He said it. Kojak said it after all that I have done for him. Can I deny it? If I do, he will ask me to show my penis.

'Show us your willy if I am telling a lie. Show it to us if you have one, you neuter! Mery, is a neuter...'

'No, he is not,' a voice came from behind me. It was Rabbit. 'You are the neuter.' He stood up to Kojak. 'You are a rotten sack of shit to go around lying about Mery, and your breath smells of dog poo.'

'How do you know?' Kojak was visibly trembling.

'Because Mery and I masturbated together last night, thinking about your mother's pink fanny.'

'Mery,' Kojak turned to me. 'Admit it, are you a neuter or not? Remember my father,' he pointed out the Dog. 'He will take you to the Turkish baths.'

'Mery, answer him.' Rabbit said. 'Tell Kojak he is a neuter himself.'

Rabbit has appeared in my life like a beautiful autumn sun, but Shawes Dog is already approaching us, walking slowly, with his hand on his dagger. Nothing could be worse than refusing Rabbit's help at this degrading moment of my life. 'Kojak, you smelly son of Shawes Dog, you are a fucking liar,' I said. It was worth it for the satisfaction it gave me, never mind the consequences.

'Bring me your mother, Kojak, and then I will show you my cock, but I will not take it out to fuck your dirty shit hole.'

Kojak tried to raise his hand but I hit his camel face. Rabbit was quickly all over him. I put down my school bag and, like Bruce Lee, kicked his two friends. The boys ran away. 'Father!' Kojak cried out from beneath Rabbit's kicks. Shawes Dog charged at us. I raced off, thinking that Rabbit was right behind me, but when I glanced backwards I saw that Kojak had got hold of his leg. Rabbit fell over and was soon the butt of Shawes' heavy kicks. I stopped, grabbed a stone and I hit the Dog on his head. Blood streamed down his face. He was dizzy and let go of Rabbit, who ran immediately. I didn't. Kojak saw me and went to hide behind Shawes, but I kicked him in his balls harder than I ever had. The Dog took out his dagger.

'Mery! Run!' Rabbit shouted, and we went back inside our school, followed by many of the pupils who were still outside eating and drinking after-school treats. The head teacher, Shamal, and a few others, were leaving.

'You bastards, are you trying to break my head?' Shawes chased after us.

'Stop! Stop this! Don't ever make threats inside our school.' Shamal stood up to Shawes. 'Get out of my way before I open your belly,' Shawes snarled. 'Put that knife away!' the head teacher ordered him. 'You should be ashamed for fighting in front of your son, and for fighting such young boys.'

'What is wrong with fighting?' Shawes snapped at him. 'Do you want my son to end up like you sissies? Fighting is for men and not for teachers, sons of bitches. Move out of my way or I will kill you all.'

There was chaos and lots of noise. Shawes punched Shamal.

'Father!' Rabbit yelled, trying to run to his father's aid as Aras, the maths teacher, held on to him. Shawes was about to stab Shamal when the caretaker jumped on him from behind. The fight spilled out into the courtyard, and the crowd encircled the two men fighting over the knife. Shamal and the head teacher tried to grab Shawes, but he was powerful and murderously angry, and easily shoved them away. Kojak was standing alone, crying, full of fear and shame. I could not help pitying him for growing up with such a father. There was an agonizing groan as Shawes Dog stabbed and slashed the caretaker, before Shamal and four others were finally able to coordinate their attack and get Shawes face down on the floor.

Shawes Dog was dragged into the head teacher's office, followed by everyone else. I stayed by the caretaker, who was covered in blood. Kojak came to me, still crying, threw the squashed five dinars to the ground at my feet, and ran away.

The last thing I remember was Shawes Dog's bloodied eyes staring at me, and his lips moving slowly, 'I will get you, Mery.'

A wet dream

The police took Shawes away. It was my fault. I had turned Kojak into an orphan, sent the Kurdish Dog to an Arab prison and, worst of all, caused the appalling death of our caretaker. The bitter loss for his wife and children hurt me the most, for he had been such a kind, gentle man. I prayed to God to forgive my sins. It was hard to concentrate. My mind was churned up like butter with contradictory thoughts jostling for attention. Yet, maybe his death wasn't entirely my doing. Perhaps, on second thoughts, this was simply God's will? It was His will that dictated how I lived. As Rashaba said, 'Our fates are written on our foreheads and we cannot do anything about it.' Although I believed my faith in God was as strong as ever, doubts were accumulating inside me, with the impulse to no longer passively accept such a fate.

Kojak and his mother left Qala, and I imagined I was rid of them forever. He did not see me watching their departure from our rooftop. I spat three times after he had gone, and I thanked God for helping me to put the sixty dinars back into Rashaba's pillow without being spotted.

I introduced Hiwa to my family, and Mother laughed when I told her I had nicknamed my friend Rabbit. I started to reveal many of my secrets to him, telling him about Grandfather's house, my treasure box and its portraits of Gugush, the Azeri pop singer from Iran, Najwa Fouad, the Egyptian belly dancer, Saira Banu, the pretty Indian actress, Jean Gabin, Gary Cooper... Lastly I showed him Gringo.

'Gringo is my hero,' Rabbit said.

Being Braders was one thing, but this made me jealous. 'No, he's not,' I said, seizing the poster. 'Gringo is my hero first of all, then yours and everyone else's.'

I did not tell him I had written letters to Gringo, about Rashaba's hidden money, and my uncles and father once being Peshmerga. *I will tell him these things at the right time. But not about Zao'Adin trying to make me Hiz. I will never tell him about my shame.* When Rabbit came to my defence and fought Kojak for calling me a neuter, he thought of this as no more than a random insult that had to be avenged. I had to hide my defect from him, though it hurt me to keep secrets from my Brader. I thought it best this way to keep our friendship safe.

Rabbit saw Happiness's necklace. 'Could I try it on?' he asked.

'You can keep it,' I said impetuously. I had waited years to find another friend that I could trust implicitly, that I could be open and carefree with, and I knew Happiness wouldn't have minded at all.

Rabbit's family had rented a house a few doors from ours. He invited me for a special occasion. Out of shyness, I was initially reluctant; after all, Shamal was one of my teachers. Yet the moment I stepped into his house, I felt I had entered a new world. The entrance to the courtyard was covered in vine leaves hiding bunches of black grapes. The house had two bedrooms on the ground floor, one used as the sitting room, and the other was a bedroom for Rabbit, his brother and sister. I was amazed to learn his parents slept on their own in a room upstairs.

Colourful balloons were hanging everywhere, and there was a plastic table and six chairs in the centre of the garden. A few guests were chatting away, and children were running about. Shamal was carrying an iced cake with ten candles on it. He welcomed me with a smile, as if he had known me for a long time. Rabbit's mother, Jwana, Beautiful, was also a teacher and was, indeed, stunningly attractive. She too shook my hand and even gave me a kiss on my cheek, which made me blush. Rabbit's younger brother, Ashti, Peaceful, was nine years old and lived up to his name. He had the kindest face, but most of the time he seemed to keep to himself. Finally, I met the birthday girl, Khorataw, Sunshine, who was a few months younger than me. She had black hair down to her waist, dark eyes with unusually long lashes and a lovely full-moon face. She was wearing a pink crown on her head, the family's princess, and the patterned roses on her dress made her shine like a spring rainbow.

Shamal's family were proudly Kurdish, but they didn't dress like the Kurds I knew. Rabbit and Peaceful wore T-shirts and trousers. Shamal was wearing pin-striped black trousers and a red shirt. Jwana looked elegant in a white pleated skirt and a white blouse. With the red rose in her black hair and the gracious, almost regal way she served drinks and greeted guests, it was no exaggeration to say that she was like a Kurdish version of Sophia Loren in Vittorio De Sica's *La Ciociara*.

Peaceful played his violin and everyone began to sing: 'Shady rozh la dayk bunt...' I did not sing. I did not even know we had 'Happy Birthday' in our language. There were so many things I did not know. I had never been to a birthday party before, and did not realise there were people in my country who celebrated birthdays. I had never come across parents being so open with their children. They talked and joked together, like friends. The many rules of my world did not exist in Rabbit's. Looking at Sunshine, I began thinking about my sister. I doubted whether Star would ever have a birthday party or be allowed to wear a crown on her head. More likely she would have to cover her head with a scarf. Sunshine received presents, kisses and congratulations from family and friends. 'What would be the most precious present for my darling?' Shamal asked.

'A kiss from my father on this cheek and from my mother on this one,' she pouted, her eyes sparkling merrily, and her parents kissed her cherry-red cheeks. 'And a ride on my horse,' she added. Shamal dropped down onto his hands and knees. 'C'mon then,' he called. Sunshine sat on his back and he crawled around the garden. I could hardly believe what I was seeing, my English teacher being a horse! Peaceful played his violin again and everyone, including me, sang 'Happy Birthday...' and this time in English. Sunshine was helped onto the table, and encircled by us, she danced to the claps and the music. I was carried away by the singing, but above all, I was overwhelmed by being among Rabbit's loving family.

I could barely comprehend my own change in fortune, not that I paused to think too much about it. As soon as Rabbit and I had saved enough money, we headed into town, which was another way of saying we went to the cinema. When two could get in for the price of one, we had to sit very close to the screen, or sometimes on the floor if the benches were full. The discomfort wasn't a problem, but what I hated was that we two-for-one customers had to wait in the foyer until the trailers ended, which was really frustrating as I loved to watch the trailers. Worse still, we also had to miss the first five to ten minutes of the actual film, which was unbearable. I begged the usher on the door to let us in. The one at the Hamra Cinema must have seen us there every week, but pretended not to know us. He had one completely white eye, and looked like the Cyclops in *The Seventh Voyage of Sinbad*.

'Never mind the trailers, but please let us go in before the film starts.' If we were lucky, such pleading sometimes worked in other cinemas, but it never did with ugly Cyclops.

'Why do you insist? Go back before I hit you with my stick,' he snapped at us. We saw many films without seeing the beginning, and had real difficulties understanding the plot, sometimes until the end.

Once, in Hasiraka market, as we were heading home, we came across a man struggling with two bulging suitcases. 'Can I help you?' I asked. The man was suspicious. 'I just want to give you a hand, sir,' I explained. 'Never mind, if you don't want us to help,' Rabbit added.

'Oh, yes please,' the traveller relented, puffing his cheeks. 'I need to get to the bus station.' Rabbit and I lifted one of the heavy bags, carrying it in turn on our backs. We pushed through the crowd to the station for Kirkuk-Sulemany. The traveller just made it on time for his bus, and as we were about to go, he held up his hand to me. 'I would like to buy you a Pepsi or some honey cakes, but have no time, so please take it.'

'No need, sir, I did not ask to help you for money,' I said.

'I know and I appreciate that, but please take this.' He insisted, before either of us could say no.

'Twenty-five cents!' Rabbit exclaimed. We went straight to the teahouse to buy a Pepsi, and gulped it down between us. We felt so happy, this was our own money. It was the first money I had ever earned, the sweetest twenty-five cents ever.

'Another three or four bags and we could make enough to go and see *Godzilla*,' I said. We looked into each other's eyes, reading each other's thoughts.

From then on, after school on most afternoons, Rabbit and I went out to the station and worked as porters. We carried anything we could, bags, cases, sheep and goats, and dragged anything we couldn't. We ended up having regular clients, mainly farmers and merchants, who would be faced by a group of kids eager to earn a few cents, but would look for the Braders to do the job.

During the summer holidays and over the years we made enough to go to the kebab house or to treat ourselves to sandwiches and Pepsi while watching another film. We had our photos taken putting our arms around each other's shoulders, bought T-shirts and, for the first time in my life, in 1983, I bought a pair of jeans. I bought a dress for Star, one for Mother and even managed to give some money to Rashaba. It did not make us rich, especially during the winter months when fewer people travelled, but for a while we felt well off, until the war escalated and things slowed down again. But we loved the job. We had the freedom to choose when and how we wanted to work, with no one to boss us around. Best of all, our work allowed Rabbit and me to spend most of our time together. We had become inseparable, except for going to Takya, the House of God, Rabbit never came there.

We felt grown-up when we finally said farewell to our primary school and were relieved when, during our second year in secondary school, Shamal was transferred to work there. For the exams, Rabbit and I studied in Al Murabaen Park. We ended year after year with top marks in all the subjects except for Arabic language. We had learned it well but still could not enjoy it. When, in September 1985, Rabbit and I started Year Three and our studies got harder, we gave up being porters. We were given a little more pocket money and I also earned some cash from Flathead for looking after his wife by sleeping in his living room. We had enough to go to cinema at least once a week.

Popcorn often came to say hello while we were at the bus station. We also saw him outside our new school and, a couple of times, he turned up in the park, where he would sing us moving songs and encourage us to study hard.

'What do you know about studying? You are an ignorant illiterate!' Rabbit teased. But Popcorn challenged him, particularly when it came to poetry and the Yezidi faith, which Rabbit and I knew little about. Popcorn also advised us not to worry about enrolling in Saddam's Youth Army. 'You could learn how to shoot,' he said. 'Living in this country, that could be useful, but how and against whom you use your gun is what matters.'

Rabbit and I were obliged to wear military gear, and over the two weeks of half-term holiday, we had to attend a tough military training in Maaskar Khalid, Iraq's strongest base in the Kurdish region. I hated it, but Rabbit thought we needed to take it seriously and reminded me of Popcorn's advice that it might come in useful.

On the first day, I was asked to take off my hat. When the officer from the Special Forces saw my long hair, he ordered for my head to be shaved. I tried to explain, 'I am a dervish!' But I was grabbed by my arms and taken to the camp's barber. The two army students let go of my arms. I wanted to escape. The barber had a beard, which was not allowed in the Iraqi army, except for Yezidis. I told him I was a dervish and had to keep my hair long. He walked to an officer, and after a chat, he came back with good news.

'It is fine, you don't have to cut your hair, go back to your training,' he said with a smile. I could have kissed his hands for helping me out in such a moment.

We started at five in the morning with physical exercise, followed by jogging, combat techniques and shooting. We were given many seminars about loyalty to the government, above all 'our' leader and the Arab world's bravest warrior-president, Saddam Hussein. We were reminded of the ghastly consequences if we ever opposed the government or joined subversive groups. We had to swear on the Qur'an and in the name of Saddam that we would use the guns to defend him and our country. We also had to swear to fight Kurdish traitors and not hesitate to kill them on the spot. If we learnt about a family with a Peshmerga son or sons, we had to inform the government, even if this was within our own family, or else we would be hanged too. We were asked to spy within our neighbourhoods and report on any clandestine activities or anti-government political discussions. Rabbit and I looked at each other, but put our hands on the Qur'an and swore, 'I will,' one at a time.

During a break, Rabbit told me that he had had a wet dream the night before. 'It was a fantastic feeling,' he continued with a shiver, and both his voice and his facial expression changed as if he was re-living it, as though he had made love for real. I could not share his feelings, as I had never had a wet dream. 'She had a light transparent green top, no knickers,' Rabbit licked his lips. 'I was naked. She took off her clothes and was more beautiful than all the trees, plants, flowers and birds in the jungle. She kissed me and then sat on top of me. She was hot, very hot. I came inside her within seconds and I must have made a noise, because the next moment, I felt my mum's hand shaking me, to come to this damn training. 'It is getting late,' she was saying, but I was all wet between my legs. It was a nice dream though. Guess who I had it with?'

'Give me a clue.'

'American actress. I was Tarzan and we did it in the jungle.'

'Blonde?'

'Yes,' Rabbit said, getting excited again.

'Bo Derek?'

'No.'

'Ursula Andress?'

'Younger generation.'

'Brooke Shields?'

'Yes, you got it,'

'That is cheating. Brooke Shields was in *The Blue Lagoon,* not a Tarzan film and not blonde, either!'

'Mery, do you masturbate? I started recently, wow, it's amazing.'

'I am a dervish, we are not allowed to do such things. That's a big sin.'

'Nonsense. You are not a real Muslim but a hypocrite,' Rabbit said, and it hurt me. 'You use Islam when it is convenient to you. A true Muslim stands by the words of God and the Qur'an and won't go to the cinema, will not watch television and won't have photo collections. Mery, you are a false Muslim.'

'That is not right. I am faithful, but I love cinema and will not give it up for anything in life, not even for…' I could not finish. I was about to say an unforgivable thing. Rabbit picked up on it. 'Say it, Mery! You will not give it up even for who? For God? My Brader, either be an obedient Muslim and live according to the Qur'an, or enjoy cinema and forget about God and the Hereafter.'

'That is blasphemy.'

'I agree. Therefore we should not talk religion, but should cherish life. You don't know what you are missing. It is nice to masturbate, and good for you. It helps you be more creative and less aggressive…'

'Rubbish. Sex is very bad, it is the devil's temptation to turn you into an infidel,' I said, hoping he would go no further.

'It is scientifically proven that sex benefits you, and since we are not allowed to have sex, at least let us be free to masturbate. What harm can that cause?' He held up his hand. 'Oh, my hand! Sorry I fucked you,' he joked.

'My father hates science,' I said.

'What about you?'

In my heart I agreed with Rabbit. I was fascinated by science and would have loved to experience sex and masturbate, but I could not get an erection.

'I have an idea. We masturbate together. We could do it while watching someone sexy on video like Bo Derek, Raquel Welch…'

'Stop it, this is disgusting.' *I will never do it, even if I can have a hard-on.* In my mind, each one of those women was the princess of a fantastic kingdom…

'I know, you want Claudia Cardinale, your favourite,' Rabbit said, to cheer me up. He was right. I was mad about her, even more so since I had seen her in *The Leopard*. But to mention her in relation to masturbating was too much. I jumped on Rabbit. We had never had a physical fight before, but I lifted him up and threw him on the ground. I sat on his tummy and tickled his sides. Rabbit suffering, shouted, 'Motherfucker…' a few times and laughed hysterically.

'Never again mention Claudia Cardinale like this! Never!' and I tickled him some more.

'I won't, I promise. I won't…'

There was an awful shout. We had totally forgotten the training, where we were not allowed to have fun. We were punished. The officer made us run around the square five times under the baking sun, then drag ourselves through mud and dirt, before he forced us to eat the rotten corpse of a frog. We both vomited.

From then on, we didn't miss a single session of the two weeks of intensive shooting training, and by the end of it, I had won praise for my nerveless aim, which had left my target riddled with bullet holes – even the tiny bulls-eye had been pierced with a satisfyingly neat cluster. Rabbit joked that it was beginner's luck. But he hadn't been lucky, he hadn't hit the target once.

My fight on my fifteenth birthday

My auntie, Flathead's wife, was as delicate as a butterfly and I nicknamed her Papula, 'Butterfly'. For everyone else she remained Nasik, 'Sensitive', and she was. Like a chameleon, she transformed constantly. Her look went with her mood. When happy, she was delightful. She looked glorious and changed her clothes, the colour of her lips and her hairstyle, a couple of times each day. Even when she was miserable or defiant, her beauty never deserted her. She was a real extrovert and straight to the point, very unusual for Kurdish women. She detested house chores. 'I was not born to be a housewife' was always on her lips.

Papula had a perfect body, what we call 'Made by God's own hands.' Within her confined world she behaved like a queen and was not prepared to give this up when married. She was one of those people whom you either loved or loathed, and as time passed, she made many enemies within our family. I was attracted to her because she spoke English and loved films. When alone, we spoke in English, but mine was not as good as hers. She helped me to learn the alphabet, which was why, on the first day of meeting Master Shamal, I could read it by heart. She was most upset about giving up her studies at secondary school because Flathead did not let her continue. She had always dreamt of becoming a model and often dressed up, and would strut and sashay like she was on a catwalk, asking me if she looked beautiful and sexy.

After the death of the caretaker, I asked Papula if I could give her address to Gringo. Papula was corresponding with a friend of hers in Turkey, who was studying medicine at Ankara University, and, for whatever reason, she kept this secret from Flathead. I thought it would be an ideal arrangement for her to receive my letters. *When Gringo sends me one, she will be able to give it to me away from the eyes of my father and everyone else.* Papula accepted at once, and I immediately wrote another letter with her address.

Flathead bought a ceiling fan which he hung above his bed. I thought this was so that even during the summertime he could sleep in his room and make love to his wife. She rarely came out, and Mother considered this normal. She said, 'This is what most brides do for the first months after their wedding.' But Mother was wrong too.

Soon Flathead did not want Papula to go to her mother's house in his absence. He wanted to find his wife at home when he arrived. Papula protested, but Flathead did not listen. He also did not want Papula to sleep alone. He suggested that I slept on the sofa in their living room on the nights he was away. 'This is perfect,' he said, 'because if I come home late in the night, Mery could go to his bed.'

'Mery,' Flathead took me aside, which worried me. 'Never, for any reason, leave my place at night. My wife must have no visitors. You spy on her, if she talks to any man in my absence, you report it to me.'

Rashaba hated his favourite son sleeping under the same roof as this scandalous woman, the one who did not wear a scarf, who had bare arms, who unbuttoned her blouse to expose parts of her chest, who wore skirts and trousers and often went around flashing her legs and her round buttocks. He considered Papula the ultimate disgrace, and whenever she passed him in the courtyard, he looked away and prayed to God for forgiveness. Even though Papula was a gift made to my grandfather, who was his idol, he did not want me to eat food from the same plate as her. On one occasion Rashaba asked me if I had ever seen her naked. I was shocked at this. He warned me to close my eyes if she ever got undressed in front of me, and I promised I would.

Papula and I became close friends. We played characters from fairy tales and films, yet this was not in the way you might imagine, for she always wanted to be the Prince and for me to take the role of Princess. 'I would marry you, Princess, if I were free,' she said. She liked to dress up as a male, and be the sort of caring man she longed to know. She dreamt of a romantic husband to love, but was forced to live with Flathead because of their arranged marriage. With my constant anxieties over my sexuality, at the beginning I was reluctant to play this role. I was worried that by doing so I would give hints of my secret to Papula, but she was irresistible, a masterful mistress in the art of seducing me to comply with her wishes and I had to go along with it. *Playing her game is a better distraction than having her question my reluctance, and I seriously need her protection.*

I opened myself to her like a ripe fig, and stories poured out of me as though the fig had been squashed and the seeds forced out. I revealed to her most of my childhood horror, about Zao'Adin and the monster's men killing Old Zorab, about my fear of paedophiles and particularly Shawes Dog, and how Happiness's death continued to haunt me. She was a patient listener and didn't force me at all. It was wonderful to be able to talk about such things, which I could not have mentioned even to my Brader, but of course, I did not tell her my main secret. Papula became a new light in my life, and helped brighten the time I passed at home.

I moved my treasure box into her room. I was looking for a secure place. 'In the cupboard, under the bed or behind the makeup cabinet, where would be the best, do you think?' I asked.

'Anywhere,' Papula answered. 'Your father would never step into the whore's room!'

A whore! I asked Papula why she used the word 'whore'.

'Oh, but your father makes it absolutely obvious that this is what he thinks of me. Sometimes I am surprised that he allows you to sleep down here, but I suppose he cannot overrule your uncle's wishes.' Flathead had a wooden storage box in an alcove behind Papula's wedding Boraq. I thought it would be the best place to hide my treasure box. I was about to close the lid, but then spotted the glint of something metal poking out of a sock. I looked carefully and saw that it was a pistol. *Does Papula know about this gun?*

'Do you have anything in this box?'

'Only your uncle's useless stuff.'

To start with, sometimes, well beyond midnight, Flathead woke me up and sent me to my bed in our room or on the rooftop. 'Mery is fast asleep. Let him be,' I heard Papula complaining. Flathead knew that was purely an excuse and only gave up when Auntie rejected him. 'I am tired and don't want you on top of me.' Occasionally, in the quiet of the night, I could hear Flathead's heavy breathing as Papula implored, 'You hurt me...don't bite my nipples...don't squeeze my thighs...' She also did not seem to like kissing.

At Papula's request, Flathead turned up with a television and a video player. We had never had one and at the local teahouse I was not allowed to watch it, so I knew how lucky I was to have had the chance to go to Happiness's house to watch *Rawhide, Gunsmoke, The Avengers, Bewitched, Kojak* and a few other programmes, all of which I adored. I would wait impatiently for the entire week to see the next episode, and would cry when a series came to an end.

The family celebrated the arrival of the new technology with a feast of takeaway kebab provided by Flathead, but Rashaba didn't join in. He called television the devil's weapon. He said he needed to work much harder to buy us a place of our own and get out before we turned into Infidel Number One with a place secured in the centre of hell. *But is he referring to the television or to Papula, the scandalous woman?* Flathead ignored him. He set up the television in the living room.

'Why do you keep a gun?' I asked Flathead, when we were alone.

'Have you told your auntie?'

'No.'

'Anyone else?'

'No.'

'Good, you are smart. Keep it a secret.'

'The government will hang you for it.'

'Oh yes, listen to this one,' Flathead said, giggling in anticipation. 'A Kurd and an Arab are about to be hanged by the Iraqi Mukhabarat, secret police.'

'I didn't realise they also hanged Arabs?' I was surprised.

'Of course they do, often, but that is not the point. Listen to the joke: Before hanging them, the Mukhabarat asks, "What is your last wish?" The Kurdish prisoner replies, "To see my mother." He then asks the Arab, "What is your last wish?" The Arab turns to the Kurdish prisoner. "I don't want this Kurd to see his mother," he answers.'

Three years after Flathead's wedding, Mother gave birth again. Rashaba wanted his third son to be called Ali. Though it was the most sacred name in Islam, after our Prophet's, I didn't like it for it reminded me of Kojak. Fortunately, Hercules wanted my brother to be given a Kurdish name, so he intervened, as was normal for uncles to do in our culture. He chose Shorsh, 'Revolution', reflecting his wish for a proper Kurdish revolution under a charismatic leader, such as Mahatma Gandhi or Nelson Mandela, who would lead us to victory.

I nicknamed Shorsh Maymoon, 'Monkey'. As he grew, he crawled everywhere and was into everything. Star, at the age of five, had to become a mother to Monkey. All she really wanted to do was play with her friends, but Monkey would not let her be. Flathead loved Monkey very much. He brought him a Superman toy from Baghdad, and often put him on his shoulders and ran around the courtyard calling, 'Hey, look everyone, Monkey is flying like Superman.'

One late afternoon on my way to Takya I came across Trouble. He was riding a brand-new bicycle and I was worried he had stolen it. 'I bought it this morning to use for my new job. You want a ride?' Of course I did! 'Guess what, Mery!' he said, as I sat on the bars of the bike, enjoying the cool breeze. 'I am also tending Grandfather's garden. Don't tell Mum or Dad about this, nor our uncles. But it makes me feel good to care for it.'

'Hercules is still convinced one day we will go back and live in the big house,' I said.

'It would be nice, it is such a special place.'

'How much did you pay for this bicycle?'

'Twenty-five dinars.'

'Where did you get the money from?'

'I have not paid it in full. My boss is my guarantor, and I will pay back monthly.'

'You must be careful. You don't want to end up losing it like Antonio in *The Bicycle Thief*. Do you remember how much he suffered for his bicycle in that film?'

'That won't happen to me, my boss is a powerful man and he knows how to look after me,' Trouble said, as he pedalled away faster.

'Aren't you scared to work for the Arabs in the big house?'

'They don't know who I am, and they are good friends of my boss.' I wondered who Trouble's boss was, but did not ask. I did not want to spoil such a rare moment. We had barely spoken a single friendly word to each other for years.

A week later, on the occasion of the Eid festivities, my parents and uncles, Star, Monkey and I went to visit my grandparents' graves. Papula did not join us. She refused to pay her respects to my grandfather, to the man who had caged her by accepting her as a gift in marriage to Flathead on the day of her birth. Trouble arrived on his bicycle with a bunch of fresh red roses, which must have been from Grandfather's garden. He bent down by Grandfather's grave, kissed the soil, whispered a few words, moved to Grandmother's and placed the bunch of roses.

Trouble was approaching a decisive moment. At the age of eighteen, unless you had secured a place to study at the University in Baghdad or Mosul, you had to enrol in the army for compulsory military service. This was bad news for Trouble because he was not a student. Once in the Iraqi army, whether voluntarily or not, the only way out was in a coffin. The country was constantly at war, and we all knew that anyone who deserted the army was hunted down and executed.

Trouble's alternatives were either to escape to the mountains to become a Peshmerga and fight the government, or become a *Jash*, militiaman, whom we knew as Kurdish traitors. There were two Jash groups. The first were those who took up their gun and went to fight the Peshmerga, their own people. These were paid a good monthly wage for serving Saddam. The second were those who did not pick up a gun but only registered as a Jash to avoid military service. A Kurdish Jash leader, and there were many, provided them with the Jash identity card and, in compensation, took their monthly wages for himself. Each Jash leader registered up to a few hundred Kurds, and made millions of dinars out of them. The money blinded these leaders, burning their hearts. They were agents of the government's policy of divide and rule and cared nothing about their people's desperate desire for freedom.

Trouble kept at his gardening job and was pleased to have avoided military service. 'At what price?' I said in shock when I saw his new ID and heard about his role. 'Whether picking up a gun or not, you are a Jash, and like all the Jash, you are a coward and a traitor, worse than our enemy. It is unforgivable. You bring shame on our grandfather and the rest of our family.'

My uncles and my mother were also desperately disappointed in Trouble. 'It's easy for you to say,' he retorted. 'You are not in my shoes. What choice do I have? Go to the war and get killed. I don't want to die for Saddam. Maybe you would like me to go to the mountains to join the Peshmerga and have you all arrested and hanged?'

Rashaba agreed with Trouble. This way he did not jeopardise the family's safety and he could still do his job. *I am sure this is not from his heart, unless Rashaba has forgotten he was once a freedom fighter.* But Trouble became my enemy. 'You will pay dearly for calling me a traitor,' he said, as soon as we were left alone.

The government outlawed the wearing of sharwal, so when I went into town, I wore jeans and a T-shirt and left my hat off. I had bought a couple of pairs of jeans and a few denim shirts in a jumble sale, and a week before my fifteenth birthday, Rabbit and his family gave me a nice pair too. Rashaba didn't allow me to wear these clothes, so I asked Papula if I could leave by her living room door, which led out directly onto the side road. She agreed, and let me hide my clothes in her cupboard. Apart from hiding my treasure box in her place, this was to be another one of many secrets I would share with Papula. One day while we were alone, after having watched *Singin' in the Rain* on the VHS, we played and danced in the courtyard, soaking ourselves under the water cascading from the hose. I ended up hugging her. Strangely enough, I did feel some desire for Papula. It was not an erection, but a feeling of complete absorption in another being.

On 11 March 1986, my fifteenth birthday, Papula wore my boyish clothes and dressed me up specially. This time, she wanted me to be her bride. A couple of days earlier, we had seen *The Deer Hunter*. She had not stopped talking about the beauty of Meryl Streep and the wedding scene, and I was in complete agreement, both about Meryl Streep and the perfection of the scene, which made the Russian roulette game between Robert De Niro and Christopher Walken all the more powerful because of the strength of their relationship. Papula sat me down in front of her make-up cabinet. She covered my face with her wedding veil and went into the living room. Left alone under her veil, I began thinking that, *although I have just turned fifteen, I still have such a long way to go before I can be an independent, free-willed adult.* Thanks to a combination of the government's repressions and Rashaba's rules, there were so many things I could not do. I drew the veil away and scrutinised my face in the mirror, for the first time realising that at last I had grown up.

Papula came back with a bottle and two glasses. She poured some beer and handed a glass to me.

'You drink?' I asked. I was shocked. 'Why not?' she smiled. 'Today you are fifteen, so you are a man now. Here, let's drink to you.'

It was hard to believe that I really was a man, given my defect, not to mention the fact that I was dressed up like a woman. *What if Papula gets me drunk and I end up in her bed?* What a stupid thought; *she is only having fun and playing a game with me.*

'I don't like alcohol, and anyway, it is against my religion, and you are a woman.'

'Oh! I thought you had watched many films and learned about women's freedom, so you wouldn't worry about such a small thing as a man and a woman drinking together.'

'I do respect you, but you already have enemies, and this will only make it worse. What if Rashaba learns that you drink?'

My father's opinions did not seem to concern her, as she blithely carried on. 'Cheers, Mery Rashaba, my princess! I drink to you and to our long-lasting marriage.'

I was upset, and grabbed her hand. 'No! You should not drink this stuff,' I snapped, pushing the glass away and spilling the beer. She slapped my face through the veil and then pulled it off. 'Right!' she exclaimed. 'In that case, we are divorced!' We both stood in silence, too embarrassed to look at each other.

'Can I be left alone?' I asked, after a while. 'I want to get changed.'

'Sure, you are a man now and need to hide yourself,' she teased, and went into her living room.

What did she mean? Does she know something about my illness? I took off Papula's wedding dress. That had made me look like a girl with my long hair. I knew I wasn't a girl and this was only play-acting, *but what am I?* When I stared into the mirror, a grown-up, sexless teenager looked back at me.

The war is close

Kirkuk, June 1986

Rough-faced traders stood outside their shops or by their carts in Ahmed Agha market, noisily hawking their fish, vegetables, animals and rugs, pitching for customers and promoting alleged bargains. The procession of old cars bumping along in both directions, the dust, the smell of rotting rubbish by the roadside, made the air stink. I pushed my way through the crowd. Some of the men semeed distracted by my looks, dressed as I was in tight jeans and T-shirt, with my hair loose. *They must think I am a girl and are puzzled to see me walking around on my own.* It was the perfect disguise to keep the paedophiles away. They mostly targeted boys. A boygirl was the only way I could think of myself. A fake boy at home when Rashaba was around, and a fake girl outside. Rashaba did not worry me. He was too busy working and he never came to the town centre.

There was a peculiar power in being able to cross gender boundaries, but I did not dress up like this for vanity. It was one way I could begin to challenge the rules that restricted my life, a form of defiance towards the narrow-minded people around me, who conspired to prevent many young people like me from being free. Free to dress as we wished or to enjoy the small pleasures of our city. But I could not possibly express this openly. When I left the house I had to keep to myself. I did not look left or right in case some of the men recognised my rebellious attitude, when they would shout and whistle at my independent manner and provocatively feminine behaviour.

I wish Rabbit were here. He would stand up to anyone who insulted me. When Rabbit was present, naturally people hassled me a lot less. But this morning, strangely, Brader did not turn up to our meeting.

Three months earlier, after my fight with Papula over the beer, I had been very upset and did not go to see Rabbit as we had planned. From the day we had met, that was the first appointment I had ever missed with him, and I regretted it terribly. Later, Rabbit told me they had put up balloons, and that Jwana had made a cake. All the family were waiting to give me a surprise. That would have been my first birthday party ever.

It was on that same day that I met Aida. I had dressed in my new clothes and left via Papula's living room door without saying goodbye, since I simply couldn't face talking to her. I went directly into town and posted another letter to Gringo, the tenth I think, since I had learned English. As I arrived in Republic Street, a taxi pulled over. A striking-looking girl, wearing tight blue jeans and a rose patterned T-shirt, got out of the car and walked into the Orzdy department store. I was transfixed by her, and without thinking I changed direction and followed her into the store. She was a perfect likeness of Susan George in *Twinky*, and I instantly fell in love with her.

That evening I was so excited to tell Rabbit about Aida, my first love. I was so sorry when Rabbit mentioned the birthday party, and I apologised to my Brader and his family many times. 'Mery, forget it,' Rabbit had said, to calm me down. 'We will celebrate your sixteenth birthday next year, it is not a problem.'

Ever since that day, though, Rabbit had started to miss our meetings. Something did not feel right. This morning he had disappeared when he knew very well how much I wanted him to come into town with me to see Aida. His mother believed he had gone to my house. I looked for him all over Qala. He had always let me know if his plans had changed, but recently, I had to admit, he had been behaving oddly.

Maybe he is jealous of Aida? Thinking about it, his behaviour towards me started to change soon after we went to Orzdy so that I could point her out to Rabbit. *Or maybe it's my fault for not keeping our appointment on my fifteenth birthday?* Lost in these thoughts as I walked down Republic Street on that sweltering afternoon, I saw my city in a different light.

Kirkuk had been built by the Babylonian Emperor Nebuchadnezzar II. Three hundred years later it was visited by Alexander the Great. Even then, the Greeks had been excited by the bitumen tar that poured out of the earth here, but it wasn't until this century that the vast oil reserves began to be exploited. I grew up in one of the richest oil cities in the world, with a million inhabitants, but it was also cursed by its abundance of 'black gold'.

Kirkuk was at the centre of a dispute between Saddam Hussein and the Kurds, and it was heading towards its darkest days because of the hatred created by the monster amongst its different ethnic minorities. Kirkuk, the city of my birth, a city sitting on a time bomb.

That day, Kirkuk appeared like a meaningless image, a discarded still from an old newspaper page, drained of colour, save for those menacing reds and browns on the imposing posters of Saddam that hung from almost every building on both sides of Republic Street. A summer sandstorm covered the sky with sickly yellow clouds, making the air dangerously dusty and hard to breathe. The people were bustling around as usual, but despite their raucousness, they seemed lifeless, trapped by the city's tense atmosphere. They looked fearful, as if entangled in the cobweb of the dusty heat, engulfed by the sandstorm blowing in from the southern Iraqi deserts.

This oppressive mood was not unusual, this was just how everyday life had become in my city. Kirkuk smelt of blood, the result of a political situation that was beyond my comprehension at the time. I was not as ignorant about it as I would have wished to be. Over the years, talking to my uncles and learning my family history had taught me a lot. I knew the problem was due to the monster with thousands of heads that was thought to be impossible to destroy. Each time a head was smashed, another dozen were born. A monster which had total control over us, who watched over us both inside and outside of our homes, and gobbled us up if we made a wrong move. The same one Rashaba warned me about when he forbade me to talk politics. Ever since, I had always thought there must be a way to destroy it, but how? The terror created by the beast made us believe that only God had power over him. Yet God's greatness did not seem to help ease the deep fear everyone had, and most seemed convinced that God was on his side.

My people had been brainwashed to believe that they were born to obey. Not for us the carefree life of American people which we witnessed in films. Their homes, families, birthday parties, New Year celebrations and holidays, their rivers, trees, mountains, animals, freedom... Everything looked so precious, so beautiful!

Did I say beautiful? Weeks could go by without hearing anyone utter this word in my city, except perhaps in the films I saw at the cinema.

Even in the middle of horror and misery there was always something that kept you going, and for me, apart from seeing Aida, it was the hope that I would soon receive a letter from Gringo.

Aida, my Christian princess, worked behind the counter in the womenswear department in Orzdy, the newly opened store which was run by the government. It was fascinating to see female employees, young women, dressed in European styles and serving customers. Most were Christians, though there were some Kurds and Arabs too, but none were as splendid as my Aida. She was a free soul, always dressed in her unique way, as if she were from a different world. From the day I first saw her I would fantasise so much about her that if I were a writer and could create magic with words, I could have written a whole book about her and whisked her off into my wonderland. Aida was different from Papula. This was not about having a sexy body. Apart from her gorgeous features, what I most liked about Aida was her sense of freedom.

I spied on her. I learnt about her life, her family, where she lived and what she did on Fridays, her day off. Aida was the daughter of a Christian Iraqi father, an engineer in the Petroleum Company, and a French mother. Given her father's position I couldn't understand why Aida was working when she was so young. *She should be at secondary school. The department store is not the place for her. She is a princess, but in the wrong world, and I am to be her prince and save her. I will take her away from all the ugliness into a magic world just for the two of us.*

I always shivered at the sight of Aida. I did it again now. *I am too much in love with you,* my mind sang to her as we exchanged a look. That day Aida was Brigitte Bardot in *And God Created Woman*. She wore her silky blonde hair over her bare shoulders, and was wearing an almost transparent, sleeveless golden dress, making her shine more than the lights around her. She was serving a woman covered with a black cape, and the contrast between them was as stark as day and night.

You are stunning. I am mad about your golden hair, your blue eyes are my life's light, your smile is honey and I would die to kiss your lips. I cannot pretend that such thoughts were particularly original, but they were powerfully new to me. We never spoke, but only exchanged looks and, recently, a few smiles. I would go in pretending I was looking at the clothes. This went on for three months. Every time I was in town, I had to see Aida and I was longing to talk to her.

What would I say? Aida, might you become a Muslim so that I can marry you? Does it really matter if she is Christian or a Muslim? But of course, if she refuses to convert to Islam I will not be able to marry her. To marry her! How could I think of such things when I can't even have an erection? I will need to have an operation, to become a boy. This was how I planned our future, thinking of her at the end of every day, before going to sleep only to dream about her. Even though I wasn't sure if I could ever become a real boy, I could not stop myself from going to see Aida, *and today I will find a way to talk to her.*

I came across an exquisite, pale blue scarf embroidered along the edge with a strip of rust-coloured silk, just like in the springtime when the sky is kissed by an orange sunset. I picked up the scarf, by way of an excuse to talk to Aida, but it felt so precious in my hand, it gave me an idea of what to do with it. I was nervous and as I stepped towards Aida, I saw flashes of romantic films, moments where the hero approaches the heroine and finally tells her he loves her. I had never been so close to her and it was too late to go back. I put the scarf down on the counter. I wanted to say something, but words wouldn't come.

'How much?' I finally mumbled in English.

'You are buying this because you want to talk to me?' she replied in English. I was speechless. 'It's fine,' she said. 'I know you come here often and have wanted to talk to me for a long time, right?'

'Yes, princess.' Aida laughed and I realised what I had just said.

'Yes, Lady Aida.'

'You know my name too?'

'I love... I love your name.'

'Aida was a captive lover of an Egyptian Pharaonic officer. My father loves that opera. He named me after her.'

I couldn't believe I was talking to Aida. I was breathing her breaths, sucking her soul into mine, and was floating in her mesmerising charm. She was the captive and I the Pharaonic officer.

'Do you know the story?' she asked.

'Er, no.'

'It's very sad.'

'What happens?'

'In the end, the two lovers die in a prison cell.'

'I prefer a happy ending, where possible,' I said, entranced by the light in her eyes. *I will ensure that will not be her fate,* I promised her silently, as though I really could be her knight in shining armour. *I will save you and we can escape to our kingdom.*

'Are you a boy or a girl?' she asked.

'I don't know.' I was about to panic. 'I mean, what do you think?'

'A boy, and a handsome one.'

'Thanks,' I said, wishing I really was. At least Aida seemed to have no doubts.

'How come you have long hair?'

'You don't like it?'

'Oh, I do, your hair looks really nice. It is just unusual, isn't it, for a boy in this country?'

'I am a dervish.'

'What is that?'

'A devout religious person.'

'Oh! What is your name?'

'Mery.'

'Like our Virgin Mary?' She giggled. 'Just a joke.'

'It is actually Merywan. I was named after a Prince from "The Twelve Riders of Merywan". You can call me Mery.'

'Mery the Prince?' she said, and she seemed impressed.

Is this another one of my daydreams? I wish Rabbit could see me. I wish you could see me, Gringo. I am here and am talking to Aida, the heroine of all my filmic fantasies. She picked up the scarf. 'Is it a present?' she said. I nodded. 'Who is it for? If I may ask.' *For you, when I kiss you for the first time.*

'For your girlfriend?'

'Yes. I mean no! I will let you know. It's a surprise.'

'You speak good English.'

'I learn from school and films because I want to go to America to meet Gringo.'

'Who is he?'

'You don't know who Gringo is, the cowboy? He's my hero and he is the best...' I imitated Gringo, twirling the pistol and shooting left and right. Aida found this funny. 'Do you always speak English?' she asked.

'Yes, often, but not when my father is present. He doesn't allow me to.'

'Why?'

'It is the language of the infidels, he says.'

'So you are Muslim?'

'Yes. You?' I knew very well she was Chaldean-Christian and that was the one thing I did not like about her. She held up her necklace and displayed the silver cross. 'I am one of the infidels,' she said, with irony.

'Yes, but you could convert to Islam if you marry me.'

Aida was taken aback, but smiled. 'So, what do you say?' I asked.

'I say there is a long queue,' she answered, as she put the scarf in a carrier bag and handed it to me.

'What?' I felt bad about the long queue, thinking she had many boys wanting to marry her. 'What queue?'

'Behind you, there is a long queue.'

I turned around, there were five women customers waiting to be served. I paid all that I had, half a dinar, the price of the scarf. I picked up the bag and left. Aida called me back. She handed me a coin, twenty-five cents.

'But it cost five hundred.'

'I know, it is my discount for you. Have a drink.'

The minute I walked out onto the street and before I had the chance to enjoy the feeling of love, and the fact that I had spoken to Aida, I heard footsteps behind me. *I am being followed.* I thought it could only be Mukhabarat men. With the threat of the monster ever present, I feared they were sent to get me for some reason. I shuddered within myself. I felt sure they would grab me by my neck. I regretted the way I was dressed and wished that my hair was tucked under my hat, so that I might blend into the crowd. My heart raced, though I reasoned that they couldn't be the Special Forces as they were not wearing the uniform.

The Special Forces were brutal. They were privileged with the power to do anything they wished against civilians, especially non-Arab citizens. At least they were easy enough to avoid, dressed in their military gear. The alternative was worse, Mukhabarat, the intelligence agents, the main branch of Saddam's secret police, the most vicious, ruthless mini-monsters. Nobody knew who was in the Mukhabarat, and when or where they might sting you.

Jam, the stamp and coin dealer

They were right behind me. 'Inglisa, she is English!' one of them said. 'There are no English in Kirkuk,' his companion answered. I sighed with relief that they were not Mukhabarat after all, but two teenage boys. They shot comments about me back and forth, like a salacious game of table tennis. 'Look at those buttocks. I am dying for them... Oh, imagine squeezing her to you from behind, holding her pomegranate tits, licking her neck...' They did not care about my reaction because it was considered indecent for girls to speak to the male sex publicly. Even imploring men to desist from hassling or pinching them would have resulted in people believing the girls enjoyed what the men were doing. That was why very few, like Aida, ventured around town alone, wearing European clothes, and even she made sure that she always travelled by taxi.

The best I could do was to ignore the boys and quicken my pace. They did the same. I didn't plan to go alone into a stranger's shop, but the anger they caused made me push open the glass door and step inside for the first time. It was halfway between Republic Street and Al Hamrah Road. A prime position for trade and right in the heart of the city. This was only a few minutes walk from Ordzy, but on that day, even walking fast, it had felt like a never-ending journey.

Many times I had stared through the window, and I had come to call this shop 'Wonderworld' because of the interesting displays of stamps and money from all over the globe in the window. Amongst them were two small paintings. One was a view of the River Thames in London and the other depicted the Eiffel Tower in Paris. In the lefthand corner there was a small desk and a chair where the owner usually sat reading, or sorting his stamps and coins. On the desk were an open book, a Philips music system and a few cassettes.

The owner must have seen me many times before, standing outside reading the names of countries that I could only dream of visiting. What I most loved about his shop was listening to the foreign music he was always playing loudly, mostly soundtracks, often those which Ennio Morricone composed for *The Good, the Bad and the Ugly* and *Once Upon A Time in the West*. But he also played music by other great composers too, like Ravi Shankar's scores for Satyajit Ray's *Pather Panchali* and Richard Attenborough's *Gandhi*. As I walked in, Shirley Bassey's voice boomed over the speakers, singing 'Goldfinger' by John Barry from the James Bond film, starring Sean Connery as 007.

The shop seemed to be deserted. I stood looking out at the street in case the boys appeared again, then took out Aida's scarf and hid it under my T-shirt, leaving the carrier bag on the table. I was surprised by a man's voice behind me and turned around. 'If you have finally decided to enter after looking in my window for months,' the man said, with a smile as he walked in from the storage room, 'you must want one of three things: to buy a stamp or a coin, a refuge because you are hiding from someone, or you are here because you wish to become my friend. My name is Jam. Nice to meet you,' and he held out his hand.

Jam appeared to be around twenty five years old. He was wearing jeans and a T-shirt and had handsome features with dark green eyes, his luxuriant black hair combed back off his forehead. His manner was not at all threatening and he seemed to have a warm personality. In the past, standing outside his shop and staring through the window, I had seen him sitting at his desk, looking, in my opinion, like a mix between James Dean, Giuliano Gemma and Jean-Paul Belmondo.

'So, which one of the three has drawn you onto my boat?' Jam asked, still holding out his hand.

'I am Merywan Rashaba.' I shook his hand. 'I like your shop, and I love the music you play.'

'Thank you Merywan, I'll take that as a compliment.'

I felt relaxed in his company, like finding a dear old friend who could easily be trusted. One reason was that he did not seem bothered about my looks.

'Do you speak English?' I asked, in English. 'Yes,' Jam answered, in the same language. 'Do you mind if I talk to you in English? I am going into Year Four in secondary school and need to practise.'

'Please do.'

I apologised for taking up his time. He offered me a drink, and when I accepted, he poked his head outside and called for two Pepsi from the man in the tea hut to the side of his shop.

'How can I help you, Merywan?'

'Can I see that atlas in the window?' The truth was I wanted to stay and speak to Jam some more. 'Sure.' Jam put the old atlas on the table and kept himself busy sorting out sets of stamps. I flicked through the pages. 'Do you know how far America is from here?'

'Not sure in kilometres, but I imagine it must be about ten to twelve hours' flight.'

'Have you been to America?'

'No, I haven't. Although, I did live in England for a few years.'

'Excuse me for asking this, but is Jam your real name?'

Jam grinned. 'My name is Janga, short for Jangawar, "Warrior", but Jam is fine.'

'Doesn't that mean jam as in fruit jam?'

'Yes. A funny name isn't it? I got it from my English lady. She loved jam on toast and kissing me, she thought I tasted like jam.'

I smiled, before we both collapsed into laughter. The man brought the drinks, Jam paid him and he left.

'Your wife is English?'

'Oh no! If you refer to the lady that called me Jam, I met her about five years ago on a journey to Rhodes, in Greece. By the end of the two-week holiday, I was in love with her and decided to follow her to London...' He told me no more and sipped his Pepsi. I looked up at the painting of London on the wall. I now realised why it was there. 'Did you like London?' I asked.

'It's a fabulous city,' Jam said, 'very interesting on all levels and a wonderfully creative centre for performing arts and films.'

'Sorry for asking so many questions. You don't have to answer me if you don't want to, but I am keen to learn about the world.'

'At your age I felt the same. I loved films, and when I saw them I found it very hard to grow up in this country. I wanted to travel, to see the outside world.'

I was so pleased to hear Jam saying this, it seemed we had much in common.

'Why did you come back?'

'I would have stayed in London if it wasn't for my father's sudden death. My mother wanted me at my father's funeral and I could not refuse. I suggested to my mother that she sell the shop, but she wanted me to take over. To begin with it was a real burden, but soon I found a new world within these four walls, through the stamps and the coins, so I became a stamp dealer like my father, and my grandfather, who was the first to start a stamp shop in Kirkuk, if not in all Iraq.'

It was incredible to me that he would leave England and come back to Kirkuk to sell old stamps and coins! *Who on earth would spend money on buying these things, when they cannot even be used for sending letters? Unless he has some other reason for staying here and does not wish to talk about it, at least not on our first encounter.*

'You may think this is a crazy business,' Jam said, with his easy smile.

'I don't understand what could motivate anyone to spend money on these things,' I said. 'I am sorry, but I am just being honest. I would never lie to you,' I added. It seemed like a strange thing to say after only having met this man a few minutes before, but he inspired such trust that it came completely naturally. Jam bowed his head, accepting my promise, and then continued our conversation by asking me whether I had ever collected cards, such as cards of footballers or actors.

'Yes, and especially those of Gringo, you know who I mean?'

'Clint Eastwood?'

'Jam, you are my friend,' I said, and shook his hand again.

'Well, collecting stamps is like that, but it is a bit more than a hobby, it is a passion. Do you know this word passion?'

'Not exactly.'

'What do you love most in life? I don't mean your family, but something you really care about, and you almost feel ill when you're not able to do it or to have it?'

'Cinema! Going to the cinema is what I love most. I want to act and make films one day. When I watch films, I completely forget everything around me.'

'You have the passion of an artist, a performer, a filmmaker, that is great. Well, similarly, others can be passionate about stamps, for some feel elated just to touch them, to read the stories behind them. For example, this set was issued by South Africa in 1979 for the

Centenary of the Zulu War. You could say it was a war against the British enslavement and invasion. Have you seen *Zulu*?'

'Yes. I like that film.'

He then picked up another one with as much care as someone handling a newborn. 'Look at this, a Penny Black. It's the first stamp in the world. The first one to be posted was sent from the city of Bath in England in May 1840. It was posted four days before the stamp was actually issued, which makes it extremely valuable. Unfortunately, this is not the original. If only it were, it would make any stamp collector delighted just to hold it in their hands. Did you know that for all their industrial revolution, Empire and inventions, Britain's greatest export to the world is stamps?'

I shook my head. In a matter of minutes of talking to him, I had learned more about the world than in the whole of my life from Rashaba. I would have stayed longer to listen to him, but I felt I was taking up too much of his time. 'How much for this atlas?'

'Oh, that is an expensive one, eight dinars. You can have it for half price. I like to treat my new clients.'

'Thanks, I will think about it.' I shut the atlas.

'Nice talking to you, Merywan.'

'You too. I will be back.'

As I left the shop, my first thought was how much I wanted to tell Rabbit about the short yet enlightening time I had spent with Jam, *but mostly I want to tell him about actually talking to Aida.*

The sudden rattle of gun fire nearby interrupted my reverie. I was so startled that I could barely move. In the middle of the day, on Republic Street, a shooting was almost inconceivable.

Abu Ali

The gunshots came from the opposite side of the street. The noise was too deafening to be just some children's game. The crowd, as one, instantly turned in alarm. I spun around too, trying to see where the firing had come from. A young man, not much older than me, was pointing a pistol in a man's face. The man was wearing the typical khaki outfit of a Ba'athist, a member of Saddam's political party. He also wore military boots, dark sunglasses and a cap, with a moustache that curled around his mouth down to his chin. *No doubt a gun is hidden under his jacket, as these guys never go around unarmed.* Although defenceless at this moment, he stood upright and faced the young man, in spite of the obvious danger.

'Is he going to kill Abu Ali?' the tea-seller nearby hissed to his friend incredulously. Abu Ali's two guards, standing on each side of him, holding their AK-47s pointed at the ground, seemed frozen with tension. The slightest move could have caused the young man to shoot. This unbelievable scene brought everyone, including those passing in their cars, to a standstill. The silence was deafening.

I am sure I recognise the young man. I want to be wrong. But where have I seen him, and why does he want to kill Abu Ali? To dare to try and kill one of the monster's men, in the middle of the city and in front of everyone, was simply unheard of.

Hercules had warned me about Abu Ali. 'He's one of the most dangerous figures in Kirkuk,' he had said, in between lifting barbells to his chest. 'Abu Ali's power comes from handing over innocent Kurds to be eaten by the monster. In compensation he gets the same privileges as the Arab Mukhabarat. He is also paid a lot of money for each victim. Thanks to his brutality, Abu Ali has become infamous and is feared in every household. Abu Ali has no mercy for anyone, especially for his own Kurdish people. If he casts his eyes on you, sooner or later he will get you, whether you have done anything wrong or not. So, Mery, stay out of Abu Ali's way!'

And here I was, only a few metres away from him, the Mukhabarat's hunting dog in my city. I ached to run away from there, but was rooted to the spot, and could do no more than try to make myself invisible. I had to see. I was like a helpless fish caught on a line, being drawn towards Abu Ali. I dreaded that he would turn my way and look me in the eyes, and the young man holding the gun worried me too. *What if he recognises me and asks for help? It would be so much better to hide or look down demurely, as most girls would, but I can't.* Although I disapproved of fighting and killing, I could not help but wish the young man would pull the trigger and kill Abu Ali.

The young man pulled the trigger, and shouted out something like, 'Long live Kurdistan and death to the Kurdish traitors.' But there was no sound, no smoke... the pistol was empty, or perhaps it had jammed? Quickly, he tried again, and for a third time, but to no avail. The young man's heroic posture collapsed. Abu Ali, stunned by his apparent luck, slowly recovered as he realised that no bullet had penetrated his traitor's heart. In a flash, he pulled the pistol from the young man's grasp, and with it, brutally bashed his face. His two bodyguards followed suit, kicking and punching the young man as he fell, then smashing their gun butts into his body on the ground.

Hundreds were watching, but not one dared to raise a finger. People faded as if they were part of a badly painted tableau, doing their best to make themselves dissolve into the background. They were terrified, like me, of being associated with this young man and taken away. Abu Ali turned around quickly and threw a glance in our direction, perhaps searching for the young man's accomplices. The crowd backed away a few steps. The tea-seller next to me lost his balance and trod heavily on my toes. I yelled out involuntarily, then hastily put a hand to my mouth.

I did not think I had made much noise, but in that sea of silence, it was enough to make everyone turn towards me. Abu Ali did too, looking straight into my eyes as though he were going to eat me alive. I became aware, with a sickening certainty, that I recognised Abu Ali. *I had met him before. But where?*

I could not move, although I was only too aware of the risks of attracting the attention of Abu Ali. *I could be killed, and what a dreadful death it would be at the hands of the Mukhabarat!*

The people around me noticed that he was staring at me, and slowly they dispersed, parting like the Red Sea in the film *The Ten Commandments*, exposing me as the solitary target of a vicious predator. The crowd was of such a size that, had we acted together, we could have disarmed Abu Ali and his men, albeit a few of us may have lost our lives. But I knew that if he should come for me, no one would stand in his way. The fear of the monster had become all-encompassing. Rashaba's old saying, 'Hold on to your hat so that the wind won't take it away' had become the only way to survive in the face of our enemy.

A four-wheel-drive white Toyota screeched to a halt. Two more guards jumped out. They dragged the young man like a sack, and threw his body into the back, where it landed with a dull thud. Abu Ali and his men got in. As the car pulled away, Abu Ali, sitting in the passenger seat, stared at me until the car went past. I was terrified to read his lips clearly mouthing, 'I will get you, Mery.'

A tremendous and fearful commotion, like an earthquake spreading along a fault line, suddenly replaced the stillness. Police cars and army Jeeps appeared from all directions, and men poured out of them and began hitting and arresting people randomly. We simply ran, frantically, anywhere but here. Shops closed, cars turned around in panic, music was silenced and all the noises of ordinary life disappeared. Instead there was a stampede, shouts mixed with sirens and gunshots, and the rat-tat-tat footsteps of the armed forces chasing us, simply because we were guilty of being in the wrong place at the wrong time.

A policeman was close to catching me when he hit a man on his head with a gun butt and knocked him out at once. I sprinted down alleys and dodged up side streets and just kept running, too scared to look back.

It wasn't until I got to the bridge, and stood there breathing heavily, straining to look normal and melt into the workers crossing the bridge on their way home, that I realised where I had seen Abu Ali before today. I stopped and held on to the parapet, stock still as though under an evil spell, stunned by what I had just discovered. *Abu Ali is Shawes Dog! Yet, surely this cannot be true. Kojak's father is in prison for murder, serving a life sentence… It is vital that I ask*

Rabbit. He must know. I really need to see him, but where is he?

As I gazed into the dry river, doubts clouded my mind again. *Is this purely my imagination, twisted by fear and exhaustion, playing tricks on me?*

The realisation that Abu Ali was in fact Shawes Dog engulfed me like wildfire. I wanted to protect myself by denying it, by rejecting it. I tried to forget it as I thought of Gringo, my hero, of my uncles, my brother Monkey and Star, Rabbit, Papula, Jam and Aida, my love. But nothing seemed to erase the nightmare. Abu Ali's heartless gaze followed me everywhere my mind went.

Abu Ali could easily come after me at any moment, and with his power, it's only a matter of time before he gets me. I am no longer safe in Kirkuk. I must escape to America. Will Rabbit know if Shawes Dog is still in prison? I must have repeated this all the way to my friend's house. I kept glancing over my shoulders, wary of the Dog appearing from one of the alleyways like an evil spectre.

Sunshine, by now blossoming into a pretty teenager, opened the door. Rabbit and Peaceful had gone to find a job for the summer holidays, it transpired. 'Where?' I asked miserably, wondering what could have made my Brader do this without me. Sunshine said that she had no idea. 'I must see Rabbit,' I said. 'I will send him to your house the minute he comes back,' she kindly assured me.

I took out my boyish clothes from Papula's cupboard and got dressed in black cotton trousers and a black shirt. I hid my hair under my new hat, changing into the look deemed acceptable by Rashaba. *The appearance I will adopt from now on whenever I go out for fear of meeting Abu Ali or of attracting dangerous attention to myself, the look that will make me feel like one of the crowd. I should avoid going to the town centre, except of course to see Aida.* I opened my treasure box, flicked through my photos, and, when I came across the monster's portrait, spat on it. I then found the black-and-white photo I was searching for. It showed Rabbit and myself outside our school, both of us grinning. Standing behind us was the young man who had faced Abu Ali with the gun. I put it in my pocket.

I waited and waited, but Rabbit did not turn up. It had been a while since I last read the Qur'an. I sat down on the veranda, opened the holy book and prayed to God that I was wrong about Abu Ali, even though I knew my instincts were right.

The next morning, I went back to Rabbit's house. Jwana opened the door. She was surprised to see me, she said, as she thought I was away, working with Rabbit and Peaceful on a building site. I did not want to worry her, but I found it incredible that Rabbit, without saying a single word to me, could have gone away for the entire week. I decided I should go to Rabbit's place of work, but the family did not know where he was, apart from that it was about an hour's drive south of Kirkuk in the Iraqi desert. There was nothing I could do. I had to wait for Thursday, the end of week, for my friend to come home for Friday, everyone's day off work. *I must have deeply offended Rabbit for him to disappear from my life, but how and when had I done so?* I went back over our most recent meetings and I began to feel guilty about my infatuation for Aida. This was the only new circumstance in our lives that could explain Rabbit's unusual behaviour.

That wasn't the principal reason why I stopped going into the city centre to see Aida, though; it was fear of meeting Abu Ali that made me stay away. I did not even go out in Qala. *But if Abu Ali is Shawes Dog, he already knows where to find me.* I was terrified that he might turn up at the door at any moment.

On Thursday afternoon, I went to Rabbit's house again and hung around outside. At last, I saw Peaceful arrive, but he was on his own. 'Hiwa decided to stay on at the building site to look after the materials,' he explained, 'and not have the day off, for an extra half dinar.'

I could not take it out on Peaceful. He knew nothing about Rabbit being upset with me. There was no public transport to their workplace. But I was getting desperate.

Later, at the Hasiraka market teahouse, Peaceful pointed out Rabbit's boss to me. Standing in front of him, I had to stop myself from laughing, so closely did he resemble Louis de Funes, a French comedian. I asked for work, but he had a full team, he did not need me. I offered to work for less money, but it was no use. I begged Louis to give me a try. He finally relented, on condition that I would not be paid for the first week.

The desert scorpion's sting

'...Bena dai, bard bena, give me a stone, well done, now cement, hurry up...' These words were sung as a mantra, to a monotonous melody, and could conceivably sound exotic to a visitor, especially against the silence of the Iraqi desert. But as much as I loved music and singing, after listening to this every day from dawn till dusk for three weeks Louis' singing about his work and building materials began to drive me crazy.

Sitting on the rough ground, one of the assistants launched handfuls of cement at Louis. He would catch it, spread it on the wall, pick up a white stone, examine it, and place it on the thick cement. When he reached the end of one line and before moving on to the next, he fixed the stones securely in position with his bare hands. This job took a while, and in order not to disturb the rhythm, he added new words to his song, first about himself and his pride in his work, 'Well done, I got it, I placed it...' and then some romance, 'dear Layla, my sweetheart, my heart burns, kiss it, soothe it, one more kiss...'

We were a small team. There was Louis, the builder. Louis' son, ten years old, the youngest amongst us, was responsible for bringing pots of water from a tank to fill up the barrels, which were set next to the cement-mixing man. He was the oldest in the group, and stood the whole day out in the open under the searing sun. I was doing the donkey work, nothing masterly. I would lift a tray of cement, put it on my head and take it to the cement-launcher. Then I collected the empty tray and went back to refill it. By lunch break, my neck felt as stiff as a log. One man broke stones the whole day with a sledge-hammer, two others carried stones from him to Peaceful, who was the stone-launcher. Peaceful searched in the pile of stones around him and offered the most perfectly formed ones to Louis.

Rabbit was one of the stone-carriers. He considered the boss greedy. We could have done with four other workers, but Louis was too penny-pinching to hire more. I realised this was not a job for a human being. I dragged myself back and forth for the entire day like a mule, for only five dinars a week. Although I did not like the job or the Arab desert, I was happy there because no one suspected me of anything, and I was with Rabbit, my dear Brader.

Rabbit seemed shocked when I arrived, but I spotted Happiness's necklace around his neck and knew our friendship was safe. At lunch break, he was the first to break the silence. He said he thought I would not like being away from the cinemas and from seeing Aida for the whole summer holidays.

'I would go to hell with you,' I said.

'It all happened so fast,' Rabbit explained. 'I just had no time to come and see you. I'm sorry.'

I know his excuse is a lie and I hate feeling that he is hiding something from me. I had not seen him for more than a week, but he seemed to have grown up and become serious. He was distracted and spoke little. But he had not abandoned the combing of his candyfloss hair and was still ticklish.

'On the morning I went to town on my own, I actually spoke to Aida,' I said, and waited to see Rabbit's reaction. He put his thumb up, still chewing. He was genuinely pleased. 'Are you jealous of my love for Aida?' I finally asked him. Rabbit laughed, but it sounded like a bitter laugh, then he spoke, 'No, Mery. I can't wait for the day to dance at your wedding.'

After work, in the afternoon, we went for a walk in the desert as the shadows lengthened and the sun became an intensely orange ball which bounced just above the horizon. We were silent for a moment, before Rabbit asked which film I had seen on the day I spoke to Aida. I did not answer him directly, but instead asked, 'Do you have any news of Shawes?' This puzzled Rabbit. He looked into my eyes, perhaps for the first time that day.

'Why?'

'I met someone in town and I think it was Shawes.'

Rabbit burst out laughing as if I had said something ridiculous, and despite myself I couldn't help but feel like a fool. It was only when I recounted the events of that day that his laughter abruptly halted. 'I met Abu Ali. I met him on the day you did not turn up to come with me to town. I am sure he is Shawes Dog.'

'Sure, sure?' Rabbit asked, with irony.

'Well, not one hundred per cent, but he stared at me in the same way Shawes did on the day he killed the caretaker, and I think he even said the same words.'

'What words?'

'I will get you, Mery.'

Rabbit put his arms around me. He apologised for laughing, explaining that he had not realised it was so serious, and I could tell that he was genuinely sympathetic to the anxiety I had suffered during the week that he had been away.

'Where is Shawes?' I asked.

'The Dog is in prison and he will rot in his cell until he dies.'

'Are you sure?' I asked. Rabbit put his hand on his heart. 'I am sorry,' I said. 'I must've been seeing things.'

Rabbit reassured me that Shawes Dog was not going to reappear. *I have to believe him. After all, if Shawes Dog is out and really is Abu Ali, he would be a threat to Rabbit and his family too.*

'Abu Ali is a powerful man,' Rabbit said. 'He used to be a Peshmerga in the mountains, with fourteen younger ones under his command. One day last year he poisoned all his comrades and came back to join the monster's forces. He was paid a lot of money and given a position that made him feel like a king in Kirkuk. If his eyes land on you, it is up to him if you live, not up to God. Mery, I am glad you are here with me and a long way away from Abu Ali.' *How can any commander betray his men, or anyone betray his friends for money? Now that same person is the master of my life and that of all the people in my city. What is God there for, then? How can God let people like him live?* I had so many questions, but the best I could do was to suppress them before the Almighty punished me by confronting me with Abu Ali again.

'I did not go to see a film because I had spent all my money on a scarf, which was really the only way I could think of speaking to Aida,' I said, finally answering his question. Rabbit shook his hips and called out, 'Wow, Do Badan, *Two Hearts*,' a reference to an Indian film featuring a tragic love story that we knew well. I grinned ruefully, but told Rabbit about our conversation. He was flabbergasted that I had actually asked Aida to change her religion in order to marry me.

Since the second year of secondary school, and when Rashaba was not around, Rabbit and I had only spoken in English, and we continued to do so on the building site. Soon, during our lunch breaks, Louis made us crack up laughing as he tried to imitate us. He did not know a word of English but kept up a whole conversation which made no sense whatsoever between himself and the old cement-launcher. We were building the walls of a new military barracks. It was in the Iraqi desert, not that far from the Tigris River near Tikrit, the birthplace of Saddam Hussein, some fifty kilometres away from the Kirkuk-Baghdad highway. We slept on site in the open. At night we did our best to protect ourselves from the deadly poisonous desert scorpions that might crawl into our beds, though they seemed to be everywhere. Rabbit was particularly fearless of them. When we found one while we were working one day, he held it up by its sting and, after enjoying himself by scaring us with it, he called Louis and asked if he wanted to have a new assistant for free. We laughed at the joke. He then squashed it under his foot. If he caught one after work, he would throw it into the fire that we used to cook our dinner, saying, 'Boss, would you like an Iraqi kebab?'

For the first three Fridays, Rabbit didn't leave the site. *Surely he would prefer to go home on his day off, it can't be just the money!* I found this disturbing and intriguing. I offered him the half dinar that he would get for looking after the materials, but he didn't want it. I would have gladly stayed behind with him, but I couldn't miss the Thursday dance, and Rashaba was waiting for my wage. On Thursday afternoons, Rabbit would get on the pickup with us. He would always sit on top of the driver's cabin. Then, after about five kilometres he would bang on the roof for the driver to stop and would jump off and run all the way back to the building site. 'He has gone mad,' Peaceful said, seeing his brother behaving so strangely.

Each Saturday, on my return, Rabbit asked me over and over for news about his family. 'Why don't you ask Peaceful?' I said. 'He doesn't talk unless I pay him,' Rabbit answered. Only when he had been reassured that all was well would he ask me about the films I had seen on my day off.

I always saw one in the cinema, and one more in the evening at home with Papula. The film I was most eager to tell Rabbit about was

Yilmaz Guney's *Yol*. I watched it on video. It dealt with the Kurdish situation in Turkey and was therefore banned in Iraq. I had to act out the story of each film he had missed, from the beginning to the end, and I had to tell it in colour. 'Only if the film was in colour,' Rabbit joked. When I finished, I tried my best to persuade him to go home, but he would not, until, he asserting enigmatically, the end of the summer holidays. I knew he couldn't be staying here only for half a dinar and for the love of the desert scorpions, but he refused to explain.

On the fourth Thursday, in the morning, we had a work inspection on the site. An Army Jeep from Saddam's Special Guards arrived, which shut Louis up for once. He was not far off shitting himself from fright. He asked us to bow our heads to salute the gentlemen. He went around with the Major to show him the progress.

'I feel like a Jash, traitor,' Rabbit whispered. 'What do you mean?' I whispered back. 'We, Kurds, are helping to build military bases for Saddam's army,' Rabbit lowered his head further. Up until that moment I had not considered that we were helping Saddam's army to kill our own people. *I wish I had never come to the desert to work on the damn military base. I loathe myself for every pot of cement I carry on my head that is used to build these walls.*

'Once finished, this base is going to be yet another one equipped with the latest weapons from around the world in exchange for our oil,' Rabbit said, with a sigh.

'While our people are totally forgotten,' I added.

'The Peshmerga will never defeat this massive army,' Rabbit reflected, ruefully.

'That's not true, Brader. I believe in the Peshmerga and they will win.' As the inspection ended, Louis told us to line up again. The Major needed a strong man to build a wall around his garden. Rabbit was chosen for the job. We helped him load stones onto the back of the Jeep and then they drove away.

On his return Rabbit was very disturbed. *He must feel a complete Jash, not only by helping the enemy to build their military bases, but to decorate their gardens as well.* To my surprise, the minute Rabbit made it back, he let me know in a grumpy voice that he had changed his mind, he wanted to go home with us at the end of the day. I was delighted but also worried by his dark mood. I smiled and whispered in his ear, 'Up Kissinger's bum.' This time he did not repeat it after me.

During the one-hour lunch break we shared our food as always, but Rabbit did not eat. '*The Birds,* by Alfred Hitchcock, is opening tomorrow in the Alamen Cinema,' I said. 'I've seen the trailers. I can't wait to see it. Do you want to come with me?' But Rabbit was only half listening.

I went away to pee, then washed my face, hands and feet. I lined up with Peaceful, Louis, his son and the rest of the group for our midday prayer. Not Rabbit. Every time I stood in the direction of Mecca and faced God, I wished Rabbit were next to me, but he never came. And whenever I asked him, he replied that he couldn't be bothered. He usually lay down for a rest, but instead he remained seated where he was, while anger visibly boiled up inside him. He even turned against me. 'Why do you make so much fuss about hiding yourself for a pee? Just do it like everyone else, like this.' He pulled down his trousers, took out his penis and went for it with everyone there. I was upset, but I loved him, and did not want to add to his frustrations. 'Out of respect for everyone else, I like to do it further away,' I said blandly, trying to conceal my annoyance.

The afternoon dragged interminably as I counted down the hours to four o'clock. Louis was at the height of his singing '...dear Layla, kiss me...' when out of nowhere – shirr – he farted so loudly that it was impossible to ignore. He abruptly stopped singing and looked in dismay at us, while we all froze and waited for his reaction, each one of us on the brink of cracking up. Louis' fart was the most embarrassing thing that could ever have happened to him. 'Ahm, Ahm, this bloody bad cough!' he said, trying to cover it up with a coughing sound. We burst into laughter. 'What are you laughing at? Are you shameless? Haven't you heard anyone with a bad cough?'

'What a bad cough, Boss,' Rabbit called. 'It was explosive.' More laughter followed. Louis grimaced and started singing, which meant for everyone to resume work. 'Layla ghyan, wara day...' Again, shirr. This time we were so overwhelmed that we doubled up with laughter. 'Damn the aging process that brings all these defects,' Louis said, shaking his head. He wasn't old. He was in his mid-thirties. In other circumstances he would consider himself very young and might talk about getting a third wife.

'What aging process, Boss? It is all the chickpeas you eat for lunch,' I said. He threw the round ball of cement he was holding, but I ducked.

'It is four o'clock,' the cement-mixer anounced, from beneath his white veil of cement dust, resembling an Egyptian mummy for all the world. There was a shout of hurray from everyone but Louis. 'Let's carry on for ten more minutes, I need to finish this wall,' he said. I was quick to interrupt him. 'Boss, no overtime on Thursdays, we work six days a week here. What does ten minutes change?' and I began to shake my dusty cloths.

'Hey Mr Long Tongue, if you can spend six days here, why can't you stay ten more minutes?' Louis said.

'Because it is Thursday, Boss, and we all want to go back to Kirkuk. Isn't that right?' I called, and everyone shouted their agreement.

'Or is it because you want extra money for your overtime?' Louis tried his best to make himself sweet. 'Fine, we will stop on the way and I will be really generous. I will get you a Pepsi each, OK?' We exchanged surprised looks. 'A Pepsi each and one more of your *shirrr...*' Rabbit said, laughing.

'Shut your filthy mouth or I will cement it shut for you. Give me a stone, hurry up...' Louis started singing again. We had to accept his offer and work the extra ten minutes, which we all knew only too well would really mean at least another half an hour.

Finally we dusted ourselves down, and, while washing our faces, I splashed Rabbit with water from the barrel and poked a finger into his side. Rabbit jumped out of his skin and swore, 'Hey, motherfucker!', leaving us dissolving into tears of silent laughter. I looked at my Brader. I never understood why Rabbit and I had such respect and love for each other, but I was convinced that we were such good friends, nothing in the world could have parted us, and we were prepared to die for each other.

'Thanks, Rabbit, I don't remember the last time I had so much fun.'

'Thanks to Boss's explosions,' he answered.

'Laughing too much is a bad omen,' the cement-launcher warned us.

'I am really glad you are coming home with us,' I said, as I put my arm around Rabbit. 'We will always be friends, won't we?' I asked. He only nodded.

An open-backed Chevrolet pickup, loaded with a few bits of building materials, had arrived to take us home. 'Hurry up now,' the driver shouted. 'We want to make it to Kirkuk before nightfall.' In a matter of seconds we had jumped into the back of the truck. Louis, with his son on his lap, and the cement-launcher, sat in the passenger seats. Most of the men lay down, hoping to catch some sleep. As always, Rabbit took his place on top of the driver's cabin, and this time he was not going to jump off after five kilometres, but go all the way home.

'With God's help,' the driver prayed before turning on the ignition, but the engine resolutely refused to rumble into life. He tried again, no use. 'Push! Get off, you boys. Push!' he shouted. Everyone jumped down from the back of the truck and set to work, gradually pushing the Chevrolet through the desert sand, and on the third attempt the engine roared and blew a few smoky explosions out of its exhaust, reigniting Rabbit and my laughter. 'Jump in, I am not going to wait. Hurry!' the driver insisted. We leapt in and the car took off.

I was happy to leave the damn desert. If it was not for being with Rabbit, I would have never taken that awful job. I was tired but did not want to go to sleep. I sat next to Rabbit on the driver's cabin as the car bumped along the desert track, creating a cloud of dust behind it. After half an hour's drive nearly everyone was asleep, rocking and jolting about with the car as Rabbit and I watched from our vantage point a top the driver's cabin, giggling at their dancing bodies. When we hit the highway we were met with the satisfying sensation of speed, as the Chevrolet accelerated onward. Rabbit was distracted.

'Aren't you pleased to go home?'

'I am,' he answered, unconvincingly.

'And to be with me?' I had to ask him this, even if it was a painful question.

'Of course I am, Brader.'

'Why do you always sit up here?'

'I want to fly,' he said. 'I want to be the highest flying bird in the sky above all the others. Like this.' Rabbit stretched his arms as if they were wide wings, expressing his desire so poignantly that I couldn't help just then but to wish he had flown away too. 'Open your wings, Brader, and fly away with me,' he called, as he turned to me. I lifted my arms as wide as I could, flapping, feeling a sudden rush of happiness with the wind in our faces, imagining that I could fly all the way to the United States of America, to Gringo. The car raced ever faster, northwards to Kirkuk, and Rabbit and I whooped louder, 'Woo-hoo! We are flying…' Rabbit, absorbed in the moment, clambered unsteadily to his feet, and as we passed stray cars, onlookers stared wide-eyed, and children waved in excitement. I waved back, but not Rabbit; he was gone. I was worried he might fall off the car and kill himself. I got hold of his legs and asked him to sit down. 'Let me go, let me fly…' he resisted.

Why does he want to fly away so desperately?

The wind had blown most of the dust from our dirty clothes when the driver poked his head out. 'Checkpoint!' he shouted. 'Get down, wake up the others and keep quiet.'

Like good children, we quickly obeyed. The familiar tension was in the air and, just as every Thursday afternoon when we approached the checkpoint, fear took hold again. I hated the checkpoints. They were like the desert scorpions, always ready to sting you.

Rabbit, what is wrong with you?

At the checkpoint I could see that war was drawing ever closer. An anti-aircraft machine gun was mounted on the side of the barracks, there was a tank by the road and several soldiers stood guard. Other cars, taxis and a couple of buses were being checked at the same time as us. The passengers were lined up, the men separated from the women and children and all thoroughly searched. We were fine, since we had nothing but building materials on board, and everyone provided a valid ID. Rabbit broke the silence. '*Shirrr*, Ahm, Ahm, this bloody cough,' he said and laughed. *What the hell is he doing? Doesn't he realise we are not allowed to laugh here?* Louis poked his head out of the window. 'You idiots, you want us dead?' he said, but it was too late. A soldier, searching the engine of another car, lifted his head and glanced in our direction. Rabbit saw the soldier, but he carried on laughing.

'Rabbit, shut up,' I said, but he would not. *Has he gone mad? He is really asking for it.* He only stopped after making sure the soldier had seen him. With a headshake, the irate soldier signalled to him. Rabbit jumped down and stood upright, as if to attention. The soldier searched Rabbit. This was provocation. He had already searched us all. *I pray to you God, don't let him touch Rabbit's side.*

'Why did you laugh?' he asked. Rabbit shook his head. He spoke good Arabic but always pretended not to know the language when he was faced with authority. 'You son of a bitch! Speak,' the soldier barked, grabbing Rabbit by his throat.

'He doesn't speak Arabic,' I dared to say.

'You don't? You filthy child-eating Kurd,' and he poked Rabbit in his side. Rabbit jumped. 'Hey, you motherfucker!' he shouted and laughed.

Now he is in real shit. The soldier turned to me. 'What did the Kurdish bastard say?' *The Arab soldier doesn't understand Kurdish, or is he pretending and wants to implicate me too? I'll try my luck, but if he does speak Kurdish I am fucked.* 'He said he suffers from tickling.'

The soldier stared at me for a second but it felt like a lifetime's threatening gaze. He slung his gun down from his shoulder and gave his order, 'Get out you filthy Kurdish motherfuckers. I will make you laugh. Line up.' He pushed and hit one or two of the guys and in no time had us in a line by the roadside. *This is it, he will shoot us all in one go with his AK-47.* Shooting us there and then did not mean much more than killing a handful of Kurdish flies to the Iraqi Special Forces. The other soldiers and the people were now all staring at us. Another soldier hurried Louis, his son, the cement-launcher and the driver. They had at least had a few seconds of relief before they too faced gunpoint.

'Is he going to kill us, Father?' Louis' ten-year-old son asked, raising his arms in surrender. He stood to my left. He wet himself sobbing. 'Shush,' Louis said. His son cried louder. The soldier stepped backwards, staring at us. The tension was building in our faces with every step he was taking. Then, rather than spraying bullets, he turned away and left.

The few seconds' wait became unbearable. The late afternoon sun felt as hot as Midsummer's Day. The flies around were like winged scorpions. The silence! Not one of us was able to say a word. We bit our lips, we swallowed, we hoped to get away. *Are we going to die?* This must have been the question in everyone's mind. I turned to my right, to Rabbit, and wished he would look at me just for reassurance, *even in death we would be friends.* Rabbit did; he was obviously sorry for having got us all into this mess. He was about to say something to me but Louis spoke first. 'I will never forgive you if they kill us,' he said to Rabbit. 'I will come after you in the other life and will take my revenge, even if you are in the lap of God.' He was as white as a sheet. His lips were shaking, his eyes twitching. He had a fly buzzing around his face, but he was too scared to lift his hand and swat it, instead, he kept blowing at it to shoo it away. His son sobbed.

'If we die, my dear boss,' Peaceful said, to everyone's surprise, 'it is because of your stinky farts and not my brother's fault.'

Rabbit was pleased, he winked at Peaceful with a gentle smile. Peaceful smiled back. Louis was furious by now and spoke through his dirty teeth, 'As for the rest of you, that is, if we live, you will have no fucking Pepsi for your overtime and will be paid at the end of next week. Now laugh, hahaha!' Louis cackled cynically. There was little or no objection, everyone was dumbfounded at his reaction, we just wanted to get the hell out of there.

'What?' I protested. 'You pay my wage today, it is the end of the week.'

'Shut up before I sack you, too,' Louis snapped back.

We fell silent when we saw a Captain coming out of the barracks with the soldier. Three others, each armed with AK-47s, followed them. The Captain commanded his men to line up, to point their guns at us and to load. He lifted his right arm. *Was he about to order our execution simply for having laughed?* Louis threw himself down by the Captain's legs. He kissed the Arab's leather boots and pleaded, 'They are only kids, sir, and usually good kids. They were not laughing at your soldier but at an awful defect that I had, a stomach ache. We are hard-working people. We are building a military base for President Saddam Hussein. Don't kill us now, please have God's mercy and let us finish the job. We will crawl on our knees like dogs, we will eat dirt but we will not laugh again, ever again in your presence, or the presence of your men. Please, sir?' Louis grabbed his son by his arm and pulled him to make him prostrate himself too, before continuing melodramatically, 'This is my son, sir. He is only ten years old, but you can ask him, who he loves more, President Saddam or his father?' He turned to his son and he himself asked, 'Say it son. Say who you love more, President Saddam or me, your ugly father?'

'You,' his son said, loudly. Louis slapped him. 'Say Saddam, you bastard.'

'President Saddam,' his son sobbed.

'See, sir, we all love our president, God's peace be upon him.' Louis was so frantic, for a moment he confused Saddam with our Prophet Muhammad. He was convinced we were destined to die that day, and he was the only one who could save us. What's more, he was right, because there was absolutely nothing else we could have done.

'Please, sir,' Louis carried on, and shook his son again, 'Say it son, say who do you love?'

'I love Saddam,' the child cried.

Louis was pleased with his triumphant performance, tears and saliva smearing his agonised face. Despite the fact that he was begging for our lives I despised Louis. I hated to hear a Kurd falsely declaring his love for Saddam. Louis did not even have the courage of Old Zorab, who so bravely stood up to the monster's men. Louis was like Rashaba, a Kurd who only wanted to protect his hat from the wind. *Would I do this if I had to beg for my life? If I am not doing it now, why would I ever? I am standing at gunpoint and about to be killed at any moment.*

The Captain, with his hand still raised, listened to Louis, genuinely interested, especially when he heard Saddam. 'You really love Saddam, don't you?' the Captain asked, pointing to a poster of Saddam on the side of the barracks. Louis smiled, thinking he had him now. Still on his knees, he looked up as if looking up to God almighty and quickly sang, 'I do, I do, I dooo... Yes, sir, and I kiss your feet.' He kissed the Captain's feet. 'I kiss your hands...' Louis was about to get up to kiss his hands but the Captain kicked him in the face, rolling him backwards.

Shit! We are done for. Louis and his son were back in the line. The Captain walked to the side. His four soldiers already stood opposite us, only waiting for his signal to shoot. I could envisage the bullets leaving the barrels of the guns in slow motion, heading towards us...

A horrendous noise cut through my body, the sound of being shot, of death hitting me, turning out my lights. But it wasn't bullets, it was the jarring sound of a Jeep's horn. It had just arrived at the execution scene. The Captain ordered his men to hold their fire, split seconds away from wiping us out. He ran to the Jeep. He spoke animatedly with a man in the passenger seat, who I could not see well because he was in the shade and the sun was right in my eyes. He hurried back and came straight towards me, removing my hat to let my hair unravel. He returned to the Jeep, and I could see him nodding.

He asked his soldiers to lower their guns. The minute the Jeep started to drive away, all the soldiers including the Captain saluted most respectfully. As the car passed by, I saw enough to recognise the passenger who, for whatever mysterious reason, had spared my life and those of my companions. It was Abu Ali.

Stop calling me Brader

The Captain slapped Rabbit across the face. I held my breath and prayed God that Rabbit would not respond. 'I am not going to kill you this time,' the Captain said. 'But my soldiers will enjoy a ride on a Kurdish donkey, and they will carry on until I hear you bray.' The Captain went back into the barracks. Three soldiers dragged Rabbit to the side. They pulled up his trousers and pushed him face down on his bare knees onto the gravel. Peaceful was about to react. I held his hand. 'Don't, you will both be killed. Rabbit is strong. He will survive.'

Peaceful, eyes wet with tears, watched his brother being humiliated. The irate soldier climbed on Rabbit's back. A second one started to kick him in his buttocks and the third, pulled him like a donkey and shouted at him to bray. Rabbit dragged himself along for a few feet, but soon started to shake as tears rolled down from his eyes. The first tears I had seen in his dark, kind eyes. Still, they did not let Rabbit go. Instead, the second soldier also mounted his back. The other soldiers around jeered and teased in Arabic, 'Hurry up Kurdish donkey, bray...'

I put my hat on again and closed my eyes. *Please, God, Rabbit is my best and only Brader, God, help him, save...* I had not completed my prayer when Rabbit released a loud bray of pain that went on and on. We were all sickened, and I could even see sadness in Louis' eyes. 'He deserves it,' Louis said, but I was sure he did not mean it. For this was no way to treat a human being. The soldiers laughed triumphantly. 'Let the donkey go,' the Captain called, from the window of the barracks.

The soldiers shouted and everyone hurried back into the pickup. Rabbit could not move. Blood ran down his bruised knees. The irate soldier kicked him. I'd had enough. I stood in front of the soldier and stared into his eyes, my lips trembling and words of Allah and our Prophet streaming through my mind. The soldier gave me a kick too, a sign that I was allowed to help Rabbit.

'C'mon Brader, let's go home,' I said, trying to prevent myself from bursting into tears. Rabbit was heavy and since he could hardly stand, I put his left arm around me and with Peaceful we made it to the pickup.

Before Rabbit managed to get in, Louis held him by the collar of his shirt. 'You're finished working for me,' he said. Rabbit got hold of Louis' hand and, despite his state, he made the effort to reply, '*shirrr*, what a bloody cough.' This time no one laughed. Rabbit tried to climb up onto the pickup. I asked him to sit with everyone else, but he wouldn't have it. With my help, Rabbit was once more sitting up on the driver's cabin. 'Sorry I couldn't protect you, but I prayed God to save you,' I said. Rabbit nodded but did not seem to appreciate it. He looked at me in a new way, as if he wished I never existed. *I must be mistaken. Rabbit would never think that of me. I have never done anything to hurt him. I love him.*

Trying to recover lost time, the driver pressed on and drove faster. We reached the dried-up Khasa River to the south of Kirkuk, and looking at the horizon, with such good visibility I could see the silhouette of Qala, like a massive mushroom, rising above the city. The others, exhausted from the week's hard work and their close encounter with death, were all asleep again, except for Peaceful, who sat silently. Bending forward over the windscreen, I could see Louis and the cement-launcher asleep too. I turned to my Brader again; his face shone in the sunset. I tapped his shoulder to get him to look at me, and he did. I bent my head down onto the windscreen and banged on it right where Louis was asleep. He jumped up, shouting in panic, 'I love Saddam.'

I laughed and saw Rabbit smile. 'I am not going back to work either,' I said. 'I only managed to stay in the scorpion desert for four weeks because of our friendship. Brader, we will find a new job.' Rabbit turned to me. He pointed in the opposite direction. 'That way is to Baghdad, Arab's land, and this way is to Kirkuk!' he said, and we both simultaneously, nose to nose, whispered, 'Kurdish land.'

'You speak Arabic but don't want to speak it, and you are right. God, I hate the Arabs. I wish I could kill them all,' and I meant it with all my heart. He looked at me for a while. 'I don't hate the Arabs,' he said. 'There is good and bad in everyone.'

'There isn't any good in the Arabs. Look what they have just done to you. If only the Qur'an had never come down to us in Arabic.'

'Those are Saddamists and you should not blame all the Arabs because of them.'

'Saddam is an Arab and he kills us because we are Kurds, not because we are not good Muslims.'

'That is too much hate for a true Muslim,' Rabbit said, defiantly. 'Is that what your religion teaches you?'

'What do you mean your religion? You are a Muslim too, aren't you?'

'Shush,' Rabbit was afraid someone could hear us talking. We were silent for a bit.

'Would you come to Takya tonight to watch me dance?' I asked.

'I have better things to do with my time.'

'You should come just for once. You will feel great to be in direct contact with God.'

'I will not.' He glanced at the others, as if wanting to reveal a secret, but first, he wanted to make sure no one was listening.

'Mery, perhaps you should know. I don't believe in religion, in Islam or Christianity or any of them.'

'You what?' I was shocked. 'But you are Muslim?'

'I was born a Muslim, but I am not one.'

'Are you not afraid of God?'

'There is no God.'

'What did you say?'

'You heard me very well. There is no God.' Rabbit marked his words clearly. 'That is blasphemy. Don't say it again.' I was getting angry, and I did not want to be, with Rabbit. 'There is a God and he has just saved us from getting killed, especially you.'

'There is no God. Not for me, and I am not sure if I was saved.'

I moved away from him. 'God is up there watching us, don't blaspheme or he will punish you, and me too, because I am your friend.'

'Tell me who made us?' Rabbit asked.

'God, of course.'

'Who made God?'

'God was always there.'

'God was never there.'

'Shut up, Rabbit! God is the greatest and he was always there from the beginning.'

'Why should your version be correct and mine wrong?'

'I don't know. But you are wrong, very wrong.' I could hardly breathe. I just wanted to escape from this conversation, but it was impossible. 'If God did not create us, who then?'

'Do you ask because you have doubts about your creator?' he said, which irritated me even more. 'I don't know now,' he carried on. 'Maybe one day I will. But for now, I am convinced that God did not. Maybe one day you too will have the answer.'

'God created us and he wants you to obey him and go to Takya to worship him.'

'If what you say is true, and if God wants me to worship Him, then God himself needs to come down and tell me that. If I hear it from God himself, I will start praying five times a day and become a much more faithful Muslim than you. But I don't want any humans to represent God because no one has the right to do so. Unless you can provide concrete proof, written by God. He must know how to read and write to prove that he exists, and to let me know that he has designated the many Prophets, their disciples and followers to speak on his behalf. If and when God provides me with this proof, then I will ask him: Why should you, God, randomly choose another human being, our equal, above all of us, to represent you? Isn't that discrimination, dear God? You should not permit yourself to discriminate against members of your flock. But unfortunately neither I nor anyone else will ever have a chance to address these questions directly to God, because God does not exist.'

'Rabbit, I am getting really upset.'

'OK, I may be wrong, but can I stay away from Takya and all that religious stuff and still be your friend?' Rabbit wanted to shake hands. I hesitated. 'Repent,' I asked. When he shook his head, I moved further away.

'See? Your God is making you fight with me,' he said, 'just because I don't believe in him. He is not a just God, is he, to make two very good friends fight?'

'You are no longer a friend of mine,' I answered, and it felt like a knife slicing my heart in two. 'You are against my God, therefore against me, and you are Kafr, an infidel.'

'I am against no one, but I want to be free to think and to say what I believe. I don't want to hurt or provoke you, but to be true to you, and to myself.'

'You are insulting Islam.'

'No Mery, don't falsely accuse me. I am not against Islam or any religion. I respect them all and I ask for them to respect me too, and to let me be free. If I am wrong I am the one who will be burned on the day of judgement for my blasphemies. So accept me for what I am, tolerate my opinion and respect my freedom.' Rabbit had revealed another side of himself, one that I despised. Suddenly, I realised how little I knew him. 'I spoke the truth because I trust you. Please, don't tell anyone about my thoughts with regards to your God. There are ignorant fanatics out there. I could be killed for this.'

'I will not betray you.'

'Enjoy the dance at the Takya tonight.'

'Why don't you believe in God?'

'I don't need him, it's as simple as that. Do you know why God created us? Do you, Mery? I will believe in your God and pray five times a day, if you can tell me why. Just give me one good reason!' I tried to say something but could not come up with any good answer, nor could I even remember reading about it in the Qur'an. I was intrigued. 'I don't know why God created us, and do not want to question God because I am a good Muslim,' I answered, but I was not convinced myself, merely saying something to cover the embarrassment of not having a proper answer.

'You saw what just happened to me,' Rabbit said. 'Are these people created by a different God than yours? Are you telling me there is more than one God? A God who created people like Saddam to enslave us and kill us, and another God who created us to be submissive forever in the name of being faithful Muslims?'

'Allah created us all,' I said, and raised my hands, praying for forgiveness.

'Why did he then create good and bad? You may answer that he created only good, but the bad are the followers of Satan. Well, what about beautiful and ugly, healthy and sick, rich and poor, powerful and weak? Would you say the ugly, sick, poor and weak were created by Satan, too? Mery, my Brader, if you just give me one, only one good reason, then I will become the servant of Allah now and forever.'

'Stop calling me Brader, for I am not your friend any more!' I shouted, waking up every man in the back of the pickup. We both knew this was the end of our five-year friendship.

Why had God created us? What for? Would I ever know? Is there an explanation? Please God, help me and let me know the reason or I will doubt your existence, too. No, no, forgive me, You are up there, but I need to convince my once-Brader because I want him to become a good Muslim like me. I am hopeful, God.

We sat silently next to each other, staring ahead. I did not want to show him that in my heart I was crying at the loss of my only and best friend because of God. I took off my hat and let my hair free to dance in the wind as the pickup speeded into Kirkuk.

There is no God but Allah

Rabbit limped ahead, assisted by Peaceful, as we headed home in silence. I held on to my scruffy bag and kept some distance from them. I could not watch him making such painful progress and not be able to help, but what was really worrying me was that soon we would be close to Rabbit's house, and I did not want him to go home without making peace. I walked over to them, relieving Peaceful and putting Rabbit's right arm on my shoulders. I asked Peaceful if he could leave us alone and he did, hurrying off ahead of us.

'Rabbit, please, just repent, and God will forgive you for what you said. God will understand that you said it out of anger.'

'It's been a while now that I wanted to tell you this secret. I don't need to repent, because God does not exist.'

'Qul hua Allah u…' I started to recite Surat Al Ikhlas from the Qur'an. Rabbit did not let me finish. He completed the rest. 'Do you know it?' I asked in surprise.

'Of course I do. There is no God but only Allah… I have read the Qur'an a couple of times, and guess what?' He stopped, and I did the same. 'Each time I read the Qur'an, I got more and more shocked about all the calls for violence. Kill the infidels! The macabre threats of burning in hell for ever. But what I most dislike about Islam, the so-called religion of peace, is the lack of any democracy or freedom. Your Prophet Muhammad made sure to leave no choice but to follow him and obey his orders. Do as I say or else you will burn in hell, and you will burn for eternity if you oppose my words, for mine are the words of God and they can never be questioned or altered. What is the difference between that and Saddam? Muhammad and Saddam, just the same, two men seeking power, to expand their empires, they terrorise without ever taking into consideration people's feelings about what they want to believe and how they wish to live.'

'That's enough, Rabbit, enough!' I was so angry that I was shouting and wanted to punch him in the face. 'If you dare to compare Prophet

Muhammad to Saddam, I will... I will...' But I just couldn't say it. I slipped off his arm and let him trip, almost falling. 'You are possessed by the devil,' I said, instead. 'You must be a devil worshipper, or a communist?'

'I am neither of the two but a simple human being, free from God and evil. For me they are both the same.'

'You must believe in something.'

'I do, but you seem not to tolerate it.'

'You are not allowed to be an infidel and blaspheme.'

'You are not allowed! Hear yourself, Mery? You are not allowed, not allowed to be free-thinking. Are you becoming another Saddam?'

'That is the end.'

'I am not what you call a fucking infidel. I am an atheist.'

I had never heard that word before and did not know what 'atheist' meant. Pride and embarrassment overtook me and I stubbornly refused to ask Rabbit what he meant. Instead with my last sentence, I shut the door. 'Can I have my necklace back?' I asked, and Rabbit took off Happiness's necklace and handed it over.

'You are an infidel.' I said. 'Until you repent and become a faithful Muslim, you are no longer my Brader.'

'Call louder if you wish to have me killed for being an infidel. But I am content now, for I no longer have to keep this secret in my heart from you. I have not told anyone about this, not even my family,' Rabbit said, and he pointed ahead.

Master Shamal, Jwana, Sunshine and Peaceful came running. They embraced Rabbit and helped him home, glad to have their son alive. *I wonder if he truly does not keep other secrets from me? Has he done this to break up our friendship? But why would he?* I sighed, knowing our friendship was over, made sure that my hat was well tied around my head and strode off purposefully towards home.

It was almost getting dark when I rushed in to find Mother in the courtyard with her arms held up towards God, trying to persuade Monkey to move back. My three-year-old brother sat right on the edge of the rooftop, at least seven metres above the ground, holding a ball. He was laughing happily as if playing a funny game. His legs were dangling over the edge and he was swinging them to the rhythm of his laughter.

'Monkey go back, go back...' Mother kept calling while Rashaba, as a faithful Muslim, on the veranda, was praying. Monkey raised his hands and let the ball go. Mother screamed. The ball came swishing down, hitting the hard ground and bouncing back up again half way between the two floors. I shouted, 'Monkey!' and ran up the uneven stairs. I passed Star on my way; five years old by then, she too was crying for Monkey's sake. Rashaba kept praying undisturbed and in a loud voice said, 'Allah u Akbar...'

I called to Monkey at every step and looked up, hoping he would stay still. By then Monkey had stood up and was only a breath away from losing his footing and falling down two floors onto the rock-hard courtyard. Now that his ball had gone he was no longer laughing, but crying and scared.

'Monkey, don't move!' I said, as I reached the rooftop, and I lunged to grab him by his arm. I pulled him back to me and kissed him. 'I thought you were going to fall.' I thanked God for helping me and brought him back down in my arms. Mother was recovering from her shock, pale-faced. As I reached her, she grabbed Monkey and hit him. 'How many times have I told you to not climb up to the rooftop?' she said angrily. I pulled Monkey away from her. 'Your father will blame me if something happens to you and I have to blame Star,' Mother was saying to Monkey, but it was to all of us really. 'How can I be looking after you and Star, get food ready, bake bread for others, do cleaning...' She went on with her endless list of tasks, then turned to Star. 'You must keep an eye on your little brother at all times.' Star came rushing to me for protection. 'Monkey doesn't listen to me, what can I do?' she said, in her sweet voice.

She is right, what could she do? She is only a girl, and Monkey would defy her. I bent down and gave Star a kiss. Monkey, hiding behind me, was still whimpering when Mother grabbed him again, but this time she kissed and hugged him. She found some sweets in her pocket and Monkey quickly stuffed them into his mouth, chewing them as tears fell down his hot little face. I put a hand on Mother's shoulder, to show her support, but she pushed me away. 'You are late,' she said.

'We had some problems at the checkpoint.' I took her hands and kissed them.

'I missed you,' she said, and pulled my hat from my head and ruffled my hair. 'You go away for one week but it feels like a year to me. Could you not find a job in town instead?'

'I will. I am not going to work in the Arab desert again.'

'Are you all right?'

I wanted to tell her what had happened between Rabbit and me, but I couldn't bring myself to do so. I went to Papula's door and found it locked.

For the entire time I was away Flathead had stayed at home, apparently due to illness, though I suspected he did not want to leave his wife alone while I was in the desert. He did not bother to go and see a doctor. He was worn out and hardly smiled, except when he was drunk. He drank more Arak and often fought with Papula. She was annoyed by his presence and, several times, right in front of me, told him off. Papula pinched my cheeks and told me to quit the building work because she missed me and, instead of her husband, she wished I would stay at home.

'Your uncle got better,' Mother said. 'He has gone back to work and must be in Baghdad by now.'

'What about Papula?'

'Your uncle allowed your snake auntie to go to visit her family, and I had to accompany her to her mother's.'

Star and Monkey started playing together with their Superman and King Kong toys. I confronted Mother. 'Mum, why did God create us?'

'I don't know,' she answered, a bit perplexed. 'You should ask your father, good Darwesh Rashaba, who would rather see his son die than interrupt his prayer. He should know.'

'Don't say that, Mum, it's blasphemy. Remember the story of Imam Ali? Instead of cutting short his prayer, he allowed himself to be stabbed to death.'

I sat down next to her and put my hands on my head thinking about Rabbit and how, for the sake of religion, we had ended our friendship. 'I won't be paid until next week,' I said, in frustration.

'It is only a week.'

'Only a week? Where will I get money to go to the cinema?'

'Shush. Your father will hear you.' Mother came closer. 'Mery, how many times do I have to tell you to end this cinema business! Dervish and cinema, I have never heard of that before,' she said, shaking her head. Rashaba, still on the small carpet, shouted from the veranda. 'What was all that noise?'

'Monkey was about to fall…' I answered, but he cut me short.

'Fine, I will put a small gate on the steps to stop him from going up.'

'You have been saying this for months,' Mother said, in a low obedient voice so as not to irritate him further. 'Your fault, woman.' He pointed his finger at her. 'You should keep an eye on your son. Mery, we need to go to Takya to worship.'

'Yes, Father, I will quickly wash my face.'

'First, bring me your wage.'

'I will be paid at the end of next week.'

'Why is that?'

'Our boss did not have enough cash.'

The devil worshipper

I missed lying in the open under a million sparkling stars. Papula preferred sleeping in her room, while Mother had stopped us sleeping on the rooftop, for fear of Monkey falling off. It was unbearably hot in our room, despite leaving the window wide open and not covering ourselves.

'...ninety six, ninety seven, ninety eight...' Mother kept counting Rashaba's latest savings, including the wages taken from Trouble and me. As always, during the night when it was so quiet, I could hear the sound of the dinars. I couldn't sleep. I was thinking about Rabbit. *What can I do to make him change his mind?*

Rashaba was getting itchy and panting, almost as if he was on the brink of orgasm with every number approaching hundred.

'Ten thousand dinars,' he said, excitedly. 'No,' Mother answered. 'You are wrong. There are nine thousand five hundred.'

'Oh yes. Yes. Five hundred more and I will find an agent to look for a house, finally a place of our own, God willing, and move out of this nightclub,' he said, which annoyed Mother. 'Wife, say InshaAllah.'

'God willing,' Mother obeyed. 'Are you sure it is safe to keep all this money in your pillow?'

'Where else can I keep it, woman? In a bank, or with your drunken brother?'

'Don't say bad things about Arsalan. He is going through a hard time and could do without your insults. My brother is an angel, and he is unlucky to have such a spoiled wife.'

'Why are you worried about the money's hiding place?'

'Ardalan has recently asked me, "What do you do with your money?" And I found him looking around suspiciously.'

'I will cut your troublemaker son's throat like a lamb if he touches this money. He would have to kill me first before he takes my money, do you understand?'

Whenever Rashaba said anything bad about us to Mother, he

called us 'your son', or 'your daughter.' On the rare occasions when he was pleased with us, when taking our wages, he proudly said 'my children', but never 'our children' or 'our money'. It was always 'my money'.

'Now put my money back in the pillow and keep it safe until the day I make the last five hundred. God willing, in a few months' time, we can buy our house. Wait!'

I closed my eyes. Rashaba looked over at Monkey and Star, deeply asleep, and then me. He went back to lie next to Mother.

'Does Merywan ask you about my money?'

'No. But he does ask why you always work and never spend time with them playing.'

'He is a coward. Tonight in Takya he refused to headbutt the wall. He failed me. I think Zao'Adin was right, your son is not a proper son,' Rashaba said, darkening the room further with his words, and with them, the light in my heart. I loathed hearing him once again question my sex.

'God forgive us,' Mother spat around me to keep away the evil eye. 'Please, God, don't record it as a sin, but make Mullah Zao'Adin and my husband wrong about my Mery.'

'Why should I be wrong? Has he ever had a wet night?'

'No.'

'Have you ever seen him with a hard-on?'

'No.'

'Isn't he always hiding his penis from you?'

'Yes.'

'Why is he doing this?'

'Because he is not circumcised.'

'No, because he is a neuter.' Mother seemed to have no answer.

'He must be,' Rashaba added. 'I was not much older than him when I got married to you.'

'My poor Mery.'

'It is your entire fault, stupid woman. In your heart you wished for a girl when you were pregnant with him. God grants children. You should not have been tempted by the devil to wish for a girl. You had to bring bad luck and God's punishment on us, for girls are all born sinners. You and I will go to hell and will burn in the eternal fire if you have given birth to a neuter child.'

'Don't you dare call Mery neuter again,' Mother said, defying Rashaba for the first time ever.

'We will be ruined if we don't do something about it,' he answered. Mother sobbed quietly. 'As soon as I have bought us a house, I want Merywan to be checked by Sheikh Baba,' was the last thing he said before he turned over and went to sleep.

He made me feel like I was the filthiest child alive, born with the most horrible sins. And to think that I might not be able to marry Aida, never be prince Sinbad, to take my princess on adventures, only made it worse.

I woke up late that morning. The house was deserted and I felt very lonely, particularly as Papula was away. I put my legs up on the courtyard wall in the sunshine, contemplating my upside-down world. I was thinking about Rabbit, about the terrible things Rashaba had said the night before, but mostly I was dying to go into town to see Aida. Yet at the same time, I was also reluctant. *Is it right to give her hope of love and marriage when I am sexless? Nonetheless, I want to see her. Abu Ali no longer worries me because, as Rabbit said, he obviously is not Shawes Dog, or else he would have come to my house to get me by now.*

Popcorn appeared, with his rattan basket hanging from his arm, moving silently like a ghost. 'Can I have a drink of water?' he asked, as he sat in the veranda's shade. I passed him a pot of water from the earthenware jar, and sat next to him. He noticed my bad mood. He picked up a handful of popcorn and offered it. 'For free,' he said. I shook my head. 'You know, Mery, you are different from everyone else and I like you very much. Can I ask why you broke off your friendship with Rabbit?'

'I don't want to talk about him.' We both fell silent and he munched some popcorn. 'Is it true that you, I mean Yezidis, worship the devil?' I asked hesitantly.

'If you want to put it that way.'

'What do you mean?'

'I am a Kurd like you, and I have the same God but a different religion,' he said. 'We don't worship the devil, but unlike Muslims and Christians, we revere him no less than the other archangels created by God. For us Yezidis, it is not Satan who is the source of evil. Evil comes from the hearts and minds of people themselves.'

I disliked what he said about evil and God having created the devil, but nevertheless I wanted to learn, in the hope of finding a good answer for Rabbit. 'Rabbit wants to know why God created us. Do you know why?' I asked.

'After creating the universe,' Popcorn said. 'my belief is that God was sitting up there without much more to do. To overcome his boredom, he needed an antagonist, someone to challenge him, to fight him; that is why he threw the one you call the devil from heaven. God created humans and gave them powerful brains so that they can make up their own minds whom to follow, God or his enemy, your devil. But God was soon bored of this too; after all, he had a greater power over his enemy and he himself had created him. Therefore, God, started to send down different messengers, different prophets to proclaim different religions. He knew very well this would be the cause of hatred and wars within his human race, and that he finally have some excitement. God gets his thrills from seeing Jews hating Muslims, Christians hating Jews, Muslims hating Christians, Muslims hating Yezidi, Sunnis hating Shiites, Catholics hating Protestants, and so on.'

'Is it God's will that they all hate each other?'

'Everything we do is God's will.'

'Does that mean God has created us for his fun?'

'If God created us, I have no other explanation as to why he did so.'

'If God has given us minds to allow us to choose whom to follow, then everything we do is our doing and not God's decision.'

'God has given you the ability to think, to make choices, but if you choose not to follow his commands, he will burn you in hell for eternity. Does that make sense to you, Mery? Wasn't it easier to not give us a choice, and have us all obey him?'

'What are you getting at?'

'Perhaps God did not create us, and he did not give us our brains.'

He confused me no less than Rabbit had a few days earlier. I really liked Popcorn and did not want to lose his friendship, too.

'Popcorn, why don't you become Muslim?'

'Mery, why don't you become Yezidi?'

'Islam is the ultimate religion.'

'Who says so?'

'Prophet Muhammad, in the Qur'an, reporting God's words.'

'What if your Prophet was wrong and the words were not God's, but his own?'

'That is blasphemy.'

'To you, but not to me.' Popcorn picked up his basket and left, but before walking out, he turned. 'I thought you a cleverer person, Mery. You should make peace with Rabbit.'

I wanted to shout back, *I will never make peace with an infidel,* but I restrained myself because I was already upset that I had offended him too because of my religion.

I could no longer stay in, imprisoned by my painful thoughts. Papula was not home yet. I knew of a secret place in the bathroom, where she left me a key. Once inside Papula's room, I collected my treasure box from its hiding place and picked up Gringo's poster, placing it in front of me. After looking at a few other film star photos, and spitting at the monster's portrait, I froze when I came across the picture of Rabbit and myself, with our arms around each other. The young man I had seen acting so courageously in Republic Street was standing behind us in that photo. I wish I had shown it to Rabbit. I then wrote another letter, which I entitled:

If I can get a passport

Kirkuk, July 1986

Dear Mr Clint Eastwood,

In other circumstances I might have cried with sadness as a result of losing Rabbit's friendship, but since I have promised myself not to shed tears for anything in life, I turn to you, Gringo, to let you know how lonely I feel without him, and to ask why he is doing this to me.

I have now made up my mind. It will only be a matter of weeks before I take my father's money. Yes, you may say it's a dishonourable thing to do, and I would agree with you, but I have no choice. I am going to be ruined if Rashaba has me examined by Sheikh Baba.

First I must find out if I can get a passport and a visa for the United States. In the meantime, I would like to ask you if you believe in God, and if you know why God created us. Do not take this as an offence. This is most crucial because with a concrete answer I could convince Rabbit. He doesn't want the usual mantra. We are here to worship God and to avoid the devil. He asks for a provable explanation, just like electricity, which was invented to give us energy and light, cars, which get us from one place to another in less time, the telephone, which enables us to communicate, and all the rest. Talking of phones, if you ever write to me, would you be so kind as to let me know your number? We have no phone at home and very few people have access to this service, but I could call you from the central telecommunications office. I would love to talk to you. Imagine that, Mery Rashaba on the phone to Gringo?

You should write me a letter urgently to advise me what to do next because if I don't move fast, my father will soon spend his money on buying us a house. You need to know that if I take his money, the pain may kill him, but if I don't, I may have to kill myself. As always I will end by thanking you from my heart for allowing me to talk to you.

Write me at least one letter, please?

Mery Rashaba

I kissed the poster and put it away, back in the safe box along with Happiness's necklace, and placed it at the bottom of Papula's wardrobe. I changed into my boyish clothes and, as I took the comb from Papula's desk to arrange my hair, I found half a dinar note on her make-up cabinet. I did everything to avoid taking the money, but I needed it so much. In the end, I convinced myself I was only borrowing it, and was going to give it back to Papula the following Thursday, when Louis paid my wage. Half a dinar makes five hundred cents, more than enough to post Gringo's letter, the bus ride, and a cinema ticket. I know I should not have done it, but I could not resist. I took the money and left.

Aida and me together forever

As we passed over the bridge, I gazed out of the window of the minibus at the dry riverbed, thinking about Aida and what I would tell her. I will give her the good news that I am no longer going back to work in the desert and am going to see her almost every day.

By the store's entrance, I came across Uncle Hitchcock, who snapped my picture with his Canon AE-1. He was a well-known street photographer, only a couple of years older than Jam. His professional name was Uncle Camera, but after seeing *Rear Window*, I nicknamed him Uncle Hitchcock because he was a Kurdish version of James Stewart, always quiet, gentle and solid. I was a good customer to him, as in those days not many people spent money on pictures. I wished Gringo could see those pictures one day, because words alone would never be enough to describe my life and that of my city and my people in the way Uncle Hitch depicted them. Observing people's lives through the lens of his camera brought a love of photography to my life. I could not even dream of having a cine camera or a video camera because they were banned in Kirkuk, so Uncle Hitch was the only one recording our daily lives through his black-and-white snapshots.

'I have enough money for another one,' I said. 'Could you please wait for five minutes?' Uncle Hitch may not have understood my intentions, but still kindly agreed.

I shivered as I walked in. Aida was as beautiful as ever, only this time I clearly saw a warm, welcoming smile as she looked up and her eyes rested on me. I could only salute her from a distance, replying with my own smile. I looked around impatiently, and when she was free, I walked over to her and heard what I was so much hoping for.

'Mery! I haven't seen you for weeks.'

'I am sorry, I should have let you know. I have been on a job outside the city.'

'I missed you,' she said, biting her lips.

'You did?' She nodded. 'I missed you too, and have been thinking of you all the time.'

'I like your hat,' she said, but I instantly took it off, I could not hide my hair in Aida's presence. 'Don't worry, I think it's wise of you to attract less attention. Are you going away again?'

'No, no more. I want to stay here with you forever.'

She smiled and put her hand on mine on the counter. I trembled, feeling her delicate fingers. 'How old are you?' I asked, already knowing the answer.

'Sixteen. You?'

'Also sixteen.' This was a lie, as I was in fact only fifteen, but it was a white lie, not as bad as hiding my sexual illness from her.

'Why do you work here at such a young age?' I had wanted to ask her this question from the first day I met her.

'Is there anything wrong with that?'

'Not really, but your father is very rich, he is an engineer in the Iraqi Petroleum Company.'

'Oh my God, you know everything about my life,' Aida said, with a grin.

'I also know you are an only child and loved by your parents.'

'We need money, lots of money, and urgently.'

I could get her thousands of dinars. 'What for?' I asked.

'I can't tell you yet, but as soon as I am sure of it, I will. I promise.'

'Why do you think God created us?' Aida was surprised at my sudden enquiry.

'Is this a cross-examination of my faith in religion?'

'I just want to know your opinion, the truth.'

'Which God? Yours or mine?'

'Do we have different Gods?'

'Of course we do, yours is Muslim and mine is Christian.'

'OK, your God.'

'My God says be good and you have a place in heaven, be bad and you go to hell.'

'My God says the same thing.'

'Does he? Why have two Gods if they say the same thing?'

I looked forward to telling her Popcorn's view on this, but not now. I will when we are married. 'Do you believe in heaven and hell?' I asked.

'Heaven is where I can be myself and hell is when I am not free.'

'Free to do what?'

'To walk on the street without having thousands of eyes staring at me, to have the same rights as men, and to be free to love you without worrying about our religious differences.'

'Did you say something about loving me?'

'Yes, I did.'

'Yay!' I exclaimed with a skip. I was over the moon. But seeing a few customers and staff staring at us, I calmed down. I also saw Uncle Hitch from around the corner waving his hand. *Shit! I have completely forgotten about the poor photographer.*

'Aida, I would like to have you with me all the time, forever.'

'Me too, Mery, but how?'

'I want us to have a picture taken together.'

'No.'

'Shall we bet on it? I will look at you for five seconds, close my eyes and then you ask me about any detail of yourself. Three questions. If I get them all right, I win, if I get one wrong, no picture...' Aida agreed. She turned round so that I could see her earrings, the back of her hair... I closed my eyes.

'The colour of my fingernails?'

'Gold,' I said, correctly.

'The clip on the back of my hair?'

'You have no clip, but a ponytail tied with a thin blue ribbon.'

'Right. This one is the last and I will make it difficult. What am I thinking?'

'Mery is madly in love with me.'

'You win,' she said, and squeezed my hand in hers.

It's so strange. I a Muslim, and she a Christian, and yet I feel most comfortable with her. I trust her so much that I could reveal all my life's secrets if she asks me to. Well, all except one. I beckoned to Uncle Hitch and we had our picture taken, Aida and I standing next to each other, holding hands. I wanted to put my arm around her and, to tell the truth, I would have loved to have given her a kiss, my first kiss... I stood there gazing into her eyes.

'Perhaps you should go now, your friend is waiting for you.'

'I'll see you soon,' I said, and walked over to Uncle Hitch.

'Where is the scarf you bought from me?' Aida called.

'Next time I will have it with me,' I answered.

I spent eighty cents on each picture: a copy for Aida, and one for myself. The normal cost was a hundred, but Uncle Hitch agreed that it was not at all an exaggeration to consider Aida one of the most stunning girls in Kirkuk, if not in all Iraq or the entire world, and well worthy of a discount of twenty cents for the chance to take the princess's picture. He also asked if he could be the official photographer at our wedding, if it ever happened. *Aida loves me! Yes, she does...* I was walking along but felt like I was floating above the ground. *Aida has painted my life with magic and I am flying.* I went straight down Republic Street into Jam's stamp and coin shop.

'You've changed your look,' Jam said, as I greeted him.

'Safer this way,' I answered, sadly.

'In this country the more invisible you are, the better,' Jam said casually, as if he had known danger all his life. 'Afraid of anyone in particular?'

'Yes, Qayshbaldar, a monster,' I said, but soon smiled. 'Sorry, that was a bad joke. My father really, he doesn't allow me in the centre of town, and I can't have my hair showing in public.' I wanted to go further with Jam, and speak about subjects that were banned. I was hesitating. Jam came to my help. 'Something bothering you?'

'Yes. I don't know if I should ask you this. It's about religion, so maybe you don't want me to?'

'If you want to lose your partner, wife, husband or fiancé, talk sex,' Jam said, with a grin, 'talk religion or politics if you want to lose friends and family. Sex, religion and politics, the three most important subjects in our lives that we should be most free to discuss, but we are not. So, be prepared to pay a price for discussing these complex subjects. Or else ignore them, which is even worse.'

After such an introduction I was almost tongue-tied. 'Is it true there is no democracy or freedom in Islam?' I asked.

'Is this a confidential conversation?'

'I promise,' and I put my hand on my heart.

'Why should I trust you, Merywan?'

I saw that it worried him to talk to me openly about this subject.

'Because I trust you for asking such a question in the first place, because I am not a spy and because I love Gringo,' I said, and walked to the shop's door. 'You don't have to talk to me, if you don't trust me.' I was ready to leave. Jam walked over to me. He locked the door and hung up the 'Closed' sign. He indicated with his hand to follow him into the back room. *Now this is a real challenge of trust, for me to go in there with him, with the shop's door locked and us two alone.*

'Not only in Islam,' Jam explained, as I sat opposite listening carefully. 'Because of religion our people are still not ready for freedom and democracy, and I believe that the real disasters are yet to come.'

'Does religion lead to war or peace then, in your opinion?'

He pointed to a painting on the wall, a portrait of a man around fifty years old. 'My father.' Jam said. 'He believed that humanity's most dangerous invention is religion. "The root of all evil," he called it. "All religions have the same purpose," he would say, "to make a group of people believe they are the chosen, the pure ones, superior to the others, and this inevitably sows the seeds of hatred." Finally, to answer your question, religion claims to promote peace, but in fact it fosters war.'

'So why did God create us and give us religion?'

'Now I understand why you were hesitating to ask in the first place,' Jam said, as he considered his reply carefully. 'I am not sure if I can answer you to your satisfaction. Let's say God has created us to worship him, but God made a mistake by giving humans brains. He should have made us like all the other species, without the distinction of such an extraordinary mind to enable us to question. Since we have brains but are not allowed to question God's actions, there is rebellion. That is human nature and even God can't stop it. Therefore some of us, after long reflection, research and consideration, came to the conclusion that God did not create us and God does not exist.'

'What about you? I mean, do you believe in God?'

'I believe in and venerate nature, but I don't believe that God created it. Yes, I am an atheist.'

Rabbit had used this same word, but what did it mean? I asked Jam about it.

'Atheists do not accept that God, or any deities, exist. Maybe I could better describe my feelings as those of a Darwinist. Do you know who Charles Darwin was?'

'No.'

'A Darwinist is someone who believes we are not the descendants of Adam and Eve but that humans evolved and developed in a natural process. Maybe you have heard about the Big Bang, the enormous explosion that happened billions of years ago when the universe was first created?' I nodded. 'Well, we are all made of the same things, the same elements. When I say 'we' I don't mean only all human beings, but everything: trees, rocks, mountains, animals, stars, oceans, minerals, everything in our fantastic solar system and beyond. Do you follow?'

'Yes, I think I do. What are we made of?'

'OK, what is water, scientifically speaking?'

'H_2O.'

'Correct. From two atoms of hydrogen and one of oxygen. We humans, and everything else in this universe, are made of the same atoms, but with millions of different combinations, therefore we have different forms and functions in life.'

I was struggling to comprehend all this in another language, but I really needed to understand these ideas. 'Does this mean nature created religion too?'

'Yes, nature created human beings and they invented religion. Zoroaster, the Mede Prophet who was born thousands of years ago around Mount Ararat, was, most probably, the first to mention a single God as a supernatural power and as the creator. Zoroaster was human, created by nature, made of atoms, and he invented the idea of God the creator. That effectively means that nature has created itself and everything within it, including God and religion.'

'Who created the Big Bang?' I wondered, thinking aloud.

'Well, I am sure one day we will have the answer. I don't know if it is going to be in our lifetime. Don't forget that modern science is relatively young; it has only existed for a tiny amount of time compared to the age of our universe. Yet science has already, in a few hundred years, made incredible discoveries. If it managed to prove religious doctrine was wrong about the earth being flat and to put a man on the moon, sooner or later it will find an answer to your question. But I am certain: the answer will not be that God created the Big Bang! At least, not the same God who supposedly created heaven and hell.'

I had to think about this. *Not long ago, I would have been offended by a simple blasphemy, and now Jam wants to prove to me that God does not exist! But if I embrace freedom for myself, I must change and learn to let others be free as well, to accept that they can have different views from mine. At the end of the day no one can enter someone else's grave, as Rabbit said, and it is not for me to judge other human beings,:that role can only be accorded to God Almighty. Now that I am learning to be more tolerant, could I make peace with Rabbit? I would like to. I miss him dreadfully, and, after talking to Jam, I feel ashamed about offending my Brader because of religion.*

'Do you think I could get to America?' I asked, changing the subject and surprising Jam.

'Is that why you want to learn English?'

'Yes. I want to go there and study filmmaking.'

'Filmmaking! Wow! That's different! Do you have a passport?' I shook my head. 'Well, you can't travel without the damn document!' he said, adopting a sardonic American accent that reminded me of Cary Grant in *Bringing Up Baby*.

'Can I get one?'

'How old are you?'

'Fifteen.'

'You are a minor, so you would have to travel with your father, or at least he would have to give his consent.'

'Could my uncle?'

'No, your uncle can't.'

'My father will never allow it and would go mad just hearing my ideas for the future. He wants me to become a dervish.'

'A dervish! Maybe by paying a back-hander to the passport office, you could get away with your uncle. But you are a Kurd and, consequently, unless you are strongly associated with someone in the government, you're not allowed to travel abroad.'

'Well, obviously I have no government connections.'

'So you can't go.'

'Can you help me?'

'Me! No I'm sorry, I can't, and you should really wake up! You're living in a dream world. You are too young and it would cost a small fortune.'

I went quiet, thinking, I was right to write all those letters to my Gringo.

'I will go to America. Gringo will help me out, I am sure of it.'

'I think that you're just kidding yourself. It's wishful thinking, though it would be nice if it happened for real,' Jam said, chuckling.

'It's not funny, Jam, this is urgent. It's a matter of life and death. I must try to get to Gringo, I have a strong feeling he will get me the treatment I need to cure myself. He is my only hope.'

Jam paused thoughtfully before asking, 'Cure what?'

'I have a serious problem, I can't talk about it.'

'Look, when you are eighteen and complete your studies, you won't need your parent's consent. As for the authorities, you could just bribe them to get you a passport for a two-week holiday in Western Europe. Once there, you make your way to Gringo.'

'That's three years from now. I could be dead by then.'

'Well, in that case you have to find an illegal way to cross the border. For this you will need a trustworthy agent.'

'What is an agent?'

'Someone who can smuggle you out across the mountains.'

'I don't know any agents.'

I did not get the help I was looking for from Jam, but I felt that he understood and appreciated the urgency of my situation.

'I will make it to America, no matter what. I cannot live in this country, and there will be two of us going,' I said, as I got up to leave.

'Who is the other traveller, may I ask?'

'My girlfriend, Aida.'

I was lost in my thoughts, as if I were walking up a dead-end street. After Jam had made it clear how difficult, or rather, how impossible it would be for me to travel abroad, for the first time I questioned my intentions, my dream world and myself. *What would I say to Aida? I can't go to America to be cured, and I can't be with you because I am sexless. No, no! I must go to Gringo, or else I might as well be dead.*

I reached the Alamen Cinema on time and had enough money to pay for a full ticket, so I sat down to enjoy the film. Finally the lights went out, and once again, I was safely lost in the darkness of my magic world. I had seen dog actors, lions, horses and bears, but to have birds playing roles was just remarkable. *How on earth did Hitchcock do it?* I remembered my mother's words, 'Dervish and cinema, I've never heard of that before.' *It's a sin to be in the cinema, in the house of the devil, and yet I love it so much. I truly am a confused Muslim, just as Rabbit once described me. I don't care if I am committing a sin. I need to see* The Birds.

I had already spent more than half of Papula's money, but I could not resist it. I bought a new ticket, a sandwich and a Pepsi and went back inside for the four o'clock screening and watched the film again. *Thank you, Alfred Hitchcock! What a film!*

My first kiss

On Thursday afternoon I came across Uncle Hitchcock in Bazaar Hasiraka, outside the builder's teahouse. I covered my face. 'I don't have money,' I said, between my hands. He waited and once I relaxed, snap, he took a shot. 'My gift for you and Aida,' he said, searching through his brown bag to hand me an envelope. 'I rarely come across people smiling into my camera. You are both very photogenic. How is the princess?'

In the envelope I found two copies of Aida and myself, standing next to each other hand in hand. 'Aida will love this, thank you. She is fine.'

'Remember, I am your wedding photographer.'

'You bet.'

He wished me good luck and moved on. I hid the photos under my shirt. The Chevrolet pickup arrived from the desert with the same team of labourers and a couple of new faces to replace Rabbit and myself. Rabbit appeared, supporting himself on a crutch, limping. He looked my way briefly. We had not talked for an entire week. Louis paid Rabbit his wage. I wanted to wait until he and Peaceful left. But Louis saw me. 'Dervish Merywan, I have already paid your wage to your father,' he called. Turning away, he forgot about me. 'I want my money,' I said, and grabbed his arm. Louis gave me a shove, nearly knocking me off my feet. I was going to jump him, until Rabbit barred me with his crutch.

'Here, have half of my wage, Mery,' he said.

I felt so ashamed, *how could I have been so stupid as to call Rabbit an infidel? There is hardly anyone as good as him and, if God has any justice, Rabbit should be the first to go to heaven, even if he does not obey God.* I had blasphemed in my heart and for the first time I did not repent. *This is the moment to make up with my friend.* 'I was wrong to attack you,' I said. 'I now understand people can have different views, even about God and his existence. I am sorry.' I held out my hand.

'If you were truly my Brader then you would have accepted me for what I am and not how you want me to be,' Rabbit answered, with bitterness. 'Like I accepted you for what you are.'

What does he mean by saying 'for what you are?' He has never given me any sign that he knows about my sexual defect.

'You have not been a true friend,' he went on. 'You have kept secrets from me. That really disgusts me. I don't know if I can ever call you Brader again.'

Who had told him my secret? I was still standing there with my arm outstretched, offering him my hand and wishing he would welcome my apology. 'Rabbit, I was wrong to insult you, and I say it again, I am sorry, what else do you want me to do to get your friendship back?'

'Too late, you brainless fool, the damage is done.' Rabbit had never insulted me like that before. But this was only the start. 'You are not a pure Muslim yourself, but full of fear and cowardly pretence to be faithful to your God.'

'You are being a bit harsh,' I said, and let my hand fall slowly to my side.

'I am not sure if I can have a…,' Rabbit could not finish. I feared what he was about to say, but provoked him to spit it out. 'A what? Say it, what am I to you?'

'Nothing but a shit neuter,' he said, quietly.

I had goaded him to be honest, but he broke my heart when he said that. It would have felt better to be struck by lightning. I didn't think about why he was doing this to me, I slapped him so hard that it brought tears to his eyes. He did not fight back, and prevented Peaceful from having a go at me. Instead, Rabbit seemed pleased that I had struck him. He smiled and shook his head, tears rolling down his face. *What is going on with my Brader?* But I could not ask him this. He had insulted me worse than Kojak ever had. 'I hate you!' I yelled at him, 'I never want to see you again, you… you candyfloss shit hair.' I turned and ran off, without looking back.

Aida's home was in Arafa. This was Kirkuk's most attractive district. An area of asphalted and lamplit roads, smartly tiled pavements, red brick, western-style houses, open parkland and thousands of trees. The British had built the district during the time they were in charge of Kirkuk's oilfields. After they left, the houses were mostly occupied by Christians and Kurds. Recently, Arabs from the south were settling there in greater numbers, and they chopped down many of the trees for firewood.

Aida lived in a two-storey detached house surrounded by a well-tended garden with flowers and roses to the front, dotted with orange, lemon and peach trees. I had never met a girl on her own before. I was in the park not far from her house. I begged God to make it go smoothly. *The last thing I want is to give my princess a hard time.* Earlier that morning, I had got Aida's scarf out of Papula's cupboard. I had it hidden under my shirt with the envelope. Aida turned up with her fluffy white dog. Unlike us Muslims, the Iraqi Christians loved dogs and most had them living in the house. Milky barked at me even before I could say hello to Aida.

'Your dog must know that I am a Muslim,' I said. Aida laughed.

'His name is Milky. He barks at everyone at first.' She bent down and caressed Milky. 'Milky, meet Mery.' She gave him a kiss on his head. Milky stopped barking and sniffed my legs. 'Hi, Milky, would you be so kind as to let us be alone for a bit?' I asked, talking for the first time to a dog. Aida let the dog off the lead. We went to a secluded part of the park, away from prying eyes, just the two of us. Aida took off her shoes. 'I like to feel the softness of the grass under my feet. It's fresh and tickles me and I feel connected to mother earth. You should try it, it's nice.'

I slipped off my shoes and left them on the grass. 'I have the photo,' I said, and I showed it to her. 'Aida, I love you,' I confessed with all my heart.

'You said you are going to America to meet your Gringo. Or was that another of your fantasies?' she asked. I touched her hand slowly before I pushed my fingers through hers. She squeezed my hand.

'Are you going to answer me, or are you on another planet?'

'I was Aladdin, and you were Princess Jasmine, flying away on my magic carpet.'

'Well, I'm sorry to wake you up, but what about going to America?'

'It is my life's dream, but I could not go without you. Please, say yes to America. I think I can get enough money to pay for both of us.'

'I am going to America too!'

'Wow! That is amazing – just like that, you will agree to come away with me?'

'For good,' she said. 'And for real. I will never come back to Iraq. My father has applied for a United Nations visa for all my family to leave the country legally. We are allowed to go because we are Christians, but we must leave behind our house and all our belongings. There is a good chance that we will leave in a month's time.'

'Really?' I had not expected this.

'Yes. That is why I need to work. We need money for the journey, a lot of money. I will miss you, Mery,' Aida said, with tears in her eyes. I knew I should have felt happy for her, but I was saddened by this news. I had dreamt of Aida and me leaving together. I was definitely going to go to America, even though I was a Kurd and was not allowed to travel abroad. 'In a month's time?' I asked, shakily.

'Yes. My father says the war is coming closer. We should leave before disaster strikes. Iraq is heading towards very unhappy days. Until meeting you, I could not wait to get out of this dump. When I first saw you coming into the department store I did not want to look at you, to give you hope, because I was getting ready to go away. Yet you kept on coming back again and again.'

'Did I do wrong?'

'Every day I would go to work with the desire of seeing you. You made me happy. I wanted to tell you about going to America immediately, but I was not sure. My father believes we will go soon.' We walked for a little longer in silence. I tried to absorb the shock. 'Aida, I could help you with some money if you want.'

'I want you to promise that you will come to me in America!' She wiped away her tears.

I kissed her hand and put it on my heart. 'I promise you, my love. I will see you in the land of dreams and opportunity. I would go to the top of the world to be with you.' I kissed her hand again. 'I will leave the country the day after you go. But if, for some reason, I can't make it soon, will you wait for me? Or will you find an American boyfriend and forget Mery?'

'I will never forget you.'

'Then I want you to convert to Islam.'

'Why?' she asked, raising an eyebrow as though this was a mild surprise.

'Because I want us to get engaged before you leave. We could go to a Mullah on our own.'

'If you truly love me, then why don't you become a Christian?'

'My father would never allow me to do that. He would disown me. Also, Islam is the ultimate religion. If I become an infidel, I mean Christian, we will both burn in hell in the hereafter. If you become Muslim then we will have a safe place in heaven.'

'Would you go to hell with me?'

'Of course, but why not choose heaven, with the bountiful gardens, food, rivers...'

'And the virgins!' Aida said, and giggled. 'I don't have the same religious beliefs, but, because I love you dearly, I will think about it.'

I kissed Aida on her lips. Kissing someone in public before, or even after, marriage was unheard of, but I could not resist it. I was lost in Aida's beauty. I felt light-headed. Suddenly we were flying, free, far above all the ugliness surrounding us. I wanted to stay in her arms and kiss her forever. Then she brought me back down to earth, reminding me how dangerous this was if anyone saw us. Aida was no longer smiling, she was nervous.

'I am very sorry, that was foolish,' I said.

'I liked it, but don't do it again. In this country even just kissing could cost us our lives.'

'I won't.'

'We will kiss and kiss when we are in the land of freedom, in America,' she said, and smiled again. 'I have to go now. Milky!' she called to her dog.

'When will you let me know about our engagement?'

She caressed my cheeks. 'For you, Mery, I will change to any religion, but first I must let my parents know about your proposal. Don't worry, they are not Christian fanatics and they may well accept it, but they need to know. Is that OK?'

'Of course it's OK! I will wait, it's fantastic! But when will I know your answer?'

'When you next come to see me in Orzdy?'

'Tomorrow.'

'Tomorrow, then,' she agreed, and left.

If Aida becomes Muslim, surely Rashaba would be very happy to accept our engagement, since converting an infidel to Islam is the greatest thing a Muslim can achieve. The entire family would be gifted with heaven in the next life. What could make Father happier? Watching her pick up her shoes and run on the grass, I licked my lips with my tongue. *Had I really kissed Aida? 'Aida!'* I called. She stopped. I ran to her. I pulled the scarf out from under my shirt.

'Here it is, I bought it for you. I wanted to give it to you on the day of our first kiss.'

'Give it to me in America.' She winked at me and ran away with Milky.

I spent the rest of the day and that night thinking about my princess and my bright future with her in America. *What if I never make it to join her?* The painful doubts came back to me. It was late, well beyond midnight, Star and Monkey were fast asleep and Trouble was out again, yet I was still awake. I had Aida's scarf on my face, breathing in every trace of her on the fragile fabric. It was then that I became aware of the unusual sounds coming from my parents' bed. It was mostly Rashaba; he was puffing and panting as though he was running a marathon. I opened my eyes. In the moonlight I saw him on top of Mother. A duvet covered them, but I could make out his up-and-down movement as it gradually became more frantic, his breathing heavier and heavier. Suddenly he collapsed, motionless, and within moments he had started to snore.

Was this making love? It certainly wasn't like Kim Basinger and Mickey Rourke in *9½ Weeks,* a film that I had recently seen on video at Papula's. *How would Aida and I make love? I will decorate the room with roses and sunflowers. She likes them very much. I will light perfumed candles and play soothing music, or we will listen to the natural sound of the sea, the wind and the birds. First, I will bathe her, wash her all over and massage her body. Then I will cover her from top to toe with thousands of warm kisses. I will embrace her and make love to her in all possible and imaginable positions night after night, day after day. Aida and I will walk arm in arm on Ocean Beach in California and kiss...*

I could barely wait for the sun to rise and for Rashaba to leave for work, on the day I was due to receive the news from Aida of her family's approval of her conversion to Islam and our subsequent engagement. I ran fast, down the hundred steps of Qala and on, until, opposite the old bridge, I jumped aboard a minibus that took me to Orzdy. I went in. It was still early morning but Aida was busy, serving two women. 'You will have my answer soon,' she said. 'After I have finished with these ladies.' The sweet smile on her face reassured me, but I remained impatient. I wanted to hear it from her immediately, but I never did.

Shouts of alarm erupted outside the store. There was a rattle of shutters being brought down, orders being bellowed. It was too late, the monster's men were coming inside. Panic was all around us now, as customers and employees ran to get away, their fear making them recklessly smash things in their way. I held on tight to Aida's hand as we bolted in the direction of a side door to get out of the store. One of the Mukhabarat's armed men barred the way. He was swift and brutal, smashing me across my head with his revolver. Everything went dark, as Aida screamed, 'Mery...'

I came to some seconds later, blood streaming down my face, barely able to think as my head throbbed viciously. I crawled sideways between racks of clothes, expecting to be hit or shot at any moment, but the Mukhabarat man had moved on, and was now yelling at the few customers who were left, kicking and pushing them out of the women's department. I hid between a row of long dresses, as employees were forced to face the walls at gunpoint, everyone but Aida.

From my hiding spot, crouched on my knees near the floor, I was the only one to see Abu Ali go for her. Blood blinded my eyes as I tried to stand up. *I will not let you down, my love.* I was weak and dizzy, and couldn't regain my feet, maddened as I was by the sight of Abu Ali tearing at Aida's fresh summer dress, the sunflowers ripped and shredded. He forced himself onto her on the store's marble floor.

She turned my way and I am sure she saw me tortured, watching the last agonizing moments of her life. *You don't have to implore me with your gaze, my princess, I now know I am not a prince, I am not Sinbad, I am not Superman but a coward, a shit neuter as Rabbit called me. I have no strength and am not a brave hero to come to your aid, to save you from the monster's men. As I watch you lose your sweet smile, your beautiful face creased by despair whilst being devoured by an evil, hideous man as your light fades away, I can do nothing but hide myself miserably away. I do not deserve your love, my dear Aida.*

Abu Ali finished his filthy job. He took out his pistol... *God, please, God! Aida is not a Muslim but she was going to convert. Please, God, save her, you created Aida too...* I was still praying when he pulled the trigger.

When darkness fell over Kirkuk

Abu Ali held the gun in his hand, before nonchalantly slipping it into its holster, buttoning up his jacket and walking out of the store, followed by his men. The shutters were lifted, the employees stumbled back inside, still wary and expecting the worst. Aida's manager and two colleagues hurried towards where she lay, twisted and lifeless on the floor. I did not have the courage to look at her face, her torn body. I moved in the opposite direction, dazed, picking up a cotton handkerchief as I passed and pressing it to my head, hiding my face. Nobody stopped me in the confusion, and I wandered out of the main doors into the street.

The sky was dark with heavy clouds, but nothing could have made life darker. Traffic was chaotic as usual; already shopkeepers who had seen the Special Forces and heard the shot were pulling down their shutters. Shoppers who had been trapped in the other departments were still shuffling out of Orzdy as the police arrived to hit and arrest any runners for no other reason than being fugitives from fear. I hurried towards Jam's shop. He saw me coming. He did not ask questions, but quickly took me inside, locked the door and pulled the curtains across. He tried to sit me down, to clean my face, to dress my wound. I pushed away his hands and got to the door. *This can't be true. I can't live with this.*

'Let me die. Let the fucking police shoot me,' I said.

Jam pulled me back and pushed me into his storage room, though I tried to resist. He shut the back door and locked me in. I sat on a chair in the dark and slowly pulled out Aida's scarf from under my shirt, putting it on my face. I did not cry. I felt nothing but emptiness inside. I stayed there, motionless, for a long time.

When the chaos outside had calmed down, Jam brought me a Pepsi, but I could not drink. He asked me if I had anything to do with the girl in Orzdy. I stared into his eyes, *I do not care if he is a Mukhabarat or a spy, I have to let it all out.* Falteringly, whispering, I told him what had happened.

'I loved Aida; I am a coward for not saving her.'

'A coward for not standing up to a dozen of Saddam's monsters armed to the teeth?'

We looked at each other. He had openly called Saddam and his men monsters. He could have been hanged for that if I betrayed him to the secret police, but he knew I would never do that.

'I am sorry for your girlfriend. I'm really sorry. There is nothing you can do but wish her spirit farewell and let her rest in peace.'

'She will go to heaven.' I just did not know what else to say.

'You can cry if you want to.'

'She wouldn't want me to cry, she loved me,' I said, slowly rocking back and forth in his chair in the dark corner of his shop.

The only sound now was the torrential rain that poured down upon this ill-fated city, the drops bouncing knee-high off the tarmac, cascading off the roofs and streaming from drainpipes to flood the overflowing drains. Jam unlocked the shop door, opened his umbrella and offered me a lift in his car. I did not answer or shelter under his umbrella. I was saturated almost instantly, not that I cared. But I did not want to be alone. I wasn't sure where I wanted to go and what I could do with my life without Aida. When we reached his old black Chevrolet Pontiac, I jumped inside without saying a word.

He drove in the rain down Republic Street. Orzdy was shut as we slipped by. Two policemen with guns in hand stood guard, sheltering as best they could outside the main door. I was thinking about Aida, her family hearing the terrible news, the future parents-in-law whom I would never get to meet. 'I was so selfish for doing nothing, for watching them pluck the rose of my life.' I cupped my hands to my mouth to stop myself from sobbing.

'When it comes to the monster's men,' Jam said, 'there is nothing to be done. Stop blaming yourself. Does anyone know about your love for Aida?'

'Only Rabbit.'

'Who is he?'

'He used to be a dear friend of mine.'

'Did Abu Ali know about your relationship?'

'I don't think so. Maybe. I don't know.'

Did Abu Ali do this because he is after me? But if he wants to finish me off why didn't he simply kill me at the same time as Aida? I was too shocked and could not think straight. But I knew I detested Abu Ali with a vengeance greater than I had ever felt in my life. I put Aida's light blue scarf to my face and listened to the desolate sound of the rain. Jam started to recite:

> I am a Dolphin diving in and out of you
> My deep and vast blue ocean,
> Separate,
> We can never be
> For I Dolphin cannot live
> Without swimming freely in you,
> My magical swirling blue ocean.
> The power and the beauty of love…

I thought he was referring to Aida and myself. But Jam was recalling his own experience, reminding me that love and loss, however painful, is not unique. 'Kathryn, my English girlfriend, whom I followed to London, turned out to be married. She only wanted to have some fun while on holiday. I accepted this and we managed to stay friends, but soon she moved to Bolivia with her husband, a businessman. I never saw her again. I am still hurt when I speak about her. But since we have come this far, let me show you something.' Jam opened the glove compartment and took out a picture. 'That's Kathryn and me on the beach in Rhodes.' I turned over the print. There were some handwritten lines in English on the reverse. 'It's 'Imagine', by John Lennon. Do you know The Beatles?' Jam asked.

'Yes. Master Shamal, my English teacher, likes their music.'
'That was Kathryn's favourite song. Can you read it?'
'I can try,' I answered and started to read:

> Imagine there's no heaven
> It's easy if you try
> No hell below us
> Above us only sky
> Imagine all the people

> Living for today…
> Imagine there's no countries
> It isn't hard to do
> Nothing to kill or die for
> And no religion too
> Imagine all the people
> Living life in peace…

I could read no more. The lyrics resonated so much that I had to look away to hide the tears rolling down my face. I was imagining Aida and myself in that peaceful world. Jam wordlessly picked out a cassette and put it on, letting the opening chords of the song 'Imagine' fill the air between us. I had never heard anything more moving. It was to become one of my favourite songs. Those profound words were in such stark contrast to the searing pain in my heart and the oppressive atmosphere of Kirkuk. I felt as if we were in the closing scene of a film as we drove through the storm in Jam's car, but it wasn't supposed to end like this.

'I wish there were a way to turn back time,' I said, as we crossed the bridge towards Qala. 'I wish I could find a way to kill Abu Ali.'

'I think you should go to America,' Jam said quietly.

I had to concentrate hard to stop myself from crying out *Aida and me in America, the land of hope and freedom.* After a while, I turned to him. I was so upset with Jam for saying what he knew damn well I could not do. I did not want to shout at him, so I asked if he could stop the car.

'Very funny,' I said, as I got out and slammed the door shut.

'Mery, don't misunderstand me,' Jam called, winding down his window. 'I was not joking. I meant it.' I could not hear him now and carried on through the puddles and the rain.

Star was crying. She was sitting alone in the courtyard, cuddling King Kong and talking to him, like he was her closest friend. I wanted to give her a kiss, but she flinched from my touch, which I presumed was due to my sodden clothes, until Mother revealed the real reason she had recoiled from me, 'Your father believes Star is grown up now. She needed to be cut.'

It was a grim homecoming. I couldn't tell them where I had been or what had happened, I just had to hear the news of more horror, this time inflicted by our own family. Star, who was only five years old... *Why?*

'Who did it?'

'Mullah Zao'Adin,' Mother answered.

I went to the box in Papula's bedroom. I took out Flathead's pistol. I checked it to make sure that it was still loaded. I tucked the gun into my trousers, hiding it under my shirt.

With a gun on me, I wanted to make myself invisible as I sloshed through the puddles of Qala. It was not so difficult, the storm clouds had washed the streets and taken the people with it.

Why should I be scared of him? I have a gun and I know how to use it.

Something flew towards me at such speed, I reacted as much by instinct as thought, grabbing it just before it hit my face. It was a haluk. Looking at it in my hand, I recalled all the painful times I had had to sit on the side of the pitch watching Kojak play with my Haluken set, and I remembered how Zao'Adin threatened to reveal my secret to Shawes Dog if I did not let him fuck me.

A young boy ran up to me and held out his hand. His friends were standing there, waiting for me to return the haluk so they could get back to their game. I could see the bat at the base and I was tempted to throw the haluk to hit it. But I was carrying a gun and I was on my way to play another game, so I handed him the haluk, wished him good luck and continued on my way.

Outside the house, I glanced to the left and right, checking that the road was empty. I took out Aida's scarf and covered my face. I pulled out the gun and knocked on the door. His wife opened it. I put the gun to her face. 'Quiet!' I hissed. 'I am not here for you. If you shout, I will kill you.'

I locked the door behind us and pushed the woman ahead of me. I knew the place well and where to find my man. I kicked the door in and his wife went ahead, wailing faintly. I was back inside the Madrasa. Zao'Adin managed to pull up his underpants, but his trousers were still around his ankles. A boy of about ten years of age was with him. He started to cry. 'I did not want him to touch me.' He pointed to Zao'Adin. 'He said he would take the devil out of me.'

'Stop crying and sit over there.' I indicated. The boy shuffled away. I put the gun to Zao'Adin's head. 'God help me,' the hypocrite muttered.

'What were you doing to that boy?' I asked.

'God forbid me...'

I cut him short, kicking him ruthlessly in the belly. 'Your Mullah husband is a paedophile,' I told his wife, as she collapsed against the wall to stop herself from falling. I pushed Zao'Adin down onto his knees. 'Tell your wife how many children you have abused in the name of Islam? Speak, you bastard!' I said, pulling back the hammer.

'One, maybe two... I don't remember.'

The lies merely stoked my anger, and I was ready to blow off his ugly head. 'Tell her exactly how many?'

'Seven... eight...'

'Tfu, tfu and tfu,' the wife spat in his face three times, indicating her repulsion, and her request for divorce.

I kicked his leather bag in front of him. I told the boy to turn away. 'Don't worry, I will let you go home soon, but first I need to free you and all the other children from this sick man.' The boy turned, but he continued sobbing. 'Get your razor.' I said. Zao'Adin did so, looking up at me imploringly, terrified of my next move. 'Cut off your cock! Take it out and cut it.' I picked up a cushion and through it shot him in his leg. He shrieked and begged me for the love of God to stop. I wanted him to cut it off, however much he whimpered and moaned. I shoved the gun into his mouth. 'Do it, you pig.'

His hands trembled along with his body as he pulled down his underpants and took the razor towards his penis. His wife looked away and kept crying. Zao'Adin was utterly humiliated. I did not let him do it. I felt death would be too gentle an escape. He needed to live and suffer the consequences of his filthy abuse. I kicked him in the face, hearing his nose crack beneath my shoe, then took the hand of the shaken boy. I cared about him, and was pleased with myself for saving him from Zao'Adin.

I led the boy outside, and, once in the street, I told him he was safe and free now. He nodded and forced a smile, but he still looked warily at me, and ran off without turning back.

A woman's touch

'Mery, you are not a neuter! You are normal!' I thought I heard in my delirious, dreamy state. When I opened my eyes I was staring up at some moving propellers and imagined that I was still lost somewhere in a nightmare, being chased by Abu Ali. Gradually, the ceiling fan came into focus, and then, stepping in front of it, there was Papula. She was cleaning my face with a wet cloth. The sight of her made me wish I was normal, but I did not say this because I did not think Papula knew about my secret.

'Where am I?' I asked instead.

'In my bed,' she replied, tenderly.

Time seemed to stay still for Papula. She grew more beautiful by the day, but to the great disappointment of Flathead and my mother, she did not give birth to any children. It was not clear if it was she who was infertile, as Mother suggested, or my uncle. I had never been so close to her before, her face only a couple of fingers away, her breasts, like ripe red juicy pomegranates, seemed about to pop out from the unbuttoned collar of her purple dress.

'It's fine, Mery. You are not a neuter,' she said calmly. I gawped. I was speechless. *So she had said this earlier, it was not my imagination.* 'You should stop tormenting yourself. You are normal,' she added with her sweet smile.

'What do you know?' It was useless to pretend otherwise; I had to ask.

'Your trousers were wet, you must have peed on yourself...' I abruptly pulled up the blanket. I was completely naked and in Flathead's bed! 'I am sorry; I had to take off your clothes. At first, I did not look at your... I promise.'

She knows!

'You were sleep-talking, saying, "I am not a neuter, I am not." You mentioned Aida, then a dog called Abu Ali, and you did not want him to take you away to a monster. I cuddled you and you went back to sleep in my bed. I have sometimes thought of you as a girl, but never as a neuter. I had a good look at you and I am glad I did.' I turned away, wanting to vanish into the emptiness of the room. Papula has seen me naked. She has examined my ugly penis.

'Mery, my dear, how much I care for you.'

'I am not a lesbian.'

'Oh, don't be silly!' She giggled. 'You are a boy, a handsome boy. It's just that you are not circumcised.' She inhaled my scent deeply. 'I am seeing a doctor about my infertility because your uncle wants a child. I could ask him to sort you out too?' She squeezed my hand. 'Should I just not care, like most people around you, and see you ruined? I am not a bad person, as your mother and your uncle think of me. You have a special place in my heart, and I am not trying to take advantage of you. I genuinely want to help you, and to do so you need to see my doctor. Mery, your secret is safe with me. Trust me.'

Papula went to her make-up cabinet, picked up her comb, and laughed. 'Your uncle left me that money for the doctor. What should I say to him, when he comes back? I didn't go because Mery stole your half a dinar?'

'I borrowed it. I'm sorry I did it without your permission. I will pay it back.'

'You still don't trust me, do you, silly?' She came back to the bed and put her arm around me. 'Don't worry about the money. When in need I can give you more, and I will pay for your visit to see my doctor.'

I took out my treasure box, and sat crossed legged on the floor opposite Gringo's photo. I wrote another letter to tell him about what had happened to my Aida… I also needed to have a chat, to let Gringo know of Papula's suggestion to see her doctor, and to give him the latest news about our Mullah. After my visit to him, Zao'Adin's scandalous story was spread all over Qala. His wife was so appalled that she immediately moved back to her family and made sure that everybody knew why she had to leave her husband. Two days later, he was found hanging inside his Madrasa. We could not be sure whether he was murdered to pay the price for his evil acts or if he had committed suicide, but I was pleased to learn that he was no longer a threat to the boys and girls of Qala.

I was also glad that Star did not meet the same sad end as Happiness, but after experiencing the brutal cut she changed, and never regained her winning smile. Rashaba didn't want to believe that Zao'Adin was a paedophile, and forbade us to talk about this shameful subject within the family. My mother went pale as Rashaba spoke, and looked tearfully towards Star and me, but she could say nothing. Papula was adamant that the hypocrite deserved his awful death.

If Papula were a man or had a warrior's freedom, I was sure she would also train me to fight like a Jedi so that I could kill Abu Ali, who was as monstrous as Darth Vader. She liked Gringo very much, but at that moment she was mad about Han Solo, and was equally enamoured by his friend Chewbacca. I knew it was hard and perhaps I was daydreaming once again, but I really believed that Gringo and I could do it. *How wonderful it would be to have you at my side, planning to kill Abu Ali! Not only because he took away the rose of my life and left a gaping hole in my heart, but also because he is sure to strike again. In this lawless land, sometimes, like Charles Bronson in Death Wish, it is necessary to take the law into your own hands. Not that I need to tell you this, Gringo, after seeing you in* Dirty Harry...

My mother would not let Papula out of the house unless she wore the black cape. Before, when they had gone to the doctor, Mother had not left Papula alone for a moment, and had done all the talking. Now Papula wanted me to accompany her instead. She felt freer going out with me. She looked great in her skirt and blouse, with her hair loose, and I could easily imagine her walking down Republic Street and enjoying the attention, men's eyes scanning her curvaceous body as if she were on a catwalk. But after experiencing the horror of what had happened to Aida, who had been betrayed so terribly by her beauty and sense of freedom, I said to Papula that I would be happy to accompany her, but only if she consented, against her wishes, to wear a headscarf and a long coat that would attract less attention. Papula pulled out a stylish silk scarf and agreed, with a saucy wink, that as long as she was going out with me, and I visited her doctor, she would forget about making other men jealous.

As we passed the entrance to Orzdy, people were strolling inside, completely oblivious of what had happened there. It was exactly as

Jam had foreseen; they were unaware that there had ever been a girl called Aida working in the store. Papula was keen to go in, but I made her change her mind. 'I want you to meet a friend of mine. He has a shop, and you will not believe what he is selling.'

'Women's underwear?' Papula said, giggling.

'No.'

'You tell me.'

'I want it to be a surprise. But don't make jokes. He cares about his shop very much.'

Jam was inside, displaying sets of stamps in the window, and came out to meet us when he saw me. I introduced Papula. Despite Papula not flaunting her body as she might have wished, her charm and her beauty transfixed Jam. I had seen Jam serving other female customers before, when he had always been polite and reserved. But with Papula, he was different; he lingered there, looking deep into her eyes, exchanging warm smiles. He even invited us in and offered us drinks. I apologised and explained that we had an appointment and were running late, so he waved farewell.

'He is handsome, your shopkeeper,' Papula said. 'Is he married?'

'No, but he has a girlfriend.' I did not know whether Jam had a partner or not, but I did know that I did not want them becoming romantically involved. Perhaps I was jealous about the way Jam and Papula's eyes had met, or maybe I wanted to protect my uncle's honour. Whatever the reason, I was glad we did not go inside his shop.

'Is your doctor a nice man?' I asked, changing the subject.

'He is the best,' Papula said, and gave a triumphant smile which I did not quite understand. 'My doctor also performs complicated and illegal operations, abortions and stitching up of deflowered girls who might otherwise be killed for having lost their virginity.'

We were almost at the corner of Doctor's Road, which, as its name suggested, had long been home to the medical profession and now harboured several private clinics, when I nearly stopped dead in fear. I thought I saw Abu Ali striding towards us, surrounded by his usual retinue of four guards, but it turned out to be another Ba'ath Party officer, with a similar Saddamist moustache and darker skin.

'Today is Wednesday,' Papula said. 'I just remembered. Dr Hakan closes early. We must hurry up.'

Dr Hakan Khanoghlu had recently graduated from Ankara University in Turkey and was not much older than Jam. He was charming. His white medical gown, the stethoscope around his neck, and his precise moves, gave him the aura of an eminent man. He was from Kirkuk and spoke Turkmani, which is slightly different from Turkish. I was panicking inside and suddenly unsure whether I wanted to be checked over by this Turkman doctor.

'I shall see Merywan first,' Dr Hakan said. 'Do you mind waiting outside?' he asked Papula. 'No,' I objected, holding Papula's arm.

'I don't want to be examined. I have changed my mind.'

'It's fine, Mery. I will stay. I am sure Dr Hakan won't mind?'

'Of course not,' he consented. He opened a curtain on the side, revealing a bed in the corner. 'Here, Merywan, come and lie down. Let me see if I can help you.'

'Thank you, but I don't want you to sort me out.' I got up to get out. Papula stood in my way. 'I don't want him to see me and touch me.'

'Fine, I will not look at your private parts,' Hakan suggested. 'I will only talk to you.'

'But don't touch me,' I warned him, as I slowly moved on to the bed. He put his hand on my stomach. I got up again. 'OK, I won't, I am sorry. I will just ask you a few questions. They are simple questions, but you may find it difficult to answer, and you are welcome not to if you don't feel like it. OK, Merywan?'

I agreed.

'On your way coming to see me, what were you hoping for?'

'For you to help me out with my problem.'

'What problem?' Hakan asked. I hesitated. 'Your auntie talked a lot about you during her last visit, but she did not mention that you had a problem. I would like to hear it from you.'

'I thought my auntie was not allowed to talk to you, as my mother always did the talking?'

'You are quite right. She cleverly left a letter on my desk about her worries with regards to her infertility, and in it she also mentioned you and what a good friend you are to her. Anyway, what problem, Merywan?'

'Mery, open up!' Papula said.

'I am a neuter. I am not sure if that is what I should call myself, or if I should say a 'boygirl', as my mother calls me.'

'We say 'hermaphrodite', if that is what you are referring to. If you are one, would you like to become a boy or a girl?'

'My father would prefer me to be a boy, but Mother would be happier if I were a girl.'

'How about you?'

'I feel that I am a boy, but I don't mind, as long as I am not a neuter.'

'You are not circumcised, is that correct?'

I nodded.

'You have something down there, except that you feel nothing and don't perform boys' usual…' He looked at my auntie. In the presence of a woman, he seemed embarrassed to go into details. 'You know what I mean, Merywan?'

'Yes.'

'That is normal. One out of ten men experience impotence, which is not being able to get an erection, during their lifetime. Do you ever touch yourself, down there?'

'No. Only when I wash, but I don't like to touch and look at myself.'

'You have told me a lot, and I think I can help. To start with, I can already say that you are not a neuter.'

I heard Doctor Hakan perfectly well, yet I can't believe my ears. I am going to ask him again, praying that he will not change his mind as I so desperately need to hear this news.

'What did you say?'

'You heard me correctly, Merywan. You are not a neuter.'

'What is wrong with me, then?'

'I will come to that, but in order for me to help you properly, I need to be able to examine you.'

'Mery, please let Dr Hakan do his job,' Papula said. 'He will save you from all the anguish you have been going through for so long.'

'She is right. You need to be helped, and soon, or it will be too late.'

'You can touch me, if you stand behind the curtain and promise you will not look at me,' I said, covering my eyes with my hands. 'But please wait, first I need to pee.'

Hakan pulled the curtains, letting me urinate into a white ceramic pot. It sounded strange, but it was better than wetting myself.

'You now need to take off your trousers and your underpants. You can cover yourself with the sheet... Are you doing it?' the doctor asked, from behind the curtain. I did not answer. Papula came in. 'You will be fine, my dear,' she said, as she caressed my face, which was sweating. 'We are ready, doctor,' Papula called, and smiled reassuringly. I closed my eyes again.

'I shall also wear gloves so that you will not feel my skin.'

I jolted as though I had been electrocuted when he placed his hand on my penis. He was the only person I had willingly allowed to touch me there for more than six years. It did not take him long. 'That's it. Finished,' Hakan said. 'You get dressed, and I will have a word with your auntie.'

From behind the curtain I could hear him giving his verdict to Papula. 'Merywan has a mental block caused by a childhood trauma,' he said evenly. 'Physically, Merywan doesn't have much wrong. He has an unusually tight foreskin and due to the fact that he is not circumcised, the size of his penis is smaller than normal because of the skin preventing it from growing. But his problem is mostly due to his mental state. His mind is quite disturbed, full of fear, mainly about his sexuality. In an ideal world, he should see a psychiatrist and have a few sessions to unblock his mind and free him from his fear, but in this country I would not recommend seeing a psychiatrist. I will give you a cream. Merywan should rub it on his penis at least twice a day. This will soften the skin, but that is not enough because he needs to overcome his psychological confusion in order to be able to get an erection. If this works, perhaps in a couple of months I could circumcise him.'

I could wait no more. I stepped out from behind the curtain shivering from the relief of what I had heard, from the incredible discovery. I could hardly raise my hand to shake his. 'Thank you Dr Hakan,' I heard myself say, but I was already tumbling towards the floor.

Dr Hakan splashed water on my face and I began to regain my senses. I reached out for Papula's hands and kissed them. 'Thank you Papula, you are the best. I mean it with all my heart.

'Don't make me cry,' she smiled. 'You have no idea how pleased I am. I knew it, and I was right. We should thank Dr Hakan.'

'My pleasure. My pleasure,' Hakan repeated.

'After applying the cream, if I am able to have an erection, will the circumcision be necessary for me to be a real boy?' I had to ask this because I did not want him to cut me. Dr Hakan considered. 'The Christians are not circumcised and they perform their manly duty with no problems,' he explained. I was so relieved. 'Merywan, would you be fine to wait here?' he asked. 'I need to examine your auntie and check her progress.' I nodded and once again thanked the doctor for his kindly, considerate advice and reassurance. Papula lay down on the bed and covered her abdomen with the sheet. Dr Hakan drew the curtain. 'If you have a child, what would you like it to be, a boy or a girl?' was the last thing I heard Dr Hakan saying to Papula.

Fly to the land of freedom

My Gringo, I now know I am not a neuter. I'm getting used to the idea that I am a boy and am taking Dr Hakan's instructions seriously by applying the cream he prescribed for my tight foreskin twice a day. Sadly, so far I have not experienced much feeling down there. Papula thinks this might be due to the fact that my mind is still too busy with the loss of my beloved Aida… After visiting Dr Hakan, I completely trusted Papula. She advised me to watch erotic films on her VHS, and, to encourage me further, she often talked to me about sex. Not her sexual life with my uncle, as she seemed unhappy about that, but how she yearned to experience sex freely with someone she loved. I tried my best, but I just couldn't rid myself from the thought of Abu Ali raping and killing my Aida so brutally.

A week later, I sat on a chair posing for Jam with my hair falling over my shoulders and with Aida's scarf around my neck, in the small back room of 'Wonderworld'. I had seen people having their portraits painted in films and was flattered to have this chance, to feel the eyes of an artist studying my face. Jam had shown me a portrait of Kathryn, which was the last painting he had worked on, many years ago. It was still only half-finished, since it was too painful for him to complete it. I was moved when he told me that I had inspired him to paint again after so long. As far as I could discern, he was a talented artist, able to achieve real beauty with tiny brush strokes, and to convey character very effectively too.

We talked as he painted, sometimes absent-mindedly when he concentrated on mixing colours. I remembered that he had mentioned Charles Darwin, and I asked Jam to tell me about him.

'He was an Englishman who changed the way we think about the world for ever,' Jam said. 'He's the man who wrote about how different species developed and evolved their amazingly diverse characteristics through natural selection.' Jam reached over to his bookshelf and handed an imposing volume to me. I read the title: *On The Origin of*

Species by Charles Darwin. 'It took him more than twenty years to write that book.'

'Can I read it?' I asked.

'That is my only copy and it is not a good idea to take it outside the shop, but you are welcome to read it in here.'

'Thanks,' I said and opened the book that Jam loved so much.

'You can relax now,' he said, turning intently to his brushwork. Jam explained that he was a pointillist. It was fascinating, because close-up I only saw dots of different sizes and colours. When I stepped back, my face appeared on the canvas. *Jam is right to believe he does not need God to create miracles.* He put down his brush to serve a gentleman who bought two sets of Australian stamps, and when the man left, Jam told me that it was time to leave, picking up his jacket.

'What about my portrait?'

'We can finish it another time. I have a surprise for you. I am taking you to a special place,' and he went to the door.

'I would love to, but I promised Papula that I would get back. She is waiting for her kebab.'

'You must be a good friend of your auntie.'

'I am. Why do you say that?'

'No reason in particular, but it must be nice for you to have a woman like her around.'

As we got into his car I asked him, 'In Islam, it's a sin to go to bed with a married woman. Is it the same for an atheist?'

'It is called adultery, and it's a problem whatever your religious beliefs are. Are you telling me that you are having an…?'

'No.'

'Do you intend to have such a relationship?'

This one was much harder to answer because the answer was probably yes. I had even had some fantasies about Papula.

'Sex is,' Jam said with a sigh, as he drove towards Tsiin district, 'one of the most important subjects in our lives. Family, relationships, happiness, success, civilisation… at the end of the day, it all comes down to sex, and we are not allowed to practise it freely. We live in such an ignorant and intolerant society, I wouldn't have been surprised if you had answered yes. If you can, you should avoid seeing a married woman. I had two fantastic weeks with Kathryn and she was married, but that was in Europe. Here, it is different, and often it ends up in bloodshed, as you know. Of course it is not easy, especially when, at your age, you are not free to have sex with girls because they must stay virgins until their marriage.'

'Would you allow your daughter to have sex before marriage?'

'Yes I would,' he said, turning to me. 'I would not suggest anything I wouldn't do myself. The Kurdish philosophy is: Why should I do it if people aren't doing it? That's wrong. We need to learn from the British: If you don't do it for yourself, no one else will. That's your individual freedom.'

'What is individual freedom?'

'As long as you and your actions don't physically hurt me or damage my life, you should dress as you wish, colour your hair and have it long or short as you like, listen to the music you prefer, love the person you love and vice versa. None of this is disrespectful to others. Freedom is your birthright as a human being, and expressing yourself freely is the only way to force our brainwashed society, dominated by traditions and religion, in the right direction. And if you feel like giving your daughter the freedom to bring home her boyfriend and sleep with him in the next room, let her do it, and ignore what the others say. Don't live your entire life falsely just to satisfy other people. In short, live and let live.'

'Individual freedom!' I said, and pulled off my hat to release my unfurling hair. 'I like the sound of that.'

'We should all be free if we want to have a free country. If I don't practise and respect my personal freedom, how can I lead people and call for the freedom of an entire nation? That is where our leaders get it wrong: they all look like puppets and move like robots, they talk about the same things and behave in the same way, they lack personality and imagination. They are not the best models for our people to follow. If they are leaders, they should be the first to break free of the chains and free themselves. It is paradoxical, isn't it, to call yourself a leader and fight for the freedom of others, when you are not free yourself – that is why, perhaps, we are where we are after centuries of struggle and wars, because we have the wrong people leading us.'

It was getting dark. Jam drove into a narrow alleyway. He

parked the car and we walked to a detached house. He knocked and a middle-aged lady with tattooed lips opened the door. She was not dressed in the typical black cape and her head was not covered. She wore thick make-up and a lot of jewellery around her neck, wrists and arms. She looked at me in surprise.

'He is a boy,' Jam said. I felt elated, as this was the first time ever someone had so confidently identified me as a boy. We followed her into a spacious guest room, dimly lit and with dense smoke clouds curling towards the ceiling. Two-dozen men lay around on oriental rugs and silk-covered cushions, smoking shisha and drinking Arak. They were facing a small, raised, mosaic-tiled stage where musicians played Arabic music, a woman was belly dancing and another was singing. My eyes opened wide when I saw several young girls serving food and drinks. They were probably around sixteen, and were dressed skimpily, their flesh shimmering through pink and green linen waistcoats and baggy trousers. This was such a novel scene for me that I could only compare it to a Bollywood film that I had seen, with a touch of 'Arabian Nights' and the powerful whiff of incense unpleasantly mixing with the smell of smoke and male sweat. The lady beckoned us to sit opposite the belly dancer, and two of the girls instantly brought us fruit and drinks. Jam put the shisha in his mouth and started to smoke.

'My suggestion is,' he said, 'if you are desperate for sex, rather than ending up in a mess by sleeping with a married woman, you should go with one of these gorgeous girls. You will pay some money, but it is much better than getting yourself killed.'

I turned to look at the girls. 'Are they whores?' I asked.

'They are Kewaly, Arab gypsies, and by tradition, they are known for their music and belly dancing. They also sell sex and do a real favour to society. Without them it would be chaos. We should be grateful for their unique service.'

'Are they Muslims?'

'They are, but you shouldn't worry about that. Muslims are also human beings and like everyone else, they too have a desire for sex, except they don't have the courage to break the chains and enjoy their individual freedom, so they have to do it secretly, and most of the time in this way. I would prefer to go with a woman for love, but when

I can't, this is the alternative.'

One of the girls touched Jam and the other put her hand on me. She caressed me and kept a warm smile on her young face.

'Do you want to make love?' Jam asked.

'With whom?'

'With me! Mery, wake up! With one of the dancers.'

'Are we here to have sex?'

'Yes,' he answered, patiently, 'but that's not the only reason. I also want you to meet the Godfather.'

'Marlon Brando?' I asked, as a joke.

'The man who can fly you to America,' Jam said. He gave me one of his charming smiles and winked.

'Do you really mean it?' I looked deeply into Jam's eyes, as if I was asking him to give me back my life.

Jam nodded convincingly.

'Swear?'

'I swear on my heart.'

This truly was the greatest surprise. I felt a real spark of hope, yet I could not find the words to express my joy. I got hold of his hands to kiss them, to show him my immense gratitude, but he shushed me benevolently, at the same time rising to his feet to greet a powerfully built man with a bald head. It was immediately obvious why Jam called him Godfather, although his voice was nothing like Mr Brando's. He greeted me too, and we sat down. He only had to nod at the girls for them to move away.

'Do you speak Arabic, Merywan?' Godfather asked.

'I do.'

'First, the cheap way,' he said. 'You go via the mountains, from Iran to Turkey and then by boat to Greece. In Athens you get a Greek passport and fly out direct to America. This could take you three months.'

'How much?' Jam asked.

'Five thousand dinars. Two thousand paid in advance and the rest paid on arrival.'

'What are the risks?'

'He will be going with a group of five others and will be accompanied by one of my men. If they get arrested, I can get him out and try again. The worst-case scenario is that he may get shot by the Iraqis, the Iranians or the Turkish border guards while they are crossing. I cannot guarantee his safety.'

'What is the expensive way?' I asked.

'Fly directly from Saddam International Airport in Baghdad to Washington DC. This is getting much tougher since the restrictions on travelling because of the war, and the increase in demand.'

'How much?'

'There is a long queue for this route. Some passengers are prepared to pay up to twenty thousand dinars, and obviously they get priority. But for the standard ones, the fee is ten thousand dinars. That is inclusive of passport and everything, and all paid on arrival.'

'The risks?'

'Nothing much, but you would need to cut your hair.'

Damn it, why should these offers always come with conditions, and such serious ones? I have to go to America, but I do not want to cut my hair. I went quiet. Jam turned to me. 'What do you think, Mery?'

'I prefer to fly direct, but I have only nine thousand five hundred dinars.'

'I could pay the remaining five hundred,' Jam offered.

'Thanks Jam. I have to think about cutting my hair.'

'I would need two passport-sized photos,' Godfather said. 'For now, you could pull back your hair, but once we are ready to fly you to America, you have to cut it. I wish you well,' he mumbled, as he left us alone.

We both followed him with our eyes, as Godfather walked to a girl in the centre of the room and danced with her.

'He is an Arab, how can you trust him?'

Jam was exasperated. 'That is called racist, and I would like to think you are not racist or prejudiced. After all, Godfather trusts me, and I am a Kurd. Stop this paranoia and enjoy the evening.' The belly dancer finished her performance, and another girl took her place. She came up to Jam. 'Hello, my love,' she said. She put her face next to Jam's and rubbed noses. 'Shall we go?'

'Yes,' Jam said. 'First I want to fix up my friend. He is a virgin and I want him to have a special treat.'

'Do you want me to choose him a princess?'

'You are the expert.'

She kissed Jam on his lips and went away. I wanted to tell Jam that I could not have sex because I was impotent. But I just could not bring myself to tell him my secret, and I did not want to disturb his erotic evening.

'Do you come here often?' I asked.

'Once every two weeks, when I need some intimacy and pleasure.'

His belly dancer came back with a much younger woman wearing transparent pink baggy trousers and a pink waistcoat. She had a pink veil on her face, but from what I could see she could not have been much older than I was.

'Princess Yasmin for…' she addressed Jam.

'Prince Merywan,' Jam completed her sentence.

He got up and went away with his girl, leaving me alone with Yasmin. She extended her hands and I took hold of them. She led me to another room. We could still hear the music and Yasmin danced to the rhythm. She handed me a glass of Arak, which I sipped at, though the taste was horrendous. She slowly stripped, starting with her veil. She was dazzling. Kohl-lined dark eyes, oval face and full lips. She had dots tattooed on her forehead and a beauty spot on her left cheek. She took off her waistcoat and exposed her young but well-formed breasts. She came close to me and rubbed her breasts on my face. She pushed down her trousers and flicked them away. She danced dressed only in her pink knickers.

My lips were getting dry and I could barely believe what I was seeing. Lovely as she was, I yearned to see Aida instead of her. Yasmin took hold of my hands, helping me to take off her knickers. She unbuttoned my shirt and pushed me down on the bed, then eased my shoes off my feet and, with a smile, removed my trousers. She was about to pull down my underpants, when I grabbed hold of her hand to stop her. 'It's not your fault,' I said weakly, 'but I am not ready for this.' Yasmin looked at me, mystified. *She can't possibly know how terribly I miss Aida, and how much I am tortured inside, unable to forget the haunting image of her staring at me in that last moment of her life.*

When I made it back to Qala, luckily, the local restaurant was still open serving the few late night costumers. I bought a portion of takeaway kebab for Papula and headed home, fantasising that my dream of going to America might finally come true, and wondering if I would ever be able to exorcise Abu Ali from my mind.

Heroes never give up

'In America you could achieve something,' Jam said as he drove.

'Here, you will never be allowed to blossom. But I need to know how you will get all that money.'

'I will tell you about the money when the time is right.'

Jam stopped by a roundabout with a huge poster of Saddam. We had to wait for a military convoy to pass. 'Do you know where the Mukhabarat's Headquarters in Kirkuk is?' I asked.

'Why do you ask?'

'Abu Ali is a member of the Mukhabarat.'

'Mery, wake up from this obsessive dream.'

'I can't forget. Even if I make it to America, and succeed in my goals, I will come back for him. I will not have peace until I free Aida's soul from his dirt.'

'Aida would be happy to learn that you have made it to America. That will free her.'

'I can get hold of a gun,' I replied, emphatically.

'Forget it, Mery. Just forget it.'

'I can't, Jam, I just can't. If I have one day left in my life, I will live to kill him.'

'Revenge can be a bitter victory.'

'Whose quote is that, Jam?'

'Mine, and I can see you don't like it.'

'I don't.'

'You stubborn Kurd,' Jam said, with a rare, exasperated tone.

I thought we were going back to his shop, but he made a diversion. He pushed a cassette into his car's system. It was the soundtrack of Excalibur, 'O Fortuna', from *Carmina Burana*, one of my favourite pieces of music, by Carl Orff. He slowed down at a street corner. 'I have only a few seconds,' Jam said, nervously, 'I am pretending I am waiting for the traffic to move on. If I stop here too long we will be shot. Look to your right. Do you see that big building? Well, that is the

Mukhabarat's Headquarters, the most protected building in Kirkuk. I must keep moving,' he added, as we accelerated from the junction and his demeanour became more relaxed again. 'Did you see all the barricades on the road? There are at least five checkpoints before you make it inside, and dozens of gunmen guarding it. It's a dead-end journey and I do not wish to see you in there. Did you also notice the machine gun on top of the roof? They would have shot us if we had lingered any longer. If I had driven to the right without prior permission we could have both been killed on the spot. That's why I turned left,' he said, with a wry grin. 'Forget about Abu Ali and think only of going to America.'

'Heroes never give up,' I said, glancing back towards the Mukhabarat's Headquarters, and then turned to Jam, 'have you seen *Escape from Alcatraz*, with Gringo?'

'Yes, and I have also seen *The Great Escape*.'

When we got back to the shop, Uncle Hitch was waiting outside. I had arranged for him to meet me there. In the back room of Jam's shop, I sat on a chair. I tied up my hair behind my head to make it appear that I had short hair. Uncle Hitch took my photo. 'I will give the passport-sized pictures to Jam tomorrow, and don't worry about the payment. It's my gift to you.'

'Thank you, but I can't accept. You have already given me several gifts,' and I put my hand in my pocket to pay him. He shook his head.

'I did not have a chance to express my sorrow to you.' Uncle Hitch put a hand on my shoulder, 'I am very sorry about Aida's death.'

Whenever I thought of Aida, the desire to kill Abu Ali returned as strong as ever. I knew I would never be able to rid myself of it.

'Shall we finish your portrait?' Jam asked.

Uncle Hitch left. I changed back into the colourful shirt that I wore to pose, loosened my hair, and with Aida's scarf around my neck, I sat down again, facing Jam. 'When will I leave for America?' I asked, as he picked up his brushes to paint. 'Godfather says he needs a couple of months to secure you a passage.' This came as a shock. Two months is longer than I had anticipated. What if Rashaba were to buy a house in the meantime? I hid my disappointment though, as I didn't wish to seem ungrateful. 'I have seen that film, *The Passage*, many times,' I said.

'I thought it was awful.'

I was surprised by Jam's comment. No matter what, I did not like anyone putting a film down. I couldn't believe that anyone ever wished to make a bad film. But I had to accept and respect Jam's opinion. He was free to think as he wished; it was his personal freedom, after all.

'Do you think I will be as lucky as James Mason, to make the passage safely?'

'Hope is the last thing to die, as they say,' Jam answered, and he asked me to keep my head still while I talked.

I thanked Jam for all his help and foolishly started to believe that, although I was still in shock, and mourning the loss of Aida, perhaps everything else might turn out as planned. I was still oblivious to the next catastrophe waiting to strike, not at the hands of Abu Ali, but of Rashaba. Trouble had seen me going into Jam's shop. He had spied on me.

'Your portrait is almost finished, but it needs to stay in the shop for a couple of days for the oil colours to dry and…'

Jam did not manage to finish his sentence, because at that moment Rashaba and Trouble stormed in. There was no escape, they had caught me in the act. They were there for a fight and came well armed. Jam tried to reason with Rashaba, but he was pushed aside and Trouble pointed his knife at him. Rashaba slapped me as hard as he could, grabbed me by my hair and dragged me behind him. Jam dodged Trouble and tried to pull me away from Rashaba. But Rashaba held a wooden baton. Jam shrieked as he was hit on the head, before collapsing onto the shop floor.

My mother gaped when she saw me being dragged into our courtyard with my hair down, wearing a blue flowery shirt and Aida's scarf around my neck, but Rashaba warned her with a stern glance, and she said nothing. He picked up a piece of hose and whipped me all over. I yelled in pain. Mother had Monkey in her arms and was holding on to Star. Both my little ones sobbed, but Mother did not intervene.

Papula ran out and tried to stop Rashaba. He just pushed her away.

'When your drunken husband comes home,' Rashaba grunted, 'he must sort his snake wife out for turning my son into a shameful girl, for turning him into an infidel. I am not going to let him sleep in your cursed house again, once your husband is back.'

Trouble was happily heating up one of the kitchen knives on the stove. Rashaba stripped me of my jeans and tore apart my shirt, leaving me only in my white underpants. He picked up the red hot knife and burned me on the top of my wrist. Smoke rose and there was a sickening hissing sound as the burning metal was pressed into my skin. Rashaba was still holding on to Aida's scarf, and he was about to set fire to it when Papula cried out and snatched the scarf from him. I no longer felt the pain, seeing the scarf safely in Papula's hand. But this was not enough. Rashaba asked Trouble for scissors.

'No,' I begged, for the first time since he had started to beat me.

'Father, burn me all over, but don't cut my hair, please...'

Trouble came back with the scissors. Rashaba asked him to hold my hands. I punched Trouble in the balls. Rashaba bashed my head, nearly knocking me out, and brought the scissors close to my hair. I got hold of his wrist and pushed him back as we wrestled for control of the scissors.

Papula threw all the shoes and slippers she could find at Rashaba. She came for him and started to hit him on his back, but he glowered and pointed the scissors towards her and he must have cut one of her hands, because Papula screamed. She had to back away, and ran out of the main door.

Rashaba pushed the scissor points into my hand and I started to bleed. I could no longer hold his wrist. He grabbed a full hand of my hair and was about to cut it. Someone got hold of him. 'Darwesh Rashaba, call "Allah u Akbar" and let Merywan go...'

Popcorn! He was the first person Papula had come across outside our house. He did not let go of Rashaba's wrist. Popcorn called 'God is great' several times, assuring Rashaba that I was going to be one of the finest dervishes, and that to cut my hair would take that chance away forever. 'You have punished him enough,' Popcorn pleaded. 'Merywan has learned his lesson. Call for repentance, Merywan. Let your father know you will never dress like that again or have your hair loose in the open.'

There was no point arguing that I had only looked like this in private while I had my portrait painted in the back room of Jam's shop. Rashaba would never understand.

'I promise you, Father. Please, don't cut my hair...'

Rashaba gave me one last blow with his bony hand. The late afternoon sun was totally eclipsed, and the world turned dark.

It was all so quiet that I felt like I was in a different world, one that was far away from Rashaba. I was glad to open my eyes and see Papula, in a white, knee-length, flowing summer dress. She was sitting by my side holding my hands. Her hand was bandaged. She answered with a sad, sweet smile. I was on her bed. I lifted my arm and wiped the tears from her face with my branded hand. She showed me Aida's scarf and gently laid it on my face.

'How long have I slept?'

'Since yesterday afternoon,' she said, smiling through her tears. Her hand was no longer dabbling away the sweat on my brow but engaged in a gentle caress around my face. She touched my eyebrows, cheeks and nose. When she caressed my lips, I swallowed and quivered inside.

'You have such beautiful full lips, I envy the girl who will kiss them,' she said. 'Have you ever kissed a girl?'

I couldn't bring myself to tell her of my first kiss with Aida. I took her hand and kissed it. 'Rashaba will not let me sleep with you again, once my uncle is home,' I said. There was a long pause. We kept staring into each other's eyes in silence, trying to read the strange thoughts rattling around our heads. 'Papula, were you cut when you were little?'

Papula's eyes opened wide. 'Do you mean my clitoris?'

'Yes.'

'No, I am not cut.'

'You are lucky.'

'I would be, if only I were married to someone who had a bit of imagination and knew how to appreciate me. I am wasted on your uncle. He never plays with me. He just jumps on me and in a few minutes, bang, it is done. He doesn't care how I feel, and I don't remember the last time I had an orgasm with him.'

'If only I could be a normal boy, I would give you a great orgasm,' I said, squeezing her hand.

'Now, shut up Mery. You are making me horny. Turn over, I need to rub more cream on your back,' she said, pulling off the sheet.

I did not mind her seeing me naked. She rubbed cream into the bruises which Rashaba's whipping had left all over my body. I was full of pain and grief, but at that moment, feeling Papula's hands on me was the best thing I could have wished for. It offered me an escape, and this was a new and wonderful sensation that no amount of religion or philosophy could replace. I knew only too well that I could not bring Aida back, and since my relationship with Papula had become so intimate, although Aida was always in my thoughts, she no longer appeared in my dreams and daytime fantasies.

'You have a nice bottom, no wonder so many men wanted it,' Papula said. 'Not as lovely as yours,' I replied, slowly turning to lie on my back and grinning at her. She blushed slightly, then asked in a matter-of-fact way. 'How's it going down there?' She pointed between my legs. I shook my head. 'Mery, when you rub in the cream, you need to stimulate yourself and get an erection…'

'I can't do it. I have tried,' I said, as I turned to her. She must have seen the pleading look in my eyes. She made me sit on her bed.

'Mery, I can't possibly do that for you.'

I felt embarrassed and covered my face.

Papula opened her make-up cabinet and got hold of a magazine.

'Here, look at this. I will not come in until I hear you calling.' She walked out into her living room and closed the door behind her. *It is an issue of* Al Moed! *That will not help.* I threw it back on the bed and it fell open. *Ah! The cover is a false one. It is a porno magazine.*

'Any luck?' Papula called, after a while. I did not answer. She peeked in to find me hiding under the sheet. She uncovered my head. 'I will do it for you, but this time only,' she said. She handed me the magazine and started to rub the cream on me. I looked at the naked women and men on the pages, but my mind was with Aida.

'Who are you thinking about, Mery?'

'Aida.' I did not want to lie to her. My mind was in such conflict between Papula and Aida. She grabbed the magazine and threw it away. 'That's not good,' she said. 'Forget about the horror of what happened to Aida. I want you to think about me, your Papula. For once I am not your auntie. I want you to desire me. I desire you, Mery. I want you. I feel you…'

She pushed herself against my body and tightened her hands around my penis while staring into my eyes, trying to seduce me with her gaze. I wasn't feeling at ease at all, but a powerful sensation drew me towards her even more. I could not help but feel her soft thighs touching mine while sitting by my side, her hair tickling my chest, her hand stroking my penis. It was hard to let go and completely relax. I thought I saw Flathead's eyes moving in his portrait on the wall above Papula's head.

'It would help if you took down my uncle's portrait.' I said, hesitatingly.

Papula did not bat an eyelid. She stood above me, in her white dress, her red underwear, her olive skin shining through; she was much sexier than my favourite pose of the gorgeous blonde girl in the magazine. She put the portrait aside and started again. This time I just could not look away from her. I desired Papula. I could feel her every little touch, her hand delicately rubbing me, her breasts dancing to the rhythm of her gentle fondling.

'Are you with me, Mery? Mery...' She caressed my neck with her other hand. 'Mery, are you with me?' she said again, as she bent down and kissed my nipples.

'Yes.'

'You feel my hot, juicy lips?'

'I do.'

'Who am I, Mery?'

'You are Papula. You are my Papula.'

'That's good, Mery. Think about me, about your Papula.'

Starting from my chest, she went down kissing me. She kept on my stomach for a while and I felt shivers throughout my body. The moment took over and there was no stopping it now, although I knew I was committing an unforgivable sin. I could not resist any longer, so began to unbutton her dress and kiss her nipples. Papula closed her eyes. I gently made her lie down. I breathed in her perfume. I kissed her eyes, nose and cheeks and finally kissed her sweet lips. She responded and put her arms around me. We kissed and kissed.

Down below I was about to explode from the sensations of feeling her warm body against mine. I was dying to go inside her. I was about to help myself with my hand. 'Not yet,' she said, and placed my hand on her clitoris, 'touch me first.'

The more I touched her, the more she was lost. She had to bite my hand to stop herself from gasping out loud. She spread her legs slightly and I felt her nails dig deep into my back as I pushed inside her.

It could only have been a few minutes later, but the next thing I became aware of was an intense feeling of anxiety, as I struggled to work out who I was, where I was and why Flathead was beating me up. It was only gradually that I realised I was deep within a vivid nightmare. As I opened my eyes, I found Papula soundly asleep next to me, her face so innocent, so peaceful.

How could I have had sex with Flathead's wife?

Outside there was a sudden spine-chilling cry, followed by a thud in the courtyard. Then terrifying screams from my mother. I ran to the window and pulled the curtain slightly, just enough to see Monkey, my little brother, had fallen from the rooftop. He was lying in a pool of his own blood on the stone-paved courtyard, his ball still bouncing about.

Can I be in your film?

In our room, I picked up the Qur'an and spoke directly to God. 'I hope You truly exist because on judgement day, God, I shall face You, point my fingers at You and tell You, God, that You had no right to create me without my consent, to put me into the most miserable life full of injustice, fear, uncertainty and pain. You are to be judged for torturing me throughout, for giving me no choice as to whether or not I wanted this life in the first place. For playing with me like a toy from the minute I drew breath on earth, for experimenting on me as if I were a mouse in a laboratory, and most of all for Your constant vengeful ways, Your nasty games with the devil, whom You also created for Your own selfish pleasure. And because of it, You turned my life, and those of countless other millions, into hell on earth. In the name of all those innocents, and especially for taking Monkey's life at such an early age, I condemn You to burn in Hell forever. Did You hear me, God? Do You exist or are You nothing but a fake created by humans to fool each other, an invented fraud? Give me a small sign, anything to prove You are truly around us and watching over us. Here, this is Your sacred book in my hand, the Qur'an, the holiest of all books, which should not be touched without the ritual of mentioning Your name, holding it against my forehand three times, each time followed with a kiss of devotion on its Holy cover. Well, when I picked it up earlier, I did not mention Your name, at least not in a nice way, and nor did I kiss it. Like any other book, I am simply holding it in my hand. Actually, I am angry at this book, because if You are nothing but a fable, a human fantasy, then the words attributed to You in the Qur'an are equally fallacious. You and Your holy book have brought nothing into my life but misery and suffering, and taught me nothing but hate. I hate You and Your Qur'an.'

I threw the Qur'an, which made a thud as it hit the wall, before it fell to the floor like a dead bird, its pages fluttering open. 'Prove to me that You have created me. Blind me now for throwing Your words on to the floor. Strike me with Your deepest hate, but stop this gruesome game, stop taking the people I love away from me to punish me. Why should they pay for me? Why should Monkey die because I made love to my auntie? Why are You such a cruel God? No wonder Rabbit compared You to Saddam Hussein.'

I picked up the holy book again. I put it to my eyes three times and kissed it. I begged the Qur'an for a miracle. *Bring back my little brother.*

Mother hit herself and sobbed uncontrollably. She howled for Monkey to wake up, running around the courtyard, pulling out her hair and digging her nails into her face, making herself bleed. She cradled and kissed Monkey's inert body, but he did not wake up. Mother did not need to blame Star. My sister was in shock, she kept repeating she was looking after Monkey, and she just didn't know how he got onto the rooftop. Poor Star felt guilty for the death of my brother. I folded Star in my arms to comfort her and stop her from hitting herself.

Papula did not come out, and I only saw a glimpse of her through the window. I did not know where Rashaba worked, but Trouble was easier to reach. I ran to Grandfather's big house in the hope of finding him there. I had to slow down and approach carefully. At a distance I called out to the Arab guard that I needed to talk to the gardener's assistant. He pointed the gun at me and instructed me to stay where I was, which I did. Trouble came out, annoyed at my appearance at his workplace.

'Monkey has fallen from the rooftop. He is dead,' was all that I coud bring myself to utter, before running disconsolately back home.

My family wore black for three days as we mourned little Monkey. It started with the boiling of large pots of water, and neighbours coming and going, helping out with washing Monkey for the last time. Trouble was amongst those who lowered Monkey's bruised body, wrapped only in a white cotton sheet, into a small grave next to my grandparents. The new Mullah called for the prayer, and despite all my despair with God, I could not stop myself from praying.

Rabbit did not pray. I had not seen him for weeks, but had not forgotten him, and was saddened to learn that his knee had got worse and he had needed an operation, which had not proved successful, leading to the amputation of his leg. On the way home, Rabbit approached me. 'I am sorry for insulting you so cruelly,' he said. 'I very much regretted it.'

'I am sorry for breaking our friendship because of God. I was wrong, and I deeply regret it, too.' We walked for a while silently.

'How is your leg?' I asked.

'Different,' Rabbit said. 'It took me a while to get used to a crutch, but now I have mastered it.'

'I was terribly sad when my mother told me they had to cut off your leg. I wanted to come to visit you, but I couldn't bring myself to. I was blinded by God's hatred.'

'It's fine, Brader, you were with me. You were always on my mind.' It felt so good to hear Rabbit talking to me as a friend again. 'You were always in my heart,' I said. We shook hands. 'I am sorry about Monkey. Good health to you and the rest of your family,' Rabbit said, and he hobbled away to walk alongside his father and brother.

Rashaba came home too late. It was a sin to delay the burial; the earlier the dead were sent to be judged by God, the better for a Muslim. I was saddened because Rashaba did not give Monkey one last kiss. Not that he ever hugged or kissed him. Rashaba wept silently. I wondered if it was because he had not made that damn gate to prevent his youngest son from falling, or was it partly because he never spent any time playing with him when he was alive, and now Monkey was gone forever.

Trouble and I helped our neighbours to put up a large tent in the open space opposite the house. The same space where we had celebrated Flathead's wedding was now used for Monkey's funeral. The Mullah read the Qur'an and dozens of men from the neighbourhood walked into the tent to pay their respects. Trouble stood outside welcoming the visitors. I offered tea on a tray and was glad to serve Rabbit, Master Shamal and Peaceful.

The women gathered in the courtyard. I greeted Jwana and Sunshine. Jwana kissed me on the cheeks. To her I had always been Rabbit's best friend. I was really shaken and was grateful for such reassurance. I wanted to spend more time with them, but I had work to do. I excused myself and went to refill the glasses.

'Mery,' Sunshine said. Her voice sounded familiar but also

stronger, more purposeful. 'This may not be the right time to ask, but could you please come to our house again? I would like to show you something.' Sunshine's features had changed little from when I had been present at her tenth birthday, but she had grown up since I had last noticed her. She wore a black dress, her hair was still long, and with a few freckles on her cheeks, she looked like a European. Despite the tragic situation, she could not hide her lovely, open smile, which broadened as she waited for my answer.

'I can only come to you after the funeral ends, is that OK?'

'Of course, thank you.' She shook my hand, and as she did so, her eyes encountered my scorched skin. 'What happened to your hand?'

'Oh, I stupidly burnt it on the stove.'

As Sunshine walked back to Jwana, I wondered what it was that she wanted from me. *Whatever it might be, I am pleased she has invited me to her house.*

I was in the tent when I saw Jam, Uncle Hitch, with his camera dangling around his neck, and Popcorn, walking towards us. I was relieved to see Jam on his feet, and felt a surge of joy at seeing these three funny-looking men, three Kurdish amigos, my best friends, who had come to Monkey's funeral. I served them tea.

'I am sorry about your little brother,' Jam said.

'Thanks. How is your head?' I felt guilty for causing Jam all that trouble.

'Not too bad,' he answered, sipping his tea.

'I can't go to your shop for a while.'

'I could talk to your father?'

'No, he is far too ignorant to understand your world. Once he is back at work, he will soon forget about me. Is there any news of Godfather?'

'He has your photos. And by the way, I have your portrait.'

It would have to remain a secret for now, away from Rashaba's eyes. I thanked Uncle Hitch for coming and Popcorn for saving my hair. 'You should be grateful to your auntie,' Popcorn said. 'She is the one who fetched me in time, and it's better if you don't show your hair in public.'

I instantly touched my hat as I nodded agreement. I looked up at the Mullah reading the Qur'an and across at my friends. Most did not believe in praying, but they did not have the freedom to express it. To do so would have been social suicide. Before leaving, Jam handed me my portrait. I so much wanted to take it out, to look at myself on the canvas, my first ever portrait, to appreciate Jam's creation, but I did not, fearing Rashaba's presence. I only half smiled at Jam and with a nod I expressed my gratitude. I hurriedly walked away with the portrait to leave it in Papula's living room.

Mother cried for hours that night, clutching Monkey's Superman toy. I kissed her hands. 'Monkey died because of me,' I said. 'I am the doomed one, and bring only tragedy. I wish I had never been born.'

She clung to me and sobbed more. I helped her to lie down on her bed. Rashaba was fast asleep. Star was not. 'Mery,' she said.

'Could you sleep next to me?'

'Yes, my little Star,' and I lay down.

'Will Monkey go to heaven or hell?'

'Monkey will go to heaven.'

'Will we ever see him again?'

'Yes, he will join us again, and will be part of our family, when we too, travel to the next life.'

Star turned to look at me. 'Why do we die?' she asked.

'To go and see our grandparents and Monkey. They would feel lonely if we did not.'

'Could you sing me a lullaby?'

I had to whisper it. I was afraid of waking up Rashaba. Halfway through the song Star put her soft hand on my face. 'I love you, Mery. I don't want you to die,' she said, and closed her eyes. I kept singing in a whisper, and after a while, she drifted off to sleep, disturbed no longer by Mother's muffled sobs.

Papula was in her room and had the door locked. I tried to open it. I called her a couple of times but I had to give up. I lay down on the sofa in her living room. It must have been around four in the morning when my uncles walked in. Flathead woke me up and asked me about the tent outside. I told him it was Monkey's. Hercules collapsed silently on the sofa in shock. Flathead had again brought home some sweets for Monkey and Star. He put his arms around me and cried, which made me loathe myself even more. *How could I have made love to his wife, to the wife of an uncle who has only ever been kind to me?*

If I confess my guilt and ask him to get his gun and shoot me, he would shoot Papula first. There is nothing I can do but accept that I have badly betrayed him.

After the funeral, as promised, I went to Sunshine's house, where I was warmly welcomed by her and all her family. Then Sunshine excused herself and left the room. 'She has a surprise for you,' Shamal said, pleased by whatever his daughter had in mind for me. But Rabbit shook his head. *What is making him concerned about Sunshine's surprise?*

'How is your film world?' Shamal asked, politely.

'Fine, all trapped in here.' I tapped my head.

'Under your hat.' Shamal smiled. 'Keep at it, son, you will get there. You have all the right qualities, and one day you will find the right people to appreciate them.'

'How about you, Master Shamal, aren't you bored by teaching us?'

'On the contrary, I love my job dearly. Teaching is a serious responsibility. How and what one teaches can affect people for the rest of their lives.'

He was right; long ago he had shone a beacon of light into my heart and my mind, for which I will be eternally grateful.

'Sunshine is ready for you,' Jwana said, as she came back. Master Shamal beckoned me with his hand to follow his wife. Jwana left me at the door to their bedroom. I knocked. 'Come in, but first close your eyes,' Sunshine called, from inside. I did as instructed and shut the door behind me. 'You can open your eyes now,' she said, in the darkness, 'and turn the light on.'

Sunshine, covered in a white sheet, stood on her parents' bed. She slowly pulled down the sheet, revealing her head, then the rest of her. She was dressed like a princess, wearing a crimson dress embroidered with golden thread. She threw the sheet to the floor and with a bow, gazed into my eyes, then announced dramatically, 'Father, I would pick up the tears and bring them back to your eyes if I could. I would lick the wounds of my brother, shot by the arrow from the enemy's lines, to bring him back to life, if I could, for he died to defend you, to defend your honour and to prevent me being married to Mam. But, I want you to know, dear Father, I love Mam and he is as innocent as your daughter. He has nothing to do with my brother's death. Please

Father, do not part us unjustly, because separated, Mam and Zin will not survive.'

It took a few seconds for me to digest how convincingly Sunshine had played the part of Zin and delivered her lines, how confidently she recited the piece. 'Well done,' I said, applauding in admiration. 'It's Mam and Zin isn't it. It is tragic, but still I like it very much, and you really brought Zin to life.' She jumped off the bed to face me. 'Do you think I could be in one of your films?' she asked.

'You are very good,' I said, and she blushed.

'I love acting,' she said, with a passion which suggested that nothing else existed for her. 'After my studies, I will go to drama school.'

'We don't have one in Kirkuk.'

'No, but by then you will be in America and I could join you?' She raised her eyebrows spontaneously as if questioning my next move, while waiting for my answer. I was taken aback and did not know what to say. She came closer and slightly shook her head as if to say 'talk'. The light in her eyes struck me. 'Would you go to the cinema with me?' I asked, after a while.

Flathead was alone, waiting for me in our room, when I reached home. I was shaking inside as I stood opposite him. 'I have my pistol on me,' he said, 'I took it out this morning to have it serviced.' Then he asked about Papula's movements, and particularly whether she had stayed alone with Dr Hakan in his clinic. I praised my auntie for her honourable behaviour, but Flathead cut me short. 'Do you know why I am getting my pistol checked?' I shook my head. 'Because I will kill her and any man who touches her... like dogs in the street.'

'Yes, Uncle,' I said, struggling to keep my expression neutral. But inside I was screaming that Papula was innocent, it was my fault, it all happened because of my problems.

'You are my eyes, Merywan, don't cheat me,' he said, looking so intently at me that I was sure my guilt would be clear to him. *But what is he thinking? Does he suspect me of sleeping with his wife?*

'Swear on my life you are telling me the truth,' he demanded. *I do not want to swear on Flathead's life. Despite everything, he is still too dear to me, but if I don't, then Papula could die because she has betrayed him and slept with a man. A man? I can't believe that in a matter of weeks I have gone from being a neuter to a boy, and now to a man, a man who has committed adultery.*

'I swear on my heart,' I said, and put my hand on my heart. This was the first time I had ever sworn on my heart while I was lying, but to save Papula I was prepared to do a lot more.

Later, in their living room, Flathead, Papula and I sat to eat dinner. The atmosphere around the table was tense and I prickled with discomfort. Even though kebab was her favourite, Papula did not eat, but only played with her food. 'Why is my portrait not on the wall?' Flathead asked, as he was eating. 'It fell down,' Papula answered nonchalantly. 'Isn't that right, Mery?' This was the first time she had talked to me since we had made love. 'Yes, Uncle, it fell down,' I said. Papula gave me a tender smile. 'Couldn't you put it back on the wall?' Flathead muttered. 'I didn't know how,' Papula said. 'But you put up Merywan's portrait,' Flathead answered, irritated. 'Mery did it himself. He can't have it in their room because of his father. I can take down his portrait, if you wish? Actually, I will do it now,' and she rose from the table. 'Sit down!' Flathead shouted. 'I will do it.' Papula insisted. 'Sit down, I said.' Flathead banged on the table with his fist. 'Merywan's will stay where it is, but mine should be up as well.'

'Uncle, I will put your portrait back up. Please enjoy your meal.' There was a moment of awkward silence until Papula started lamenting. 'Poor Mery, he was burned because of you. He won't be able to sleep here again. Mery, show your hand to your uncle.'

'It doesn't matter.' I did not want to show my wrist, but Papula did it for me. 'His father burned him because he sleeps here to look after your wife,' she complained. Flathead got up and strode out into the courtyard, calling, 'Darwesh Rashaba…' I gave Papula a look to make her understand that I did not appreciate her inciting him like this, and followed him outside.

Rashaba stood on the veranda and Mother blocked Flathead's way. 'Take out your anger on me, Brother,' she said, protecting her husband firmly. 'I have had enough of your husband,' Flathead roared. 'Darwesh Rashaba,' he called. 'Merywan will sleep in my house and, if you stop him, I shall have you kicked out of the house once and for all, you dumb idiot.'

'Don't call my father an idiot, Uncle,' I yelled at Flathead. It was the first time I had ever been upset with him. 'He is my father and you should show some respect.'

'I understand, Merywan,' he said, turning towards me. 'I too would be hurt if someone called my father an idiot, but that is because my father was a great man. What I don't understand is what he saw in this idiot to make him his son-in-law,' he fumed, storming off to his living room.

Rashaba nodded at me. He showed his appreciation for the way I defended him. I knew I had him on my side again.

The war is here

Kirkuk, September 1986

As the summer holidays came to an end and the start of the school year arrived, we were faced with a new nightmare. Arab Saddamist head teachers were appointed to almost all the schools in Kirkuk, with the instruction to spread terror, and to spy on their students. Anyone who dared to do anything but praise Saddam would be branded a traitor to the state. The punishment was severe. The new head would call the Mukhabarat and make the dissidents disappear. It did not depend upon whether the student was brilliant in class or had never even been given a detention. All that mattered was that we were Kurds. If we were not collaborators like Abu Ali, we were vulnerable and had to be vigilant about every action. Kurds could trust no one, not even in their own family. The school was no longer an educational institution but had become another recruitment centre for the government to find traitors.

The new term began with a group from the Juvenile Brigade marching into the school's morning assembly playing Iraq's national anthem on somewhat battered brass instruments, as usual. This was followed by the wretched salute to the flag. I was in Year Four of secondary school, which the Americans call Tenth Grade, and was looking forward to resuming my friendship with Rabbit. He was in the row ahead of mine, standing two students away, to my left.

This tiresome routine was unexpectedly interrupted by the appearance of Abu Ali. He strutted in, followed by his usual retinue of guards. Then the young man I had seen at the Republic Street shooting was brought in. He was blindfolded, badly bruised and moved as if he were unbearably tired.

There were more than five hundred students, two dozen teachers and three caretakers standing in the courtyard, but the silence was so complete that the sound of Abu Ali's military boots hitting the concrete made everyone's heart race, mine most of all. He paced up and down, all the while staring at the floor.

The Mukhabarat's routine strategy, when people were arrested, was to make them name at least two accomplices, any two, as long as they were Kurds. This was not going to save you, but could bring the torture to an end with a welcome death.

The young man knows me and he is here to point me out. Why else have they come to my school? Normally the Mukhabarat would turn up in the middle of the night and snatch people out of their beds. The young man's blindfold was taken off. He walked along the line with painful steps, staring intently into each student's terrified eyes. If he singled you out it would mean certain death, and I was sure that, like mine, everyone else's heart was nearly jumping out of his chest from fear of being chosen. *Will I be the only one he would point out, or will he choose Rabbit as well?*

The young man moved closer. He did not point at anyone before getting to our class. *I am not surprised. He is keeping himself for Rabbit and me, playing the dirty game for Abu Ali's enjoyment.* At last Rabbit turned and glanced my way. We looked at each other across the rows as if to give a final farewell. *But I don't want to die, not yet. I want to go to America, to meet my Gringo.* I pulled down my hat. I kept my eyes on the boy and did not look away. He didn't stop until he reached where Rabbit was standing. He indicated, but it was not very clear whom he was pointing at.

Is it Rabbit or the student next to him? Rabbit limped forward, out of the line. Master Shamal made a move, but before he had time to intervene, the young man said, 'Not you,' and condemned Azad, another student standing next to Rabbit. Two of the guards seized Azad. He cried out as he was dragged away. The young man turned his gaze back to me. I almost stepped out of the line myself. But the he did not stop as he passed me. Instead he smiled. *Why on earth at a moment like this would he smile at me?* He chose Niaz, the classmate next to me, and despite his desperate pleas, Niaz was also dragged out.

Selfishly I was relieved that I was not chosen. *Maybe Abu Ali is not here for me after all?* It was just about possible that the two victims were the young man's accomplices. But the coincidence that they were both standing next to Rabbit and myself was damning. Azad and Niaz may just have been in the wrong place at the wrong time and ended up as two more gifts from Abu Ali to the monster. Maybe this was a warning for all of us at the school to witness what could happen if we dared to oppose him. Abu Ali had become as fearsome as God, and had the power to decide who could live and who must die. At the end of that day, I left school and never went back.

I had arranged to go to the cinema with Sunshine after school, but when I went to her house, it was Rabbit who opened the front door. He stood in my way, defiantly holding onto his crutch. 'I don't want my sister to fall in love with you,' he said, facing me. *He must really loathe me to look at me with such hostility.*

'I am not a neuter, if that is what worries you?'

'I never thought you were one,' he said, which pleased me. 'I just don't want you near Sunshine.'

'Rabbit, I have no intention of falling in love with your sister.'

'She will fall in love with you, though.'

'She won't.'

'She will, Mery. You are that kind of person; everyone falls in love with you.'

'Do you still love me?'

'I do, but you must stay away from my family.'

'I am leaving for America.'

'Is this another one of your fantasies?'

'No, for real.'

'You've been saying this for years.'

'I am waiting for news from Godfather. Jam, a friend of mine is helping me…'

Rabbit put his hands to his ears. 'I don't want to know about your plans and contacts. I hope you go before it is too late.'

'Too late for what?'

'You saw the boys taken away from our school? That can happen to any one of us. Go now, Mery, and save yourself. And don't tell anyone I gave you such advice.'

'You once told me real friends keep no secrets. Are you hiding something?'

'No.'

'Sunshine, I can understand! But why stay away from your family!'

'We have already felt the pain of missing you, I don't want to go through that again.'

Rabbit's answer did not convince me. I took out the photo and handed it over to him. 'I would like you to keep a copy too, it is one of my favourite shots with you,' I said, waiting to see Rabbit's reaction. 'Thanks,' he replied. 'I always loved this photo.'

'Do you recognise that boy standing behind us?' I asked, sure that he would.

'No.'

'He is the one who was brought in by Shawes Dog to our school, to name two students.' I said Shawes and not Abu Ali purposely.

'You mean he was brought in by Abu Ali?' he said, evenly.

'Yes, Abu Ali.'

'That man is a real plague on our people,' Rabbit said, with a deep sigh. 'Mery, stay away from him.'

'Have you come across him in the past?'

'Yes, more than once, but what would he want with a cripple like me? I am worried about you, my friend, the wind seems to blow in your direction. Try to stay out of his way until you go to America.'

'I still have doubts about Abu Ali,' I said, although I knew this risked upsetting Rabbit. 'I sometimes believe he is Shawes Dog and is playing with me.'

Rabbit laughed, to my embarrassment. 'If Abu Ali were Shawes Dog,' he said, 'he would have taken both of us and my father away the other day at our school. After all this time, Kojak and his dog father still haunt you. Go to America.'

'My brother doesn't want to let you in, am I right?' Sunshine asked, as she walked out.

'I think I am Brader again with your brother,' I said, waiting for Rabbit.

'Friends,' he answered, and shook my hand, but only a cold handshake. 'Have a good time, sister,' he called after us, 'and stay away from Mery.'

Following the tension and threat of brutality that the day had brought, walking side by the side with a girl only a few months younger than myself, wearing a dress with a delicate floral design, high heels and her long hair down to her waist, made me feel almost light-headed, and I started thinking that we could have been in a European film. We might be an attractive young couple on the streets of Rome, Paris or London, or even better in Hollywood, about to star in a romantic comedy. Perhaps this was my best way to escape, to forget the awful reality, but in any case, I felt very glad to be with Sunshine. She was clearly happy too, like a free spirit glowing in the morning light. I noticed people turning around to look at her. She was the first girl to go to the cinema with me. She behaved as if she had known me all her life, and did not hesitate to put her arm in mine, to hold my hand and sometimes pinch my cheek. I was so fortunate to have her for a friend, but I was also reluctant to get too close.

'Rabbit has changed a lot since you two stopped being friends,' Sunshine said, as we walked down the steps from Qala into Kirkuk.

'He doesn't go out to the cinema, in fact he hardly goes out at all, and he doesn't like us talking about you. Do you know why?'

'I thought we had made up, but I must have hurt him a lot. I didn't go to see him when he had his leg amputated, so I don't blame him for finding it hard to forgive me.'

'My brother is not the type to brood and harbour hatred. We are all sad for him, but I can't get him to tell us what is wrong. I have found him alone sometimes, crying. Maybe you could talk to him?' I wasn't aware of Rabbit's sadness, hidden behind the walls of his family's house, like a cloak of darkness. 'I will do my best,' I said. Sunshine smiled in gratitude.

Sex, love and treason

I tried to keep my mind busy by flicking through the photos of my heroes, but I could not concentrate. Seeing the monster staring into my eyes from his vile portrait was poisoning my thoughts, contaminating me with fear. I picked it up and spat at it again. A knock on the living room door disturbed my miserable reverie. *Flathead is the only person who uses that door to the side street, but he left for Baghdad last week, and anyway, he has his own set of keys.* It was far too late, at midnight, for a social visit. The likes of Abu Ali would never, ever knock politely and the Mukhabarat would come down from the rooftop, or kick the door open. *So who could it be?*

I went to see who it was, but before I knew it, Papula had emerged from her room, hurried past me and opened the door without a moment's hesitation, just as if she were greeting a friend in the daytime. I was bemused, as Papula never bothered to go to the door, and there she was only in her gown, giving me a quick nod and smile of reassurance.

Dr Hakan stood outside, waiting to be invited in. 'Hello Merywan,' Hakan said. He was relaxed, as if he were at his own house, which made me feel that I was the one who was in the wrong place. 'Well done,' he said, walking towards me and patting my head gently, 'and congratulations. Your auntie told me everything. You are a real man now!'

'Good night, Mery,' Papula said, as she walked into her room with Hakan, and closed the door.

It all happened so fast, I wondered if I had imagined it. *Is this another one of my visions? This is no time for a doctor to come and make a diagnosis! She is not even allowed to go alone to his clinic, and yet she is on her own in her room with him! I should ask for an explanation and look after my auntie, and I must ensure she is not cheating on my uncle. As a good Muslim nephew I should kick down the door, stride into the room to get Flathead's pistol and shoot them both in bed.*

That way, I will save my uncle's honour. But even though I loved my uncle dearly, I could not play that role. I had moved on from all that piousness. Then I recalled Papula's appointments behind the curtains with Hakan in the clinic that had always taken so long. *So this is why she had wanted me, rather than my mother, to accompany her! This is why she helped me out, and maybe also the real reason she had sex with me. I am to cover for her secret love affair.*

After pacing the room impatiently, I could not hold back anymore. I went to the door. *Damn my nervousness! I cannot just barge in on them.* I bent down and, like Mark Lewis in *Peeping Tom*, who watched his victims through the cine camera's viewfinder, I peered through the keyhole. Hakan and Papula were on my uncle's bed, naked, passionately making love.

I was torn between love and hate for Papula, and could no longer take it. I had to surrender and let them carry on. I sat down on the sofa, put my fists together and bashed them against my head many times over. I just could not bear to think my Papula, my sweet butterfly, was in the arms of another man next door. That was an awful night and I wished I had never witnessed anything.

The next day, in the brothel, Jam and I met Godfather again. His news made me almost forget all my troubles. He placed an envelope on the low table between us, and after a brief exchange of pleasantries, he moved on to talk to a group of businessmen on the other side of the room, leaving the envelope behind. Inside was a brand new Iraqi passport bearing my photo and a new name. Jam and I looked at each other. *It is happening. I will soon be on my way to you, Gringo. How far is Washington DC from where you live?* I should ask this in my next letter to Gringo. Of course I would have preferred to see a Democratic Republic of Kurdistan passport with my own name, Merywan Rashaba, but for the moment this false document was my pass to freedom, and with that hope in mind I kissed it fervently. Godfather came back and explained that he would keep the passport until the day of my departure – only a matter of weeks, and on that day he must see the money. I reassured him, and Jam once again acted as my guarantor. Godfather told me that he needed to talk to me alone, and with Jam's approval, I followed Godfather into one of the rooms.

'I did not want to do this in public,' he said, as he took my measurements, even recording my shoe size. 'You need to keep quiet about this, not a word to anybody. You could get yourself killed and me too if the plan is discovered. Do you understand, Merywan?'

'Yes.'

'What do you most like in America?' Tell me a name, one that you can remember, as you'll need a password.'

'Could it be an American actor?'

'Of course.'

'Clint Eastwood.'

'Gringo?'

'Yes.'

'No, no, no...' Godfather shook his head. Suddenly I was worried that he hated Gringo, for some reason. 'You like Gringo?' he asked, facing me with his big head. *If I say Yes will he slap me, and throw me out of the place? I can't say No because I love my Gringo.*

'Yes, Gringo is my hero.'

'Fantastic!' he said with a wide, toothy grin, and enveloped me in his huge frame. 'Gringo is my favourite.'

'No,' I replied, with a smile. 'He is my favourite first and then he can be yours, too.'

'Have you seen *Joe Kidd*?' he asked.

'Yes.'

'*The Outlaw Josey Wales*?'

'Yes.

'*Bronco Billy*?'

'Yes.'

'All brilliant films! Mery, I will get you to America, I promise. And when you go to Gringo, you tell him Godfather sent his regards and says you are magnifico!'

'Sure I will.'

'Now go and enjoy the evening. One last thing, your password! You mustn't reveal it to anyone, not even Jam, do you understand?' I nodded. 'And you have to cut your hair.'

Sometimes you have to give away something very precious to achieve your goal. No dreams are fulfilled without real sacrifices, and in my case, it had to be my hair.

Like James Coburn in *Pat Garrett & Billy the Kid*, I found Jam in his own earthly paradise, with four belly dancers surrounding him. The women had their hands all over him as he smoked the shisha, and he seemed to want nothing but that. I did not wish to disturb him, so I decided to go and wait in the car. By the door, someone grabbed my hand. I instantly recoiled, fearing Abu Ali.

'Marhaba, hello,' Yasmin said in Arabic. 'Marhabten, hellooo,' I answered warmly, making her understand that I was willing to go with her.

In her private room she started to dance again and slowly stripped both herself and me. She offered me a glass of Arak. *I have never tasted anything so revolting. How can anyone possibly enjoy this?* Yasmin urged me to have another sip. I had to swallow the disgusting liquid. It was alcohol, but I was a prince in the Harem and could not refuse my princess's advances. Yasmin, wearing only her pink knickers, jumped to the bed. She danced in the candlelight, offering a far more intoxicating proposition than the alcohol. We kissed and pleasured each other, before lowering ourselves onto the bed to make love.

'How did it go with Yasmin?' Jam asked, as we drove through the darkness of a moonless night and the deserted streets of this heartless city. I did not answer, but smiled and looked down, feeling a sense of both embarrassment and joy. 'Could we listen to "Imagine"?' I asked. Jam put on my favourite song again, and I lost myself in its words. I was so dizzy. *I am not made for drinking Arak.* Jam parked the car outside our house. He knocked on the door and after a while we heard a voice. 'Who is it?' Papula asked. Jam answered quietly. She opened the door.

'Merywan is drunk,' Jam said.

'I am not drunk. I am fine.'

Jam let me go, but fortunately Papula got hold of me before I fell over like a broken scarecrow. They helped me on to the sofa in the living room. 'Thanks for looking after Mery,' Papula said.

'Yes, Jam, would you like another shot of Arak?' I shouted, and Papula tried to shush me. 'She drinks too, you know?' I said. She put her hand over my mouth.

'No thanks, it is getting late,' Jam ruffled my hair. 'It was a pleasure to have a drink with you, Mery. Good night!'

'My pleasure, Jam,' I muttered, under Papula's fingers.

She cleaned my face and started to unbutton my shirt. She sniffed me. 'The scent of a woman,' she said.

'Yasmin, an Arab princess.'

'I thought you did not like Arabs.'

'I like their whores, they are excellent fuckers.'

'Don't be horrible.'

'I wonder who are the best, the Kurdish whores or the Arabs?'

'You should respect the women who allow you in their beds.'

'I hate you.'

'Because I don't want you in my bed?'

'Because you go to bed with every man you meet. Why didn't you ask Jam to stay, and take him to bed too?'

'He is a very handsome man.'

'See! I knew it, you don't love, but only look for sex.'

'Lower your voice!' she said, as we heard the scrape of a window from upstairs. 'Your father will strangle you if he sniffs Arak on you.' She collected a jug of water and tipped some into her hands and washed my face.

'Oh, you suddenly seem to care for me?'

'You know I always have.'

'You just seduced me in order to blackmail me so that I will cover your dirty...'

She put her hand on my mouth again. She was really upset now.

'It was I who helped you overcome your problems and gave you a new life. It's thanks to me that you and Yasmin had fun tonight. I did it because I cared for you, and I still do. It was not easy for me to touch you and to let you come inside me. I helped you from my heart, rightly or wrongly. I wanted to do you some good. I love Hakan and he was my first boyfriend, but I could not be married to him because I was engaged from my birth. I was a gift to your grandfather.'

'I'm sorry, Papula, for what I said. And I'm sorry for you,' I added, caressing her hair, despite her refusal to accept my pity. 'I have never really considered this until now. My grandfather was a special man, but he should have refused such a gift. They had no right to treat you like this, almost like... a slave.' I stopped, surprised at what I had said. Yet it was true, her freedom had been denied just because she was female. *How lucky I am to be a boy and not a girl.*

'I have asked your uncle for a divorce more than once, but he refuses. And in this damn country, women can't make that decision. At the beginning I respected Flathead because I thought he would understand me, and after fulfilling his father's wish, he might let me go free, but he got worse when I asked for a divorce. I have not made love with him for months now, and have never wanted to sleep with him. Every time he climbed on top of me, I felt abused, worse than being a whore. How would you feel if you were raped again and again? You don't know because it has never happened to you, thank God, but you need to know, If it wasn't for my love for Hakan and meeting you, Mery, I would have killed myself long ago.'

I was taken aback. 'Papula, I'm sorry,' I said again. 'I didn't realise it was so bad for you.' I paused, trying to think clearly. I opened my arms to indicate that my whole life was bewildering. 'It would be easier if I just followed the right side of my brain, the side that asks me to hate you and wants me to kill you for loving someone else.' Papula held my face in her hands. She was crying, but was no longer upset with me. 'I had never loved anyone but Hakan until I met you,' she said. 'I love you too, very much, and I was happy to make love to you as I felt that it could help you, but it will not happen again, so don't be confused. You should go to America, and I will be glad to do anything I can to make your dream come true.'

'I will help you too, in any way I can,' I said, 'and instead I will listen to the left side of my brain.'

'What does it tell you?'

'I love you too, and really don't want you to get hurt.'

'Thank you, Mery.'

'I will respect your love for Hakan, but, Papula, this cannot go on forever. Once I go to America, he can't come to you. Trouble will sleep here and he will tell on you, and Flathead will kill you if he learns you are sleeping with another man. Papula, you should run away with Hakan.'

'We are going to. As soon as Hakan secures an agent, we are leaving for Turkey. He has friends over there. We are going to live in Istanbul. He says it is a wonderful city. You must come to visit us when you go to America and become a famous actor. Will you, Mery?'

'I will.'

'Promise.'

I put my hand on my heart. 'Have you told him we slept together?'

'No, that is going to remain my secret, one of the nicest memories I will take to the grave with me,' she replied. 'I will not make love to Hakan until you leave for America, if this makes you happy?' *Yes, that would make me happy.* 'I have no right to deprive you of being with your love. Is he coming tonight?'

'No.'

'Can I sleep with you one last time?'

'Yes, you can, Mery,' she smiled, 'but it's sleep only. And for the last time.'

My great escape

Kirkuk, October 1986

Dear Mr Clint Eastwood,

There is now absolutely no doubt that I am a young man! So far I have made love to Papula and Yasmin. Luckily for me, two beautiful women, but nonetheless one was my auntie and the other one an Arab prostitute. That is what comes of living in a culture where sex outside of marriage is forbidden. I have now committed every possible sin except for killing, and I am still struggling with my religion. I just cannot accept that God does not exist.

I am convinced that if Sunshine and I made love her family would not kill her for losing her virginity. Not that I ever want this to happen, because I am soon going to be on my way to America. I asked Godfather if I could depart earlier but he thinks that, as long as I have the money, I will go in the next three weeks. I can't wait to get there and start working as an actor in the film industry. The idea of putting a foot inside one of the Hollywood Studios makes me shiver. MGM! Paramount! Universal! Columbia Pictures! Walt Disney... these names have brightened my daytime dreams. I'm sure you know them all very well, but for me the idea that I could soon be walking through Beverly Hills and, with a bit of luck perhaps, one day walking by your side along the red carpet into the Academy Awards ceremony.

I promise, the first money I earn, I will spend on buying a new leg for Rabbit. He keeps advising me to get out of the country because life has become impossible here, and he is perfectly right: every day is lived as if it may be the last.

Away from Sunshine and Jam's shop, I spend most of my time watching films at Papula's place. We have seen Steven Spielberg's fabulous *E.T.* We were intrigued by Stephen Frears' *My Beautiful Laundrette,* especially the lovemaking scene between Daniel

Day-Lewis and Gordon Warnecke. Flathead can't have known about the film's contents when he bought it on the black market. Papula and I disagreed about *Passion*, Godard's exploration of the nature of work and his love of filmmaking. I found it an interesting depiction of the filmmaker's world, but Papula thought it too slow and rather boring. When I saw *Soldier Blue*, my heart was broken and I believed that your people treated the Native Americans atrociously. They suffered terrible injustices, just as my people and I are suffering now at the hands of the occupying powers in our land. Unfortunately we did not manage to finish watching Fellini's *8½* because the video player broke. But I loved this quote from Marcello Mastroianni: 'Accept me as I am, only then can we discover each other'.

You may wonder how I remember all the film titles, the directors' names and the lead actors. That's easy: from very early on I made notes about every film I watched, including television series. I keep the information with your portraits in my treasure box. There are so many other films I would love to tell you about, but I don't think I can fit them all into this letter.

I don't know the exact time and the date of my arrival, but I think I will most probably land in Washington DC, because I will be travelling as the son of a diplomat who works at the Iraqi Embassy in the United States. Immediately upon my arrival I shall ask for your phone number and call you. I am sure it won't be hard to find it. You are very famous.

Wish me good luck, my Gringo. This is my great escape.

As always I end by thanking you from my heart.

Mery Rashaba

Write your story as if it were a film

When I went out again into town to post the letter to Gringo, I was wearing my boyish clothes and I kept my hair hidden under my hat. Although I was inconspicuous and should have been able to pass unnoticed, even small sounds seemed to startle me. Everywhere, I saw the monster's men in uniforms, police, militia and Special Forces, and I suspected Mukhabarat in everyone I passed. I wished that I could almost disappear, like Claude Rains in *The Invisible Man*.

At the post office, I was pleased to see Purtuqal, the Arab employee. As always, he was friendly to me and smiled. I paid and waited until he dropped my letter in the basket, telling me as he did so his good news. His son had obtained his aeronautic degree and was soon to fly an aircraft. I congratulated him and left. I went to the Hamra Cinema. They were showing *Dog Day Afternoon* with Al Pacino. I bought a ticket and walked over to the usher. At first the Cyclops routinely tore the ticket, but then he grabbed my arm and pulled me back to face him. He took off my hat.

'Hey, don't. I am a dervish...'

'Merywan Rashaba?' he interrupted me. There was nothing strange about him knowing my name. He must have seen me hundreds of times, and like the ushers in all the other cinemas, he knew me well. He handed me back the split half of my ticket and pointed to the exit. I did not understand, so I looked towards the exit, but I could see nothing unusual. 'What is it?' I asked. 'Out,' he responded, with his usual curtness, 'you are not allowed in this cinema again. And don't ask why!'

I headed to the Alamen Cinema. I was stopped and refused again. The same thing happened at the Atlas and at Khayam. Finally at the Salahadin Cinema I found out what by now I suspected. I was banned from going to all the cinemas. I asked who had imposed the ban, but the usher shook his head silently.

What is going on? Who is so determined to take away the greatest joy of my life? I decided to go to Jam and tell him that I feared my life was in danger.

Jam was painting in the back room when I arrived. I glanced over his shoulder at the portrait and did not recognise it. 'My father,' Jam said, pointing to the picture. 'He was a real patriot.'

'I am banned from going to the cinema. I have been to every cinema and the result was the same.'

'Then stay away from the cinemas.'

'I can't. Life means nothing to me without cinema.'

'You exaggerate.'

'No I don't. It is thanks to films and my heroes that I am still alive. Jam, do you mind if I ask you a personal question?'

'Of course not. Go ahead.'

'Are you a member of any underground organisations?'

Jam stopped working and turned to me. 'Don't ask me that again. This is what the Mukhabarat wants to know, and if you are a member, you are supposed to keep it secret until death.' I apologised, but Jam noticed my uneasiness. 'Why this unusual question?' he asked, and carried on working.

'You should stay away from me. If you are a member, I don't want to endanger your life. I sometimes feel like I am being followed and could be taken away at any moment.'

'Thanks for your concern, I appreciate it and think it's very wise to stay alert, but the fact is, that unless you work for the Mukhabarat, you are followed. Even people who work for the government may be vulnerable. We are all pushing our luck.'

'I have always been unlucky.' The cinema ban had shocked me and made me feel very negative about my situation. In moments like this it was easy to overlook my blessings, one of which had been meeting Jam himself.

'Listen, soon you will be flying out to America, and that should not be underestimated,' he said, raising one eyebrow. 'Where will you get the money from to pay Godfather?'

'I can't tell you yet.'

'Mery, I must know. We cannot afford to risk anyone's life if this plan is unrealistic.'

'I will take it from my father.'

'Wow! That is a great deal of money.'

'He has spent his life saving it to buy us a house.'

'He can't buy a house in Kirkuk, not unless he is an Arab.'

'I know, but he wants to change our ethnicity from Kurd to Arab. He doesn't care.'

'That would be stealing. You shouldn't do it. He could have a heart attack from losing his life savings.'

'What other choice do I have? Anyway, I don't consider it stealing, but only borrowing, because when I get to America I will work hard to make lots of money so that I can pay him back three times over. And buy a new leg for Rabbit.'

'You care a lot about Rabbit.'

'I let him down badly. I need to do something special for him. I will help him out and together we will travel all over America.'

'That sounds very nice.'

'Especially if you join us too.'

I flicked through the books on his shelves and picked up one.

'*Oedipus Rex,* by Sophocles,' I read in a loud voice.

'Have you read it?'

'No.'

'It is a Greek tragedy. You should know it if you want to make films.'

'Has it been made into a film?'

'Yes, and there are different versions. My favourite is Pasolini's *Oedipus Rex.*'

'What is it about?'

'A man is destined to become the king. By doing so, he ends up marrying his own mother.'

'He makes love to his mother?'

'Yes, and the rest you should read.'

I placed the book back on the shelf. 'I don't have the mind for reading at the moment,' I said, and sat down on the chair and looked up at the ceiling. A spider was busy making its web. *How lucky, the tiny creature does not have to worry about the monster and his men.* 'I wonder why I was born as a human and not a spider?'

'You could be one if you get to play Spiderman.'

'Jam, this is really bizarre, isn't it, to be banned from the cinema?

Do you think this has something to do with Abu Ali?'

'If Abu Ali is after you, you would not live to see tomorrow. I think it's more likely to be someone from your family, perhaps your father, or your brother.'

Trouble! Of course. Who else could it be but my own brother? He knows how much I love watching films. He has not forgiven me for calling him a traitor, and his spying for Rashaba was not sufficient revenge. He knows all the ushers very well, and his Jash identity would give him enough authority to threaten the ushers with all sorts if they did not please him by preventing me going into the cinemas.

'Jam! I think you are right, it could be my brother. I will do as you suggest then, since nothing else can be done, and stay away from the cinemas, even though it's heartbreaking for me to abandon my magic world. As long as I can get out and go to America.'

Jam turned around again, searched through some boxes and picked out a brown leather bag. 'Here, have this,' he said, handing me the bag.

'What is it?'

'A notebook and a Super 8 cine camera. I bought it in London but have never used it, and I doubt I ever will.'

I opened the bag and took out the cine camera. It was a Canon, still sealed in plastic with a little sac of silica salts. I had never seen one before. 'This is too precious,' I said.

'It is yours.'

'Why me?'

'You want to make films? Well, here is your chance.'

'What is the notebook for?'

'You first need to write your story.'

'I don't know how to write a story.'

'Write your story as if it were a film.'

Long before the end of his normal working day, Jam put down his paint brushes and decided to close the shop. He asked me to go with him, and when we got into his car, I thought we might be going to see Godfather. It turned out he wanted to introduce me to an artist friend. I was holding on to the bag in my lap and was already thinking about the story for the first film I would shoot with the Super 8.

'Keep the cine camera in a safe place and out of sight, especially from the monster's men. They won't like it,' Jam said.

'Nor my father,' I added.

He drove on to Atlas Street and then, halfway along, he turned off to the right. He skirted around the block and through narrow, dusty alleyways, eventually coming to a halt in a dead-end space behind a huge building. It was deserted, but he asked me to stay in the car. He walked to a door in a long, high wall, and tapped on it three times. It was clear that the door was not used very often. A man of around his age opened it. He embraced Jam and kissed him on both cheeks, as good friends do. I assumed he was the artist. The friend looked over at me, so I knew I was the subject of their discussion. His friend seemed troubled by something, but Jam appeared to be insisting. He gestured for me to get out. When I did, I saw the friend glancing left and right in case we were being watched. *We must be doing something illegal here.*

'Samir, my dear friend,' Jam introduced us.

We shook hands, but Samir looked at me suspiciously. 'Come in. It's better if we don't stay out here too long,' he said, moving aside for us to pass. He locked the door. 'I have an Arab mother and a Kurdish father,' he explained, as he strode ahead up a couple of dozen stairs lit by a dusty light bulb, 'I have in me Shiite blood, Sunni blood, Christians, Turkman, even Jewish, Armenian and some Persian. If I go back further, no doubt I'm part Babylonian, too, and most probably one of my great-grandmothers was fucked by Alexander the Great. I am a real fucking mix, so what does that make me, Merywan?' He stopped and faced me.

'An artist.' What else could I say?

'Yes, an artist,' and he started to climb the stairs again. 'An Iraqi artist who wants to have nothing to do with the shit out there!' he gestured, 'and who is content to be nothing but a fucking Iraqi, and to be here between these walls. An artist who definitely does not want to have any complications. Do you understand, Merywan?' He stopped again to face me. He was obviously shit-scared to have me there. I did not feel at ease, and turned to Jam for reassurance.

'Samir wants to know if you can keep a secret?' Jam asked.

'I can. I swear on my heart,' I answered, putting my hand on my heart.

'Fine,' Samir said, and moved on. We came to a landing. On the wall I saw a large poster of my favourite film, *The Good, the Bad and the Ugly*, exactly like the one I kept in my treasure box. It was not hard to guess where we were and why Jam had brought me to this dark place.

There were more posters on the walls as Samir turned a corner and opened the door to my kind of heaven , the projection room. The reels spun on the magic machine that fed the strip of celluloid past the shimmering light, bringing its frozen images to life.

'This is my peaceful paradise,' Samir said, proudly. 'I feel best in here, apart from when the fucking power cuts off and turns it into a pitch-dark hell hole. But today we are lucky, we have light and Merywan, a new friend.' Samir said, talking to the projection machine and patting it gently, as if talking to his love.

Once we entered his hideaway he relaxed with an easy smile, which reminded me of Norman Wisdom, the British comedian, so I promptly nicknamed him 'Norman'.

'Merywan. Here, have a look!' Norman called, pointing to one of the rectangular holes in the wall. For the first time I saw the big screen from the projection room. 'Ah, *The Lost World*. I love this film,' I said.

Turning around to thank Norman, some figures behind him caught my eye, hideous, mutilated human torsos stacked along a shelf on the back wall. They were so authentic that I had to suppress a scream. One had half its face cut off, and the inside of its head was clearly visible. Another one's belly was open, with its guts hanging out. There was a woman with one breast and an open chest and a man badly burned from head to toe. They reminded me of the victims in *The Texas Chainsaw Massacre*, and were truly horrible to look at.

'These anatomic sculptures are Samir's work,' Jam said. 'He is a talented sculptor.'

'I thought they were real.'

'They are made of resin. I make them up.' Norman said, blowing some dust away from the burned man's face. 'You don't have to fear them, they are good company. When you make your films, and if you need someone to help you with creating fucked-up and blown-up bodies, people covered in blood and scars, that's me. I would love to work in the film world. You can come here anytime you want, but it must remain a total secret,' Norman added, anxiously.

'I won't tell anyone, I promise,' I answered.

'OK. Stay and watch the rest of the film, it has a happy ending.'

'I have seen it many times, thanks. I need to talk to Jam.'

'Yes, and I need to give Jam some more soundtracks.' Norman picked up a handful of music cassettes and handed them over to him.

'So this is where you get your music from?' I asked.

'Yes, thanks to Samir,' Jam said, taking the tapes and leaving a few blank cassettes in their place.

'When you come here,' Norman explained, on our way out, 'you knock three times. If I don't open, you must leave, and if someone else answers, you must pretend to be an apprentice from the kebab house. Can you do that, Merywan?'

'Yes, he can,' Jam answered for me. 'Merywan is an excellent actor.'

Once back in the car I immediately asked Jam if he trusted Norman.

'What are you worried about?'

'Paedophiles and monster's men.'

'Samir is not one or the other, and you can trust him as much as you trust me. If you ever need help and I am not around, you can turn to him.'

'I always wanted to work in a cinema, but could never dream of doing it because of my father. Thanks to you, Jam, today I got a cine camera and got to go inside a projection room. I can't tell you how grateful I am.'

'Hopefully it won't be too long before you're on a film set. For now though, do you want a lift back home, or do you want to go to see your princess Yasmin?'

'Home please. I want to go and see Sunshine.'

The last ride

My first filming had to be done secretly, but it wasn't a bad start. Rabbit opened the door to their house. I couldn't believe my eyes, as he had cut his candyfloss hair very short. He was not in the mood for talking about his new look.

'I liked your long hair, but you look good with it short, too,' I said, as I walked in. Rabbit stayed behind, checking to see if I was followed.

'Hey Rabbit, I've been banned from going to the cinema.'

'What, all of them?'

'Every one. Does that surprise you?'

'Not really. I sometimes wonder how much longer you will live.'

'Don't worry, Brader, I will not die in your arms.'

As if in a rehearsal room, alone on the rooftop, Sunshine was practising lines from *Romeo and Juliet*. This was the perfect opportunity for me to test my cine camera. I pointed it at her and with a wondrous feeling I started to film Sunshine. When finally she saw me, she stood still. She opened her arms and called, 'Mery, has the wind carried you to me, or is it going to take you away?' and she gave me an exaggerated bow. I turned off the machine and applauded.

'Can we watch your film?' she asked, eagerly.

'I wish we could. Sorry, but there's no film in the camera and no film stock available in Kirkuk.'

'An imaginary world in an imaginary film.'

'I was just practising, but you looked great. Could I leave my notebook and my camera with you? I don't want them at home. I am worried about my father.'

Sunshine agreed at once. I unbuttoned my shirt and unwrapped Aida's pale blue scarf that I secretly kept around my waist. I was going to put it in the bag, when Sunshine took hold of it. 'Oh, that's pretty,' she said. 'My favourite colours,' I answered, and wrapped the notebook in the scarf and put them in the bag with the camera. I wanted to do something special for Sunshine, something different, like happy lovers might do in a film, and the best I could come up with was to take her for a ride on an Arabanchi, an ancient Ottoman Empire-era horse-drawn carriage, one of which was still in use in Kirkuk.

It was an early autumn afternoon and the sky was a deep blue ocean, like Persian lapis lazuli. Sunshine and I sat at the back under the black leather cover. The horseman used the whip on the horse very occasionally, but mostly it was for whipping the children who hung on to his carriage to get a free ride. Two kids of around seven played the drum and sang. It was a joy to watch them performing so amusingly, at least until they stopped halfway through a song. Our time had run out for the few cents I had paid them. They jumped down, while the carriage kept going.

'That was very nice, thank you, Mery,' Sunshine said, as she waved to the two boys. Without their music, the sound of the horse's hooves seemed so much louder, clacking on the road and echoing off the walls. *How little it takes to be happy, to be so close to Sunshine, feeling the warmth of her body, and to see her so full of joy, there is nothing else I could desire, except, of course, to go to America.*

On the old bridge we came across Uncle Hitch. I called to him and he ran along and jumped into the carriage, instantly snapping Sunshine and myself. 'Glad to see you, smiling beautiful girl,' he said. 'Life is shining when you smile. You should smile too, Merywan. I have a job for you. I need an assistant for the four days of Eid. The money is not much but enough to buy you a few more cinema tickets.'

'I can't go to cinema any more, I have been banned.'

'Whatever next! But still, will you accept my offer?'

'I have a plan,' I said, suddenly excited. 'Can you imagine a girl photographer?' I asked Uncle Hitch.

'I don't understand,' he answered, 'but I like it. Go on.'

'I would like Sunshine to be involved. What do you say?' I asked her.

'I would love to.'

'I can just see how it will all work out.'

'Get to the point.' Sunshine was intrigued.

'I am in.' Uncle Hitch clasped my hand.

'But Mery has not told us what the plan is yet,' Sunshine said.

'Mery comes up with crazy but fantastic ideas and I am sure this one is going to be good too,' Uncle Hitch answered.

'We must go and see Jam at once,' I suggested.

We stopped the carriage outside the shop and went inside. Jam was at his desk.

'OK, here is my idea,' I said. 'Sunshine and I are going to work for Uncle Hitch. Jam could paint life-size film heroes, leaving a hole where the face should be, and we will take photos of people posing through these pictures. I am sure it will work, and could be fun too. Uncle Hitch will provide the cameras for us, make some money, and so will you too, Jam, as I know business isn't as good as it used to be. What do you say?'

'Artistically, it's maybe not so rewarding,' Jam said with a grin, 'but still, I am in. I think it could work.'

'Well, we shouldn't waste any time,' Uncle Hitch said. 'It is already the second week of Ramadan,' and he snapped a shot of Sunshine standing between Jam and myself.

We went out to search for a location for our new enterprise. The first site we considered was the roundabout at the end of Al Alamen Street, but then realised the area had become a prohibited zone because of the presence of the Mukhabarat, the police station and a militia centre... After looking at several other potential pitches, we agreed to set up our base at the west end of the old bridge. It was just the right position, very crowded, and we had the ever-present citadel as the ideal background.

A few days later we displayed Jam's life-sized figures. At my request, the first one was of my Gringo. It did not take long for the crowd to gather around and soon we had our first customers. It was an immediate success and Sunshine, working as a woman photographer, was the highlight. Many young men had their pictures taken only to flatter her, asking her how could she do this job, whether her parents were from Europe, as Kurds would never allow their daughters to be so free, and if she had a boyfriend? She was very friendly and enjoyed the repartee.

It cost one hundred cents for each photo, not that affordable for most people, but the novelty of posing as one of their heroes was just too tempting. They also had a great laugh at their friends and families – Kurds, Turkman, Christians and Arabs of all shapes and sizes, as they became transformed into Gringo, Superman, King Kong, Tarzan and Hercules. At the end of the day we had made a lot of money. Uncle Hitch generously shared all the profits among the four of us and we packed the life-sized pictures into Jam's car.

As Sunshine and I walked home over the bridge, I pointed towards Qala. 'That house was my grandfather's.'

'Don't point,' she said, lowering my hand. 'You know that is not allowed. The monster's men could suspect you of something.'

'I wish I could have filmed some of the people posing behind the posters with my cine camera.'

'You don't have film in the camera and filming in the open is forbidden.'

Over the following days we had many familiar faces posing. The first was Master Shamal, then there were Jwana, Peaceful and Rabbit, Dr Hakan and Papula (the visit of whom I had to arrange, and I had to cover for her to be able to come out), my mother and Star, Trouble and Norman, the projectionist and even Cyclops, the usher. We were complimented by most, except for Rashaba, who adamantly refused to pose but happily took most of my wages. Uncle Hitch made a rule that we should take an extra shot of family and friends for nothing. I wanted to exclude Trouble from this generous offer, as he was behind the selfish cinema ban on me, but I was worried he might ban me from being a photographer, too.

Soon after I had taken Norman's photo, and to my joy, had got him to agree to allow Sunshine into the projection room sometimes, we had a nasty surprise. Suddenly, the throng moved aside, leaving Uncle Hitch, Sunshine and myself alone in front of three armed Mukhabarat men. Two of them stood guard as the third walked from left to right examining the posters. He turned to Uncle Hitch and then to me. He gave us an abrupt fake smile, exposing his yellow teeth, as he nodded his head. I was relieved he had left out Sunshine. With our cameras hanging around our necks, we were escorted to a four-wheel-drive white Toyota parked on the roadside. The engine was running. I recognised it as Abu Ali's. The third Mukhabarat jumped into the passenger seat and the others gestured to Uncle

Hitch and me to get into the back. *Finally, my day has come, Gringo.* The two sat at the end, leaving the back doors open and pointing their guns at the street. The car drove away and the last thing I could see, amongst a crowd of faces, was Sunshine's alarmed face watching us disappear.

I was sure that Uncle Hitch, sitting in the back of a Mukhabarat car, considered the ride to be his last, as did I. We kept silent. The two at the back signalled to cars behind us with their guns, warning them not to overtake. They drove us towards Republic Street. *This is not the way to the last station, Mukhabarat's Headquarters.* My heart sank. *They are on their way to pick up Jam from his shop.* We passed Hamra Cinema, not turning left at the crossroad towards Jam's shop, but straight on all the way to Arafa. *Is Abu Ali waiting for me in Aida's house?*

Looking into the distance, I could see the ever-burning flames of Babagurgur in the middle of the oilfields. The flames that symbolised our hope of freedom. While they continued to burn, our hopes were alive, but sitting in the back of Abu Ali's car, it was only a very faint hope indeed.

We did not go to Aida's house but turned up a side road heading towards open parkland, which was only found in pockets in this part of Kirkuk. Soon after we passed the spot in the park where Aida and I had our first kiss, the road rose up a hill darkened by dense thickets of tall pine trees. We came to a checkpoint, but were let through immediately.

From there on we could see no other cars, except those belonging to the monster's men. I spotted a few army posts along the road, *so we must be going to a secret place*. We came to another checkpoint at a gate surrounded by an electrified barbed-wire fence at least three metres high. The guards raised the barrier. Through the trees I could see an imposing three-storey building that was very different from the average buildings around Kirkuk. Built out of red brick, with a dozen large windows arranged either side of wide central doors, it overlooked a paved terrace surrounded by gardens with exotic plants, and fountains. Peacocks were running around freely and, for a moment, I wished I could change places with them.

We were escorted along a spotless pathway. I could not believe that such luxury and elegance existed in my city. Under any other circumstances I would have loved to visit this place, which had once been enjoyed by the English people who owned our oilfields, but was now used by Saddam's elite. As we passed two armed guards at the main door, I realised that the building made me think of the German mansion in *The Dirty Dozen*.

There were opulent chandeliers, illuminated multicoloured marble tiles, polished tables and chairs that glinted with golden inlay work and expensive-looking leather sofas. Finally, when we reached the back of the house, two bikini-clad girls were walking together, laughing. *I must be daydreaming again.*

We were led to the side of an open-air swimming pool. Young women in bikinis splashed about or lay on sun loungers. A few children ran around too; others were playing and swimming. For the first time it occurred to me that the monster's men were also humans, fathers with families. *How can they inflict so much horror on the lives of innocents when they have children of their own?* A band under a canopy was playing Arabic pop music to entertain Iraqi Muslims who were celebrating Ramadan by sunbathing, drinking alcoholic cocktails and kissing foreign girls. *So this is how some Muslims celebrate our religion's most sacred month of fasting and praying?*

A scar-faced, ugly Arab, dressed only in swimming shorts and holding a cocktail glass, saw us standing there with the third Mukhabarat. He left his two girls and came towards us. Much to our amazement, he informed us that these were important friends visiting him to help him celebrate his promotion to be the head of Mukhabarat in Kirkuk, and he wanted us to take some nice shots. He invited us to help ourselves to drinks and food and to make ourselves feel at home.

Flabbergasted and deeply relieved, I relaxed momentarily, until I spotted Abu Ali among his guests. He too was in shorts, surrounded by semi-naked girls, drinking alcohol, grinning happily. *How can he be such a leech, to sell the blood of his countrymen, and enjoy the life of a king, even as his own people outside are butchered? This is it, the place where heaven and hell meet.*

Abu Ali seemed unaware of my presence, but nothing could have made me relax and trust that I was safe among those vile men.

'Ask before you take any photos,' Uncle Hitch whispered, wide-eyed, barely able to speak. 'Smile and thank them, even if they don't answer you.'

'I am thirsty, can I take a drink?'

'Don't Merywan, let's finish our job and get out of here. We are playing with fire.'

'Who are these girls?' I had to ask. I had never seen women like them in the flesh.

'Russians, Egyptians, Cubans, Filipinas and, please, no more questions. Put a new twenty-four film in your camera and let's start.' I slowly approached the first two men, who were with three girls. I smiled and nodded. I pointed at the camera. 'May I take your photo, sir?' I asked in Arabic, in the politest manner. The men posed with their arms around the girls, clinking their cocktails. I took a few shots and thanked them for their permission. Uncle Hitch, on the other side, was busy taking more pictures. I would have liked to be closer to him and was doing everything to stay as far as I could from Abu Ali. I took a few more shots of Arabs and their pet girls. Wearing my hat under the baking sun, I could feel sweat rolling down my face, but it was mostly from the tension. I observed the swimmers and wished I could dive in too. Uncle Hitch was having a hard time with a big-bellied, drunken Arab who threw a bottle at him as he approached them to take their photos. Half a dozen waiters glided around, always available with trays of vividly coloured drinks and a dazzling variety of food, like being at a party in Monte Carlo. I could not resist and stopped one of the waiters. 'Water, please?' I asked. She handed me a crystal glass with ice and water and slices of lemon. I was about to take a sip when a Mukhabarat in shorts took the glass from my hand, drained it in one gulp, and motioned me to follow.

He led me exactly where I did not want to go. Abu Ali with his girls and friends posed. I lifted the camera and adjusted the focus. I was about to click the shutter when on his lips I read, 'I will get you, Mery!'

My hands started to shake. I tried to gain time by pretending I needed to adjust the focus again but just could not keep still. 'I am sorry, I have run out of film. I will be back soon,' I said, and walked across to where Uncle Hitch was working. 'Can we change sides, please?' I asked. 'Don't ask me why.' Uncle Hitch went to Abu Ali's group. I was watching anxiously to see how Abu Ali would react. He did not make any fuss and gladly posed for Uncle Hitch. *Did he really say those words or is it my over-active imagination again, my deep fear of Abu Ali, playing tricks with my mind?* There was a sudden outburst from the scarred face of the Ugly Arab. The music stopped and everything went silent. The waiters froze in their places, people in the pool swam to the side, and we put our cameras down. All the attention was on him as he called for a blonde girl, Russian presumably, to come closer. The girl was petrified; whatever she had done was unforgivable. 'You spilled my drink onto my slippers,' the Ugly Arab said. He laughed and his guests echoed him loyally. The girl facing him was slowly stepping backwards. 'Come here,' he roared at her. 'I am sorry, sir. It was an accident. I'll get you another drink,' she said, but her lips puckered from fear. 'Lick my slippers,' he barked, gruffly. 'Sir,' she said, and she must have wanted to add something, but the Ugly Arab took out his revolver. The girl crawled to him, bent her head down and licked his slippers. He laughed more, and the guests followed suit again. The girl looked up, surely believing that this abasement was enough, but her expression was desperate, horrified. The Ugly Arab grunted, he aimed the gun at her head, but then changed his mind and shot in the air. 'Music,' he called. The party started again.

Before leaving, the third Mukhabarat gave us fifty dinars, a huge sum of money, and took away all the films we had shot. 'You have seen nothing and heard nothing,' he threatened us. 'I suggest you forget about this visit.' We were left outside the forbidden zone in shock, and made our way back.

When Jam saw us he breathed a deep sigh of relief. He gestured to the back room. I found Sunshine there alone, leaning against the wall. She appeared so distraught that she did not notice me walk in.

'Sunshine!' I called.

'Mery!' she said, and ran to hug me, for the very first time.

'Please don't ask, I had to take some photos and that is all I am allowed to say.' I dried the tears on her face. She slipped her hand into mine and we walked into the front of the shop. Uncle Hitch paid everyone, much more than we had made on any other day. 'Mery, don't forget your share,' Uncle Hitch said.

'I don't want it, thanks.'

'Why not?' Jam asked.

'It is dirty money made out of innocent people's blood,' I answered, irritated. Jam put his share back, followed by Sunshine. Uncle Hitch picked up the dinars from the table. 'I understand,' he said. 'I will give it to the war orphans.'

Sunshine was still holding on to my hand. 'Can we go to the cinema?' I asked, as we left Jam's shop.

'You are banned,' she answered.

'Ah, but I have access to a private viewing room.'

I explained to Sunshine that we had to enter the building very discreetly and that she must not tell anyone about my private viewing room, absolutely no one, including Rabbit. I also warned her about the disfigured bodies, but to my surprise, once inside she evidently found them amazing and did not hesitate to touch them. She complimented Norman on his artistic skill. Norman was happy to have us in to the projection room, where we watched *Fitzcarraldo*, but he only had one chair for Sunshine to sit on. I stood behind her, though I couldn't see very well. Sunshine got up and asked me to sit.

'What about you?'

'Please just sit,' she said. I did and she sat on my lap. I was embarrassed, I turned to Norman. He winked at me. 'I shall leave you for a few minutes,' he said and walked out. Sunshine stood up again, turned and sat on my lap facing me. She took off my hat, letting my hair fall down my shoulders. 'I love your hair,' and she touched it.

'I love yours,' I said.

'OK, now listen, Mister. You go to America, I don't mind. I will wait for you, as long as you promise you will not forget me and that I will see you again.'

Just like Aida and I had once promised not to forget each other.

'I am not coming back. Not until we have our own country.'

'In that case, send for me and I will join you.'

'Do you mean it?'

'Yes, I swear on my heart,' she said, putting my hand on her heart.

I was a bit shy because I felt her breast in my hand. 'And I would like to kiss you, Mery Rashaba!'

'What are you waiting for?' We kissed for a long time.

Norman came back in. We stopped kissing.

'Glad to see you are enjoying the film,' he said and smiled, before adding kindly, 'As if I wasn't here.' We kissed again.

The death of another princess

Flathead's gun is still loaded, Gringo, and I am holding it to my chest. I swear on my heart, on my love for Sunshine, I will kill Abu Ali or anyone who lays a hand on her. I would rather die than let her down as I had let Aida down. I put the gun back in the box and went to sit next to Papula in the living room, where she was watching TV. I gave her a tender kiss on her cheek.

Saddam owned ninety-five per cent of the television stations. As I watched one of them showing footage of him gracing another neighbourhood with his presence, I remembered one of Flathead's jokes and laughed. Papula turned to me, she wanted me to share the moment.

'The rumours are that many families have put a poster of Saddam on their television screen. That way they do not have to switch on the TV and save electricity. Saddam, trying to portray a popular image, pays a visit to a family. As you know, he generally goes for the kids, to terrify them from an early age, so he bends down and puts his arm around a five-year-old child. The child's parents stand aside, wanting the earth to open rather than be in the presence of Saddam. They watch the president and their son chatting. "Do you know me?" Saddam asks the little boy, with his false smile, trying to show himself the sweet father of the nation. The boy studies Saddam's face. "Yes," he answers, confidently, "each time you appear on our television, my father spits on your face."' The Iraqi news never mentioned the thousands of families forced at gunpoint to leave their homes in areas that the government wanted to Arabise. It did not acknowledge the hundreds of political arrests taking place every day, or that the war against Iran, now entering its sixth year, was destroying the country's economy and had long ago reached a stalemate. Also the city's walls were covered with the black placards that represented martyrs, soldiers killed on the front line. When Saddam started the war, in his stupidity, he believed it would be over in a matter of months, but the kick he had given the Iranian Mullahs got stuck in their behinds, and he did not know how to get his foot out.

'I wonder if I will live to see the end of Saddam,' I said.

'He has seven souls,' Papula sighed. 'He will never die.' She wasn't alone in this belief, as most had convinced themselves that Saddam was indestructible.

'Hitler died,' I said.

'Yes, but not our evil Hitler.'

'Is Hakan coming tonight?'

'No. Soon it is Eid, your uncle may come home anytime. How is Sunshine?'

'She is great, my princess. We kissed.'

'I knew it, I knew you two would end up together. Oh Mery, I am so pleased for you.'

In the past, she might have embraced me but now she kept her distance, which was better for both of us. I left Papula and went out to Takya for Laylat Al Qadr, the 'Night of Power', the night on which Prophet Muhammad received the first revelation from Allah. This is the night when Muslims all around the world stay awake to pray, to ask for forgiveness. That was exactly what I was going to do, to cleanse myself. *I want to go back to being a faithful Muslim and, even if I go to America and work in films, I will still keep my faith.* I had read in the Qur'an that Allah forgave his last messenger's followers if they repented on this holy night.

I sat next to Father and read from the Qur'an. I played the drum and danced with the dervishes. I prayed the entire night. I begged Allah to help Papula escape safely, to give guidance to Trouble and for Hercules to find a nice wife. To help Flathead give up drinking, for Jam to fall in love again and stop going to prostitutes. I prayed for Popcorn, Uncle Hitch, Master Shamal and his family, especially my love, Sunshine, and for Rabbit to accept that love. I begged Allah to protect Sunshine and keep her away from the hands of the likes of Abu Ali. Finally I prayed for good news from Godfather.

I had never fasted during Ramadan before, only pretended for Rashaba's sake. According to Jam, I could damage my health by not drinking any liquid from sunrise to sunset while living in a country where the temperature often reached 45 degrees. *I can not understand the benefit of this practice of fasting in my religion, but I am not going to question it. No matter how harmful it is to not eat and drink from dawn till dusk for thirty days, as a good Muslim I am going to fast, and not masturbate ever again, or look at Sunshine with sexual desire.* In Islam, desiring sex is forbidden.

Women are considered 'tilth' and men are allowed to visit them when they wish to reproduce, but only once they are married.

Sunshine was having breakfast. At her house no one was fasting, they were all carefree infidels. But I had to close my eyes to this because I loved Master Shamal's family and it was not for me to judge them, but for Allah. They were truly surprised when I refused to eat or even drink a cup of tea.

Once alone, I gave Sunshine the pile of paper I had taken out of my treasure box earlier.

'What are they?' she asked.

'Copies of all the letters I have sent to Gringo. I want you to read them because you should know about my life up to this point. I wish to keep no secrets from you. But I must have your absolute promise that no one else will ever read them.'

'I promise.'

'When you finish, you can keep them in my bag with my notebook and my cine camera.'

'Yes, sir!' She saluted me.

'Please, this is serious.'

'No problem.'

I made it clear that I did not want to kiss her, to hold her hands or to touch her again until we were married.

'We will need to get married immediately then,' she said. 'How can I live without feeling your lips? I want to kiss you all over right now.'

'Please, I am fasting and these sinful words could tempt me. Do you have a scarf to cover your hair?'

'Have you gone mad, Mery? If you think this is funny, I don't.'

'I am not trying to be funny. I am now a true Muslim and should have a wife who obeys Islam's Sharia law and her husband.'

'I think we should postpone the wedding,' Sunshine stated, evidently concerned about my new-found religious fervour.

Jam turned up at the photography site bearing bad news. 'I have seen Godfather. You won't like it, Mery. Further delays, only a matter of a few more weeks. With a bit of luck, you should be leaving before the New Year.'

I spent the rest of the day feeling very grumpy. Sunshine tried her best to cheer me up.

'I really appreciate Norman's projection room, but what about all the other films?' I complained. 'In Hamra Cinema they are showing a new one starring Gringo that I am dying to see, and now this shit news, more and more delays before my escape to America.'

'I have an idea,' Sunshine grinned, 'but first I want one of your smiles. That won't affect your fasting. C'mon Mery, you can do it!' *God forgive me!* We asked Uncle Hitch for a few hours off work. We went to Jam's shop and changed in the back room. Sunshine put on my clothes, my first ever suit, which I had bought second-hand with my photography money, and I wore her pretty new dress. I was worried that we may be watched and risked discovery, but Sunshine thought otherwise. For her, with our radical new looks, and as long as we used Jam's back door to go in and out, we had nothing to fear.

Sunshine, a young man with a hat and a moustache that we bought from a toy shop, and I, a girl, wearing high heels, sunglasses and red lipstick, audaciously went to the cinema. With our cunning disguises we bypassed the Cyclops without any problems. I was delighted when we got in to the Hamra Cinema, for our first film, *Honkytonk Man*. I loved the relationship between Gringo and his nephew and did not realise that the actor playing him, Kyle Eastwood, was actually his son in real life, until later in the day when I added the information to my film notes. Gringo's character was very powerful. A man battling against time. Once again he had somehow given me the strength to persevere.

We also went to see Agatha Christie's *Ten Little Indians*. In the past I had seen it as one of the best murder mystery plots in film, but in that last viewing, it also made me think about my life. I saw myself as one of the characters, except the mystery of my life was not really ready to unfold… yet. Over the coming days, we saw a few more films in our disguises. The minute the screenings ended I wanted to watch them all over again. I could never tire of my filmic fix.

I had written most of the above in my last letter to Gringo, congratulating his son for his great talent and for having Clint Eastwood as his wonderful father, and not someone like Rashaba. I also told Gringo that this was to be my last letter because Jam was alarmed when he learnt recently that I was writing to him. According to Jam, I should not have trusted Purtuqal, the friendly Arab postman, or indeed anyone, with letters to Gringo. I could not comprehend Jam's concerns about this. *If the Mukhabarat had got their hands on my letters, I would have been dead and buried long ago.*

A couple of days after the end of the festivities, when the time came for Flathead to go back to work, I had my last dinner with them. The atmosphere was different, similar to the time when Papula had first arrived as a new bride. Flathead was very nice to her. He had bought kebabs, 7 Up and baklava, Papula's favourites. Over dinner, he told us several jokes and made us laugh. *I feel sorry for Flathead as this is the last meal he is going to share with his wife.* I was going to leave them alone in the hope that they might spend one final night together, but Flathead got up from the table first. He had to go and see his boss to make sure the cargo was loaded, because the next day, he was going to leave early.

The minute he walked out and shut the door, Papula gave me her news. 'Hakan has sorted everything out and we are leaving for Turkey in five days.' She was elated. 'Remember Mery, your promise, you will come to visit me in Istanbul, won't you?'

'Of course I will.'

'You must come with Sunshine. Oh, Mery, it is going to be so wonderful, we will visit Hagia Sophia and take the boat to travel on the Marmara Sea through the Bosphorus Strait, and under the suspension bridge that connects Europe to Asia, all the way to the Black Sea.'

'As this is your last night together, try to be kind to my uncle,' I said, and wished Papula good night and good luck.

Long before it was Father's time to go to work, and as daylight was just creeping across the sky, there was a ghastly scream. It was not a dream, I realised, as another fearful shriek rang out. I opened my eyes and glanced around. My family, except for Trouble, who was out with Hercules to help him load his cargo, were stirring themselves awake, looking seriously alarmed.

I ran down and was the first to make it to the courtyard. The screams were coming from Hercules' gymnasium and I rushed to the window, where I was momentarily paralysed by what I saw. Papula had poured naphthalene over herself and set it alight. She was in the midst of an orange and blue fireball, burning all over and jumping and jerking uncontrollably. The sight was too dreadful to put into words.

My father, mother and Star joined me, all deeply distressed and feeling utterly helpless. Rashaba ran to bring a hammer to smash open the door, which she had locked from the inside. The sickly sweet smell of burning flesh filled the air. Papula ran out, screaming hysterically, her body still alight. Mother screamed too. She was in a panic like everyone else, and all we could do was run around helplessly. I grabbed a blanket and threw it over Papula, but it fell off her, as she could not stay still. With Father's help, we finally managed to cover her as she writhed in agony, and at last the flames relented. But it was too late.

She was so badly burnt that she could no longer move her charred and blistered body. By the time Flathead came out of their room, Papula was lying there dead.

Strange, Flathead sleeps in the room next door but he is the last one to arrive, or was he too drunk to wake up? This is not the time to ask such questions.

We all looked towards him, his distraught face twisted with sudden grief, which he suddenly slapped hard with both hands, as if trying to wake himself up to the shocking reality of that grisly morning. He slowly stepped back, retreating towards his living room door, still staring at his lifeless wife. He turned away, punching and kicking the wall with all his might. My mother ran to him, trying to stop him from doing himself an injury. She was joined by the neighbours, who had rushed into the courtyard having heard the panic and commotion. Everyone surrounded Flathead to console him. Not Rashaba, though. To my surprise, my father held the sleeve of his shirt to his nose to avoid the stench of Papula's burned flesh, and then, as an alleged pious Muslim, he duly recited the prayer for the dead.

There was a sudden change in Flathead's mood and he started ranting, calling Papula a sinner who had done no good to herself or anyone else by the horrendous way she had ended her life. Her act was inexcusable, he declared, as her body lay smouldering on the floor. He did not want to even hold a funeral for her. He demanded that Papula's corpse be immediately sent back to her mother, and insisted that she must arrange for their daughter's burial. I could not believe what Flathead was saying, not to mention being bitterly crushed by Papula, my dear friend, choosing this gruesome suicide. The best I could do was to escape the baying crowd in the courtyard and take poor Star away from the horror of it all. We were on the veranda when Star asked innocently,

'Will auntie Nasik go to heaven and see Monkey?'

'No,' I answered, as there was no use lying. 'I'm afraid that she killed herself, and that is the worst sin in Islam. Allah will probably send her to hell to burn forever. And you, my little Star, no matter what happens in your life, promise me never to do something so awful, you hear?' and I hugged her tightly. I did not actually believe for one moment that someone as lovely as Papula could end up in hell, but I wanted to warn Star, I did not want her to meet such a dreadful fate one day. The prospect of her growing up in our twisted society worried me beyond reason.

'I won't burn myself,' Star said, holding King Kong to her chest.

'We heard the terrible news, is it really true?' Hercules shouted, wild-eyed as he ran in to the courtyard with Trouble.

'Yes. She is dead,' Mother said flatly, sobbing, as she pointed to Papula's covered body, in a corner of the courtyard.

How little a special woman like Papula is valued in our culture, I considered sadly, as I watched my brother's reaction to this awful event. She probably didn't deserve even half of the tears that were shed for Monkey, in Trouble's eyes, but not so for uncle Hercules. He was obviously deeply distressed by the death of his sister-in-law and, standing over her body, he cried silently.

At Flathead's request, Hercules and Trouble, with the help of our neighbours, wrapped Papula in a couple of blankets and carried her outside to a car, so that her body could be taken back to her family. My mother rushed up the steps and kept crying for Papula as if she was her dearest friend. I was appalled by what I considered to be a display of false emotion for Papula, a woman who was different and daring and did not comply with her conventional way of living. I followed her into our room. 'You should not cry for her. You hated her,' I said bitterly. Mother suddenly slapped me around the face, which was the first time she had ever laid her hands on me. 'I am crying because I was not there for her,' she said. 'I had disagreements with your auntie, but never realised the pain she lived with would lead her to end her life in such an atrocious way.' She donned her black cape and left me alone.

My mother was a generous and strong person in many ways, but I had a problem with the habits of certain Kurdish women. They were jealous, envious and gossiped endlessly, gathering by their doors during their free time, eating bagfuls of sunflower seeds and chewing gum. Their childhoods had been spent obeying their parents and culture and once married, they served their husbands like slaves. Whenever it came to protest, to fight back, to stand up for their rights, for their freedom, they were incapable, and many escaped this oppressive life by simply committing suicide. But Papula was not like them; she was different, she was a fighter. I had trusted her strength and spirit; she was always an independent and liberated woman, another one of my heroes, escaping to her freedom in death. *What made her resort to such an appalling death? Poor Dr Hakan. Now the plans he made to go to Istanbul with the woman he loves so much are all shattered. Believing that my uncle has gone back to Baghdad today, he might turn up in the middle of the night, to find Flathead at home.* I remembered Flathead's gun, which made me gasp, as I was sure Flathead would shoot the doctor. Hoping to prevent another catastrophe taking place, I went into Flathead's room and opened the box, but the gun was not there.

'I have taken it out.' Flathead made me jump. I did not realise he had followed me. 'Don't worry, I will not shoot myself. I am not such a desperate husband. I had to get rid of it in case the police come to check our house because of your auntie's madness. She did not please me in life and I will not grieve for her death.'

'I wish we were able to have a proper funeral for her,' I said. Flathead did not respond. Gulping down more Arak, he looked away, resigned to the fact that there would be no proper funeral.

That night, under the moonlight, I sat by the wall outside our house thinking about all the joyful moments Papula and I had spent together. *I am sure if she had a chance to turn back time, she would forever regret what she had done and would never think of killing herself, let alone in such a horrific way, burning her beautiful body and being.* I waited for Dr Hakan to arrive, planning to stop him and to shield him from the tragedy. *I will only tell him about my uncle's presence. What if he doesn't believe me? What if he has heard of Papula's suicide?*

'He won't come!' Flathead said, approaching slowly, walking with heavy steps as if the weight of guilt pressed down on his shoulders.

'Who?' I asked, hesitantly.

'Whoever you are waiting for.'

'I am not waiting for anyone, Uncle. I am just upset. Surely there could have been a solution, why was she so tormented to have to burn herself to death? It is such a waste of a life.'

'That is right, Mery, she has not only achieved nothing, but women like Nasik who selfishly kill themselves set a bad example for others as well,' Flathead said, as he crouched down and sat next to me on the dusty ground. 'Her doctor was her last hope to save our marriage. I wanted a child and Dr Hakan was to help get her pregnant. Last night, during his shift at the hospital, Dr Hakan was found making love to another woman. The husband surprised them and shot them both, the wife and doctor, on the spot. Nasik must have heard this shocking news and felt betrayed by our doctor. Maybe she thought that our dreams of having a child died with him. I don't know. Thousands of young girls and women kill themselves in Kurdistan, she is not the only one.'

The night I will never forget

It was mid-December, and as the days were getting colder, fewer people posed for photos. Sunshine was still going to school, but when she finished, she came to work, to be with me, even though we were not so busy. Jam was trying to get news from Godfather. Evidently, the tension and uncertainty was ongoing. On New Year's Eve, Popcorn was our last client of the day. He posed behind every cut-out picture. I only charged him for one photo and offered to pay for the rest out of my commission. He left to sell his popcorn in Qaysari Bazaar. There was no Happy New Year, just another day, except that suddenly, to my delight, the sky turned white and it started to snow. It should have been a special part of some celebration, but we did not have any. The snowflakes drifted down, dancing in the gentle breeze.

'We must keep looking up at the sky, we might see Father Christmas,' I said.

'Santa Claus comes on Christmas Eve and not New Year's,' Sunshine answered.

'Do you believe in angels?' I asked.

'I do. You are my angel.'

The snow reminded me of *It's a Wonderful Life,* and I wondered if the snow, a rare occurrence in Kirkuk, would bring me luck to somehow help me get to America.

Over the following weeks it kept snowing. One day around the end of the month, it snowed so much that traffic couldn't get through. We had to pack up earlier than usual. Most people hurried to get home, but Sunshine and I enjoyed staying outside to throw snowballs at each other. Our city seemed a lot more peaceful that day, and the citadel, covered in snow, looked almost surreal.

On the way home we kept laughing because at one point, showing off about how skillful I was at skipping on the snowy road on the bridge, I slipped and landed on my bum.

By the steps of Qala, militiamen on the other side of the road were also having fun, laughing as their commander tried to force Popcorn to sing. They had him surrounded. It was as if he were a caged bird. 'Sing!' the commander was shouting, in Arabic. 'Sing, son of a donkey.' Popcorn was pulled and pushed back again. The commander picked up a handful of snow and hit Popcorn in the face. He did not sing. They put their hands into his basket and threw popcorn over his head, mixing it with the snowflakes.

What sadistic pleasure can they get from humiliating someone like Popcorn, one of the most harmless people in Kirkuk? Sunshine and I turned to each other. We couldn't leave Popcorn in the hands of such savage Arabs. The commander pointed his gun at Popcorn and demanded that he sing and dance, which Popcorn simply ignored with admirable but dangerous disdain. Having seen what happened to Old Zorab, I was truly worried now. I ran ahead of Sunshine. 'Sir,' I called, as we approached them, 'some rebels are tearing down President Saddam's poster by the bridge.'

'They may even burn the poster, sir,' Sunshine echoed me. 'There are three of them, sir. They should be arrested at once.'

'Watch out, they may be armed,' I said, putting as much phoney concern into my voice as I could.

The gullible militiamen sprinted towards the bridge. We headed off in the opposite direction, and soon we were invisible in the dense snow. Popcorn had inadvertently left his basket on the side of the road. We escorted Sunshine home and I asked Popcorn if he would like to come to my place to rest. He said that he had to leave, but first wanted to tell me something important: 'Mery, you are in greater danger than I am. You are being followed and could be arrested any day.'

'How do you know?'

'I can't tell you, but I trust my source.'

'You are talking about my life?'

'I could help you get out to the mountains,' he suggested. 'You could become a freedom fighter.'

'Popcorn, what you're saying is really alarming. I appreciate your help, but to become a freedom fighter is not for me. You know I never liked guns, and soon I am going to America.'

'Well, if you can, that's great. But until then you should go into hiding or at least stay away from the centre of town. Good luck, Mery,' he said, as he embraced me.

Popcorn had always looked out for me, but even so, his warning me like this was both touching and unnerving. I could not understand why he had not told me who his source was, but my real concern remained. *Who is my predator? Abu Ali has already had far too many opportunities to nail me. I can't possibly suspect Master Shamal, Peaceful, Rabbit, Jwana, Jam, Norman or Uncle Hitch. Sheikh Baba, one of the dervishes, Godfather? What about Rashaba, my uncles and Trouble? Surely not. Louis? No, I have not seen him since our fight over my wage. Who then? Who is following me and why wait, why not come to take me away and just finish me off?*

I was capable of suspecting everyone, including my mother, or even Sunshine, but it was the fear that made my mind play tricks on me, eating me up from the inside and twisting my judgement. Jam saw that I was in an awful state. He locked the shop and hung up the 'Closed' sign. We went into the back room. 'Popcorn believes that I am a target. Shit! My days are numbered. I must get out immediately!'

'Godfather is not ready.'

'You told me it was going to happen long before the New Year, and we are now at the end of January.'

'I can try and pressure him, but I seriously doubt that it will happen overnight.'

'I could take Father's money and go into hiding.'

'Don't. There is nowhere you could hide safely in this country. The minute your father learns his money is missing, and that you are missing too, he will let the authorities know and they will hunt you down. We must find a better solution.'

'If I am taken away, I am fucked once and for all.'

'I know Mery, I know. Perhaps you should go to Baghdad with your uncles?'

'They left a couple of days ago. They will not be back for a month.'

'Do you want to go out via the mountains?'

'Yes, anyway I can get out.'

Jam paced the room. He stretched his hand over his face, deep in thought.

'What else did Popcorn say?'

'He offered his help to get me out and he suggested I become a Peshmerga.'

'Do you trust Popcorn?'

'Yes. No. I don't know, I am confused. I no longer know who to trust.'

'Why didn't he tell you who is following you?'

'I have no idea,' I replied, desperately.

'Popcorn could well be working for the Kurdish resistance. Perhaps he tried to recruit you to become a freedom fighter. Remember, in this damn place people are not followed. They are just taken away.'

'You could be right, Jam. I am sorry if I panicked.'

'I will talk to Godfather; let's see if we can get you out as soon as possible.'

'Thanks, Jam.'

'And you stay away from Popcorn.'

Popcorn, the mad popcorn seller! Who would have ever suspected him of being a member of Freedom for Life, the most secretive anti-government Kurdish organisation? I am not angry with him, not at all. I hope to see him again and congratulate him on his bravery.

I went back to Sunshine and told her about Popcorn's warning. She too agreed with Jam and was glad I did not take up Popcorn's offer to go to the mountains. For Sunshine, our future was to be in America. I spent only a few minutes with Rabbit because he inexplicably cut me short. He said that he knew nothing about me being followed, after I had told him of Popcorn's revelation and offer, but believed that Popcorn would never tell a lie and would not use such important matters as an excuse to recruit people. He advised me to take Popcorn's concerns seriously.

It was dark and cold by then, and our road was covered in snow. I was battling against my fear, trying to answer my mind's many questions. *I am at risk like everyone else, but I am lucky because soon I will be out of this nightmare and be in America.*

Outside our house I came across Trouble, sitting in the passenger seat of a red Fiat, talking to the driver, his gardener boss. I had hated this man the minute I met him. He was also rumoured to be one of the most dangerous paedophiles in Kirkuk. His name was Dara, and he was in his late twenties. He did not look obviously threatening. But to me he was 'Pig', the animal most loathed amongst the Muslims, and that's why I called him by that filthy name.

They gave me a suspicious look. They whispered a few words and Trouble turned to me. 'Mery,' he said, with a fake brotherly smile, 'how lucky! We were looking for you. Come with us.'

'I can't, it's getting late and I am hungry.'

'Well, that is perfect, Mery,' the Pig said. 'We are going to the kebab house and I would like to treat you.'

'Thanks, but I'll be happy to eat whatever Mother has prepared.'

'Look, willing or not, you're coming with us,' Trouble said, as he opened the door and jumped out of the car to face me. 'We need your help.'

What sort of help does my Jash brother need from me? The thought threw me off guard, and he pushed me into the back seat of the car. There was plenty of snow and slush on the road and as the car's tyres ran through it, muddy splashes splattered halfway up the walls of the surrounding buildings.

'Why do you keep changing the colour of your car?' I asked as I pulled of my hat.

'Don't tell me you don't like red,' Dara teased, and they both laughed. 'You know something Mery, you could be an attractive girl with a pair of pomegranates on your chest. Do you have a willy?' the Pig said, as he stared at me from the rear-view mirror.

'Cut it off if you have one, have an operation and change into a girl. It is better to be a girl these days and avoid military service. People are shooting themselves, mutilating themselves, doing anything to get away from the army. They don't want to go to the front line. And believe me, it would be better to be a pretty woman than a Jash like me. Just have the operation and after, when you are a girl, I will marry you.'

They laughed again. I sat silently, but my thoughts were murderous. *I would have killed him before he could marry me.*

As we reached Iskan, one of the eastern suburbs, they told me to get out. I followed them into the local teahouse, which was packed with men playing backgammon and dominoes. Others were gathered around the gasoline stove. Dara and Trouble joined a few friends around a table in a round of Aznif, one of my favourite dominoes games. 'Do you want to play?' Trouble asked. The group turned towards me, as if they had just noticed my presence, their rough wild faces, glowing in the light of the stove, looking like characters from The War of Fire. I felt uncomfortable amongst them, especially as I had to sit so closely to Dara, the paedo Pig.

'I will watch,' I answered.

'Mery can keep score,' Dara suggested, and everyone agreed.

'Good for you, Mery. You will drink your Pepsi and no matter who loses, you won't have to pay,' Dara said, and grabbed my cheek. I pushed his hand away.

The tea maker brought five bottles of Pepsi, one for each player and one for me. I kept marking the points. At the beginning Dara and Trouble were losing, but they soon recovered. They asked for another round of Pepsi and yet another. By the end of the game I had drunk five. I was worried that Trouble was going to lose and make me pay, not only for my drinks, but also for his and his friends' too. The game intensified and by the time they reached the last point, both sides were close to winning, but Trouble and Dara were the ones who were eventually flushed with victory.

'It's getting late!' I said, as the antiquated clock on the wall next to a poster of Saddam, struck eleven. I was worried about checkpoints and armed patrols.

We got back in the car and I assumed we were going home.

'Don't worry about checkpoints,' Dara said. 'We are respected Jash.' *Respected by whom?* I wondered. *Traitor* and *paedophile* were the words that came to my mind. Dara parked the car outside a house. Trouble got out and knocked on a door. A man opened it and, with Dara's help, they pushed a few pots and bags into the boot of his car. There was something sinister about it that gave me an uneasy feeling. Trouble came back with two full carrier bags. Dara drove away again. Trouble wound down the window and started to throw bunches of leaflets along the road.

'What are you doing?' I asked.

'Don't ask,' Trouble hushed me. 'Here, read it.'

My tired eyes popped wide open. On the leaflets were the most dangerous anti-government slogans, calling for the Kurds to rise up, to fight the regime, to join the armed struggle in the mountains and to leave the Jash and their leaders. I was astonished. *Trouble and his Jash Pig boss are not traitors but patriotic Kurds.* I was impressed and intrigued, but I did not want to be involved. I handed the leaflet back to Trouble.

'Open your window and throw it out,' he said.

'I can't.'

'Do it.'

I did so, but quickly closed the window, fearing the monster might pop up out of the darkness and bite my hand. We drove around until Trouble emptied the bags. Outside Iskan secondary school, Dara stopped the car. He opened the boot and took out tins of paint and brushes. Trouble asked me to get out. He handed me one of the brushes. 'Write on the wall in large letters...' He glanced around and whispered the rest into my ear.

'We will be shot on the spot if they catch us,' I replied, shivering.

'Then be quick and let's get going,' Dara said, keeping watch.

'Why me?'

'Mery, just do it or I swear I'll cut your fucking hair right now,' Trouble grunted.

'Death to Saddam! Long live Kurdistan!' I wrote on the wall with shaking hands.

I was glad to get back in the car. Still it was not the end. Dara drove to another district and I had to paint it again and again. It was cold and I just couldn't cope with the tension. I begged Trouble to take me home. I could do no more. On the way back, they made a diversion towards Priadi. They checked the surroundings, making sure it was all clear. Dara pulled over. Trouble grabbed a gallon full of petrol. He ran to Saddam's massive poster in the middle of the round-about, covered it with petrol and struck a match. Within seconds the president was on fire.

'You have gone too far,' I said, once Trouble was back in the car.

'Shut up,' Trouble shouted, as Dara drove away.

'Burning a poster is stupid. They will arrest innocent people for it,' I said, though I couldn't help but feel a thrill to see Saddam burning. We did not get far before a military Jeep appeared. I saw Dara's eyes dart to the rear-view mirror, then felt myself thrown back in my seat as he hit the accelerator, driving like a madman. The road was too slippery for this, with all the snow. The Jeep roared to keep up with us, and then bullets rained down on us, until Dara veered suddenly down a side road, tyres screeching. I glanced back and thought we had lost them. But soon the Jeep was right on our tail again. I was terrified. The Jeep slipped sideways in the snow and seemed to nearly roll over. This gave us some time to get out of danger, but suddenly, there was a checkpoint, with three militiamen standing by a small fire. They aimed their guns at us. Dara wound down his window and called in Arabic, 'We are Jash, let us through, we are being chased by Kurdish rebels, let us through...'

The Jeep appeared behind us at that moment, accelerating to full speed, firing at us. The Jeep's lights blinded the militiamen, who didn't have time to check whether it was one of their vehicles. They let us through and opened fire. I turned back to see the Jeep careering into the barrier before crashing against a wall. And still they were firing at each other!

'Fuck you!' Dara shouted, excited. 'What a night.'

Trouble was overjoyed. 'Leaflets and slogans, posters burned and a few bastards killed, what an achievement,' he said, and he looked into my eyes to see my reaction.

I turned away, unsure what to say. I was elated because we had survived these audacious adventures, but also furious because we had so very nearly been killed or, even worse, captured. Dara parked the car in a garage outside Bazaar Hasiraka. He immediately started to spray it white. 'It is better if you walk home,' Dara said, 'and thanks, Mery, you deserve to be named after a prince.' I nodded to Dara. Despite my distrust of him, I admired the Pig on that night for his bravery to fight the monster's men in Kirkuk, and to give me a chance to be part of that fight and actively contribute to the plight of my people for their freedom. But, the whole experience was so powerfully frightening and unexpected, I was still shivering as we made it into the alleyways of Qala.

'Are you working for the Freedom for Life organisation?' I whispered.

'Don't ever ask me that question again,' Trouble snapped. 'But thanks for tonight, brother,' he added, calming down, 'our usual man could not make it.'

'Where do you think you are going?' an armed policeman on patrol yelled at us. 'We are dervish, sir,' Trouble answered. 'God is great,' Trouble called. 'We have just finished dancing in Sheikh Baba's Takya. And I am also a Jash.' They checked our identity under the torch beams, and finally let us go.

'Trouble, you shouldn't have put a ban on me going to the cinemas…'

'What ban?' Trouble cut me short. 'What are you talking about? That's not me. Did you try all the cinemas?'

'I went to every one, and each time I was turned away.' *Then Popcorn was right, someone is after me.* 'You must not ask me to come out with you again, and stay away from me. I am being followed.'

'Who is following you?' Trouble stopped, facing me.

'I don't know. I am not sure, it seems like someone is playing a sadistic game with me. But I don't know who and it's driving me crazy.'

'Don't worry, Brother. Dara and I have strong connections. We will look into it, and when we find the bastard, we'll take him out.'

'Will you?'

'Of course! You are my blood, a good Kurd and a born freedom fighter. I am sorry if I have given you problems in the past, but you should know that I am proud of you, Mery. I will not let the bastards put their dirty hands on you as they did to our grandfathers.'

At last, good news

Jam turned up at our photography pitch with Godfather's latest news. 'Mery,' he said, with a smile, 'the day of departure has been fixed and your flight is booked for the 15th of March.'

I did not know what to say. I was choked up. This was the best news ever. *Jam, my friend, you have done it.* It took me a while before I could speak. 'That is four days after my sixteenth birthday.'

'Perhaps it's better if you keep this to yourself.'

'I can't hide it from Sunshine and Uncle Hitch.'

'I understand. I am glad for you, it is finally happening.' Jam said, and left soon after we finished displaying the film heroes' posters. I picked up my stills camera and started to take pictures, but could hardly concentrate.

'Something on your mind?' Uncle Hitch asked, the minute he arrived.

'I may have to stop working with you soon, I hope you don't mind.'

'I am delighted for you. Say no more.'

When Sunshine arrived from school, Uncle Hitch did not give her time to load her camera. 'You are off with Merywan, he has a surprise for you,' he said, and gave Sunshine an envelope with a nod. I thought it was some money to treat us, but later discovered it was something completely different.

We headed to Jam's and, for the last time, transformed ourselves into boygirl and girlboy. In the past I had to close my eyes when she changed into my clothes, but on that day, she did not mind me seeing her. She was wearing a set of turquoise blue knickers and bra. Her olive skin glowed and, with her luxuriant dark hair cascading over her shoulders, she looked spectacularly desirable. I hugged her. I knew that she knew. 'You are leaving soon,' she stated.

'I will always love you, and as soon as I can, I will send for you.'

'When?'

'In two weeks' time.'

'Good, because I have plans for your birthday.' We continued to look longingly into each other's eyes. 'No kissing before marriage,' she said.

'No kissing before marriage,' I repeated.

We kissed for a long time.

At the Atlas Cinema, we lorded it in the family box, just for us. Holding hands, at every exciting moment we would kiss. We were watching *Hair*. I related to that film. The scene that touched me most was when Woof was forced to cut his hair in the prison. At the time, sitting next to Sunshine, with the prospect of going away to America, to my Gringo, I felt like one of the luckiest people on earth.

'Look what I have got for you,' Sunshine said, holding Uncle Hitch's envelope.

'What is it?'

'Open it.'

I did and found a small square box with Kodak written on it.

'A Super 8 film for your cine camera,' she said. 'Uncle Hitch and I have been looking for one for months.'

'I love you, baby,' I said, and I kissed the rare treasure with a smile.

I must check Rashaba's money. He might have the ten thousand dinars by now. I was alone and was about to touch his pillow when Trouble and Dara walked into our room. Trouble picked up Rashaba's pillow and put it down for Dara to lie on. I felt myself react, but wasn't sure if Trouble noticed. Mother walked in, pushing Dara off. 'Excuse me,' she said. 'Nobody lies on this one except for my husband.'

Trouble laughed scornfully, imitating Mother's words about the pillow being exclusive to her husband. He grabbed it, making a joke out of it with her. They pulled it between them. 'Let me lie on it just for once,' Trouble teased. Mother pulled harder. I was worried that it might rip and the money fall out.

'Ardalan, let go.' I said.

'Fine, I will, only if Mother makes us a drink.'

'I could make some yoghurt-shake,' she replied.

'No, I don't want that.' Trouble let go of the pillow and took out a bottle of Arak from his pocket. 'This is more like it, the dearest.' He poured for Dara and himself into two glasses. Mother held her nose and left the room.

'Mery, sit next to me?' Dara opened his arms.

'I am fine here, thanks.'

Trouble offered his glass. I shook my head. Since the midnight adventure of the leafleting and the subsequent terrifying car chase, we had started to rebuild our trust in each other. He knew very well about my patriotic feelings. We had talked many times together since we were little, about our father and uncles once being Peshmerga fighting for the freedom of our country, about our grandfathers being killed and hanged by Saddam's men. Despite him becoming a Jash, I had always been quietly confident that my brother loathed Saddam. I had learned to trust the Pig, too. Paedophile though he may be, I no longer feared that he was one of the monster's men, so I had decided to ask Trouble and his friend to let me film them, which they agreed to.

Our life was constantly lived on the edge, any one of us could have disappeared into the hands of the monster's men at any moment, yet I wanted to film, and keep a record of the people around me to take to America.

I was glad when Trouble and Dara left soon after they had finished drinking. I touched Rashaba's pillow and felt the dinars. Now that I was reassured about the money, I went out and filmed Mother in the kitchen.

'Put that camera away, now,' she said.

I had already filmed Sunshine, Master Shamal and family, Uncle Hitch, my uncles, Trouble, Dara Pig, Star and now Mother, and it was painful not to have Father in my first ever film. *Not a hope in hell.*

On my way to go and leave the cine camera with Sunshine, I came face to face with Rashaba, who had returned home from work earlier than usual. He was in a bad mood because our landlord had increased our rent. I had no time to hide the bag. I took a couple of steps back.

'What is that?' he asked, standing by the door.

'It belongs to Jam. It's a bag.'

'What is inside the bag?'

'A machine, he uses it for making stamps.'

'Can I see it?'

I pulled out the camera. 'I will tell you the truth, Father, if you promise to give it back?'

'Fine, I promise,' he said, and snatched it from my hand.

'It is called a cine camera, and it's used for turning stories into films. Jam bought it in London.'

In a split second Rashaba had slammed the camera on to the concrete floor, the sickening sound of smashing metal and plastic sending me incandescent with rage. I wanted to pick up the camera and beat him over the head with it. I knew I could not hit him in front of Mother, but I was so upset that I was sorely tempted. If I had not had the prospect of leaving for America a few days later, I wouldn't have been able to restrain myself. He picked up the camera and smashed it again, this time against the wall. Then he threw it at me, hitting me hard on the chest.

'There, have your Satan machine back, as promised.' I stared defiantly back at him. 'And no more photography work. That's not a job for a dervish. You hear me?' I nodded. I put the camera back in the bag and headed off. 'Where are you going?' Rashaba growled, from the veranda. *I won't mind taking away his money and giving him a heart attack, if indeed he has a heart.*

'To give the camera back to Jam.'

'It is Thursday.'

'I know Father, I will see you in Takya.'

Sunshine was outside waiting for me. She had greeted Rashaba on his way in. When I told her about the camera, she was quietly furious too. She examined it and said, 'I am sure the film is not ruined,' to calm me down. 'Uncle Hitch can save it.'

I could not stay with her, though I wanted to, as I had to go to the damn Takya. 'See you tomorrow,' I said reluctantly, leaving her at her door, holding the broken camera in its bag. I was sure she would stay there as always until I disappeared around the corner. Just before turning, I looked back and there she was, waving. I waved back.

I felt strange; for the first time I did not want to go to dance. It was not because of lack of faith, not at all: since the Night of Power I had repented all my sins. I continued praying, reading the Qur'an and begging God for forgiveness. I just did not feel like it.

I could not play the drum. I was too upset about the smashed camera. I took part in the dance. Rashaba went for the wall and headbutted it. He stared at me, imploring me with his gaze. Bang! I hit the wall with my head hard. He was pleased, but also defiant because he could see I did it to challenge him. He charged again and this time hit the wall much harder. I did the same. It hurt a lot more, but I did not show it. He called for Allah, and ran at the wall with all his strength. Some of the dervish stopped to watch us. I charged again, this time as if I wanted to bring down the wall. I hit it so hard that I bounced back and fell over. I got up immediately. Rashaba was very proud. He came and got hold of my hand, and took me to Sheikh Baba. 'My son, Merywan, is ready to be ordained a dervish,' he said, as he kissed the Sheikh's hand.

'I can see that,' the Sheikh answered. 'I shall be glad to give him the spiritual licence of a recognised dervish right now,' and he started to recite over me. My legs were trembling. I had a sharp pain in my head. I found it ironic that just a week before leaving for America, I had to be ordained a dervish. The Sheikh finished and called, 'Allah u Akbar,' and the dervishes echoed him in my honour.

I went back and started to play the drum. In front of my eyes, the Takya transformed into a fantasy world where my film heroes were dancing and singing, to the extraordinary rhythms of many drums being beaten simultaneously. I joined them and sang my heart out. Rabbit, and his family, the primary school caretaker, Louis, my parents, Star, Monkey, Trouble, Dara Pig and my uncles, Happiness, Papula, Aida, Jam, Norman, Dr Hakan, Godfather and Popcorn were amongst them. All dancing and singing at my wedding to Sunshine on Love Island. Uncle Hitch's flash went off repeatedly as he snapped everybody. I was overwhelmed by the presence of all the people I loved so much. Sunshine was given away to me, not by Master Shamal, but by Gringo, whom she chose because she knew it would make me so happy…

A slap from Rashaba's stony hand awoke me from my fantastic vision and brought me back to the reality of the Takya, where everyone was watching me. The dervishes had stopped worshipping, the Sheikh was infuriated and my father deeply embarrassed. It was the most scandalous thing I could have done in Takya. Instead of the traditional dance of worship, I had unconsciously slipped into singing and dancing as though I were in a Western musical.

I tried to apologise and to explain to Rashaba and our revered Sheikh about my hallucination in order to keep my dervish status, but as I started to talk, my body gave up and I fainted.

Save the film

On 11 March 1987, Rashaba left early for work. I was pleased he was not going to be around for my birthday. I was sure he did not even remember I was born on that day. It was different for my mother, as she, Star and my uncles were invited to my party, planned for the afternoon at Master Shamal's house. Sunshine and I were only going to work in the morning and later in the day would go to her house with Jam and Uncle Hitch for my first-ever birthday celebration.

When Jam turned up with the cut-out pictures, I gave him good news, 'The money is ready, ten thousand dinars. I won't need your five hundred.'

'I also have news for you. I am putting the shop up for sale. I want to go back to England.'

'That's fantastic, you can paint again and have exhibitions. I remember you telling me, your passion to paint is like a flame that never dies.'

'You in America and me in England. Maybe we could visit each other and go to see one of your films together.'

'I wanted to have you in my first film, but my father broke the cine camera.' I showed it to Jam. 'What a shame. What a waste! I will ask Uncle Hitch to save the film.'

'I can do it.' Jam put it back inside the bag. He closed it to prevent the daylight from getting in and pushed in his hand. After a while, he took out the film. 'Here, the film is saved.'

'Thanks so much, Jam, I want to take it with me and show it to Gringo,' and I put the film in my pocket.

'Where is Uncle Hitch?' Jam asked. 'I need him to take a picture of the shop.'

Uncle Hitch was never usually this late. 'He'll be here soon,' Sunshine said. 'He is our photographer for this afternoon's special occasion.' She smiled at me, and picked up her still camera to start working. I was no longer allowed to take photos, on Rashaba's orders.

'Can I let Jam know?' Sunshine pleaded. 'I am so excited. I can't keep it in any longer.'

'Jam only,' I suggested. But I think Jam realised something was up as he looked at us standing next to each other.

'Share your happiness and light up my day even further,' Jam said.

'Well,' Sunshine started eagerly, 'as we are to celebrate Mery's sixteenth birthday this afternoon, we are also going to surprise our families and friends by announcing our engagement.'

Jam's face broadened with a warm smile. 'Congratulations,' he said, as he clasped our hands in his.

Gringo was also invited. Sunshine had put up a handsome portrait of his on the wall of their living room, so that he could be present at our engagement.

Soon after Jam left, Rabbit appeared to wish me 'Happy Birthday' and to give me a gift. Sunshine had suggested it should be something from Jam's shop. We were not going to be long and he told me he was looking forward to spending some time alone with me before I left for America. Sunshine stayed to look after the business.

Jam was painting a For Sale sign to put up in his shop window when we arrived. Although Jam and Rabbit had seen each other before, they had never met properly. I introduced my friend, 'This is Rabbit. He is an atheist like you.'

'I have heard a great deal about you,' Jam said. 'Can I get you a drink?'

'No thanks,' Rabbit answered. 'I don't want to take up too much time on Mery's day. I am here as a customer.'

'Brader, you are my best gift,' I said grinning.

'What is it that you like most?' Rabbit asked, while looking around. I had expressed to Sunshine on a couple of occasions how much I liked the old world atlas displayed in the window, but it was expensive. I had been embarrassed to tell Jam, as he would have given it to me, no doubt.

'My shop is Mery's, and he can have anything he wants,' Jam said. I pointed towards the atlas in the window. 'Sure,' Rabbit said.

'How much?' and he took out his wallet.

Jam was about to answer when Abu Ali suddenly stepped in to the shop. *He would never walk around alone, and is sure to be armed, with his guards not far behind him.* We were silent now, while Abu Ali casually looked at the stamps. I could feel his brutal energy. Rabbit went pale. Jam fought back his nerves and signalled to us to keep calm. Abu Ali moved towards the coins and notes. His gaze was fixed on one in particular. Jam wanted to block his view. 'Can I help, sir?' he asked, but Abu Ali kept staring in the same direction. He finally spoke, 'I want to see that note.' Jam handed it over to him. 'Iranian Tuman?' he said, sarcastically.

'Iranian, yes, you are right, but from the time when the Shah, our good friend, was in power.'

'How much for our enemy's money?' He marked his words as if bargaining for Jam's life.

'Three dinars. You can have it for half that price. I like to treat my new clients.' Jam's voice started to tremble. *He must be cursing ever seeing that note, never mind displaying it.* 'You can also have this old dollar, an American dollar, President Saddam Hussein's best allies?' Jam said, but he saw no reaction except for Abu Ali's sickening smile and a headshake.

'I found the Iranian note and gave it to him to sell for me,' I said, facing Abu Ali. 'It's mine.' *I know selling an Iranian note could be construed as an anti-government act, but I want to help Jam.*

'Do I know you?' Abu Ali asked, examining me. 'I have seen you before, but where?' He moved his face closer, as if he were short-sighted. 'What's your name?'

'Merywan Rashaba.'

'What is he to you?' He pointed to Jam.

'My friend.'

'I must be confusing you with someone else,' he said, and put his hand in his pocket. 'Three dinars. I will pay the full price.' He threw the money on the table and walked out with the note. Abu Ali did not go far, he stopped outside, with his back to us and lit a cigarette.

'Is he Shawes Dog?' I had to ask Rabbit.

'I am really tired of your stupid questions. He is standing there, why don't you just go and ask him, Abu Ali are you Shawes Dog?'

'Brader, can't you see how much he looks like Shawes Dog?'

'Shawes is in Abu Ghraib prison, for life,' Rabbit insisted.

'You should stop this,' Jam stepped in between us. 'We are not done with him.'

'I'm off,' Rabbit said, going to the door.

'There is something not quite right about your Brader,' Jam looked distrustfully at Rabbit as he left the shop.

There was no time to question Jam's doubts about Rabbit, as Abu Ali's four-wheel-drive appeared outside the shop. Abu Ali tore up the Iranian note, throwing the pieces on the ground. He got into the passenger's seat and simultaneously the car's rear doors were pushed wide open. A body was shoved out in the middle of the road, and the car drove away.

I was the first to run to the broken form. I gasped as I noticed a broken camera hanging around his neck. The busy morning traffic came to a standstill. A crowd gathered but hesitated to get too close. Jam pulled me back in a hurry. I resisted him and shouted hysterically, 'We can't leave Uncle Hitch in the middle of the road!' And I pushed him away.

'There is nothing we can do for him now. We must get out.' Jam grabbed me.

'We have to take him back to his family,' I said, trying to lift Uncle Hitch, his kind face disfigured by the scars of cigarette burns.

'This is a trap.' Jam got hold of my arm.

'Jam, it's Uncle Hitch.'

'He is dead and I want to keep you alive.' Jam lifted me up from behind by my waist, yet I struggled to free myself. 'We must see Godfather.' Jam dragged me. 'You have to go away today.'

'I still have four days to go.'

'You can hide in Baghdad.' Jam pushed me into his car and drove away.

Uncle Hitch would have been so proud to be the official photographer at our engagement, but that dream, along with so many others, had died with him.

'Fuck, fuck the bastards...' I shouted, punching my seat. 'Stop that, Mery, and keep watch,' Jam kept his eyes on the road but was also checking the rear-view mirror. 'Make sure Abu Ali is not following us.'

'Fuck Abu Ali. Fuck Abu Ali...'

'OK, Mery, fuck Abu Ali! But is he behind us?'

I turned around. I could no longer see Uncle Hitch's body. The crowd blocked my view. 'Do you think Uncle Hitch was a member of Freedom for Life? I know I should not ask this, but why him? Why Uncle Hitch, why?' I cried out, and buried my face in my hands.

'A British gentleman,' Jam said, feeling very frustrated, 'in one of his history books, says, "The Kurd has a curious habit of disparaging himself and his brethren." He also describes us as hardworking, avaricious savages. Abu Ali is all three, he is the worst type of Kurd. He is a disgrace to our people.'

'The time will come when a brave Kurd will finish him off.'

'And he'll be replaced by another heartless Kurd.'

'There may be another, but someone else will finish off that one too. It just takes one of us to start, and the others will follow. One can make a huge difference.'

'You sound like you are talking like your hero.'

'Yes. Gringo always wins in the end, doesn't he? That is why he is a hero, and the heroes never lose.'

I want to be a hero like you, Gringo. Islam forbids taking the life of another human being, unless fighting for Allah, but Abu Ali has just murdered another of my dearest friends.

'Can we go to Sunshine first? She must be very worried,' I asked.

'Rabbit will have taken her home,' Jam answered.

'She would not leave the cut-out pictures with no one there.'

'Fine, Mery.'

'What did you mean about Rabbit?'

'I could be wrong, but I think he brought you to the shop today for a reason. He might be dodgy.'

'No, not Rabbit. He would rather die than spy on me for the monster. He hates Saddam and loathes his regime.'

There was no sign of Sunshine. We got out of the car. We found the pictures in pieces on the pavement. 'A crippled guy did it,' a beggar said, sitting at the site. 'He tore the posters and forced the girl-photographer to go with him.'

'Mery, let's go,' Jam said.

Jam drove fast. I was overwhelmed, but was relieved to know Sunshine was safe with Rabbit. So many thoughts scrambled through my mind. 11 March, the day I was born, the day Sunshine and I were to get engaged, the day Uncle Hitch lay dead in the middle of Republic Street and the day our photography dreams died with him. The day Flathead wanted to burn down King Sherzad's house sixteen years before, the day I was to go to Baghdad and then to Gringo, in America, the day I feel an overpowering desire to kill Abu Ali.

By midday we made it to the brothel to fetch the big man. I sat on the back seat next to Godfather with Jam at the wheel as he drove to Qala. 'I have already sent hundreds out this way,' Godfather said, comfortably. 'But I must first see the ten thousand dinars.'

'We are on our way to pick up the money,' Jam confirmed.

'The money stays with you,' Godfather tapped Jam on the shoulder, 'until Merywan gets to America, I trust you, Jam.'

'Mery must go out today.'

'As soon as he hands you the money, he will be on his way.'

'My flight is booked for the 15th, today is the 11th.'

'You are going to Baghdad this afternoon,' Godfather said, 'with Jam, not me. I will arrange your way out of Kirkuk if you are worried about checkpoints. Once in Baghdad, you have a haircut, nice and short. You then go to the five-star Hotel Hamurabi on Rashid Street. Your room number is 101. Jam will stay in 102 next to you. You receive a call, someone will ask you for your password in Arabic. Do you remember it, Merywan?'

'I do.'

'Anyone else?'

'No.'

'Good. You give your password, adding your room number, 101. A waiter will bring you a black suit, new shirt and tie. Your passport is in the jacket's inner pocket. Read the details and learn your new name. You don't leave the room until the 14th. In the evening you get another call informing you that your portion of kebab is ready. Then you go out with Jam to enjoy the life on the banks of the Tigris. It will be your last night in Iraq. Are you following, Merywan?'

'Yes.'

'The next day at eleven in the morning, you must be ready to go down in your suit with your short hair, looking very smart, the son of an Iraqi diplomat. Your father, around fifty years old with white hair, and with his two body guards, both fat like me, will greet you, take you to his car where you meet your new mother. They drive to Saddam International airport. You go to the VIP lounge. And an hour later, with your parents you walk through security. Don't worry, they are well paid and won't stop you. After a five-minute bus ride you find yourself on board the aircraft. The Boeing 747 flies you all the way to Washington DC. You should be there at four in the afternoon. The diplomat keeps you for one night in his house, and after that, you will be Merywan again and free in the land of hope and dreams. Any questions?'

'Jam also wants to leave,' I was worried about Jam.

'Let's get you out first and then I will think of Jam.'

'Your people in Baghdad are not expecting to see Mery before the 14th,' Jam said. 'How would they know of Mery's arrival today?' Jam was worried about me.

'I will send out someone ahead of you as soon as I see the money in your hands.'

'Why don't you call them?' I asked.

'Never,' Godfather reacted by jumping up on his seat. 'The phone lines are all tapped, The Mukhabarat have eyes and ears everywhere,' Godfather pointed to his own big features.

'Would the diplomat, I mean my new father, help me to get hold of Gringo's phone number?'

'I don't see why not. More questions?'

'No,' I said.

'No,' Jam said.

'Fine, repeat the plan, Merywan. Word for word?' Godfather closed his eyes.

I did as I was told. I was desperate to get to America in one piece and was not about to mess it up. I hesitated slightly when it came to cutting off my hair, but I dutifully recounted every instruction. Godfather was pleased. 'It is a lot of money, Merywan,' he said, blowing his nose out of the window. 'I only take five hundred dinars for my service. Five thousand goes to the diplomat, and the rest will pay for your passport and the others involved.'

'I understand, thank you. I will remember your greetings to Gringo.' Godfather laughed and we imitated Gringo, in a duel, shooting at each other with our middle fingers, Bang! Bang...! But

I was only half smiling since I could not rid myself of the image of Uncle Hitch's broken body, and the thought of his terrible end at the hands of the Kurdish traitor.

Jam drove around a couple of times to make sure it was safe before making his way to my house. My heart raced, but I tried to stay calm. *I know, God may not forgive me for taking Rashaba's money, but I will make better use of it.* As I stepped out of the car, Trouble ran out of our house. I ducked back inside. 'My brother,' I said. 'It's better if I wait until he is out of sight.' Through the car window I saw Trouble, holding on to a bag and looking to the left. Dara Pig, in his resprayed white car, appeared. Trouble got in and they accelerated away.

'He's gone!' Jam said. 'Yes, he's gone,' Godfather repeated. He too was nervous by now, and despite his nickname, he bit his nails like a child.

Another bag of leaflets for Trouble to distribute tonight, I imagined, as I made my way inside. Fortunately for me the courtyard was empty. I ran up the stairs and into our room, straight to the pillow. Without hesitation, I grabbed it and I was about to put it in the large carrier bag I was holding, but I stopped. The pillow felt different, it felt too light!

I was not supposed to, but I had to open it. I found the pillow full of chicken feathers, absolutely no sign of the money, not even one dinar. I was devastated. *Had Rashaba taken the money out last night to pay for the new house? Surely not, I was awake thinking about Sunshine, about America, besides praying for most of the night. I would have noticed. Have they moved the money's hiding place?* I checked all the other pillows. I looked between the mattresses, inside Boraq and everywhere I could think of. I heard the horn from Jam's car beeping. I was taking too long, but I could not go out without the money. I stuffed the feathers back in the pillow and tried my best to make the place look the same as before, alerted again by the persistent beeps from Jam's car.

I heard Mother as she walked in. 'Arsalan, Baban, Mery!' She called. I was the first to run out onto the veranda. 'Your grandfather's house is burning. The flames are going high up into the sky,' she said, as if she had won the war against Saddam.

When Flathead and Hercules heard Mother, they burst out of

their room and ran up to the rooftop to join her. I followed, until I was frozen by another loud beep from Jam's car. My hesitation could not hold, however, as the urge to witness the conflagration was too great to resist. Huge billowing flames rose from the King's Castle. Flathead may not have succeeded, but someone else had.

'Am rojhi, sali tazaya Nawroza... today Nawroz is back, the ancient Kurdish celebration brings us joy and hope...' My uncles were amazed to see the house on fire and sang our song, welcoming back our New Year, dancing around Mother.

'You took too long,' Jam said, as he drove away.

'The money is gone,' I blurted out.

'What the fuck are you talking about,' Godfather turned to me.

'The money is gone,' I repeated.

'Calm down, Mery,' Jam asked, though he was not calm himself.

'What do you mean, the money is gone?'

'It is not there.'

'Have you searched everywhere?'

'I have. The money is gone.'

'This is fucked, my business is ruined,' Godfather moaned.

'This is not about your damn business!' Jam shouted.

'I have to be paid.'

'You will be, and Mery is going away today.'

'No, he is not. You have to pay first, that was the agreement.'

'The fucking agreement was payment on arrival.' Jam turned to Godfather.

'Watch out for that bicycle, Jam!' Godfather shrieked. 'Fuck, you almost killed the man.'

'The money is gone,' I carried on saying.

'I will sell my shop.'

'Fuck that, Jam, it could take ages.'

'It may, but I will pay you. Mery must go today.'

'No chance, he will not go anywhere, not until I see ten thousand dinars.'

'You idiot, you care about nothing but money.'

'The money is gone.'

A fight broke out between Jam and Godfather. Jam attempted to punch him while driving, and Godfather was ducking to defend himself. Jam threw frustrated punches, he couldn't reach him. The car veered left and right on the road. 'The money is gone...' I moaned, hollowly. Jam kept throwing punches at the big man. We all shouted at once. No one listened. 'You will be paid, you fucker...' 'Ten thousand...' 'Mery must go...' 'The money...' 'He goes nowhere...'

'The money!' I shouted the loudest, and they both turned to me.

'Ardalan! My brother must have taken the money.'

Jam stopped the car. 'Where can we find him?' he asked, looking hopeful. Godfather smiled again.

'I don't know.'

'Fuck, I can no longer buy this shit.' Godfather jumped out. He walked to Jam's window. 'Come back with the money and make sure you come before the 15th or I will have to charge you one thousand dinars for expenses and compensation.'

'Shall I pay your taxi to take you home?' Jam said, and pushed him away.

We left Godfather on the road. I climbed over to the passenger's seat and we drove to the teahouse. The tea maker had not seen Trouble and Dara Pig. We drove around Iskan, where, on the night of the leafleting, four soldiers and two militiamen had been killed in the shoot-out. I saw that my slogans had been painted over. Above the roundabout by the Priadi dual carriageway, a new Saddam poster had replaced the burned one. We searched for hours. The garage in Bazaar Hasiraka was our last bet, but when we made it there in the late afternoon, there was no sign of them or the Pig's car.

'Trouble, I will never forgive you for this.' I could have cried.

'Let's hope we find him before the 15th. If not, I'll sell my shop and pay for your trip too. If we don't make it this time, there will be other occasions, or we could go out together via the mountains.'

'What about Godfather?'

'I will deal with him. I am sorry, Mery,' Jam said, as he sat back.

'You did your best, Jam. Thank you, my friend.'

The sun was setting on my long and disastrous day as I made it back to Qala. I could still see a pillar of black smoke rising from Grandfather's house. I went to Sunshine to give her all the bad news, on the day we were to celebrate my birthday and get engaged. It was heartbreaking to face her, sitting in the living room, on the sofa, under Gringo's smiling portrait on the wall. She cried broken-hearted tears for Uncle Hitch.

'I am so sorry about our engagement,' I said softly.

'We can get engaged another time,' Sunshine answered between sobs. She opened her hand; there was a little box in it. 'Happy birthday,' she said, trying her best to smile while fighting back the sobbing that choked in her throat. I opened the box and found a small golden heart pendent with an S inscribed on one side, and an M on the other.

A miracle

It was a fresh, late-winter evening, cool rather than cold, so we could dine outside on the veranda. I could hardly bear to listen to Mother talking about finding a wife for Hercules, it made eating very difficult. *Trouble had indeed been carrying Rashaba's money in his bag, not leaflets. I wonder where he has disappeared to? Maybe he and his Pig friend have left the country altogether?* I was not looking forward to when Rashaba discovered his money was missing. *I will not mention anything, or else he will accuse me of helping Trouble to steal it.*

Rashaba strode upstairs, for once looking happy, bearing a watermelon on his shoulder. 'The agent has found us a house in Old Rahimawa,' he said. 'I went to see it earlier. It has a spacious bedroom, a small kitchen, toilet and a bathroom in the courtyard.'

'Old Rahimawa! Where Popcorn lives! That is far from Qala.'

'Not far enough for me, Merywan. It will only cost us nine thousand five hundred dinars. At last, our own house.'

'Could we stay here a few more days, until my brothers go out to Baghdad?' Mother asked. 'Fine,' Rashaba said, and put down the watermelon. 'But I have to pay for the house no later than tomorrow.' He walked into our room. Fifteen years of carefully orchestrated secrecy was about to end. I closed my eyes and waited for the storm to break, as it duly did with his thunderous roar. He was holding his pillow in his hand. 'Where is the money?' he demanded.

'Where you always keep it,' Mother answered.

'Here, see? I kept it in here.' He emptied the pillow of the feathers and chucked it at Mother, hitting her in the face. She turned as white as a sheet, as the blood drained from her face. She could not believe her own eyes, nor her hands as they dug frantically at the contents of the pillow.

'Where is the money, wife?' Rashaba grunted, and grabbed Mother by her neck, something I had never seen him do before. He picked up the kitchen knife that Mother was using to cut the watermelon. He pushed her towards Star and myself and held the knife up to our faces. 'I will cut off your heads one by one if you don't give me back my money.'

'I don't know,' Mother mumbled, a croaking sound escaping from her throat in Father's fierce grip.

'I don't know,' Star cried.

He brought the knife to my eyes. 'I don't know where your money is. Perhaps you should talk to Trouble.'

'It can't be Trouble, you son of a dog.' *Darwesh Rashaba has declared himself a dog. He has gone crazy, and he will kill us.* 'I have not seen Trouble for the whole week. Where is my money?'

'It's not just your money!' Mother shouted. 'It's our money, our money...'

He slapped her hard. Star cried even louder. He brought the knife to my neck. I struggled out of his grip and called for my uncles. Flathead and Hercules dashed out of their room. For an instant Rashaba seemed to want to fight them, but when he saw the brothers storming up, he ran into our room and locked the door. Mother wanted to stop her brothers, but it was in vain. Hercules and Flathead kicked and battered the door, shouting for my coward of a father to come out. This time I did not mind them calling him an idiot.

Mother held the empty pillow in her brother's face. Sobbing, she begged them, 'Our life savings are all gone. Ten thousand dinars! Please don't hurt my husband, he worked most of his life to save this money, to buy us a house.'

Flathead and Hercules backed away and both turned towards me.

'I swear I have not taken the money,' and I put my hand on my heart. My uncles suggested that we go down to stay in their place, but Mother wished them to leave us alone. She wanted to be with her husband. 'My father has a knife with him,' I said, holding Star in my arms. 'He might kill himself.'

Flathead and Hercules tried to reason with Rashaba through the door. They promised to help him to find out where his money was. Father threw the knife out of the window, then opened the door and let us in. He sat in a corner, and long after everyone was asleep, he was still sitting there in bitter silence.

The next day he did not go to work. The shock of losing his money had made him very ill. We thought he was going to die. Mother massaged his head and mopped his sweat. *For her sake, I pray to You, God, to keep him alive*. My uncles postponed their trip to Baghdad to support Mother in nursing Rashaba.

It seemed that he was living his last days, if not moments. Mother did not leave his side. My uncles searched all over town for two days, but there was no sign of Trouble or Dara Pig.

I should be landing in Washington DC at this very moment, I thought while lying in bed. It was long after midnight on the 16th. I was the only one awake. There was a gentle knock. Not on the main door, but the door to our room. The knock came again, slightly louder, but not enough to wake up Mother. I opened the door. I did not recognise the visitor holding a bag.

'Glad it's you, Mery,' he whispered.

'Who are you?'

He lowered the scarf from his face enough for me to identify him. I was stunned. Then he beckoned urgently for me to go up to the roof with him. 'I did not know about this,' he said, referring to the bag in his hand. 'Ardalan and I had finished with our duties in town and were called to retreat to the mountains. In the darkness of the night in the hills, we were trapped in an Iraqi army ambush. They shot at us. We did our best, but we only had two pistols. Ardalan was badly hit. He just managed to tell me to take the bag and that it was his father's money, before... well... they were his last words.' *My God, Trouble is dead!*

'He wanted to give the money to our Kurdish armed struggle, but using stolen cash was never part of our plan. I managed to sneak away through the rocks in the dark. I had taken his identity card and later burned it. When I felt safe, I opened the bag. I couldn't believe what was inside. I risked my life to bring it back, but I made it. Here, ten thousand dinars. I must go soon.'

I am glad I did not kill the Pig, as I had wished to in the past. I will call him Mr Dara, if I ever see him again.

'Ardalan told me a lot about you, Mery, about your desire for freedom, hope for the Kurds to be able to govern themselves and your warrior's spirit. You may not know this, but in a way, your brother Ardalan was jealous of you, of your strength and your fight for your personal freedom. Actually, you inspired him to become a member and get involved in the Freedom for Life organisation. Ardalan loved you, Mery. He became my friend so that I could protect you, he was worried about you getting abused by paedophiles and asked if I could keep you under my wing. He knew I was not one of them. I had to portray myself as a bully to disguise my other activities and in order to infiltrate the paedophile ranks.'

'You are not a paedophile?'

'No, Mery. I despise them, but I had to pretend, in order to save many boys like you. Your brother was not a bad person, just a young man who wanted to enjoy himself. Maybe he was born in the wrong place, the culture was too brutal for him and he could not cope with it.'

Trouble had given me a hard time, but in his heart he loved me. I felt very shocked and saddened by his death.

'I want you to remember your brother as a true patriot. He was on his way to becoming a Peshmerga. He died like a hero.'

'What about my grandfather's house?'

'Ardalan burned it down,' Dara said, before he left as quietly as he had come, via the rooftops.

I looked into the bag, which was tightly packed with the stacks of dinar that Dara had risked his life to return. I must go to Jam at once and then to Godfather. I quietly walked down the steps with the money like a scared cat. I went to the main door and opened it, then shaking my head, I closed it again and went back upstairs.

'God is great!' Father called out in excitement in the early morning, waking us all up. 'Allah u Akbar, wife, wake up, it's a miracle. We had the angels visiting us in the night to bring us Allah's miracle.'

Mother found it hard to believe, she had to look at the money several times. My parents never learned about the mysterious visitor and I did not tell them of my brother's death. I did not want them to discover that Trouble had taken their money, and played along like a good actor, appearing to accept that this was indeed a miracle.

After Dara had left, I had intended to go straight to Jam, but, of course, we had missed Godfather's deadline, the 15th, and having seen my mother crying so much alongside my father, I realised that I simply could not steal their money. *They will never know I had placed the money by Rashaba's bed, under his hand, while he was asleep.*

Rashaba recovered rapidly. He insisted on going out the same morning to buy us the house. 'God is great,' he called again.

'What a miracle.'

Mother explained Father's intention to her brothers. My uncles wished that we did not have to move away. I felt the same. I did not want to go away from Sunshine, her family, and Qala, our great citadel. At the same time I was happy to leave the house which brought back so many sad memories. I took out my treasure box from Papula's Boraq and hid it in my mum's.

'What is that?' she asked.

'My treasure box. I don't want Father to see it.'

We had so little in the way of possessions that in a matter of one hour, with our friends' help, our belongings were all packed. 'We are going on a picnic,' Sunshine said, as she helped out. 'I would like you to come with us. It will be on 21 March.'

'On Nawroz day?'

'Yes, even though we are not allowed to celebrate Nawroz, we can still go out to welcome the spring, to welcome back our New Year and to refresh our hopes.'

We finished loading everything onto Flathead's truck. My parents, after a brief chat and a quick farewell to Master Shamal and his family, climbed up and sat in the front. Star and I sat in the back on top of the mattresses. I longed to kiss Sunshine, who kept waving until we were out of sight.

We drove down the hill from the Qala citadel. I caught a glimpse of Grandfather's burned house. Thanks to Trouble, only the skeleton of the building still stood. From Kornish we made our way to Old Rahimawa on the north east side of Kirkuk. The small village had now become part of the city, due to the rapid expansion to accommodate the Arab settlers. The minute we finished unloading, I asked my uncles if I could go with them to Baghdad. They talked to Father and he allowed it. I was glad to see my parents so happy. I thanked Dara hundreds of times in my heart. The only thing I absolutely hated about buying a new house was that Rashaba had to change his ethnicity from Kurd to Arab to be allowed to buy in Kirkuk.

Rashaba could not have cared less. He was just content to have a place of his own to live in into his old age, where our landlord could not come and shout at him for the rent and where he could sleep in peace. From now on he did not have to worry whether he was working or not, he did not have to pay rent. We could live on bread and water, according to him. He was proud of his achievement as a dervish, to have gained Allah's mercy to such a degree that he was given back both his money and a house. He even bought a sheep to be sacrificed, so that we could send the meat to the new neighbours. Mother had a nice smile on her face as she put the palm of her right hand in the blood and marked the door of our house, to keep away the evil eye.

'We shall call the house Lover's Hill, in memory of my family and my village,' Rashaba said, kissing the wall.

He stayed at home sorting out the small kitchen and mending the toilet door. Then he spent the entire day going around and admiring his 'palace'. He started to dig a tiny trench in the courtyard. 'We will grow our own vegetables, Merywan,' he said, as he dug into the red soil. 'I will buy a couple of chickens and possibly a cow. We will only need bread and thankfully, your mother is expert at making it.'

With some hesitation, I suggested Star should go to school. Much to my surprise, Rashaba gave his consent immediately. I had believed he would never let Star, a girl, go to the devil's house where they taught science. He was truly a changed man, and over the following days he even bought some kebabs to treat the family.

After registering Star at the local primary school, to start in the coming year, I went out, searching for Popcorn. I asked several people and was directed to where he used to live. He would have been my neighbour, but he had not been seen around for a while. Over the kebab dinner, Father spoke to me, for the first time as an adult. 'What is Shamal's daughter's name?' he asked. 'Sunshine,' Mother answered. 'She would make a good wife,' he said.

'Merywan, do you want me to talk to Master Shamal?'

This is truly a miracle. He has completely forgotten about my neuter problem and is suggesting that I marry Sunshine! What about the way she behaves and thinks and how she dresses!

'She is the daughter of a teacher... you hate science,' I answered, dumbfounded.

'Master Shamal is a good man,' he said.

'You may not like this, Father, but since you are talking to me like a man, I wish you had not become Arab in order to buy us a house.' Rashaba almost choked on his mouthful of kebab. Mother banged on his back. He recovered. He pulled himself away and sat silently. Mother tried to get him to finish his dinner but he did not. He was too hurt. I am not sure if I did it to him or it was because I woke him up to the reality that he had become Arab. It was the worst insult a Kurd could ever be exposed to, especially Rashaba, as Arabs had killed all his family. Tears poured from his tired eyes. I sat next to him and put my arm around his shoulders.

'I am sorry, Father. I did not mean to hurt you.'

'It is not you, Merywan.' He could hardly talk for fear that he might burst into tears. 'Qayshbaldar, the monster,' he said, and cried.

Picnic with Qayshbaldar

At dawn on 21 March, the first day of spring and of our new year, I sat next to Peaceful and Rabbit in the back seat of the car. Sunshine and Jwana squeezed in alongside Shamal, and he began to drive north. Although we were not allowed to celebrate, thousands of Kurds would still head to the countryside for a picnic, so the roads would be packed. Rabbit was grumpy. He did not want to go out, and had plans to go into the city centre with me. I could not work out Rabbit's logic, as I was delighted to spend Nawroz with Sunshine and her family. It was only later that I learned the reason why he objected to the outing.

During the peacetime of the Autonomy Agreement, millions went out on Nawroz, not only Kurds, but also Turkman, Christians and Arabs, leaving the towns and cities deserted. People danced in the open around large fires. Apparently, in the same year I was born, a huge celebration took place, some twenty kilometres to the north of Kirkuk. People, using every means of transport, turned up from all over the country. Master Shamal recalled the steam train that used to travel between Kirkuk and Erbil, packed full of passengers.

'You could hardly see any part of the train, even the top was covered with people,' he said, as we passed the same place. 'This whole area was one crowd of visitors taking part in the celebrations.' Those days were long gone, but the fact remained that despite all the risks and the government's restrictions, we were out on Nawroz, proving that our dream for our country to be free was still very much alive. The countryside was green, fresh and lush after the winter rains. Because of the Kurdish-Arab war, and the significance of the date, the number of checkpoints had greatly increased. By the time we could feel the warmth of the sun, we were well into the mountains.

We settled by the nearby Gali waterfall, shaded by peach and fig trees. Peaceful played his violin beautifully. The rest of us arranged fires to cook lunch. Sunshine and I went looking for dry twigs. 'Don't go too far into the hills,' Master Shamal warned.

'There are mines around.'

'Peaceful must be worried about his coming concert,' I said, once we were away. 'I wish he was not so reclusive.'

Sunshine came closer. 'This is to stay between us,' she said. 'My brother had a terrible experience as a child, when Father was a freedom fighter in the mountains. He was sexually abused.'

'By whom?'

'A freedom fighter.'

'A Peshmerga?'

'Are you surprised?'

'Peshmerga are heroes, they don't do such things.'

'No, Mery. Apart from a small minority, they are ignorant and if it comes to it, they are no different from the Mukhabarat.'

How can she compare our Peshmerga to the Mukhabarat?

'Was your father with Barzani or Talabani?'

'Neither. He hates both, and believes the Kurdish leaders are only interested in wealth and power, just like Saddam.'

'That is not true. Our leaders are sacrificing their lives for our freedom. They are living in the harshest conditions in the mountains, all because they refuse dictatorship and want to establish democracy in this country.'

'Yes, in your dreams. Is it for democracy and freedom that your leaders are killing each other's forces with their infighting, while the enemy is wiping out our people?'

I knew she was right, but didn't want to admit it to myself, and I suggested that we change the subject.

'The truth hurts, Mery. But you should know that they not only abused my brother, they also tortured my father and beat Rabbit, when he was only ten, because of Father's different views and political ideas.'

'The Kurds?'

'Yes, our own people.'

'No more, please. Not on Nawroz day.'

I looked back at Peaceful playing his violin and reflected on the terrible atrocities inflicted on Master Shamal and his family at the hands of our own people. *I now understand why Master Shamal never talked about our armed struggle, and why Peaceful did not go to school, and I realise that Rabbit has kept secrets from me.* I was shaken by the truth of what some of the Peshmerga were capable of, and mostly, of the fact that in Sunshine's eyes they were barely any different from our enemy. I left some wood by the fire, took off my shoes and walked alongside the stream to the waterfall, despondently kicking the falling water. It was icy cold and soothing, but inside I was burning.

'I am sorry if I hurt your feelings,' Sunshine said, and took my hand as she walked along beside me.

'I'm glad you told the truth.'

'I have finished reading your letters. You are very brave to share all your secrets with me.'

'Did I do wrong?'

'No, thanks for letting me read them. I am so sorry about the loss of your family members and friends. I cried for Princess Aida and Papula. Such huge tragedies for you.'

'Are you upset with me for having made love with my auntie?'

'Of course I am! Especially when after this you say to me that we must not kiss or touch each other. What's good for you should be good for me, too. But, having read about your childhood, I can understand why you did it.'

'Will you still marry me?'

'Maybe,' she raised one eyebrow in my direction. 'But people have to make sacrifices when they marry, you know. You must never see prostitutes again, for a start...'

'I won't, I won't!' I interrupted her. I looked deeply into her eyes.

'I desire no other woman but you, my love,' I said, holding her hands in mine. 'And I will love you for ever.'

We admired the waterfall and the sound of the cascading water rushing down from the mountains, arm in arm. 'I may go to Baghdad with my uncles for a while,' I said. 'It's safer if I stay away from Kirkuk, and then we shall see what develops.' Sunshine stayed silent, but she nodded in agreement.

Just as Rabbit and Peaceful joined us by the waterfall, we suddenly became aware of a whirring noise above the sound of rushing water, and much more insistent. We looked up. Several helicopters circled above, those same giant wasps that were buzzing over our cities, stinging at will. Special Forces were parachuting down towards us, filling the sky. Sunshine and I turned to each other in anguish. *Are we caught in the middle of a battle? The army must have got a tip about Peshmerga presence in the area.*

'I told you we should not have come here,' Rabbit said. 'Let's go back to the family and pack up.'

We did not get far. Within seconds, soldiers were landing around us and appearing from all sides. Two tanks and several armoured vehicles thundered down into the gorge, and a few trucks followed, carrying hundreds of Republican Guards, armed to the teeth. The Special Forces jumped off their vehicles and took up their positions. In the blink of an eye, the narrow road, and the area surrounding the waterfall, along the stream, between the trees and right across the top of the hills were covered with Iraqi military. We tried to walk down calmly.

'Stay where you are!' a soldier barked, in Arabic.

It was still relatively early, and only a few families had arrived by the side of the waterfall, including one Indian family, the first foreigners I had ever seen in Kurdistan having a picnic. They too were evidently alarmed. It was hardly the paradise they had been told to expect. A dozen soldiers were making way for the next convoy, which was headed by a Jeep with a machine gun mounted on top. On board were Mukhabarat men, brandishing an arsenal of weapons, leaning out of car windows and the open rear doors, their guns pointing in every direction. We were startled by the ear-splitting noise of jets swooping low overhead, the sounds cracking and echoing around the gorge long after they disappeared from view. *What on earth is happening? Is Abu Ali amongst them?*

Every area was searched, every person was checked. The army demonstrated their total control, as if to show that not even a bird could have escaped them. This beautiful, peaceful, remote place had been overrun with what looked like more than a thousand men covering every inch of rock and grassland. The soldiers started waving their guns when a convoy of black Mercedes arrived. After seeing so many television reports showing similar convoys, we knew this could mean only one thing.

'We give you our blood, our souls, Sir Saddam,' the soldiers chanted.

'What is going on?' I dared to ask one of the apparently elated soldiers.

'Clap your hands and dance, for this is a special day in your life,' he answered. 'Clap your hands and shout, "long live our great leader Saddam!"'

Suddenly, a crowd of civilians appeared, cheering and dancing. I was sure they were Saddam's elite personal guards disguised as ordinary Iraqis. The doors of all the Mercedes swung open in unison and Saddam's personal bodyguards, the elite forces from the Revolutionary Command, jumped out. The cars were all the same model, with blacked-out, bullet-proof windows. Saddam himself must be here, I realised, with a terror all the more acute for the fact that it was impossible to work out which vehicle he was in. I doubted if even his guards could tell. When travelling, Jam had told me, Saddam would move from one identical car to another every so often, so that his vehicle could not be identified and targeted. Numerous lookalikes were deployed to further confound any potential assassins. Whenever I saw Saddam walking about with hardly any guards on television, I always wondered why nobody shot him. He looked like such an easy target. *How could he successfully survive and apparently thrive when more than a third of the Iraqi people were his sworn enemies? Why had the many plans to overthrow him all failed? Several ministers and army generals were caught and hanged long before they even set in motions their plots to topple him. How could this monster be so indestructible?* I would finally find the answers to those questions that day in Gali.

Saddam Hussein, the President of the Republic, the Prime Minister, chief of the army, leader of the Ba'ath political party, Commander of the Supreme Council of the Revolution, head of the Amn, the secret police and the Mukhabarat, the most brutal dictator in the short history of Iraq, the new Salahadin of the Muslim world and the biggest enemy of my people, the deeply savage monster who had tormented me for so many years, was walking up to us here in Gali, in the heart of our Kurdistan.

I never imagined, even in my nightmares, that I might one day stand face to face with the giant monster himself, the one from the portrait in my treasure box which depicts him fiercely holding on to the innocent people in his grip and eating them by the dozen. I got it from Hercules, a caricature he had acquired when he had been a freedom fighter.

'If you talk politics, the monster will find you, no matter where you hide...' Watching the horrible spectre of Saddam himself approaching, I remembered the words of warning my father had spoken ten years earlier. At first, I had believed that he was talking about monsters in fairy tales. I was wrong. This monster was real and had thousands of heads and millions of eyes and ears. He had wings and arms and legs everywhere, and gigantic jaws to crush dozens of people in one go. His appetite was insatiable, and he only ate human flesh, with a particular taste for Kurds. At that time, when I was five years old, there were not many Arabs living in my city. I had seen a few around Kirkuk coming from the villages in the south to sell their dairy products in the market, with their long dishdasha and bare feet, looking quite different from everyone else.

'Who are they?' I had asked my father. 'Arabs – the people of Iraq, our neighbours,' he had explained. 'Is the monster Arab?'

'Yes. That is why you must never say anything bad about Arabs.' Listening to Father, I had tried to figure out this giant in my head, but neither Dinosaurs nor Cyclops, King Kong nor Godzilla could compare to the fear he engendered in my heart. I envied the enemy for having such a special monster. I wished we Kurds had one too, one powerful enough to lead our fight. 'Why did God create such a monster to eat thousands of innocent people?' I had asked.

'The devil created the monster,' he answered. 'But Father, you said God created everything, including the devil? That means that God created the monster.' 'Mery, don't say that again, that is blasphemy.' 'Yes, Father.'

Rashaba's prediction had come true. Ten years on, the Arabs were taking over Kirkuk, and now their monster was visiting the mountains of Kurdistan to prove to the nation that he was truly omnipotent. I did not see which car Saddam emerged from, and my heart leapt to my mouth when I saw him only a couple of metres away.

'Monster!' I whispered.

'Who?' Sunshine asked, turning to me.

'He who is heading for us.'

I longed for Flathead's gun, for Gringo's gun, to shoot him in the head. *Saddam is the monster's main head, crushing him would destroy all the other heads at once. That is the only way to free myself and my people from this brutal existence.*

Iraqi TV camera crews were buzzing around to record the scene, but it was clear that they were also special guards, his personal crew. The dressed-up Kurds, Arabs and other ethnicities crowded around him, clapping and cheering him as if he were their Lord. He walked to the family next to us. They welcomed him with thinly disguised, fear. He bent down to a child. 'Do you know me?' he had to ask twice before the shy child answered, 'Yes, you are Saddam.'

'Say Rais Saddam, son,' the father said, with a plastic smile on his face. 'Say our bravest hero and the hero of the Arab nation.'

'No,' the child answered. 'He is Saddam.'

The father was evidently paralysed with terror, but Saddam deigned to ignore this transgression. The minute he moved away, the father squeezed the child's arm. The little one cried. Then, the Indian family cleverly asked permission to pose and take a picture with the monster.

I could see that the cameramen were trying to ensure that the soldiers did not appear in their images, so as to portray Saddam as if he moved around freely and unguarded, the same way I had seen him before on television.

'Do you think he is the real one, or one of his doubles?' Sunshine asked.

'The real one.'

'How do you know?'

'None of his doubles have such miserably false smiles.'

The moment he turned in our direction, one of his guards banged on our backs. 'Clap and cheer for Rais Saddam,' he hissed, and started to cheer. Rabbit, Sunshine and I did not. Peaceful did. He genuinely seemed to be impressed to have a chance not only to meet Saddam but also to shake hands with him.

He shook hands with Rabbit, Sunshine and finally me. I did not let go of his hand.

'Ya hala, ya hala, hello, hello,' Saddam said. 'Urbi, Arab?' he asked.

'Ana Kurdi, I am a Kurd,' I answered back in his language, looking right into his eyes. *I am the grandson of the man who was known as King Sherzad, the man who was hanged on your orders before I was born,* I wanted to shout into his monstrous face.

'Kurd and Arab are brothers,' he said, and tried to pull away his hand.

I have spent my life fearing this blood sucker, and now I am not going to let him get away without getting it off my chest. If I die, I may as well die with my head held up, as Old Zorab wisely said.

'Happy Nawroz,' I said, and smiled, speaking from my heart, as the noise died down around us.

Saddam Hussein, the all-powerful leader, was held in the palm of my hand and, for a mere moment, I would not let him go.

'Happy Nawroz,' he replied.

Peaceful's concert

Soon after sunset on that same Nawroz, Rashaba, for the first time in fifteen years, stepped inside Flathead's living room, where the television was on. It was a heart-warming occasion and a joyful way for us to end the day that we had encountered the monster. Flathead had bought sweets and a tray of baklava as well as a crate of Pepsi to celebrate our New Year. He even lit a few candles to spark the light of hope for some freedom in our hearts. Soon our attention moved to the TV screen as we watched the monster's visit to Gali. The whole family, including Father, were astonished to see Saddam parading around our Kurdish mountains. As I expected, the filming excluded the army and only framed Saddam with his puppets prancing around him.

'This is shameful for the Kurds,' Flathead spat, 'an insult to our land.' But when the TV camera panned on the role-playing Kurds welcoming Saddam, beyond them in the background, you could see Rabbit, Sunshine and myself standing there, watching, not clapping or cheering, and Flathead smiled contentedly. Then followed my brief moment with the monster.

'Happy Nawroz.'

Everyone reacted in disbelief to seeing me reluctantly shaking hands with Saddam and saying Happy Nawroz to him. 'Well done, Mery,' Flathead said, and he grabbed me and kissed me on my cheeks. 'Up Kissinger's bum,' Hercules said, and he held his thumb up. 'That was really brave, Merywan,' Master Shamal nodded.

'Mery saved our New Year,' Jwana said, patting my shoulder. 'Your grandfathers will be very proud of you, Son,' my mother said, with a broad smile, ruffling my hair. 'Let's hope the Mukhabarat will not pick up on it,' Rabbit said, through his teeth. 'Merywan meant no harm in wishing Happy Nawroz to our President,' Rashaba added, as he stuffed another baklava into his mouth.

'This Nawroz will be remembered for years to come, Mery,' Sunshine said. Instead of a kiss, she shook my hand. 'You did what all the true Kurds would wish to do. You made many hearts very happy today, including mine.'

'Thanks Sunshine, and thanks everyone,' I said, as I stood up, facing them. 'I will not forget this day because my father has made peace with my uncles, and because what I said to Saddam would have made my grandfathers proud. But above all, I will remember this moment because my father approves of my friendship with Sunshine.' I would have liked to say "my love for Sunshine" and to add a cheer, but did not want to push my luck with Rashaba.

It was a night that I didn't want to end. The people I most loved surrounded me. Our discussions covered many things, yet the conversation never strayed too far from my bravery in facing Saddam. Master Shamal invited my family to Peaceful's concert, which was planned for the end of the week. By the time Sunshine's family left, it was too late to make our way back home, so Flathead suggested that we sleep at his place. I was really surprised when Father accepted. He had changed a lot since he bought the house. In the morning I went to see Sunshine. Master Shamal, who had worked as a teacher for nearly fifteen years, and his wife Jwana who had been teaching for ten years, had both been summoned that morning and summarily sacked. The atmosphere was tense. Rabbit blamed me for his parent's awful situation.

'What has this to do with Mery?' Sunshine protested.

'He is bringing us bad luck,' Rabbit said, pointing at me.

'You are just jealous because he loves me.'

'Shut up!'

'You shut up.'

'Stop this, please!' Peaceful begged, in tears.

'I love you as my own family and have never wanted to harm you,' I said, looking into Rabbit's eyes. 'I must go now.'

'Wait, Merywan!' Master Shamal said. 'Calm down, everyone. This has nothing to do with Merywan. Jwana and I were sacked because we went out at Nawroz.'

'And I am glad we did,' Jwana said.

'Oh yes, and how are we supposed to live from now on?' Rabbit asked, banging his crutch.

'I will find another job,' Master Shamal said, with his infinite optimism. 'The car could become a taxi, if necessary. We will not die of hunger.'

'I still work as a builder,' Peaceful stood by his father.

'I assume that we will cancel Peaceful's concert,' Rabbit remarked, strangely.

'No, we will not,' Peaceful answered.

'No, we will not,' Master Shamal confirmed.

I reluctantly stayed away from Sunshine for a while, to give the family some space, and spent time playing with Star and helping out my father with the new house. It was almost a week since Rashaba had gone back to work. Somehow, it all felt different between us, and at times he talked to me as a friend. 'I have not forgotten about your Sunshine,' he said. 'I will talk to Shamal whenever you want. But there is something I need to know. I hope you don't mind me asking about your circumcision?'

'Don't worry, you were too busy, an excellent doctor has sorted me out.' Rashaba nodded, smiling broadly between his golden teeth. He seemed truly pleased about my news. 'Tonight Peaceful has his violin concert.' I couldn't find a better time to ask, 'would you like to go, Father?'

'You know I have never been to the cinema, or the theatre, and I have never watched television until last week, I was worried about committing sins.'

'Father, there is nothing wrong in listening to music. He is Master Shamal's son. Please, I would like us to go as a family...'

'Your mum too?'

'Yes.'

He turned to Mother. 'Our son wants us to go to the theatre.' *Our son, he said 'our'.*

'That would be nice,' Mother answered, with a smile, as if she had always nurtured a desire to go to the theatre.

'Fine Merywan, I will, and your mum will come with me.'

'Thank you, Father,' and I kissed his hands.

'What colour do you think would look nice on the main door?' *He actually wants my opinion.*

'Light blue is my favourite.'

'Light blue it is,' he said. 'Here, take this dinar, buy a pot of paint and a brush and four Pepsis, for you, for Star, for your dear mother and one for me. Off you go!'

'Yes, sir.'

I ran all the way to the shops and jumped in the air for joy. I was so happy. I was looking forward to getting back home and talking some more to my dad. He had become very sweet since 'the miracle' of buying the house. I bought everything needed and ran back home as fast as I could. I put the four Pepsis in the new fridge, opened the tin and started to paint the door. Father went on the roof to patch up the cracks left by the winter frosts. Mother was in the courtyard, bathing Star. A police Jeep drove up to the house and parked outside. I looked for Abu Ali, but he was not there. *The police must be looking for Trouble. Whatever the reason, having the monster's men on our doorstep does not bode well.*

'Darwesh Rashaba?' the officer called, followed by three policemen with AK-47s in their hands. 'Yes,' my father answered, and rushed down to face them. 'Do you have a cold drink for us?' the officer asked.

'Of course,' Rashaba said, in a friendly tone.

Father gave them the four Pepsis I had bought for us. I kept on painting the door, but could not take my eyes off the monster's men. Mother dried Star with a towel, anxiety flooding her eyes. We waited whilst they casually slurped their drinks. At once, the officer threw the bottle against the wall, sending broken glass in all directions, his men gleefully following suit.

'Is this your house?' he asked brusquely.

'Yes, sir.' Father answered, proudly.

'Well, not any longer. You are being deported.' The officer handed Rashaba a forced removal order. 'My father can't read,' I pleaded.

'Read it for him!' The officer grunted.

'Yes, it's the official order by the Iraqi government for our deportation,' I reported reluctantly, passing the paper into Father's shaky hands. He asked me to read it again, which I did.

'Go back and finish painting the door,' the officer ordered.

I threw away the brush. The monster's man was about to grab me, but my father stood in his way. 'You can't deport me, I am an Arab,' Father said, firmly. 'You are a false Arab and a bastard Kurd!' the officer shouted, as he viciously gun-butted Rashaba. Mother screamed and ran to her husband. Star and I did the same.

'Don't hit my father!' I yelled, but the policemen were laughing too much to take any notice. We gathered protectively around our father, something we had never done before as a family.

'Do you have a television?' the officer asked. Father could not talk.

'No,' Mother answered.

'Do you have a fridge?'

'A small one, my husband bought it yesterday.'

'You can't take it, all the electric appliances must be left behind.' In my world, being poor sometimes had its benefits. Once a year on the monster's birthday, in order to prove their loyalty, the rich paid a large sum of money, in cash or in gold, as a contribution to Saddam and his ceaseless warmongering. Many were convinced that most of the gold ended up in the safe of Sajida Khirallah, the monster's wife. She was loaded with the wealth of innocent Iraqis, and that was apparently all that she cared for.

Father broke away from us. He got hold of a pair of pliers and pushed them into his mouth. Mother and I tried to stop him but he carried on. He pulled out his teeth one by one. Blood poured out of his mouth. He held the three golden teeth in the palm of his hand, proffering the blood-stained treasure to the officer. 'This is all that we have left, sir,' he said. 'Take them, please. They are a gift for Rais Saddam's birthday. I beg you, don't force us to leave, this house is our life.'

The officer examined the teeth. 'Pure gold! But unfortunately today is not Rais Saddam's birthday,' he said. 'For these three expensive teeth I will give you a choice, and don't say the Arabs are not nice to you. Do you want to go to the mountains, or south to the desert?'

'We want to go north,' I replied. We might be displaced, but at least we would stay in our own country.

'Then you have three hours to pack up, or we will pack you up and Anfal you to hell when we get back.' The officer put the teeth in his pocket and they left.

Father collapsed on the floor in pain and anguish, his mouth bleeding. His only valuable possession was to be given to an Arab family immediately after our imminent and unexpected departure. Mother left hurriedly, in search of her brothers. Star and I, numb with shock, started to pack, desperate to be ready before the monster's men returned. I did not want my family Anfaled. I knew what that meant. 'Please, Father,' I called. 'Give us a hand. They will send us to the desert and bury us alive if we are not out in three hours.'

The government's policy of forcing hundreds of thousands of Kurds out of Ninawa, Kirkuk and Dyala, three oil-rich provinces, was called Arabisation, a policy that was part of the Anfal Campaign. 'Anfal – the plunder of the infidels' came from the Qur'an, the holy book in Ayat 37 of Surat Al Anfal:

> In order that Allah may separate
> The impure from the pure.
> Put the impure, one on another,
> Heap them together, and cast them into Hell.
> They will be
> The ones to have lost.

But my father is not impure. He has spent his life worshipping Allah in the House of God. Jam is right to say, 'No matter how faithful a Muslim Kurd is, in the eyes of the Iraqi Arabs, a Kurd remains a Kurd and an infidel.'

'I will not leave my house,' Father yelled, running around as if he were trying to hide the house in his outstretched arms. 'Kill me like you did my father and mother, my sisters and brothers,' he cried.

'I will not leave Lover's Hill.'

Mother returned with my uncles. Flathead pulled up his truck outside our door and we quickly loaded our belongings, while Father leant against the wall, utterly defeated.

'Mum,' I kissed her hands, 'tonight is Peaceful's concert and tomorrow I am supposed to go to Baghdad with my uncles. Can I stay in Kirkuk?'

'You come with us.'

'Can I at least go and say goodbye to Sunshine?'

'No.'

Our happy life in Lover's Hill had been cruelly short-lived. I put my treasure box in my pillow, a trick that I had learned from my parents.

'Mery, I will go to the concert tonight and will let Sunshine know what has happened,' Hercules said, seeing my hopelessness. 'You can go to Baghdad another time.'

We left the fridge in the room and the half-painted door wide open. My uncles had to drag Father away. He must have kissed the walls dozens of times shouting, 'I will not leave Lover's Hill for the Arabs!' He wanted to take the house with us.

My parents sat in the passenger seat next to Flathead. Star held on to King Kong while I sat on the mattresses in the back. We waved to Hercules and left our house behind.

In the busy Bazaar, people walked about like the living dead. No one dared to question why we had been forced away.

'Say goodbye to Kirkuk, little sister.'

'Goodbye, Kirkuk,' Star said.

I am leaving Kirkuk, Abu Ali, you evil bastard, and am going to the displaced people's camp, with the hope of finding an escape via the mountains out of this cursed country. But at the same time I feel sick at the thought of leaving the place of my birth, the town where I grew up and the land of my ancestors. This city where my love Sunshine, and my friends Rabbit and Jam live. How can I leave without even saying goodbye? If I were coming to you in America, Gringo, to the land of opportunity and freedom, of my own free will, I could bear the pain of leaving all this behind, but now the monster is forcing me and my family out.

I kissed Star's soft cheeks. 'How is King Kong?' I asked.

'He is fine,' she answered, in her sing-song voice.

'Star, we can't go to Peaceful's concert.'

'Why can't we?'

'Because we are going somewhere else.'

'Where?'

'Somewhere nice.'

'I don't want to go away from our uncles, from our house.'

'We have no choice. It is the wish of the monster.'

'Can King Kong fight the monster?' she asked, holding up her old toy.

No more Star, please, I don't want to cry. 'I love you, little sister,' I said, 'but I have to leave you. Whenever you need Mery, just tell King Kong. He will let me know and I will be there for you. You hear me?'

'If you have to.'

'Can you let Mum and Dad know I love them very much?'

'I will.'

'Will you wish me luck?'

'Good luck, Mery,' Star said, and kissed my hand.

At the crossroads near the Rahimawa graveyard, Flathead slowed down as he met the traffic nearing the checkpoint. This was my chance, before we came too close to the soldiers blocking the road ahead of us. I hung down from the back of the truck, ran along for a moment, and then let go.

I waved to Star, and she waved back. Though I initially held back from crying, I started to feel the tears run down my cheeks. I waved until she disappeared on the highway to Erbil.

'I wish you good luck as well, my little sister.'

How much suffering has one to endure for simply being born in one place rather than another? I have now not only lost my home but also my family and I am nowhere near you, Gringo, I thought, as I walked towards the city centre feeling heartbroken and completely lost. I really needed to see Sunshine, but first I went to Jam. He was locking up his shop before heading off to the concert. I told him everything. I told him about how my father so desperately and impossibly wanted to take our home with him. Jam was not surprised. My family were just one of the many to be deported. We got into his car. 'I had an offer to sell the shop, but it didn't work out,' Jam said, as he drove. 'It should not take too long. Hopefully, by the time you are back from Baghdad, I should have the money.'

Hercules met us outside the concert hall. I ccouldn't see Sunshine in the foyer. It was a free event organised with the help of the Town Hall, and thanks to the posters displayed across the city and word of mouth, the theatre was packed. Sunshine waved. She was sitting in the middle of the fourth row, and had kept several seats free for my family and myself. After greeting Shamal and Jwana, I sat next to my love. I apologised for my parents' absence, but did not go into details. I was not going to spoil such an important event, which their family were so excited for. Jam sat on my left and Sunshine held my right hand throughout the concert.

Peaceful looked very different on stage with his confident smile.

There was no spectacular lighting, just one simple microphone in front of his violin, and a single spotlight trained on him. The audience was not used to concerts or to keeping quiet and listening to music, particularly a performance with a single instrument, yet as Peaceful began to play, slowly his magic spread. Soon there was a hushed silence in the hall, as the crowd sat, transfixed by the mournful sound of his violin. He played popular pieces, classical sonatas and some tunes that Sunshine told me he had composed himself, playing extraordinarily well, his body moving with the rhythm of the music. Peaceful continued for almost an hour, and finished... to complete silence. Shamal was the first to put his hands together and clap proudly for his son. The audience followed and the applause reverberated around the theatre.

Jam stood up. 'Bravo,' he called several times. Others echoed him: 'Well done! Fantastic!' They whistled and clapped. Sunshine could not stand still, and the same went for her parents. Master Shamal, a true man of art, had proved his point: 'The good we get from art is not what we learn from it, it is what we become through it ... We spend our days, each one of us, looking for the secret of life ... The secret of life is in art.' It was Oscar Wilde's quote, Master Shamal's favourite one about art, but it was his son who brought it to life.

Rabbit was on the other side of his parents. He cheered for his younger brother, too. Peaceful bowed several times, then looked in the direction of his proud family. He waved to them, his face beaming. He left the stage to rapturous and persistent applause, yet there was no sign that he would appear for an encore.

Instead, a group of armed Mukhabarat appeared on stage, and the applause died in an instant. *Has Peaceful been snatched from the wings?* It was then that Abu Ali emerged, striding towards Shamal with a cruel smile and his sadistic offering: Peaceful's broken violin.

Into the wilderness

I jumped into the passenger seat. As always, Flathead drove first and Hercules followed. We were heading for Baghdad. 'How are my parents?' I asked. 'Fine,' Flathead sighed. He was missing them, too. 'They're in Betwata camp. Your mother wants you with them.'

'What about Star?'

'She cried when I left. She wanted to go back to Kirkuk, of course.'

'She will be lucky to see our city again.'

We stopped at the checkpoint. The Special Forces checked our identity cards. When the soldier looked at mine, he scrutinised my face and went away. After a while, he returned, handed back our documents and signalled to us to move on. *I am sure they have information about me. Why did they let me go?*

Flathead produced a bottle of Arak. I was worried about his habit of drinking and driving, but there was no use in irritating him. He offered me the bottle, but I shook my head. 'Listen to this, Mery. A Kurdish drunk woke up next to an Arab drunk. "Where were you born?" the Kurd asked the Arab. "In the hospital," the Arab answered. "Why?" the Kurd said, "were you ill?"' We both laughed, but the levity was forced.

'You like telling jokes about Kurds and Arabs,' I said.

'Sad things make funny jokes. That is our reality. We will never have peace with the Arabs in Iraq, the wound is far too deep. It's just like the rift between my wife and me. One of us had to die.'

'Not if we separate from Iraq and have our own country.'

'That is correct, Mery. That is the only solution. Hamrin Mountains,' He waved an arm towards the horizon, 'these are our witnesses. After all, this is the natural border between Kurdistan and Iraq. But we Kurds never learn from our mistakes. Our history repeats itself. We keep calling Arabs our brothers, when all the time they are burning our people with acid and experimenting on our Anfal, the missing, like guinea pigs in their laboratories. How can we ever be brothers? We should separate, just like your auntie and I should have done before the disaster.'

Whenever Flathead referred to his wife, he gulped down more Arak. After Papula's death he had hardly mentioned her name, but as we drove into the Iraqi desert, he was finally ready to talk about her again, and ask questions about things he had been longing to know.

'You knew it, didn't you?' he said, calmly.

'Knew what?' I played the innocent.

'That my wife was seeing other men.'

I have been forced to tell lies all my life. I am not going to do it ever again. 'Yes,' I answered, and was prepared to say a lot more.

'Thanks,' he said, and went quiet.

Ask me who she slept with and I will admit my guilt, I will tell you that I made love to her, too. 'I am sorry I betrayed you.' I hoped this would provoke him to ask more.

'It is fine, Mery. You did what any young man would have done in your place.'

What does he mean? Is he referring to me keeping it secret that Papula was seeing another man, or does he know that I slept with her, too?

'I would have done the same at your age. It was easy to be seduced by such a beautiful woman and comply with her wishes. I forgive you.'

He knows. He is talking about his wife and myself sleeping together. I cannot hide the truth inside any longer.

'Do you want to know who she slept with?'

He swerved the truck violently to the right, shifting its entire weight on to the wheels on that side. We were moments from overturning, but the vehicle did not give way. He swerved wildly back to the left, then to the right, throwing me violently from side to side time and again. I could hear Hercules' horn honking behind us, desperately trying to prevent his brother from driving so recklessly. Eventually, Flathead regained his composure and wiped the tears from his face.

'I should never have married her,' he said. 'I took her as a gift. Her beauty did not belong to me. I was greedy. I should have divorced her, let her go free, but I did not. I made her suffer, Mery. I killed Nasik. I am the guilty one and nobody else.'

'My auntie burned herself.'

'If only I had known she was in love with Dr Hakan before our wedding. If only she had told me, I would not have married her and would have freed her from my engagement and encouraged her to marry the man she loved. She told me when it was too late, and I was blinded by jealousy. I have committed a horrendous crime. I killed Dr Hakan.'

'You told me Hakan was killed in the hospital while in bed with another woman.'

'I lied. I killed Dr Hakan for sleeping with my wife.'

'How did you find out about their affair?'

'You remember the dinner we had together the night before she burned herself?'

'Yes.'

'On that trip, I came back a few days earlier. I did not go home. I had suspected her for a while and believed you were on her side. So I decided to spy on her myself. I hid in a friend's car at night, and saw a man entering my house. From the living room window in the courtyard, I listened to the murmurs of my wife making love to the stranger. I went back to the car. When he left at dawn, I recognised who it was.' Flathead took another swig of Arak. 'On the evening of that last meal together, I took out my gun. I did not go to check on my cargo, I went to Hakan's house. He pleaded, he cried about his deep love for my wife, but I did not listen and pulled the trigger, blowing a hole through his heart. I cut off his finger, with my wife's ring on it, and brought it home. I was surprised to find that she wanted to sleep with me. Then I showed her Hakan's finger with the ring and told her I had killed him. The next morning, she burned herself.'

'Why didn't you kill them in bed?'

'I did not want to end up in Saddam's prison.'

'They had plans to escape that week and go to live in Istanbul.'

'Just like the Iraqi government is blinded by the wealth of Kurdistan, I was blinded by the beauty of your auntie, and in the name of false love and greed, I destroyed her. You can hate me for what I did, Mery. I hate myself too. I did wrong and will never forgive myself. I should have just accepted it and divorced her. Take my advice, Mery. Never get married to someone you don't love or who doesn't love you.' Flathead took another swig from his bottle.

We spent the rest of the journey in silence. There was nothing more to be said. I must have fallen asleep about an hour before we reached the capital, the city I had wanted to visit for so long.

'Mery! We are in Baghdad,' Flathead said.

'Baghdad?' I shook myself awake. I was struck by the immensity of the city, the towering buildings, the red double-decker buses, the broad Tigris River with boats criss-crossing it, the gigantic monuments, the many overlapping roads and bridges, and, above all, the massive billboards outside the cinemas. 'It's Prince Sinbad's city,' I said.

'The town centre is not on our route, but I thought you might like to see it before the curfew starts.'

'Thanks, Uncle. What curfew?'

'Iranian jets often appear in the night to bomb Baghdad. Don't worry, they come to hit military targets.'

We stayed at Hotel Soran in Bab Sharji, the district of the Kurds. My uncles went to sleep soon after dinner, but I stayed by the window looking at a dramatic, red-and-gold sunset illuminating the skyline of Baghdad. As soon as darkness descended, piercing sirens rang out several times. Shortly afterwards, the city fell quiet as the streets emptied of cars and pedestrians. Only half an hour later, the anti-aircraft machine guns opened fire, turning the sky into a battlefield. Iranian fighter jets roared overhead.

'Switch off the light,' Hercules said, before turning over to resume his slumber. *How can my uncles sleep so peacefully while the planes and guns thunder overhead?* I reminded myself that they had been freedom fighters in the mountains, and had been to Baghdad countless times.

The next morning we went to unload the cargo at Saddam International Airport, the same airport from which I had been supposed to fly out to America. I watched a plane taking off, and realised it was the first civil aeroplane I had ever seen for real. Instead of me being on board and on my way to Gringo, I accompanied my uncles as they continually shifted goods between Baghdad, the airport, Kerbala and Najaf, the sacred cities of the Shiite Arabs. On our first day off, we went to Abu Ghraib. The prison was massive, much more so than those I had seen in films. There were not many people around, but armed guards were everywhere. 'It doesn't seem like it's a visiting day,' Flathead said, as he parked. At the reception I asked for Shawes, Kojak's father. The guards checked through the list of prisoners and after a while they found his name. He was indeed there, serving life imprisonment for the murder of a caretaker. *Rabbit was right! At last, I can accept that Abu Ali is not the same man as Shawes Dog.* We could not see him until Friday, the next visiting day, but I was already satisfied with what I had been told.

This was the first time I revealed my fear of Shawes Dog to my uncles. I told them everything, including how Shawes had wanted to take me to the Turkish baths. My uncles were sorry they had not learned about the Dog's story at the time. They assured me they would have given him a beating that he would not have forgotten.

We went to the Zoo in Zawra Park. There were many animals that I had never seen before: lions, tigers, elephants, giraffes. We enjoyed a few rides at the funfair and then headed towards Abu Nawas along the Tigris River. In one of the many restaurants there we had a meal of fresh fish. For a moment I felt like I was on holiday, until Flathead told me we were going back to Kirkuk. 'Your uncle Baban wants to wed,' my uncle said, grinning. 'We are going home today,' and he left to pay the bill. Sunshine's golden pendant hung around my neck. I often kissed it. Hercules caught me doing this. He smiled and winked at me.

'Uncle!' I said, looking into Hercules' eyes. 'I just want to say thank you for caring so much for me, and I am glad you are getting married soon. I'm sure you will be a kind husband and make your wife very happy.'

'Thanks, Mery, I love you.' Hercules leaned over the table. 'Let's have a go together,' he said. 'Up Kissinger's bum,' we whispered, and laughed.

We went back to the garage. A man with a bandaged arm was waiting by Hercules' truck. 'Koyra, what happened?' Hercules called to him.

'I was hit to shit by an Iranian shell, it's a miracle I survived.' Koyra greeted my uncles. 'Your truck?' Flathead asked. 'We are God's servants and are going back to him after death,' Koyra said, and turned to me. 'I know you!' He studied my face. 'I once asked you for a spoon and you cheated me.'

'It was at my uncle's wedding.' I reminded him.

'Yes,' Koyra said, holding his hand open as though he was still begging.

'Are you a truck driver?' I was surprised.

'Well, ever since this bloody war began the begging business has collapsed too,' he said.

'Have you had lunch?' Flathead asked.

'I am fine. I just want to get home. I am looking for a lift.'

'It's your lucky day, let's go.' Hercules pulled Koyra by the hand. He sat next to Hercules and I was with Flathead as we left Baghdad. Flathead was in a good mood. 'Mery, I am not going to drink Arak again while driving.'

'Uncle, you should stop it all together.'

'I don't think I can.'

'Of course you can, it is a matter of will.'

He started to sing. I felt relieved too, as it seemed that Flathead and I, each in his own way, had had a huge pain lifted from our hearts, even though Dr Hakan and Papula would remain in our thoughts.

Flathead pulled over on the highway in Daquq to have tea. Hercules pressed on, beeping his horn. 'He is dying to see your mother and give her the news about getting married,' Flathead said, acting out a loving embrace.

'That will make Mum really pleased,' I said.

'Do you know, he has never gone ahead of me before? Let's get going, shall we, Mery?' Flathead finished sipping his tea.

He drove and I took out the Arak from the cooler. 'Can I chuck it?' and I held up the bottle. 'Go on,' Flathead answered, after a pause. I threw the Arak into the desert. Flathead started to laugh.

'Listen to this, Mery. A Kurd arrives at a deep river, he can't swim and there are no bridges to be seen. He lifts his head skywards, "Please God," the Kurd prays, "for the sake of my four kids, I do not want my children to be orphans! God Almighty," he calls out, "help me cross the river safely." He jumps in, and somehow, after a long struggle, he makes it to the other side. He shakes the water off himself and he looks up again. "What sort of God are you?" he says, blowing a loud raspberry. "I don't have a wife yet, let alone four children. But thanks anyway."'

We had a laugh. About an hour from Kirkuk, we came across Hercules' truck. 'I didn't think he would go ahead without me,' Flathead said. 'That is what I call a brother.' Flathead blew his horn and stepped sharply on the brakes. 'That's a strange way to park!' he said, as we drew to a halt just ahead of the stranded truck.

On the side of the highway, the front of Hercules' truck was pointing towards a village. Flathead reversed. I poked my head out and saw Koyra, sitting against one of the wheels of Hercules' truck. He was moving strangely, his arms going up and down from his face to his lap. There was blood on the road and a few scraps of a sheep that had been torn apart.

'I told him to drive on, they are only a few brainless sheep, but he did not listen...' Koyra kept wailing, and hitting himself, despite his bandaged arm. 'What happened?' Flathead asked several times, getting more irritated. 'It was not his fault! The idiot sheep just ran on the road. Baban could not stop in time, he tried his best...' Koyra continued. 'What the hell is going on?' Flathead grabbed Koyra's hands. 'Baban stopped and asked me to clear the road of the remains of the dead sheep. He said it was dishonest to hit and run. He was going to find the sheep's owner and pay for the damage. He walked to the Arab village...' Breaking off, Koyra looked up to Flathead and pleaded, 'Arsalan, please go, just listen to me and go away. Merywan, don't let your uncle see what I have seen...'

'Where is Baban?' Flathead shook Koyra. 'Where is my brother?'

'Baban is dead.'

'What?'

'Arsalan, get into your truck and go. Merywan, don't let him see...'

I followed Flathead as he rushed to the front of the truck. And there, as we reached the cab, we saw the horror – Hercules' severed head stared back at us fom the bonnet of his truck.

'How could they do this?' Flathead screamed, his body contorting with the agony of his grief. 'How could they? My brother went to pay them...' Flathead cried out once more as he jumped into his truck. I opened the passenger's door. He pulled it back and locked it. 'Uncle, no! Please no...' I called, hanging on to the truck. He turned onto the dirt track and headed for the village, which was a couple of hundred metres away.

'Stop, Uncle! They will behead you, too...'

I jumped off and ran ahead to stand in his way, but he was lost in a hysterical tornado of rage, and barely seemed to register my pathetic protest. At the last moment, I dived out of the path of his speeding vehicle, then turned to run after him, vainly shouting, waving, begging him to stop. Flathead pressed on. Entering the village, he ran over everything that crossed his path, chickens, sheep, dogs, cows, and then, remorselessly, he sent the truck careering into men, women, young and old, children and babies. By the end, he had flattened the ten or more mud-brick houses and all that lived among them.

It was a massacre. Flathead had turned the place into a slaughter house. Finally, the truck became wedged in the ruined remains of one of the huts. A baby left behind screamed hysterically. 'Arab bastards,' he repeated, again. 'My brother came to pay you for your fucking sheep.'

I tried to pull him away. He shoved me hard, knocking me to the ground. 'Mery, get out of here! Go! This is not your fight!' he yelled, though he was not looking at me. He opened the flap of the storage space under his truck, grabbed a canister of diesel and poured it over his vehicle. He struck a match, and there was a sickening blast and whoosh as the flames devoured the metal, greedily racing along the side of the truck. Battling through the flames, he climbed back into his driving seat. I tried to reach him, but again he pushed down the lock. The fire engulfed the cabin with Flathead inside, staring impassively ahead.

There was no explosion like there would be in an action film, just a cloud of poisonous black smoke rising high above the flaming truck, which was hardly visible now, obscured by a thick, swirling pall of dust that hung over the ruined village.

Without a thought, I blindly ran from the carnage, into the desert. Into the wilderness.

The old Arab

I kept on running as fast as I could as if this might make time turn in on itself and magically bring my uncles back to life. I wanted life to be a film so that I could rewind it to when I first saw Gringo on the big screen, sitting happily between Flathead and Hercules, feeling like the luckiest and most protected child in the world. Back to the time when I rode with Happiness on the bike in Qala, when Aida and I first kissed, and when Papula and I danced under the cascading water from the hose. I did not want to stop running, or stop thinking of those wonderful times when I had been happy, for fear of seeing Hercules' severed head left on the bonnet of his truck, or Flathead burning in the fire... So many that I had loved, loved more than my own life, had died horribly. Death was following me, clinging to me just as closely as the gritty sand which lodged in the sweat around my face, in my hair, and down my neck. I was exhausted. I was no longer running, just dragging myself along in the cloying sand, doing everything I could in order not to stop, not to think, not to remember.

At sunset, I reached the Khasa River on the south side of Kirkuk. I was half-dead, desperate now for some water. I bent down to drink and felt a gun in my back. 'Arab?' someone asked, in Arabic.

'No, I am a Kurd,' I answered, swallowing, as I turned around to face death. I was cold and shivering, tormented by what had happened to my uncles.

It was not a gun, but a walking stick in the hand of an old shepherd. He wore a black cape, dishdasha and Arab turban. 'Kurdi!' he repeated, poking his stick as though searching me. 'Are you one of the missing people?' *He thinks I am a victim of Anfal who had managed to escape execution.* I nodded. 'Do you have Peshmerga brothers, or your father?' I shook my head. 'The Kurdish fighters killed one of my sons,' he said.

He will kill me himself rather than hand me over to the Mukhabarat.
'Come with me.' He indicated with his stick. I did not move.

'Scared? Because I am an Arab?'

'Sir, please don't give me up to the government.'

'Saddam? Fuck Saddam and his wife,' he said, bitterly. He pulled off his cape and wrapped it around my shoulders. He called, whistled and by waving his walking stick, he gathered his dozen sheep and moved on. After a while I followed him. As the darkness fell we reached his village, a few mud-brick houses. He had a simple hut surrounded by bits and pieces of wood and metal, including two rusty old MZ Motorbikes which formed part of a fence for the sheep. He penned in his animals, stood by the door and, gesturing with his hand, invited me in.

Inside there was no electricity, just a couple of rugs, a mattress, a few pots and plates, buckets full of water and a jar of milk. He lit an oil lamp. 'Sit?' he asked, as he poured some milk. 'Eat,' he said, offering the milk and a hunk of bread. I took off his cape and put it on the floor next to him. I went to sit in a corner, as far away as I could. *Why should I trust him?*

'What is your name?'

'Merywan.'

'Don't fear me, Merywan. I have respect for the Kurds even if they killed my son. They did it in defence of their homeland. At least they did not come to kill in my house like the Mukhabarat. You are my guest. If you don't eat, I don't. That's the true Arabic way of welcoming guests.'

My stomach was tight and my throat hurt, but I moved closer and started to eat. He carefully unfolded an apple-green scarf, as though he were opening a treasure box, to reveal several photos. He passed them to me and began to tell me his life story. 'I must look old, but I am only fifty-five,' he said. 'I am not an Arabisation Arab, but originally from this land. We had villages and fortunes, a guest house that could accommodate one hundred people and was hardly ever empty. Those were golden times, long gone. We lost it all to my own Arab people. Those are my four sons.' He pointed to one of the photos. 'The oldest was killed as a soldier by Kurdish fighters, the Mukhabarat took the other two away because they refused to become soldiers and fight the Kurds. The youngest, Rasul, a university student, was executed right in front of his mother and father. They took away our two young daughters. We never saw them again. Saddam is an Arab and a Sunni like me, but he is not a true Arab. He is evil and is against everyone, including his own people.'

I have never heard an Arab say a bad thing about the monster.

'My wife became ill and died. I have lost my family and friends, but I have not lost hope.' Abu Rasul dried the tears on his face and passed me another photo. I was astonished. I stopped eating.

'That man,' he said, indicating with a shaking finger, 'he was my dearest friend, a Brader, as you Kurds call real friends. Never mind that he was a Kurd. Before Saddam put his vile spell on us, Arabs and Kurds were not such enemies. When I think about my friend, about his warmth and his gentle manners, and then how unjustly Saddam's men hanged him, my heart cries out. "You are my Brader, Abu Rasul, and to hell with Saddam!" he used to say with a smile each time he visited us on his way to Baghdad.' Having resisted crying under the pressure of all the horrors I had lived through, I could hold back no longer. I sobbed for what seemed like a very long time. Abu Rasul waited patiently.

'Your Kurdish friend,' I pointed to the older man in the photo, 'he was my grandfather.' Abu Rasul looked into my eyes, my inherited blue eyes. 'You are the son of King Sherzad?' he asked, with a gasp. 'He was my mother's father,' I said, through my tears.

Abu Rasul pulled me to him and cried with joy. 'Merywan, through you I embrace my sons, my daughters and my Brader again. This is not a coincidence, this is the light, and my wishes are fulfilled now, for I know that one day soon we will all, Kurds, Arabs, Turkman and Christians alike, be freed from this evil tyranny.'

'I am sorry,' I said. I got hold of his hands and kissed them. 'I am very sorry, for I hated the Arabs so much that I wanted them wiped out. I was wrong, really wrong. Forgive me, please, on your behalf and that of all the good Arabs like yourself in the world, I ask for forgiveness because I was brainwashed by the horrific acts of the monster.'

'I don't blame you, my child, and no decent person should ever blame you. The cruel hypocritical Arabs of our country are deserving of hate. They cry for our fellow Arabs in Palestine and kill the Kurds mercilessly.'

'Abu Rasul, I swear on my heart,' I put my hand on my heart.

'I will never again use the word hate against Arabs. There is good and bad in everyone.'

Abu Rasul looked at the photo once more. 'Do you know that man standing next to your grandfather?'

In the photo Grandfather and his assistant were standing by his truck, smiling. Rashaba did not have his golden teeth yet.

'He is my father.'

'Is he still alive?'

'Yes, but recently he was deported out of Kirkuk with the rest of my family.'

'It is unforgivable what is happening to you,' he said. 'The Kurds are an ancient people of this land and should have their own country and their freedom. Hopefully, one day we will have the chance to live as good neighbours, as we have never managed to live peacefully together. This would be better for the Turks, the Persians and we Arabs. No one's sons would be killed again in the name of occupations and liberations.'

How much I wish all the Iraqi people had the same belief in us as Abu Rasul. He has had so much pain inflicted on him yet he does not have any hate in his heart, except for Saddam.

'Would you like some more milk, Merywan?' I shook my head. 'Did you know that when your grandfather was taken away,' Abu Rasul said, now trying to smile through his tears, 'my two sons, Rasul and Rahim, helped your uncles escape to the mountains on the back of their motorbikes, the same bikes that are now rusting outside my hut. How are your uncles? I haven't seen them for a while.'

'My uncles are gone and will never come back,' I said, and I began crying again. I found it horrible to even think about what had happened to my dear uncles. I cried uncontrollably, sobbing as I had never done while I told Abu Rasul about the dreadful deaths of Flathead and Hercules.

In the morning I had another look at the corroded motorbikes, all that was left for Abu Rasul to remember his brave sons by, and I imagined Flathead and Hercules sitting behind his sons on their way to the mountains.

Abu Rasul handed me a staff and put a lightweight black cape with a golden trim around my shoulders. He asked me to help him take the sheep to pasture. I, Merywan Rashaba, who had until this time sworn my enduring hatred of Arabs, proudly stepped out in the company of Abu Rasul. We walked along the parched riverbed, which, since it was now late spring, had dwindled to little more than a muddy stream in the middle of its course. Three hours later we were behind the main Kirkuk bus station. I kissed Abu Rasul's hands and gave him back his staff and cape. I had some money, but he insisted on pushing a five-dinar note into my hand.

When I stepped out of the taxi in Kirkuk centre, I found Jam's shop closed, with the 'For Sale' sign in the window. I knocked on the glass panel and Jam opened the door. We went to the back room. I broke down again as I told him about my uncles, about Abu Rasul and my good luck in meeting him, and how wrong I was about hating Arabs.

'Is there any news of Peaceful?' I asked, through tears.

'No. Master Shamal has spent all his savings on bribing officers to free his son. He has sold most of their belongings, and has been selling his books in the market.'

'Sunshine?' I asked, looking up to Jam, *please don't give me bad news about my love*. 'I have not seen her or Rabbit since the concert. It is a shit time, Mery. I have not been to the shop for weeks. I am only here because someone is coming to buy it today. I am going away with you. We will have to leave via the mountains to Turkey.'

'What about Godfather?'

'He is fucked. Abu Ali got to him, too.'

'The checkpoints around town have my details.'

'We go out tonight.'

'I must see Sunshine.'

'It is too risky, Mery!'

'I can't go away without seeing her. Please! Only for a couple of hours.'

With a sigh, Jam relented. 'Alright. If you don't find me here, I will be with Norman. Give Sunshine my regards and don't be late.'

I couldn't be sure what it was that made Jam and I embrace each other. I was going to see him shortly, yet it felt like a farewell.

Jam is next and then you

'Abu Ali is not Shawes dog...' I said, the minute Rabbit opened the door. He stormed at me, hitting me with his crutch. 'Hit hard, Brader, for I am a cursed person!' I shouted at him. 'You ignorant fool, you are doomed because you are a Kurd, and this misery has nothing to do with me.' Rabbit did not want to know, he kept beating me. 'I am here to say goodbye to Sunshine. Only for a few minutes, please?' I begged him, trying to protect myself from his blows.

'She doesn't want to see you,' Rabbit burst out, striking at me again.

'Sunshine...' I screamed.

A police jeep drove down the road towards us. Rabbit, unaware of the monster's men, dived for me. We grappled with each other, but were both attacked as the police kicked and pushed us on to the open back of their truck. Three more men were already sitting there, one with his hands held aloft, praying. They drove on, randomly picking up more people, whoever was on the streets and wasn't quick enough to escape, until the back of the Jeep was packed.

'Why didn't you let me see Sunshine?' I asked, but Rabbit did not blink an eye, staring steadfastly ahead. We joined a convoy of army vehicles, buses and taxis which had been commandeered by militiamen, the police and Mukhabarat, driving crazily fast towards the football stadium. We were herded inside at gunpoint, thousands of us, bewildered and scared. *Can they really shoot so many people together?*

The football stadium was packed. Rabbit and I were seated in the seventh row and could see a military band that was playing the Iraqi national anthem and other martial music. To their left, a stage had been erected on which special seats were occupied by the governor of Kirkuk; the Ugly Arab, the head of the Mukhabarat; army generals; the Chief of Police; the militia commanders; and Kurdish Jash leaders. The wives and children and the personal bodyguards of these elite men were there, too. *This must indeed be a great occasion, one that is special enough for them to bring their families along to enjoy the show.*

The Ugly Arab took the microphone and his voice echoed around the stadium. He blathered on about brave Iraq, glorious Iraq, victorious Iraq, the Arab nation… *Arab nation! Of course, we five million Kurds in the north of the country do not exist for him. How can the Kurdish Jash leaders sit there and not sweat shame?* He must have mentioned Saddam at least a dozen times in his speech before he told us that we had been invited here to see justice given to traitors.

Invited? If it had not been such a sick spectacle, I might have searched my pockets looking for my invitation.

'This is the nation's judgment,' the Ugly Arab announced, 'the honourable Iraqi people's verdict and, above all, our leader Saddam Hussein's judgment. You are here to witness our victory over the dissidents and subversives, and to share our sentence for those who betray our president.'

A group of soldiers chanted, 'Long live Saddam,' and most of the hapless, intimidated spectators were obliged to join in.

'The first traitors are the army deserters. Let their execution commence!' The Ugly Arab ordered, to a warm applause from his elite friends, the army who were all scattered around the stadium, and, of course, the spectators, most of whom had been 'invited' in the same way as we had.

A military truck drove into the middle of the pitch and halted opposite the elite. Special Forces pushed and pulled young blindfolded men, hands tied behind their backs. Some fell over, others walked in the wrong direction, disorientated. Five of them were picked randomly and tied to five poles. The others had to wait their turn, blindly listening to the terrible fate that awaited them next. At the order of an officer, five Special Forces soldiers loaded their AK-47s and pulled the triggers. The blindfolded men slumped lifelessly down the poles. The officer took out his pistol and, one by one, shot them in the head.

Applause erupted from the elite, their families and their followers. They cheered for the glory of Saddam. The bodies were thrown on to the back of the truck.

Abu Ali then appeared in the centre of the pitch with his prisoners. I was disgusted to see he was wearing traditional Kurdish clothes.

The sharwal is banned by the government, but this traitor can do as he pleases. Since we had entered the stadium, Rabbit and I had not exchanged a word, but as soon as we saw the bastard, we turned to look at each other and both spoke his name, wondering whether it was really only our bad luck that led to being picked up and brought to the show. It no longer felt coincidental.

The Ugly Arab spoke again. 'These are Kurdish traitors, members of underground subversive organisations, who act against the nation and President Saddam Hussein. Today they are receiving justice for their affiliations with the Kurdish rebels.'

As Abu Ali's guards, also wearing sharwal, lined up to shoot the prisoners, a spectator ran on to the pitch. 'I am a father,' the man, who held a violin, shouted. 'I have served this country all my life. I have done no harm to the government and my son is innocent.'

'My father!' Rabbit jumped to his feet. 'That's my father! And that prisoner must be Peaceful.'

I grabbed Rabbit's hand. 'Sit down,' an armed guard barked at Rabbit, who would not have obeyed if I hadn't pulled him down beside me.

'My son is only fourteen years old,' Master Shamal pleaded. 'He has never taken part in any subversive activity and all he loves is this violin. I beseech you, your wives and children. You are fathers, too. Here is my identity card, I used to be a teacher.' Master Shamal handed his ID card over to the officer and kneeled in front of the elite. He dragged himself along on his hands and knees, still holding on to Peaceful's violin, begging, kissing their hands.

The officer went to a General, the General passed the ID to the Governor, who gave it to the Ugly Arab, who passed it to Abu Ali. I had to struggle with Rabbit to keep him still. Abu Ali shook his head as the others had done, for he acted at the behest of the monster's men and could not do otherwise. He was there to complete their sick performance. The Ugly Arab approached the microphone. 'This man is a father, he is defending a traitor son, and therefore he too is a traitor and will be executed alongside his son.'

'Let me go, I want to be killed with them!' Rabbit yelled. I held him with all my might. Despite his amputated leg, Rabbit was too strong. 'Help me please,' I called for the crowd around us. 'Hold his legs, hold his arms, he is epileptic.' But we made too much noise. 'What is going on?' an army guard asked, walking over to us. 'He is epileptic, sir,' I answered. 'He is having one of his fits, better if I take him out and not spoil the party?'

'Be quick! Before I have you lined up, too,' and he gave Rabbit a ruthless kick.

I kept a hand on Rabbit's mouth and with the help of three men we dragged him away. Rabbit struggled fiercely to free himself. We were nearly out, but I saw Master Shamal lined up. He refused to be blindfolded and did not let them tie his hands. He stood there holding onto Peaceful's violin as the Kurdish traitors took aim, then suddenly he sprang to Peaceful, enveloping him in a final embrace as the bullets rocked their bodies, father and son slumped as one to the dust beneath their feet.

I had tried to prevent Rabbit from witnessing their tragic end, but he let out a muffled cry when he saw the horror register on my face. How can we ever be free of this monster? If God does not kill him, soon he will eat all of us. But, for now, it seems that God is definitely on his side, just as many countries in Europe and the world are.

There were more gunshots. Rabbit no longer struggled. I pushed him into a taxi and was about to get in next to him. He put his crutch to my chest. 'You idiot,' Rabbit said, in a ghostly tone. 'Jam is next on the list, and you are last.' He punched my chest with his crutch and I fell backwards. He shut the car door.

Several army vehicles drove by fast and I thought I saw Abu Ali's four-wheel-drive among them. I ran to another taxi. 'Republic Street, please,' I said, as I jumped in. I urged the driver to go faster, to find some short cuts. I was desperate to make it to Jam, but I got there too late.

A heart-wrenching scream came from Jam as he was kicked by the guards and hauled out of his shop. Abu Ali had his pistol in one hand and with the other he clutched Jam by his hair. They smashed the glass panels and with them, the stamp and coin display. I stood among the crowd watching my friend, my mentor, in the hands of Kurdish traitors. Abu Ali lit his lighter and threw it into the shop. He held up Jam by his neck to make sure he saw his father's much loved treasures burn.

I cried out, 'No, you savage Kurdish bastard...'

Abu Ali turned and pointed his pistol in my direction. Jam, his face bleeding, swivelled and knocked Abu Ali's hand away before he could shoot. 'Mery, run!' Jam shouted.

The bodyguards headed straight for me. I ran through the crowd and into one of the shops. Like Jam's, they each had doors that opened on to backyards. The guards were not as quick as I was, but I was within range, and I heard the shots whistle past my shoulder as I dived over a wall. I raced down a narrow alleyway, leapt over another wall, ran through and along more alleys, running blind, praying that I would not be trapped by high, dead-end walls.

They continued the chase, but I managed to lose them and, behaving as casually as I could, slipped into a barber shop and sat in the chair at the back. I gave the barber a quarter-dinar and requested a rapid shave. He raised an eyebrow at my 'bumfluff' beard, but seconds later my face was covered in lather and my clothes were hidden beneath a white cape as the guards rushed past the window. I lay back breathing deeply, trying to calm my thumping heart and take stock of what the hell was going on. I thanked the barber with a tip, left the shop and jumped onto a passing minibus.

The scream of sirens rang out as police cars roared past in the opposite direction. *They are looking for me. I have to stay alert and stay alive and, if I only have one day left in my life, I have to kill Abu Ali.*

The riverbed was often crowded with the poor and destitute, who went there to search through the piles of rubbish for anything useful, or simply to use it as an open-air toilet. To avoid checkpoints and army posts, my best bet was to take the riverbed and go back to Abu Rasul's village by the same route I had come into Kirkuk that morning. It was well into the night by the time I stumbled towards the village, helped by a half-moon which gave just enough light to find my way to his hut, and to avoid running into the guard dogs that I could hear barking during night patrols. I snuggled next to Abu Rasul as if laying down beside King Sherzad, my grandfather, but I was shaking all over and I started to sob at the thought of what might happen to Jam. Why did Master Shamal and Peaceful have to come to such a heartbreaking end? And what was that list that Rabbit spoke of?

Abu Rasul lifted his head and covered me with the blanket. 'What brings you back, Merywan,' he asked quietly as he caressed my hair, 'and why are you crying, son?'

I was very grateful he had woken and wanted to talk to me. With a breaking voice like that of a lost child I let my Arab friend know about the unforgivable events of that day. When I finished, Abu Rasul's first thought was to warn me about the grave danger I was in, and the absolute need to be cautious – he was really alarmed when he heard about the list Rabbit had spoken of. He raised his arms and prayed, calling for Allah's protection.

'Abu Rasul, Allah won't protect me, as I will always be a sinner in His eyes.'

'Allah forgives those who repent,' Abu Rasul responded calmly, and he began to recite from the Qur'an. 'Allah accepts the repentance of those who do evil in ignorance and repent soon afterwards; to them will Allah turn in mercy…'

'But I repented. I repented from my heart, the heart of a devoted Muslim. I prayed throughout the Night of Power and thereafter I fasted. I helped beggars and the poor and I even stopped my uncle from drinking Arak.'

'Allah will reward you for your sacrifices and your faith in Islam, and for your repentance.'

'Truly, I believe Allah is not aware of my repentance, or He has forgotten His own words in the Qur'an. Unless these are not His words at all, but just the words of men who have written them to suit their own purposes. Words that will never apply to me, no matter how faithful a Muslim I try to be, or however much I repent for my sins, because I am a Kurd.'

'There is no difference between Arabs and non-Arabs in the worship of Allah'.

I was not so sure any more but I was impressed by his faith, and I wondered how he could still pray and retain such piety after all that Saddam had done to his family. Didn't the dictator himself appear to enjoy Allah's full protection?

'Abu Rasul, you are a kind Arab and a good-hearted Muslim, so I hope you have better luck with Allah than me.'

I am not going to America

Arab Village, May 1987

Dear Mr Clint Eastwood,

I am away from Kirkuk and have no news of Sunshine. Jam is dead and I am living on the edge of life. Apart from a friendly Arab man, I feel like I am now alone, hunted by the vicious Abu Ali and the Mukhabarat. Almost all of my friends have been killed or arrested, and I lost both my dear uncles in a tragic incident. They suffered a terrible vengeance after Hercules accidentally killed a few sheep while driving his truck. The monster's men brutally murdered Peaceful and Master Shamal in a public show. I can put my hand on my heart and say they were both innocent. I wonder what happened to Brader, my Sunshine and their mother? And most of all, I wonder how Rabbit could have possibly known that after Jam, I am next on the monster's list?

Meeting this wonderful man has helped me to rethink and renounce my racist feelings towards Arabs. I now have no prejudice. He used to be wealthy, but now he only has a simple hut in a village with a few sheep. But to me he is one of the richest people I have come across, because he has a clean heart and knows how to forgive. The Kurds killed his older son, yet even so he is giving me refuge in his house.

I write this last letter because I want to rid myself of a deep-seated pain in my chest. I am most disappointed in you. You are no longer my hero, Gringo. I feel a big lump in my throat writing this, but I shall carry on. I have to let you know that I no longer believe in you and I've lost my hope in you. I am not sure if I will be able to watch another one of your films, if I ever get to go to the cinema again.

I have sent you many letters. You have not answered one, not even just to say "No!" or "Leave me alone!" You don't seem to care, and I worry that you might be a selfish person and not give a shit about what is happening to my people and to me.

I should have learnt not to generalise, but your American government's constant support of Saddam Hussein's tyranny makes me believe that little or no good will come out of your part of the world. You should know that your American money and weapons, given to your beloved monster, are used to spread terror in my country, and to take away the lives of many innocent women and children of all faiths and races: Kurds, Arabs, Turkman and Christians. Your American government has surely proved that the mountains of Kurdistan are our only true friends and allies. I no longer want to go to America but to the mountains to fight for my freedom and that of my people.

I am not blaming you entirely. My people and the Iraqi people are also the culprits in serving Saddam, but the difference is that they do it because they have no choice, whereas you do it because of greed, in order to steal our wealth, our oil.

Perhaps I was not born to become an actor, or to make films, but you were my hope. Sorry if I have bothered you with my boring letters. Part of me is also glad you did not come here, because if the Iraqis found you, they would have shot you on the spot, no matter whether you are Gringo or not. That way I feel I don't owe you anything.

My friend is leaving for Kirkuk tomorrow. He will post my last letter to you. On his return, in the late afternoon, I shall leave with him in the night to go secretly to the mountains, from where, as a Peshmerga, I will fight Saddam Hussein.

Mery Rashaba

Abu Rasul left to sell two sheep in the city. They were getting too old and only good for the slaughterhouse, and he needed money to buy his bread. He had kindly offered to take my letter to post it and to pay for the stamp. But as much as I wanted Gringo to read my angry words, I did not want to put Abu Rasul's life at risk, and decided to keep the letter.

I put on the Arab cape and took the remaining sheep to pasture along the river. The place was deserted and the day was very hot. I took off my clothes and for the first time in days, I also removed my hat, letting my hair down. I so much needed to feel the freshness of the water, to wash away the heat, the fear and all the horror I had witnessed.

When Abu Rasul came back, he had a brand-new pair of black trousers and a blue silky shirt for me, and had bought shish kebab for dinner. He wanted to make our last moments together special.

'Did my grandfather approve of our armed struggle?' I asked. 'Oh yes, very much so,' Abu Rasul answered, while eating. 'King Sherzad was one of the most patriotic men of this land. Not only for the Kurds, no! He cared about everyone's freedom equally. "Freedom is the torch and the Saddamists are the extinguishers, they want us to live in darkness," he used to say. His hope was for the Kurds to reunite, to fight Saddam, but he did not live to see that day. Merywan, you become a freedom fighter, and you will make King Sherzad and myself proud.'

'Mery Rashaba!' a voice came from outside the hut. A second later, someone pushed the metal door wide open. 'How unpleasant of me to disturb your nice dinner,' Abu Ali said sarcastically, crushing our food with his heavy boots.

I am finally facing my death. Abu Ali, a Kurd, one of my own people and blood, had come to kill me. Abu Rasul, an Arab and an old man, defended me and stood up to my enemy. 'You will not touch Merywan in my house.' My Arab friend had courage, but not a gun in his hand. 'Abu Rasul, please! Don't make me beg the Kurdish Jash for your life.'

'He will have to take me too, the traitor,' Abu Rasul said.

'I will,' Abu Ali grunted.

His guards pushed us out at gunpoint to where a dozen Mukhabarat and Jash waited. *I must be an important fugitive for so many to come for me.*

'I am a Kurd, I have no authority to kick Arabs,' Abu Ali said, sarcastically. 'But my friend Abu Ramzi,' He indicated another Mukhabarat officer, 'is an Arab like you and he is upset to learn that you called me a traitor.'

Two men kicked my friend to the ground. Abu Ali's Jash men held me. I screamed for the desert to gobble them up and save my elderly friend. I shouted out, promising to reveal important secrets if they let

Abu Rasul free, but they did not listen.

Men, women and children, Abu Rasul's neighbours, watched from a distance, as I was pushed into Abu Ali's four-wheel-drive with Abu Rasul tied by a rope round his feet to the back bumper. They drove off, leaving the car doors wide open so that I could see my Arab friend being dragged behind us on the dirt track. Abu Rasul managed to look up into my eyes before he lost consciousness.

The Kurds, the rat and the locust

'Happy Nawroz.'

'Arab?'

'I am a Kurd...'

The Ugly Arab pressed the VHS player's remote control to playback. On the television screen in a corner of his office, the footage of the exact moment where I shook hands with Saddam was repeated. The Ugly Arab was sitting behind his desk with a portrait of Saddam above his head, I was on a chair facing him and his Commander-in-Chief. Abu Ali stood to my right.

We were in the Mukhabarat's headquarters – the last station. *I am not a politician, and not involved in anti-government activities, but none of this really matters. I am a Kurd and I am not on the monster's side. More than this, I, Merywan Rashaba, dared to wish the monster 'Happy Nawroz', having declared my complete rejection of him and his men ever since I was a child.* All along I thought I had done this with no one's knowledge until the day I greeted Saddam, but I was wrong. The Ugly Arab had plenty of evidence to put a noose around my neck.

'Why don't you clap for the president, Merywan?' After he had made me watch the video over and over, he pulled out a metal basket and put it on his desk. My heart sank. 'How many letters have you written to Gringo?' he asked, as he counted them.

'Nineteen,' I answered.

'Yes. The first dates back to March 1981, but with your last one, written just two days ago from Abu Rasul's village, the only one you did not post, the total is twenty. Over those six years you have insulted our President Saddam Hussein hundreds of times. You have called Abu Ali the bastard Kurdish traitor, and in almost every one, since the day I first encountered you by the swimming pool, you call me the Ugly Arab. Here, have a look.'

All that time I had waited! I had so longed for an answer from you, Gringo. But thanks to Purtuqal, the 'nice and friendly' employee-spy at the post office, my letters never made it out of Kirkuk, let alone to America.

'Did you write these, Merywan?' he asked, as he examined the letters in the basket.

'Yes.'

'You would have been shot, or hanged, after your first letter, and nobody would have given a fuck about your age. But the Mukhabarat found them very useful. Thanks to you, our job was made easier. Each one of these had more information than any of the reports given by our spies each month. Merywan Rashaba, I will have you sent to Abu Ghraib and have you hanged twenty times for your twenty letters. I do not need to torture you. I do not need your confession. Thanks to these letters written to your hero, and the good role your friend Rabbit played in our game, we got to every bastard we were after. You serve us no more.'

Mery, don't believe a word he said about Rabbit. The Mukhabarat are famous for playing tricks during their interrogations.

'Mind you, there is one thing that you could help me with, just out of curiosity. In this one, dated November 1986, you mention a private viewing room, but you don't go into details and you keep its location secret even from your Gringo. What did you mean by your private viewing room?'

'I meant the films I watched on video.'

'Where was this private viewing room?'

'In my auntie's place.'

'Who is Norman?'

'A nickname I used to occasionally call my auntie for our film games.'

'In one of your letters you say you have lost count of how many you have sent to Gringo, and now you can tell me precisely the number you have written over six years. That is what makes me curious.'

'I called it a private viewing room to impress Gringo.'

'That is partly a lie and partly true, and the correct part is what I am after. I believe you keep copies of your letters in your private viewing room.'

'I don't.'

'You left them with someone. We thought perhaps it was Jam, but we did not find anything at his shop, at his mother's or his sisters' house. Uncle Hitch's family did not have them either, and they weren't in your uncles' rooms. Are they with Sunshine, perhaps?'

From the moment of my arrest, I had been thinking about Sunshine, hoping above all that she wasn't in the hands of the Mukhabarat too. The Ugly Arab's suspicion that she was the custodian of the copies of my letters gave me a glimpse of hope that they did not have Sunshine in their control, since if that had been the case, they wouldn't have needed to interrogate me. 'Merywan, if you lie, I will have to torture you. We already know the truth because we also have Sunshine here, but want to hear it from you.'

'What does Sunshine say?'

'She says you have not given her copies of your letters.'

'She is telling the truth. I have no copies.'

'But she says you keep them in your private viewing room.'

'I don't.'

'I will try the nice way for a bit longer. You see, we cannot let your letters make their way out of the country. If your story were to be published, it could be very damaging to our president, which means that I, Abu Ali, and everyone else in Kirkuk would have to pay for your shit. Your story must die with you. I know you keep copies in your private viewing room. So, I ask you for the last time, where is this room?'

They don't have Sunshine. If they did, they would torture her in front of my eyes and I would tell them the truth about the letters. I would have done anything to save Sunshine. 'I told you the truth about my private viewing room, and that there are no copies of my letters.'

The Ugly Arab opened a folder and took out a bunch of black-and-white photos. 'See these men and women?' he asked, as he leaned over to show me horrific images one by one. 'Like you, to start with they played stubborn and refused to collaborate. Look what happened to them as they chose to avoid the easy way out. I could have you join them in their misery, to make you tell the truth. I could have you given electric shocks like this, or get my men to tear off your fingernails, or have you sleep in shit and eat shit, or bathe you in acid, or hang you upside down and have my men stuff bottles in your arse. I could have you fucked by my men. I won't. I will be nice to you, and you to me.'

I wished I had never seen those photos. They were Kurds, yes, but above all they were human beings who were being sadistically tortured in the cruellest ways possible.

'I don't have copies of the letters.'

'Fine. I have something special for you. I will hang a weight from your balls and will gradually add more and more until your penis and balls are… separated. Remember how much you suffered to find out you were a boy? Make up your mind, I am about to call for my men.'

'I have no copies.'

They blindfolded me and took me down to hell. I was shoved along corridors and down steps to the basement, the torture chamber. I heard pitiful screams. *How many are here? I can see faces, too many jumping out in the dark, suffering from the pain inflicted on them.* I was pushed onto the floor and my feet were tied up in the air. They took off my shoes and socks and a Mukhabarat struck the bottom of my feet with a thick bamboo cane. The Falaqa torture, just as Zao'Adin practised in his Madrasa. This was not enough. My hands were chained behind me and I was raised from the floor. My trousers and underpants were pulled down. I felt rough hands on me and then the agonising pain as weights were attached to my genitals. The more I cried out in agony, the more weight they added.

I remembered the torture scenes in *Midnight Express,* and a few other films, but nothing had prepared me for this pain, intentionally inflicted. Rabbit and Jam had tried, though they had never entirely succeeded in changing my beliefs about Islam and Allah. But that day the Mukhabarat did. I totally lost my faith, for if God existed and was a just God, he would have never allowed such atrocities to take place in a world that he created. I could not tell how long I was left in that state, but when they removed the weight and freed my arms, I could no longer stand on my feet. They also took off the blindfold and made me sit on a chair in the middle of the torture hall.

'Merywan, I accept now that you have never kept copies of the letters,' I heard the Ugly Arab say, as he entered the cell, followed by Abu Ali. 'So, now I ask how do you want to die? Would you like to be executed like Jam, or hanged in Abu Ghraib?'

'I don't want to die.'

There was silence for a while. The Ugly Arab signalled to his men and they left. He came close, as if to share a secret. 'What did you say?'

'I don't want to die.'

'In that case, I want you to do something for me. It is nothing hard really. Just like we began with your countryman, Abu Ali. To start with, two Kurds a week will do.'

'I am not good at spying.'

'Do you know what we Arabs say about you Kurds? "There are three plagues in the world, the Kurd, the rat and the locust." Therefore we have to exterminate your plague. Kirkuk is ours and it will remain an Arab city. We will rid it of your infectious people and parasites. You plague of Kurds can never be good Muslims. That is why we use Anfal to eradicate you.'

Salahadin, the greatest Islamic leader, who fought the crusaders and freed Jerusalem from Richard the Lionheart, was a Kurd. At that moment I hated him, for he did not fight for his people but for his religion, like so many Kurds had done in the past. Jam was right, if we did not have our nation state, our freedom, it was precisely because we had been cheated all along by Islam. The Ottomans, the Safavids, the Muslims, all the region's empires had used Kurds to fight their battles, and then stabbed them in the back. *Religion is the cancer of our people and the main cause of our suffering, just as Jam said.*

'Abu Ali fucked your princess Aida and I was promoted to the head of the Mukhabarat, for I am an Arab from the same tribe as Saddam Hussein,' the Ugly Arab said, pushing his face into mine. 'But Abu Ali, despite his hard work and unlimited loyalties, is a Kurd. He is a rat and he remains a rat in my service. Is that right, Abu Ali?'

'Yes, sir,' Abu Ali answered, in a grovelling tone.

'Yes, what?'

'I am a rat, sir, a filthy Kurdish rat.'

'Merywan, look at Abu Ali and tell me, what is he?' I did not answer. 'Is he a rat?'

'I don't know.'

He took off my hat and grabbed me by my hair.

'What is Abu Ali?'

'He is a rat!' I shouted.

'A filthy Kurdish rat, did you say?'

'A filthy Kurdish rat.'

'That is precisely what I want you to become, Merywan. A filthy Kurdish rat.' He let go of my hair. 'Abu Ali, did you hear Merywan? He called you a rat. What would you like to do to him?' The Ugly Arab was playing with Abu Ali and me like puppets, and it was chilling to my soul. *This is what we have done for generations.* It was not without reason that some stranger had noted that the Kurds had the curious habit of loathing their own people and enslaving themselves to strangers. *Yes, we truly deserve what we get.*

'I would like to cut his hair, sir,' Abu Ali answered, and his voice stabbed my heart.

'Do it, then.'

Abu Ali walked to a table, searched through the many tools of torture, and came back holding on to a pair of scissors.

'So Merywan, what is your answer to my offer?' the Ugly Arab asked. 'Will you become my rat? If you say yes, I will not let him cut your hair and will not send you to Abu Ghraib. You have my word. Work for me for a few years and one day I will have you fulfil your dream. I will let you go to America, to your Gringo.'

I don't want the Kurdish traitor to cut my hair.

'Merywan?'

'I will.'

'I will what?'

'I will become your rat.'

'Like Abu Ali?'

'Like Abu Ali.'

'Good, very good,' the Ugly Arab said, satisfied with himself. 'I now need to test your loyalty.' He took a letter out of his pocket and read, '"Dear Gringo, my first feature film will be an epic in three parts starting from the First World War, through the days when British colonialism first reached Kurdistan, then on to Mahabad, the first Republic of Kurdistan in 1946. The last part of the trilogy will tell my people's struggle for freedom against Saddam Hussein…" Here is the part of your letter I most detest, Merywan,' he said, before continuing, "Dear Gringo, you would make me the happiest film director if you would accept the role of the Kurdish general in my film, the hero who would lead my people to crush the army of the monster..." Do you remember these words, Merywan?' he asked, as he tore the letter into pieces.

'I do.'

'In order for you to become my rat and for me to truly trust you, I will make your test of loyalty very simple. Say "Clint Eastwood is shit".' He could not have chosen anything more hurtful and impossible for me to say, especially so soon after learning that my letters had never reached their destination and I had wrongly accused my hero of not caring about me or coming to my aid. 'Merywan? Say "Clint Eastwood is shit".'

I cannot.

'Why hesitate? Gringo is American. He doesn't give a shit about you and your people, and he will never play such a role in your film because your Kurdish leaders are not true heroes. Your stupid leaders have achieved nothing except to have you Kurds killing each other for decades for their sake. Because they are greedy for power, and they never learn from their mistakes. They are now considering allying themselves with Iran in order to win the war and destroy President Saddam. Well, guess what, Merywan? Your selfish leaders want your Kurdish rat people massacred because we have a nice surprise prepared for them. If they back Iran, we will attack them with chemical gas and wipe out you Kurds, including your family. How about that, Merywan?'

That does scare me, but there is no way I can warn any of my people. I will soon have a rope around my neck, and that's if I'm lucky not to suffer a more grisly death.

'Merywan, say "Clint Eastwood is shit". Say it! If you say it, I will spare your family from the gas attack and will not let Abu Ali cut your hair. And I promise I will let you go free. Say it!'

I stayed silent. He was the last person in the world I could trust to fulfil his promise, especially after revealing such an important secret, wiping out the Kurds with chemical gas.

'Cut his fucking hair!'

Hanks of hair fell into my lap.

'One last time, Merywan. Say "Clint Eastwood is shit", and you don't have to become my rat. Say it, and I will let you have your beautiful hair. I will stop Abu Ali...'

'Fuck Abu Ali!' I finally burst out. 'He is not a Kurd, he is a bastard, and fuck you too, you are not a true Arab but an ugly Arab, a blood-sucking leech, a monster's man who will one day be destroyed. You will not break me, ever, for I am strong, and Gringo will always be my hero.'

I was no longer afraid. I was ready to face death. The Ugly Arab, disappointed with himself for not breaking me, lit a cigarette and watched Abu Ali, sickly taking pleasure in hacking off more and more of my hair.

I drifted away, thinking about the prison scene in *Hair* where they try to cut Woof's hair. I could see them singing behind the bars protesting, I was there with them, but then Abu Ali brought me abruptly back to my brutal reality.

'Do you remember this, Mery?' He pointed to a scar on his forehead. 'You should have stayed a neuter. But you are still very attractive, even more so now than when you were ten. Would you go to the Turkish baths with me?'

In his eyes I saw myself picking up the stone and hitting him on his forehead outside the school on the day he had killed the caretaker. Then he did it again, 'I will get you, Mery,' he whispered, tormenting me with the threat once more, as he had done so terribly well for so long.

'So you are the fucking Shawes Dog?' I said, and I spat in his face. He was about to slap me.

'No!' the Ugly Arab interjected. 'Cut his hair. No hitting.'

Abu Ali, or Shawes Dog as I now knew him to be, cut and cut till the scissors grazed my shorn and bloody skull. It felt as though his scissors were slicing into my heart with every cut he made. When he finished, the Ugly Arab came to me and got hold of my face. 'I will have you sent to Abu Ghraib, to hell on earth, to be hanged, Merywan Rashaba, and nobody spits at my rats,' he said, slapping me so hard that the light faded away.

I miss my long hair

With my hands tied behind my back I stood up to my hangman. I refused to have my face covered. He put the rope around my neck... I had had this horrifying vision many times during my stay in isolation. After so many days in the dirty room I still could not work out the Byzantine complexity of it all. *Isn't Shawes Dog supposed to be in Abu Ghraib prison serving a life sentence? Did Rabbit know and deceive me? Was he really a spy? But would they have killed his brother and father if he worked for them?*

I was waiting for the Ugly Arab to come back. 'Don't live to die, die to live', the sentence I remembered reading so often tattooed on Hercules' arm, came to mind once again. *That is exactly what I am about to do, Gringo – die to live – because if I fail to kill him, it will be my end.* I had never given up hope of getting away. Sitting naked on the dusty old military bed, like Matthew Modine in *Birdy*, I wished I could fly away, escape from my prison. *But to do so, I must kill him. I have to live, not only for myself, but also to warn my people about Saddam's sinister plan for gas attacks.*

I could hear the sound of his footsteps as the Ugly Arab approached. The noise rekindled a familiar dread, and I had to remind myself of the wooden spear under my pillow. He released the locks of the solid door with a rasp of metal against metal. He was back to satisfy his disgusting desires and, as he had hinted to me during his previous visit, this was to be the last time. No one knew I was there; even Abu Ali believed I was already history. *Come on Mery*, I told myself, *it's time to put aside any scruples, because it's like Jam explained about Darwin's theories: it's the survival of the fittest, kill or be killed.*

'Bastard Kurd,' he said, as he walked in. 'I have enjoyed reading your letters, especially your fascinating sex life,' he teased. 'But I am getting tired of them, and tired of you.'

I behaved the same as before, like a dog I went onto my hands and my knees and waited. He had not brought me food, as he had done on the other occasions, which confirmed my suspicion that this was to be my last day, unless I made it his last.

He was holding a carrier bag. He took off his black hat, his black suit and his underwear. He checked his gun, and then left it on top of his clothes. He picked up his thick leather belt and swung it, preparing to beat me again, but he changed his mind. He opened the bag and took out a wig. He jumped onto the bed behind me with the wig and a picture of Sunshine and myself, standing happily between Jam and Uncle Hitch, a photo that I had put in one of my letters to send to Gringo.

'I regret letting the rat cut your hair. I prefer you with long hair. Put on this wig and let me see you.' He did it himself instead and he put Sunshine's gold pendant around my neck. 'You look good, very good, and much nicer than your princess Aida. You were born to be a girl, but I am glad you are not. I don't like fucking women as much as the rat boys. You are so irresistible. Not all of the rats are special like you, Mery.' He kissed my neck. He put his hands on my chest and squeezed my left nipple and pushed his filth into me. 'I am going to miss you, bastard Kurd,' he said, as he jerked back and forth behind me. 'Your time has come. You may as well enjoy having me in you because this is your last fuck, your last fuck...' he repeated as he neared his climax.

I was passive, as usual, waiting for the appropriate time. Finally, when he was distracted by his approaching orgasm, I carefully extended my right arm under the pillow and took hold of my weapon.

'This is your last day,' he shouted breathlessly.

I did not let him come inside me. I swung my right arm with all my strength and anger and hatred, striking the spear up under his ribs with so much force it pierced his ugly heart and reached his spine. 'Your last day!' I said, 'I am not a rat. I am a Kurd! I am a Kurd...!'

He fell sideways into the wall, a look not of horror but surprise filling his face, and slumped onto the mouldy mattress, his breath coming in quick splutters and gurgles, until it petered out, and it seemed like there was no sound at all left in the world. He was gone. I had expected to be exultant. I should have felt exultant, but I just felt numb and exhausted. 'Don't live to die' came into my mind again, and I thought of my uncle Hercules, who was never given the chance, and all the others whom the Ugly Arab and my letters had condemned to death. Tears welled up, but I choked through the sobs, casting around that pathetic room for some sign of redemption. I dipped my hands into the bucket and splashed water over my face to wash away the blood, and slapped my face to think clearly. I wanted nothing more than to rid myself of his stench, but before I could contemplate this I knew I had to dress in his clothes.

His jacket was too large and his trousers were short, but wearing his hat gave me a complete disguise. I checked his revolver, which was fully loaded. I thanked Popcorn once again for advising me to attend military training. I found the keys but did not go for the door straight away. I walked up and down several times making sure that I could stand on my feet, fit enough to face the outside world, the monster's world.

The sunlight burned my eyes as I pulled the door ajar. I stepped back, blinded, and waited for my eyes to adjust to the fierce glare, which I had not seen for weeks during my captivity. I was still dizzy when I stepped outside the cell and turned around to feign locking the door. My prison was an abandoned sentry post, an isolated concrete hut surrounded by a rusting metal fence, which provided scant protection from the encroaching desert. I tightened my belt against my empty stomach and hid the revolver in my hand under the jacket. I had guessed that he would bring fewer men when he came to visit me. There were three personal bodyguards, chatting away under the shade of two palm trees. They hardly looked up as they jumped to their feet, but saluted me as if I were their commander when I approached the Jeep.

The driver ran around to open the passenger door. I pulled out the gun. 'Put your guns down,' I warned them. There was a moment of hesitation. They were surprised now because they saw my bearing was different. The driver moved to draw his gun, but I was too quick for him, and with a single shot, I killed him dead on the spot. The two others saw I was possessed with the fearlessness of someone with nothing to lose, and threw their guns into the sand. I ordered them down onto their knees, then made them crawl inside the building to the far wall of my prison chamber. 'If they take a long time to rescue you,' I said, as I locked them in, 'don't get too bored. You can always fuck your ugly Mukhabarat boss.'

Surveying the barren landscape from the compound, I knew I could have not been too far away from Kirkuk as on the horizon, I could see the flames of Babagurgur rising from the oilfields. I avoided the main road, worried about checkpoints, and kept to the dirt track, walking south, heading towards the river to take the same route Abu Rasul had shown me, the safest way to get back to Kirkuk.

As soon as I was inside the city, I hailed a taxi. I paid him with the Ugly Arab's money and asked him to stop outside the Jamhuria hospital; for fear of the driver being a spy, I did not want him to take me to my destination. Walking through the alleyways, I reached the backyard of the building, checking often that I was not being followed. I knocked three times, and Norman opened the door to my private viewing room.

'How can I help you, sir?' He did not recognise me, and was clearly nervous. 'It's me, Norman,' I said. 'Who are you?' he asked, the colour drained from his cheeks.

I couldn't blame him. In the last four weeks I had been disfigured at the hands of the Mukhabarat. To Norman, I must have resembled John Hurt in *The Elephant Man*. I took out my photo, which I had retrieved from the Ugly Arab, and handed it to him. I pulled off the Saddamist hat and put on the wig. Norman was dumbfounded. 'Mery? Shit! You look like shit, and don't smell much better.' We walked up the stairs. 'Think deep and long, Mery,' he said, breathing fast. 'Apart from Sunshine, have you told anyone else about your visits to me?'

'No.'

'Are you sure, Mery?'

'Absolutely. Not even Gringo.'

I had a quick peek at the big screen from the rectangular hole. I had not seen a film for almost two months.

'*The Great Dictator* by Charles Chaplin,' Norman said. He was shaking all over. 'What happened?' he asked.

'I killed the Ugly Arab.'

'Who is he?'

'The head of Kirkuk's Mukhabarat.'

Norman stared at me, aghast. I told him the whole story from start to finish.

'If you are found here, we are both fucked,' he said.

'Do you want me to go?'

'No. The Mukhabarat will mobilise every man they have. The army, the militia, the police, the security, the Special Forces, the Jash and the fucking spies. They will storm across the city and will not stop until they get to you. You can stay one night, two, but soon they will be here, so what is next? I mean, where will you go, Mery?'

'America.'

'What the fuck? Well, I can't get you to America. How about a second choice, somewhere you don't need a passport for?'

'Popcorn once told me he knew the way out to the mountains.'

'Where is Popcorn?'

'I haven't seen him for months.'

'Another great fuck-up!'

'Rabbit will know.'

'Who is he?'

'Sunshine's brother. He was Popcorn's good friend, too.'

Norman went to Qala. I stayed in the projection room, waiting. I was tempted to get up, to watch the film, but I could not move. I was still haunted by my experience with the Ugly Arab and his Commander-in-Chief's secret plan to gas my people, and, like a shadow surviving only on a memory of hope, my mind and heart was with Sunshine as I anxiously waited for Norman's return.

'Here, Mery, I got you a Pepsi and a kebab.' Norman said, as he walked in. 'You will also need a good wash, my friend.'

'Did you find Sunshine?' I asked, still sitting in the corner.

'No Sunshine, no Rabbit. An Arab family lives in their house.'

I took out the photo and cried over Sunshine's sweet smile. I pulled out the Ugly Arab's gun and made for the door. Norman stood in my way.

'Abu Ali is another bastard to kill!' I said.

He pressed his chest onto my gun. 'There are many thousands of fucking bastards to be killed. You are not going out of this room, not unless you kill me first. I have two children and a wife to look after. If you are seen walking out, I am fucked too.'

I went back to the corner and sat there. My hands rested on

Sunshine's pendant around my neck. Norman was growing ever more agitated and stalked around the room deep in thought.

'There must be a way.' He considered, stopped and rejected the unspoken idea. He paced again.

'Sunshine must have cried for me,' I said, in a low voice, as if to myself. 'She must have believed I was dead and buried...'

'Dead!' Norman stopped excitedly and cut me short. 'Yes, dead, fucking dead. Mery! I think I've got it. You can act, isn't that right?'

'How can that help?'

'I want you to play dead. I will transform you and get you out of town like one of my dead fucking sculptures. OK, let's think it over. Let's say you were my cousin who was terribly burned and died in the hospital. I will be taking you back to your village to be buried. We'll need to fake a death certificate, but I know a couple of doctors at the hospital I can ask. You will need to be dead when we cross the checkpoints. Could you do that? Could you play dead?'

'I almost am anyway.'

'Mery!'

'Yes, I can.'

'It will work, Mery, it will. Let's just hope we don't come across your old friend, Abu Ali.'

'Fuck Abu Ali.'

That made Norman smile, as he loved swearing. Not for nothing was Joe Pesci one of his favourite actors.

Norman spent hours on my make-up and transformation. He did it in his garage, the space he used for his artistic work, and the whole time he spoke about his good friend Jam and how much he missed him. He had me lie in the back seat of his Toyota, completely naked and totally burned, including my face and my hair. He covered me with a white cotton sheet. He was confident we would make it. I insisted on having the Ugly Arab's gun hidden in the car, in the gap between the seat and the back panel, where I could access it in case our plan failed.

He drove, nervous at the presence of so many armed forces on the roads. To distract himself, Norman kept talking about films and how he would have liked to work with certain directors. On Kornish Street, we came across a checkpoint. Norman gave the guards his story, pointing to where I lay, inert, on his back seat, and with barely a second glance, the armed men waved him on.

'See, I told you, I could be an Oscar-winning make-up artist!' he squealed when we had driven on. 'Promise you will have me on your first fucking feature film, Mery?'

'I promise.'

'Don't talk, Mery! The checkpoint I most fear is the main one out of town.'

'I have a gun. I will not let anyone take you away.'

'Alive, say take you away alive.'

'Thank you for helping me out.'

'Don't fucking talk, Mery! Keep practising your breathing. I am not doing this shit only for you, but so you can let people know about this fucking gas attack, to let the outside world know what that bastard Saddam might do to his own population now, murdering them as callously as he poisons Iranian soldiers. This is big shit, Mery, really big shit.'

'Do you work for the underground organisation? I mean, if you do, you could get a message about the gas attack to our leaders in the mountains.'

'I asked you to not talk,' he said, and turned round. 'Try to stop breathing for a while. I am going to pour some more perfume on you.' I could stop breathing for a minute or two. Norman poured the nasty liquid over me. 'Some more burned-flesh-odour perfume,' he said. Fear made him almost sing the words.

'Shit! That is the rottenest smell ever, absolutely revolting,' I said. I was glad to stop breathing.

'Shut up, Mery, and hold your breath.'

'It's cold back here,' I said, shivering despite the heat of the summer night. 'Couldn't you turn off the air-conditioning?'

'Dead fuckers aren't known for their warmth,' Norman responded, in annoyance. 'You have to be cold to the touch, remember?' He slowed down the car. 'This is it. This is my nightmare. We get out of this fucking mess, or we are on our way to heaven.'

'I don't want to go to heaven. I want to go to the mountains, and from there to America.'

'Yes, Mery, America! Oh shit, I can see Abu Ali. I wonder who they are looking for, Mery?'

'We will be OK, he doesn't know I am alive.'

'You are dead, Mery.'

'Yes, I am dead.'

'Shut up, Mery! That is it, not another word. Yes, Mery, we film people know many tricks they can't even dream of. Isn't that right, Mery? Don't answer please, just keep practising your breathing, and I will keep you on course. We have three cars ahead of us, five in the opposite direction, and hundreds of the monster's men searching vehicles, looking for you... I mean for whoever killed the Ugly Arab fucker.'

Norman described every move. I felt sorry for him. He was hiding the most wanted fugitive in the back seat of his car and had to face Abu Ali on his own. I felt for the gun.

'Here we go, Mery, the fuckers are coming. Shush... Hello sir,' he said cheerily.

Hearing the voices, I figured out that Norman had to face three armed men. I guessed he was showing them his ID and the hospital certificate. Now he was explaining how an exploding gas bottle had fatally burnt me. A soldier poked his head through the window.

'I am sorry about the awful smell, sir,' Norman said, politely. The armed forces asked him to get back to the wheel. 'He was my cousin but also my old friend, sir, my old friend.'

'Get out of the car,' Abu Ali barked at Norman.

Abu Ali opened the back door, where my feet were protruding from the thin white sheet. This was the moment of trial for Norman's artistic talent and my acting ability.

'I'm sorry about the awful smell, sir!'

'Shut up!' Abu Ali shouted, and pushed Norman away. 'Stand there until I finish.'

He does not care about the stink. His whole life smells rotten. He pulled off the sheet all the way to my belly button. *I am not circumcised. If he pulls down a little more, he will recognise me.* He held on to his nose and poked his finger hard into my stomach. I did not move. *But I cannot hold my breath for much longer.*

'Your rotting cousin smells like shit,' he said to Norman. 'Open the boot.'

Abu Ali searched the boot and slammed the door in frustration. He was already scanning the occupants of the car behind us.

Norman pulled the sheet up to cover my face and whispered, 'Not as much as you smell, you fucker.'

King Kong E.T.

The Betwata camp for displaced Kurdish Anfal victims was a hellish scene of chaos and squalor. Several hundred huts and makeshift tents had been built closely together, most of which had been hurriedly assembled by people desperate to have a roof over their heads. The camp had grown rapidly, spreading like a disease in what must have once been a peaceful and fertile valley, though now it looked more like a rubbish dump populated by humans. Here and there groups of older men chatted and played *Dama*, Kurdish chess. Others walked about or sat alone pensively, defeated by the hand that fate had dealt them. Some of the women were busy washing rugs and blankets, while others fought back tears caused by smoke from the wood fires that they used for cooking in the open. Children ran around playing noisily, somehow oblivious to their environment, dressed in clothes which were now so ragged that their families would have normally given them to beggars… But now they had nothing left to give. I found my way to what passed as the mosque – a lean-to shelter – and asked the Mullah for Darwesh Rashaba.

My family were living in a mud-brick hut, which had its back to the hills and towards the sunset, so that the view, at least, was serene. I came across Star and Mother, each with a bucket on their heads, taking water home from the communal well. Star was so surprised to see me that her bucket fell from her head, water cascading over the barren ground. 'Mery,' she called, running to me. I kissed her cheeks and Mother's hands. I took the bucket from Mother and put it on my own head.

'Mum, it's better if no one knows I am here,' I told her quietly. I knew the Mukhabarat would not look for me in the camp because for them I was dead, but I had learned my lesson. I needed to be extremely careful.

'Do you have news of Ardalan?' Mother asked.

'I have not seen him since we left Qala.'

'He is dead, isn't he?'

'I don't know. I don't think so.'

'Swear?'

'I swear on the Qur'an and in the name of Allah.' I was so totally disillusioned with Allah and Islam that I could lie while holding the holy book and not worry in the least.

My father sat silently in the dark room. I kissed his hands, but he said nothing. 'Where have you been all this time?' Star asked, stroking King Kong. 'With our uncles in Baghdad. They are fine, they send their love to you and will soon find a way to get you back to Kirkuk for Uncle Baban's wedding.'

Mother started to cry. 'Your uncles are dead,' she said. At that point, I reluctantly relented, admitted to what I knew and took some comfort from the momentary shared burden of grief. My father kept quiet. Mother lit the oil lamp. We did not have much more to add to our misery. I turned to Star. 'How is King Kong?' I asked.

'He is fine. He doesn't like it here and wants to go back home.'

'Shall I tell you a story?' Star nodded. 'There is this creature called E.T. He's from a different planet and mysteriously gets stranded on Earth. He meets a young boy, Elliot, not much older than you. At the beginning Elliot is scared of E.T. but soon they become inseparable friends. One day he finds E.T. standing at the window, pointing to the sky and calling "Home, Home…" Elliot hides a startled E.T. from the monster's men who are chasing them. E.T. helps Elliot's and his friends magically escape by flying away on their bicycles. Then E.T.'s family arrives in a flying saucer and E.T. gets to go home. And one day, my sweet Star, we will, too.'

'Can I change King Kong's name to King Kong E.T.?'

'If that is what you want.'

'Your beard is growing,' Mother pointed out.

'Yes, it is,' I answered, and pulled off the new hat that Norman had bought for me, along with my new clothes. Mother gasped, seeing my short hair.

'Why did you cut your hair?' It was the first thing Father had asked me since my arrival. 'I am no longer a dervish, Father. I do not wish to be one.' I was waiting for shouts and perhaps kicks, but he sank back into his thoughts. He took off his turban and let his long hair fall onto his shoulders. He started to pray quietly. Without his three golden teeth, he looked a lot older and more miserable.

In the morning, Star poured water from a metal jar into my hands to wash my face. They did not have running water, nor was there electricity or a toilet. I took the jar from her and headed to the outside natural toilet, a dirty hidden corner at the back by the hillside. I turned and surveyed the camp, where people moved about like ants, with no real direction. They were utterly lost, like my family, displaced and with no purpose for being there. On my way back, I heard a familiar voice.

'Well done. I got it, Layla, my heart burns. Kiss it...' Louis no longer had a whole team around, only his son and two wives, building a wall by his hut made from mud bricks, metal pieces and old tyres. I ran over to help out. 'Get lost!' Louis said, breaking off from his song and his work. 'I have no money to pay you. Just get lost.'

'I don't want money. I want to say sorry for giving you a hard time.'

'Merywan? Am I dreaming?'

Louis asked his wife for some tea and insisted that I join him. He took me aside. 'See the thousands of people around, they were all forced out of their houses and replaced by Arabs. But I am not going to accept it, Merywan.'

'What can you do?'

'I am leaving soon. I am not staying in this shit place.'

Life in the camp must be really tough if Louis complains about it.

'Where to?'

'Turkey, and then to Europe. Many are making their way out.'

'Can I come with you?'

'Do you have money?'

'No.'

'There is another way, you can go for free. The agents even pay you some money. That is how I will get across the border.'

'How?'

'By carrying drugs.'

'What drugs?'

'I don't know the name. Shit stuff from Afghanistan, via Iran. They use refugees to take it across for a free passage to Turkey.'

'What if we get arrested?'

'We will be shot. But some have made it out.'

'How do you know?'

'They never came back.'

'I will come with you.'

'We need to get to a village called Argosh on the border; there we will meet the agent. We need to carry a couple of boxes across to Semdinli, a small town in Turkey.'

'You mean to north Kurdistan, the part occupied by Turkey?'

'Well, yes, but everyone knows it as Turkey at the moment, don't they? Once in Semdinli, we leave the drugs and make our way to Istanbul. They say the crossing from Istanbul to Greece is only a matter of one night's walk.'

'When are you leaving?'

'At the end of the week, as soon as I finish this damn wall.'

'Are you taking your family along?'

'No. It's far too dangerous for women and children.'

I pulled out the Ugly Arab's gun. Louis raised his eyebrows and, for once, he was nearly speechless. 'What the hell is this?' he whispered, though nobody was nearby. 'Do you think you could sell it?' I asked. He checked the gun and put it under his jacket.

'Merywan, be careful! There are many spies around here, but I should be able to sell it, perhaps even tonight.'

I was one of the most wanted fugitives and I needed to disappear from the camp before attracting the spies and having the Mukhabarat hunt me down, so there was no way that I could risk waiting for Louis until the end of the week. After leaving him, I repeated the mantra of 'Argosh' and 'Semdinli' silently to myself to memorise the names as I walked back. I was looking forward to seeing my posters and the portraits of my heroes. I picked up my pillow and pulled out my treasure box. *Mum, I love you.* As always, I first spat on Saddam's horrible figure, but this time I did not keep it, I tore it into pieces. I unfolded Gringo's poster. I was not going to write him a letter but I needed to have a chat, to let him know how much I still wanted to get out and go to America.

My dear Gringo, over the years I sometimes had doubts my letters would make it to you, but I still wrote them because, although I was surrounded by many people, I had no one to communicate with as freely as I could with you. I wanted to burn the copies of my letters more than once. I told myself many times I should bury them since they were going nowhere. But talking to you kept me going and, above all, it gave me hope. Now I have also learnt the important role my letters could play against the monster, provided I can get them out of the country and get them published as my story. I wish I had those copies. I wish I had Sunshine with me. I am looking at her photo next to your poster, at her sweet smile and the joy of our being together between Jam and Uncle Hitch. The last time Sunshine put her arms around me and we kissed was on Nawroz night, on the rooftop of our house in Qala, under the stars. I am now a long way away from her, and I hope with all my heart that she is still alive.

The next morning I went to Louis' house to find that he had indeed sold the gun. I thanked him, pocketed the cash, and hurried back to my family's shack.

Star was the only one to run up to me and hug me. I stood in front of Father. He looked away. 'I am leaving, Father. I am going to America and I may never see you again. Please let me kiss your hands?' He put his hands inside his pockets. I wanted to hug him so much, but he shrugged and turned away. *He won't allow me near him. I have not become the great dervish he wished for.* I turned to Mother. She could not stop herself from sobbing, but she let me kiss her hands. 'Why are you going away?' she said, crying.

'I have to go, Mum. I hope you can forgive me.' She hugged me back and kissed me again. I took out four hundred dinars, the gun money. 'This is all I have, Mum. This is all I can leave for you.' I handed her the money and kissed her hands again. 'I am sorry, Mum. I have lied to you. Ardalan is dead. I am so sorry. I couldn't tell you immediately, I didn't want to add to your pain. He died for a great cause, for our people's freedom, and I know he died like a hero.' I had finally unburdened myself of the tragic news of Trouble's death, but I wasn't sure if she had registered what I had told her. She kept staring blankly at me as more tears streamed down her face. 'Stay to have dinner with us,' she said, sobbing, her body trembling.

'I must go. Please take care, Mum.'

Star was still holding on to King Kong. I crouched down to

her level. 'You remember, whenever you need Mery, just tell King Kong, OK?'

'His name is King Kong E.T. now,' she said, lifting up the old doll.

'I mean King Kong E.T.'

'Can I tell you a secret?' she whispered.

'Yes.'

'King Kong E.T. said he will take me home on his flying saucer back to Kirkuk.'

'Did he?' Star nodded convincingly. 'Star, here, you take this.' It was the only thing I had that I could leave for my sweet sister.

'What is it?' she asked, curiously. 'My treasure box. My good friends are hiding in there. If you get into trouble and I am not around, you can count on them.'

'Thank you,' she said, and held the box to her chest.

'I love you, little sister.'

'I love you too, big brother.'

I walked away. Mother followed for a while, crying. 'Mery!' Star called, running after me. I turned to her. 'Please let your hair grow again,' she said, and waved.

'I will. I promise. I miss my long hair.'

A night with the PKK

High up in the mountains I was amazed by how beautiful my country looked. Never before had its landscape appeared so mesmerising. It could easily have been a perfectly unspoiled location for one of Gringo's film sets.

For the first part of the journey, I hid during the day and travelled by night along the banks of the river Dulmawan. On the fourth day, I reached my destination. I had left the government forces behind, and was amongst our true friends, the mountains of Kurdistan. Thanks to the many orchards in the valleys, there were numerous fruit and nut trees that provided me with plentiful supplies. I consciously avoided the Peshmerga forces. I was not sure if they would have trusted the reasons for my presence in the land under their control. For the same reason, I avoided going into Argosh. I knew the smugglers would stay away from the villages, as the Peshmerga would have them arrested for smuggling drugs.

I stumbled across them in a cave, close to the border. Once they had searched me and heard about my motives for being there, they were assured that I didn't pose a threat and continued to prepare their cases of drugs. I had been expecting to meet a well-organised group of armed smugglers, but they were a miserable, dirty bunch of roughnecks.

I was the only one aiming to cross the border and the youngest of the seven. Carrying two cases on my back, which were said to be drugs from Afghanistan, the smugglers put me in the middle, fourth in the line, and we trekked across difficult terrain, sometimes climbing up steep tracks for two hours before making the descent. The plan was to make it to the other side by six o'clock in the morning. With an all-too-brief twenty-minute break, I was to walk for around eleven hours. At times I felt hungry, but mostly I felt nothing but exhaustion, my weakened body shaking from the fatigue of the journey. I staggered on, sweat pouring down my spine, keeping myself going with the thought that none of this hardship mattered. I was finally on my way to Gringo.

The midsummer night was warm and pleasant, the heat from the day still rising from the rocks into a sky lit by countless stars. I had never seen so many before, and high up here in the clear air I almost felt I could touch them. We were only supposed to signal to each other, and to maintain a stony silence so as not to alert Turkish border guards. The smugglers were knowledgeable about the narrow tracks, and more than once they pointed out minefields to our left and right. After almost seven hours, we eventually stopped for a break. I could see some lights in the distance. 'Semdinli?' I pointed. 'Deryene,' the head smuggler answered. 'Then Semdinli.'

'Are we far from the border?' I asked.

'Ten more minutes' walk and you will be in Turkey.'

'Why stop here?'

'We don't cross the border. We wait for our partners from the other side. From here on they take our cargo.'

'What about me?'

'You go with them.' And then, irritably, 'You ask too many questions. Not good. Shush...'

Flashes of light – torches going on and off – came from the other side. The smugglers lifted their cases onto their backs. 'Wait here,' the head smuggler said, and walked alone towards the approaching lights. Suddenly, he dropped his cases, and ran back towards us, warning, 'The Turkish Gendarmerie, run!'

He collapsed dead onto his face with the first shots. We ran back as fast as our tired legs would let us, each of us dropping our cases to lighten our load. I was the last to let my cases drop. Two more smugglers were brought down, and I knew that at any moment I could be the next. More gunfire came from the opposite direction. *Should I go left, or right?* I didn't know what to do. We were trapped. We were surrounded. I put up my arms to surrender. The guns continued firing spasmodically, but not at me. The Turkish Gendarmerie was now firing towards the mountains. When one of the other Gendarmes was also hit I realised I was caught between two opposing forces. The Gendarmes made a break for it, back towards safety in Turkey.

By the time I turned around, the other smugglers were nowhere to be seen. *Shit! The minefields!* I carefully stepped on to the tracks we had been using on the way to the border. I was heading to Turkey. I had no intention of going back. '*Dur,* Stop!' a female voice called in Turkish. I could understand, because it was not so different from the Turkmani spoken in Qala, but I could see no one. '*Kim sin,* Who are you?'

'Merywan Rashaba.'

'Are you Turkish?'

'No, I am a Kurd.'

'Kurmanci or Sorani?'

'Sorani.'

We Kurds from the southern part of Kurdistan, Iraq, mainly spoke Sorani, while the Kurds from the north, in Turkey, speak Kurmanci.

'Don't be scared, comrade, we are friends,' the voice said in Kurdish Kurmanci. Two girls and a young man, not much older than me, materialised from behind boulders, each wearing khaki sharwal, armed with AK-47s, hand grenades and pistols.

'My name is Narin,' one of the girls said, as she gave me some water to drink. 'We are PKK, the Kurdistan Workers' Party.'

I was aware of the PKK, but had never met anyone involved with them. I was shocked to see young girls so heavily armed.

'Thanks,' I said, as I handed back her water bottle. Narin set fire to the drug cases, and we walked high up into the Qandil Mountains with her comrades.

That night, in the mouth of a cave, Narin told me about their armed struggle while she cleaned her gun. 'The PKK was founded in the late 1970s, built on the revolutionary ideology of Kurdish nationalism. In 1984, under the leadership of Ocalan, it transformed itself into a guerrilla organisation. Our goal is to create an independent state of Kurdistan that includes all the Kurdish land in Turkey, Iran, Iraq and Syria.'

I hesitated, but had to ask, 'Turkey considers you a terrorist organisation?'

'America strongly opposes the PKK, because Turkey is a member of NATO, and was America's ally against the USSR in the Cold War. America and Turkey are wrong. We are not terrorists, though we do fight guns with guns. We want a peaceful solution to the Kurdish question. If Turkey talks peace, we talk peace. It is our birthright to have freedom and be recognised for who we are. There are more than forty million of us and in Turkey alone there are more than twenty million, yet Turkey calls us 'Mountain Turks'. They don't even allow our Kurdish language to be used publicly.

'We don't want to live by the gun, but are forced to do so, just like your Peshmerga fighting Saddam's army. I am only sixteen. I never dreamt of this life. I wanted to go to university, to become a lawyer, to help women, who are doubly oppressed, firstly by the Turkish government because they are Kurds and secondly by the males in their families because they are women. I could not follow my path in a civilised way because I am facing an uncivilised opponent. I must resort to the gun, and if necessary, will die by it. I always keep one last bullet, to kill myself with if I am captured. I would rather die with dignity than be tortured and raped by the enemy.'

The Kurds in Turkey live no better than we do under Saddam. Narin put her gun under her head and lay down. 'Merywan,' she said. 'You could join us if you wish.'

'I respect your fight, but I am no good with guns, and am on my way to America. I need to cross the border.'

'America doesn't like Kurds.'

'Sadly not, but I have a good friend there. I need to give him an important message about the fate of our people, and I want to make films.'

Narin turned my way, looking at me differently. 'Once we get back to our base camp,' she said, 'I will ask our commander for permission to help you cross the border. That's good, Merywan. You should go to America and make films. Fighting on its own is not going to win our freedom.'

I was still in the habit of peeing away from everyone, especially in the presence of ladies. I chose a spot not far from the mouth of the cave, but before I knew what was happening, a hand grabbed my mouth tightly. 'Don't move,' a male voice said, and I became aware of a group of men behind me. Around a dozen Peshmerga from the south of Kurdistan had surrounded my PKK friends from the north and disarmed them. Watching Narin and her two friends as they had their hands tied behind their backs made me feel sick. I faced the commander. 'They are Kurds like you,' I said.

'They are Kurds from the north. This is south Kurdistan. They can't be here. They should fight from their own land.'

'Kurdistan belongs to all the Kurds.'

'That's wishful thinking.'

'Let the PKK members free.'

'Who are you?'

'Merywan Rashaba.'

'Tie his hands too,' the commander ordered.

'I know him, sir,' a Peshmerga said, as he came forward. 'Mery! I didn't recognise you with your short hair.'

Popcorn! Now he carried an AK-47 instead of a basket. 'Please ask your commander to let my friends free!' I pleaded with him.

'The PKK has to conduct their fight from within Turkey,' the commander answered.

'But Turkey is our enemy, too,' I protested.

'At the moment we are fighting Saddam, and cannot afford to fight Turkey, as well.'

'Then let the PKK do it.'

'Our leadership does not want to upset Turkey and find their army at our doorstep. They may be the enemy, but we must keep them happy, and these people should not be using our land to attack Turkey.'

'What will happen to my friends, Popcorn?'

'I am not sure. Sorry, Mery, I can't help you with this one.'

I moved away from him and stood by my friends. 'Tie my hands, too,' I said, but they did not.

We walked south-east with the PKK captives and I showed my solidarity by staying by their side, rather than talking to Popcorn or the Peshmerga. We camped in the open away from the Turkish border. It was a pleasant night and the Peshmerga lit a small fire. Popcorn sat by my side. 'Mery, you can sleep peacefully. Here you are safe, a long way away from Abu Ali's game of cat and mouse.'

'Popcorn, do you know who was following me?'

'I can't tell you, but I'm sure you will find out for yourself soon enough. Good night.'

'*Shaw shad*, Happy night, my friend. I am glad to see you alive.'

A wolf howled in the distance while the Peshmerga slept soundly, untroubled by this eerie serenade. I surveyed the scene. One of the Peshmerga stood guard. *My best bet is to wait until they change shift.* It must have been well beyond midnight, and I guessed that the next person on guard duty would be drowsy after just waking up. Steeling myself for what I had to do, my heart sank as I saw Popcorn sleepily tapping his comrade on the shoulder to relieve him of guard duty. I lay and watched him covertly, waiting for him to fall asleep as he sat by the ashes of the fire, but he remained resolutely vigilant. *I could gun-butt him on the back of his neck. But I do not want to harm Popcorn.* He got up, and checked that everyone, including my PKK friends, were sleeping, then disappeared behind a boulder. I crawled over to Narin, untying her feet and hands, and she silently helped me to free the other two. They quietly gathered up their guns and we slithered away to make our escape.

'Stop! Or I'll shoot.' Popcorn faced us.

'No, Popcorn, you won't,' and I walked straight towards him.

'Mery, move away!'

'I will not, you'll have to kill me first,' and I dived on to Popcorn. Narin and her friends ran as Popcorn's shot sailed high into the air. At the sound of gunfire, the others jumped to their feet. In an instant, the commander ordered half of his men to chase after the escaping captives. Then, facing me, he went to slap me, but I reacted in time and grabbed hold of his wrist.

'I do not wish to be hit by you because I love our Peshmerga,' I said, 'and I would have done the same for you, never mind which party you are a member of, as long as you are a Kurd fighting our enemies.'

'You will be tried for treason,' he answered, and moved away. Popcorn had to tie my hands. The men returned to report that Narin and her friends were nowhere to be seen, and I smiled inwardly as I imagined them melting back into the mountains. For the rest of our journey Popcorn hardly spoke a word to me.

'Popcorn, you have to talk to your commander,' I said, as we walked behind the others, 'you must free me, I have to make it to America.' Popcorn shook his head. 'OK, then you have to get me to meet our leaders, I have important secrets to reveal to them.' Popcorn was not interested. He kept walking. I insisted, 'Saddam will gas the Kurds if our leaders ally themselves with Iran against him. It's a plan that I learnt of from the head of the Mukhabarat in Kirkuk.'

I want to marry you

I was shut in a small room in a shack on the mountainside not far from Kani Rash village. There were two Peshmerga in charge of guarding me while I waited for my trial, and I managed to befriend one of them. He was a good-hearted youth about my age. Despite his thick-grown beard, I could see that his face was badly disfigured, burned or perhaps hit by a shell during one of the battles, I imagined. 'Your voice is familiar,' I said to him.

'Is it?'

'Yes. It reminds me of someone I used to know in Kirkuk.'

'Who?'

'It doesn't really matter, it was a long time ago. What is your name?'

'Arpa.'

'Is that your real name?'

'No, it is my Peshmerga name. I can't give my real name. It is safer that way.'

'Even in the mountains?'

'Only to those who served in the Freedom for Life underground before retreating to the resistance.'

'Are you with Barzani or Talabani?'

'You'll have to guess.'

He relieved some of my boredom in captivity by providing me with books and pamphlets about the Kurdish armed struggle, and with updates on the latest in the Iran-Iraq war, the Kurdish-Iraq war and the situation in the towns. He brought me good food and was interested in the story of my life, especially my desire to go to America, but he kept any trace of his past to himself.

On a fresh autumn afternoon, we went out for one of my brief exercise breaks. By then we had become good friends, and Arpa casually slung his gun from his shoulder rather than carrying it in his hand. He was making jokes about the various political parties involved in the armed struggle, tying his turban in different ways to mimic them. 'Like this,' Arpa demonstrated, 'I will be Democratic and have a yellow scarf around my neck, the colour of the Barzani. This way, I am PUK, and will wear a green scarf, Talabani's colour...' The more I learned, the more I realised how ridiculous it was to have so many divisions among Kurds fighting for essentially the same cause. The only differences I could see were how they tied their turbans. But on that day Arpa gave me worrying news. 'The Barzani and the Talabani are united in the Kurdistan Liberation Front, and with Iran's help are planning one final assault on Iraq. There are also Arabs, Turkmen and Christians in the mountains fighting Saddam. We may not be too far away from destroying the dictator and finally enjoying our freedom.'

I wonder if Popcorn has taken my message to our leaders? And what about my freedom? I had never ceased to plan my escape, and would have attempted it long before if I hadn't worried about the consequences for Arpa.

'I hope you don't mind me asking, but what happened to your face?'

'My father threw acid on me.'

'I am sorry.'

'It could have been worse.'

'Arpa, soon the snow will fall, it will become much harder to cross into Turkey.'

'You must wait for your trial.'

'Trial for betrayal at the hands of the Kurdish armed struggle? Because I freed three PKK fighters?'

'It is not in my hands.'

'If I escape, would you shoot me?'

'Don't, Mery, please don't. I will ask my commander to radio the judge to bring your trial forwards.'

'OK, I will wait another week.'

'Promise?'

'I promise on my heart,' and I put my hand on my heart. 'But if, after my trial, they put me back into captivity, I will go.'

'And I will help you out.' Arpa put his hand on his heart.

In the morning Arpa turned up with good news. His commander

had sent a message and I was to get ready for my trial. He gave me a razor and some soap. 'It is better if the judge sees you nice and clean,' he said. 'I will bear witness that you were one of the easiest prisoners we have had. The judge is a Peshmerga and will understand.' I shaved, looking into the cracked mirror. It was more than two months since I had last seen my face. It was pleasing to see my hair growing again. There was a knock at the door, but I did not have time to reach it before it opened wide, the bright rays of sunlight framing a silhouette standing on the threshold, a pistol at its belt.

'Mery Rashaba, it had better be you and not a dream!' said a female voice.

'Sunshine Shamal! And you too!'

I hugged her with the strength all my love. I felt her face, her eyes and her lips. She smiled and cried tears of joy. My eyes filled too. I was back with Sunshine! Our arms wrapped around each other in a tight embrace, our breath mingling.

'You look different with short hair, boygirl, but I still love you.'

'You are really here?'

'I am, my love. I never lost the hope of seeing you again.'

'Do you still have the copies of my letters?'

'You can bet on that. Yes, and Aida's scarf and your notebook.'

'I love you, Sunshine. There will be hundreds, thousands and millions of kisses after our marriage, but can I kiss you once now?' I had hardly finished speaking when Sunshine pressed her sweet lips against mine and we kissed for a long time.

'Come Mery, someone else is waiting to see you.' She got hold of my hand.

'I can't. I am a captive.'

'No more, Mery Rashaba,' Popcorn said, from the doorway. 'I have secured your release, you are free.'

'Popcorn! Thank you.' And I gave him a hug too. 'Have you given my message to our leaders?'

'Yes, we sent a dispatch and explained that the bearer of the news would like to meet the leadership. We are waiting for their answer. But for now, come out, you have someone else to meet.' Standing on a new false leg and holding an AK-47, Rabbit was also waiting outside. *The man who always objected to the armed struggle?*

'You have become Peshmerga?' I asked.

'Yes, my friend.'

We embraced and shared tears. This had all happened so suddenly that I did not have time to say goodbye to Arpa. He was not around and I asked the other guard on duty to let him know where I was going.

Sunshine and I held hands and sat in the back of a Land Rover with two more Peshmerga. Rabbit, as always, sat on top of the driver's cab, and with Popcorn in the passenger's seat, we drove down the dirt track. I kept looking Sunshine in the eyes. 'How did you get out of Kirkuk?' I asked.

'When you left for Baghdad, Rabbit made contact with Popcorn in the mountains. He begged my father to leave Kirkuk…' Sunshine had to pause and wipe away her tears. 'My father didn't want to go without Peaceful. The officers he bribed kept giving him false promises. On the day my father and brother were shot, Popcorn helped us get out.'

'Master Shamal and Peaceful will live forever in my heart.'

'What about you, Mery?' She was wiping the tears from my eyes, as I did for her, while I told her my side of the story since we had last seen each other. 'Over all that time, I never went to sleep without the hope of seeing you again, without wishing you good night and saying "Sunshine, I love you".'

'The same goes for me.'

'When can we get engaged?'

'I am still wearing black for my father and my brother.'

'We can have a quiet wedding. I want us to be married before I leave for America. Unless you come with me.'

'I can't. My mother is in a real state.'

'You will join me, won't you, if I make it?'

'I will, I promise, on my heart,' she said. She became quiet and looked away.

'What is it, my love?'

'I am not a virgin.'

'I am not a virgin either. I love you. Who was the lucky man?' Sunshine looked away again. 'You don't have to tell me if you don't feel like it.'

Razga was a mud-brick village on the lower mountainside near the Iranian border, well hidden in a valley. Popcorn and I went to Sunshine and Rabbit's new house there. Jwana sat on the small raised veranda in the courtyard. She was sadly no longer the charming, stylish teacher she had been, but a broken woman. She was talking to herself as we walked in, when she lifted her head and cried out, 'When are they coming home? I want my husband, I want my son.' I took hold of her hands to kiss them, but she pushed me away. 'I don't want you. I want my husband...' Sunshine tried to make her understand who I was, but she kept calling out. Rabbit started to cry, and Sunshine and I did too, giving in to the need to grieve together. Popcorn lit a cigarette and sat smoking. Rabbit stood opposite and offered me his AK-47, while Popcorn and Sunshine looked on. *Is this a provocation, is it for real?*

'Iraq, Iran, Turkey and Syria,' I said, reminding him. 'One against the other and all united to kill Kurds. Your own words, my Brader. Four powerful enemies and you believe we can bring them to their knees with these stupid guns by killing a few soldiers from the mountains? This will only bring more disaster to our people. We need a different solution.'

'You once said the only answer to our enemy is our guns.'

'I no longer believe that. That was a different time and I am now a different person. I also once hated the Arabs, I don't hate them any more. I was once a devoted Muslim, I'm no longer one. And most of all I want to go to America, so you had better put your gun down and come with me.'

'If we put down our guns our people will be massacred by Saddam.'

'Not if you back him up.'

'Become Saddamist?'

'I would rather do that than have our people slaughtered and achieve nothing. How can we fight this monster who enjoys the world's support? If the world backs him, why shouldn't we?' Rabbit moved away. I faced him. 'Rabbit, Saddam plans to gas us all if we join the Iranians to attack him. Is that what you want? This is all wrong, our leaders should have never taken guns into their hands.'

'Shush, Mery, you could be punished for saying bad things about our leaders,' Sunshine said, which surprised me.

'I believed the mountains were one place where the Kurds had freedom. Does that mean even the mountains are no longer our friends?'

'Talking badly about our leaders is not tolerated,' Rabbit said, moving his gun to his chest.

Rabbit has changed too. He is bloodthirsty.

'Well, what is the difference between our leaders and Saddam Hussein?' I said, looking into his eyes.

'That is going too far.'

'Never far enough, Rabbit, for those who are taking away your freedom of speech, and controlling your thoughts, they take away life itself. They are brainwashing you. Haven't you heard, "those who can make you believe absurdities can make you commit atrocities?" I am going to America, I have made my decision.' Jwana suddenly burst out again. 'I want my husband, I want my son…' Sunshine sat next to her and caressed her face to calm her down. 'Mother, Mery is here, he wants to ask you for my hand.'

Jwana stopped wailing at once. She looked up. Something clicked inside her. She opened her arms to me. I went to her and lost myself in her arms. She kissed my cheeks as she always did. She studied Sunshine's face and then mine. '*Piroza*, Congratulations,' she said, with her familiar broad smile. Sunshine turned to Rabbit. Popcorn and I did too. He turned away from us and climbed up the wooden ladder, dragging his false leg behind him. I followed.

On the rooftop I stared around at the beautiful landscape and wondered how much more tragedy this land could endure. I put an arm around my friend's shoulders. 'I love Sunshine, I always will. I'll do everything for her happiness. I understand this is not the right time. If I weren't on my way to leave the country, I would have waited.'

'Mery, you and Sunshine are made for each other. I have no objection,' Rabbit said, without looking at me.

'Thank you, Rabbit. Is that from your heart?'

He turned to me, but not to give me an answer. 'Did Jam get away?' he asked instead, with sadness in his eyes.

I shook my head. I battled to ask him the most important question on my mind. I was afraid of hurting him, and he had just given his consent for Sunshine and me to marry, but since he had brought up the subject of Jam, I ventured to ask it, 'How did you know Jam was next and I was the last on the list?'

Rabbit sighed, looked away, and shook his head in misery. I could see he was struggling with himself. I faced him and decided to press on. This was my last chance to learn the truth. 'You could have at least told me, if you knew that Abu Ali was Shawes Dog?'

'The monster's men did not need me for their game,' Rabbit said, at last, tentatively beginning his confession. 'They knew everything about you through your letters. Without those letters you would have been dead long ago. Gringo saved your life, in a way. Yes, Shawes Dog was put in prison, but he collaborated with the police and spied on his prison mates. He was credited for his work. The Mukhabarat realised how useful he could be and gave him a trial period. Within a short time he had handed over many innocent Kurds. Shawes Dog was recognised as Abu Ali, and to hide his identity, he made up the story of having once been a Peshmerga commander who had poisoned his fourteen men.'

'When did he get you involved?'

'When you met Aida. I missed our appointment because the Mukhabarat took me to Shawes Dog, who was by then Abu Ali. He wanted me to spy on you and the people you had contact with. In exchange he was going to let my family and me live. He left me with no choice. He would have killed my family, your family and both of us too. He would have done the same if I talked to anyone about his plans, including my father, and especially you. Nobody would have been safe from him, even if I had committed suicide. He promised not to harm us as long as I played his nasty game. I thought he might just threaten people to stay away from you, to give you a hard time. A couple of weeks later I had to report on the first victim.'

'Who?'

'Aida. That is why I asked you to stay away from her, not because I was jealous. Shawes Dog's hatred for you was unprecedented, really crazy. On the same day you went to Orzdy to see Aida, he planned out the scene with the young man. He had already spotted you on Republic Street, and this was his way to get to you and torture your mind with the possibility that Abu Ali was indeed Shawes Dog.'

'Why didn't you leave Kirkuk?'

'I asked my father, telling him that life was becoming far too dangerous. He felt that the whole of Iraq was like hell. The only safe place was in the mountains, but not for him, after his experiences with the resistance. I was miserable and couldn't forgive myself for spying on you. I found the job in the desert to escape from an intolerable predicament. It was a stupid solution, but what else could I have done? I was hoping Shawes Dog would get killed or forget about us, and because of him I stayed in the desert, even on Fridays. But it wasn't long before he sent for me. Under the pretence of building a garden for the Major who came to inspect the site, I was taken away and given an ultimatum: I would either go back to town, or Abu Ali would kill my family.'

'Is that why you broke off our friendship?'

'I attacked your belief in Islam. Not that I regret a word I said in that regard, but I had no right to spit it out so bluntly to your face. The last thing I wanted was to hurt you. Shawes Dog was so angry. He beat me for going away without telling him. I could bear his beatings, but when I told him you were no longer my friend, he gun-butted me on my injured knee. You were his favourite pet.'

'But you did not try to make friends with me again.'

'I was trying to gain time to find a solution. I insulted you about being a neuter. I was pleased when you refused my friendship, but later that day, Shawes Dog took me in again and this time, he crushed my injured knee. I had to tell the family I was run over by a car. Two weeks later I had my leg amputated. He could have sent many people to spy on you, but he despised our love for each other and was playing the worst possible game, taking his revenge on me too. After Aida, he then asked me to find out who Godfather was. You had not given his real name in the letters, but they found the brothel. They knew Uncle Hitch had no political affiliation, but it was enough that he cared for you and that you loved him. As the list shrank and your time was coming closer, I told Popcorn to let you know that you were being followed. I was hoping you would leave for America, or at least leave town and go into hiding, but I am glad you didn't because I might have lost my sister and mother too, as well as you losing your parents and little sister.'

'What about Jam?'

'Shawes Dog asked me to go with you to Jam's shop on your

sixteenth birthday, but I had no idea that they would dump Uncle Hitch's body like that. I didn't want to go out on Nawroz day because I was supposed to go with you to Jam's shop. He had plans to arrest Jam in front of you. I had to lie, telling him I was ill in bed on Nawroz, but Shawes Dog had seen us together on television greeting Saddam. That's why my parents were sacked from their jobs, but even this was not enough. Shawes Dog was furious and decided to kill your entire family, and my family too. I cried, I pleaded with him, I promised to play his game, and Shawes Dog... he... he...,' Rabbit sighed, as if his soul were leaving him.

'I finally told my father the truth. We had to find a way to leave Kirkuk immediately. Sunshine wanted you to come with us, and I did too.'

'Why did you decide to tell your father?'

'I can't tell you about that part of the story and you should not ask me. Popcorn was to help us get out secretly. We were to leave the day after Peaceful's concert. Shawes promised he would free Peaceful if I found out where your private viewing room was. I wanted to believe him. But I did not ask you. I was scared that might be your end.'

'But when I went to Abu Ghraib prison, Shawes' name was there on the prisoners list.'

'Only his name is there. Officially he is still in prison.'

'I will get you, Mery,' I mouthed, hollowly. 'I read that on his lips many times. He played a nasty game with me.'

'After my father's and brother's deaths, I felt like killing myself, but I knew I had to look after Jwana and Sunshine. I am so ashamed for having played his evil game, for causing so much pain.'

'True Braders keep no secrets. Your words.'

'I do not ask you for forgiveness, and even if you did forgive me, I will not forgive myself until the day Shawes Dog dies. I did what I did to save people, to save you, but I got it all wrong and I am sorry.'

'I am sorry too, for I also kept secrets from you.'

Rabbit had to suffer so much because he befriended me and stood up to the Dog and his son, Kojak. What a price he and his family have paid for giving me love and respect. I kept quiet, but when Rabbit stopped crying, I said, 'Brader, I asked many people, "why did God create us?" as I wanted to find a convincing answer to help win back your friendship. I could not find an answer, but I found you again. So now I can say, Brader, that I agree with you: God does not exist.'

In the evening, Sunshine and I sat by the oil lamp in the spare room where I stayed during my time in Razga. She cried when I asked her who had taken her virginity. She realised I had worked it out.

'Abu Ali raped me. Soon after Peaceful's arrest he came to our house. Rabbit was the only one at home. Shawes Dog beat Rabbit and then attacked me in front of my brother. Rabbit cried and cried…' Sunshine's words exploded like a bomb inside me, hitting me with the most horrendous pain. I felt anger, such massive anger that I could have ripped out Shawes Dog's heart with my hands. After all that I had gone through, hearing that Sunshine had been raped by the Dog hit me the hardest. I felt as though I would never smile again. I did not know what to say to Sunshine, and when I reached out to comfort her, she cried and shivered. The trauma of revealing the awful truth was too much for her, and she recoiled at my touch.

'I love you,' I said, beseechingly, and with a tear-stained face, she leaned into my chest, and I held her close again.

Peshmerga, those who face death

Kurdistan, September 1987

I went out into the hills, taking a long circular walk that skirted around our village. It wasn't for the exercise so much as to give myself space to think, as I knew I had to make up my mind. Along the way I picked wild flowers, and by the time I returned, I was carrying a large bunch of autumn crocuses, daffodils and hyacinths.

Sunshine opened the wooden door. She was on her way to the village school, where she was working as a maths teacher for the resistance. 'Happy birthday,' I said, holding up the flowers. 'I'm sorry I have no presents for you, except these.' She took the flowers. 'I will kiss you later,' she said, and headed towards the school. I stood there and watched her, feeling so lucky to have her in my life.

Rabbit was in the courtyard cleaning his gun. 'I want to meet your commander,' I said. 'Sunshine and I have talked. I am not going to America, not while Shawes Dog still lives.'

I could see at once that Rabbit was pleased with my decision. We walked out side by side like the Braders of old. We were together again and on a mission. A group of children, led by Sunshine, holding a scarecrow, passed our way singing: 'Our scarecrow asks for water, for the rain because the fields are thirsty...' They knocked on doors and the farmers threw buckets full of water over them, as well as some coins. The children loved getting wet and making a few cents for their school. Rabbit and I waved to Sunshine, and she smiled her sweetest smile.

For security reasons, Rabbit's commander was based on a hill a few minutes' walk from the village. We crossed a couple of Peshmerga posts set up on both sides of the track before we got to the base camp.

The commander, surrounded by his men, was giving a lesson on how to avoid mines. Rabbit and I stood by and waited for him to finish, but seeing his face through the gaps between his men I could not help myself and called out: 'Mr Dara!'

Dara and his men turned my way. 'Merywan Rashaba!' he responded, and walked over to us. 'Mery, what brings you here?'

'I want to become a Peshmerga,' I said, shaking his hand. He pulled me to him and greeted me warmly. 'Listen,' Dara said, to his men. 'Today I am happy to stand next to Merywan, a brave person, who fought for his freedom at a time and in a place when most of us were hardly aware of what freedom meant. He was and remains a special person to me. Merywan not only fought the brutal regime of Saddam Hussein, but also the old mentality of some of our most ignorant and dangerous people, those who deny the existence of beauty, colour and joy. Please welcome Merywan Rashaba into our forces.'

Cheers followed Dara's welcoming speech. His men, some thirty of them, of all different ages and sizes, crowded around to shake my hand. Each one was all but buried under a mass of weaponry, with bullet belts up to their necks. Dara himself offered me a brand new AK-47 and two bullet belts. I had become a Peshmerga.

I wonder if Shawes Dog will be worried when he discovers that I am alive, have become a freedom fighter, and am now his predator.

'One more thing,' Popcorn said. 'Mery has a nice voice. Would you like him to sing?' More cheers. Popcorn got out his *Saz*, a Kurdish guitar, and started to play 'Chawt Jwana Layla', a popular folk song that we all knew by heart. I really did not feel like singing, but how could I refuse? Fortunately, after the first verse, the others joined in.

'Mery is also good at something else,' Arpa said, which really came as a surprise. 'And I am here to challenge him to a game of Haluken.' Arpa stood alone, holding a set of haluk and bat. The Peshmerga carried on singing around Popcorn, as I called out: 'Arpa,' and walked over to him. He clasped my hands. 'Mery, I owe you a game of Haluken.' He offered the haluk and bat. 'I kept them all along. Here, you can have your Haluken set back now.'

'Kojak!' I exclaimed, as I took the set from him. 'This can't be true. I had a gut feeling that I knew you from somewhere in the past. Your voice sounded strangely familiar, but now…' I stopped speaking because I was really lost for words. Arpa's voice had been tugging at my memory since I first heard it, but I had never made the connection between the boy I had most despised in Kirkuk and the man standing before me, with a full beard covering his face, much of which had been horribly disfigured and scalded by acid. I found it hard to believe, let alone accept that the son of my greatest enemy, who had turned my life into a hell, was also a Peshmerga, and one who had been so kind to me.

'You have every right to despise me, Mery,' he said, bravely. 'But it was my father's wish that I become your enemy. Actually, I admired you and your courage. The very first time I met you, I wanted to be your friend. I looked up to you as my hero. I knew it was wrong, but my father forced me to be a bully, and he taught me how to steal. All the money I took from you and the others was for him. When I refused, he beat me and burned me. Look at my hands.'

I was still stunned by his transformation and speech, but managed to mutter, 'How did you end up in the mountains?'

'I hated my father for killing the caretaker and was glad he was imprisoned, but it wasn't long before he was released to serve the Mukhabarat. He got married to a young woman by forcing her family to accept it. Then he kicked my mother and me out. When I stood up to him, he threw acid in my face. I decided to join the resistance, to do some good and try to pay back all the harm I had done under the orders of my Dog father.' Kojak pulled out his pistol and handed it to me. 'I want you to forgive me, or to kill me to save me from my shame.' He turned to the Peshmerga and announced loudly, 'I want you all to know, especially Mr Dara, that as a child I gave Mery a very hard time. If he kills me, he should not be blamed. I deserve it.'

Kojak's astonishing declaration made all the men turn our way. I took the pistol from him. Rabbit, Popcorn and the others watched intently. I weighed the gun in my hand, as I considered all he had told me. 'Let's play Haluken,' I said, and handed him back his pistol. We divided into two teams of five, headed by Kojak and myself.

I had Popcorn, Rabbit and two more Peshmerga on my team. Rabbit could move remarkably fast, despite his false leg, and was eager to win. Dara, joined by Sunshine and the others, watched the game, delighted at the challenge between two old enemies. They each cheered for a side and my familiar desire to win returned. Playing my favourite game and competing without involving life-or-death decisions was a great joy. After all I had been through, it wouldn't have mattered to me if I lost. But, modesty aside, I knew I was the better player, and after a close-fought game, my team emerged victorious, and Arpa and I shook hands in friendship.

'How did you know I was not circumcised?' I whispered.

'Mullah Zao'Adin told my father.'

'I must say sorry too, because I tried to poison you.' Arpa laughed when I said this. 'I don't blame you, Mery. That should have taught me not to be greedy, but it didn't.'

Kojak also made his peace with Rabbit and Popcorn. But Sunshine, having suffered directly at the hands of the Dog, and by reading the copies of my letters and learning how much Kojak had made me suffer too, still had doubts about him. She took Dara aside to ask if Arpa was trustworthy. Dara assured her that he had no reason to be concerned about Arpa's loyalty.

That afternoon, in the presence of Jwana, Rabbit, Dara and Kojak, Sunshine and I got married in a simple ceremony in the midst of our friendly mountains. Under a clear blue sky we all walked up a hillside outside the village to where the air was cooled by a nearby spring. Sunshine and I stood opposite Popcorn.

'Merywan Rashaba, do you take this precious woman to be your wife?' Popcorn asked.

'Yes, I do, and I will love and treasure her always.'

'Sunshine Shamal, do you take Merywan, my best friend, to be your husband?'

'Yes, I do, and I want to share the rest of my life with him.'

In our absent friends' memory, we had translated John Lennon's poem into Kurdish, just as Jam would have done. Rabbit read it out:

Imagine there's no heaven
It's easy if you try
No hell below us...

Popcorn picked up on it, improvising in his deep melancholy voice, the words echoing in the valleys all around us.

That night Sunshine and I made love for the first time. Later, she slept peacefully, but I knew that I would not catch a moment's rest that night. Part of my nervous excitement came from the joy of being next to my wife, and part of it was because I could no longer keep my story to myself. I sat by the oil lamp and read the copies of my letters. I opened my notebook, and on the night of the day Sunshine and I got married, 17 October 1987, in the middle of the first page of my notebook I wrote the first words: "I miss my long hair".

I am writing my story as if it were a film, just as Jam suggested, for you, my dear Gringo, in case I don't survive.

Over the following two days, Sunshine and I climbed up and walked through the mountains, kissing, admiring the scenery, remembering our good friends, kissing again, laughing when we remembered the funny faces of the clients posing behind Jam's painted cinema heroes. We made plans for our future life in America, which all seemed so promising, and once, high up on a mountainside, like two birds nesting behind a bush, under the warm sun and amongst the autumn wildflowers, we made love.

At the end of this two-day honeymoon, I was ready to reveal my plan. I spoke first to Rabbit, who was delighted. We found Popcorn at the Peshmerga media office. He was busy printing leaflets on an old machine. He came outside to talk and I explained my intentions in a few words. Popcorn also approved, and together we went to see Dara to request a private meeting. Dara asked the Peshmerga around him to leave.

'Do you have someone in Kirkuk you can trust?' I asked Dara.

'Yes. More than one. Why?'

'Could you ask the one that you trust most to follow Abu Ali?' Dara looked aghast when I explained my idea. 'This is not the Peshmerga way,' he said. 'We have always rejected terrorism and fought honourably from the mountains to defend our people. We never execute our enemies in cold blood, and we free war prisoners at the earliest opportunity.'

'This has nothing to do with terrorism. I am not asking you to kill or blow up innocent civilians, but to save them from the traitor who is one of our most dangerous enemies.'

'This is not a mission for the resistance.'

'Fine,' I said. 'It is my personal mission. I will do it for my friends, my family, Rabbit's family, for my wife, and most of all to save the lives of the many yet to be killed at the hands of this savage.'

It was difficult for Dara to refuse: he knew what a cancer the Dog was to our people.

'Shawes Dog is not only your enemy. He is our people's enemy, and he will be charged as a war criminal and will pay dearly when we win our war.'

'If we allow him to carry on killing our people, raping our girls, abusing our boys, we may have to wait years for his trial. How much longer must we wait? We have been fighting for centuries and we are still in the mountains. I can wait no longer. I must win my battle now. I cannot wait for us to win the bigger war. All I ask is for three more Peshmerga that I can fully trust.'

Dara looked at my friends.

'I'm in,' Rabbit said. He turned to Popcorn.

'Me too.'

'What is your plan?' Dara asked.

'I can't tell you the details until I have your answer.'

'You had better be sure of success. It sounds to me like an impossible mission, and it would be my arse I'd be risking, backing you up.'

'With your support we will bring the Dog down.'

'We will need someone very skilled to spy on Shawes Dog,' Dara said, thoughtfully. 'It will not be easy and it will take time.'

'Please keep this just between ourselves. I don't want anyone to know, not even our man in Kirkuk, until I complete my plan. To do this, I need to get information about the Dog's movements.'

'Does Sunshine know?'

'Yes, and she too wants the nightmare to end.'

'OK, Mery, I will see to it, and I am proud of you.'

The leaves on the trees began to fall, the sunshine was chased more often by thickening clouds and, to the joy of the farmers, the rain poured down, turning our surroundings into a valley of mud. There was little to do in the village except to train, as we were far away from the day-to-day war against the Iraqi army. This allowed me plenty of free time to write. Sunshine did her best to stay out of my way while I was immersed in my memories, writing about the short but intense life I had had so far. At times I just could not carry on. I would go to the window and watch the rain, listening to its soothing sound. Sometimes the memories would drive me to tears, and I was grateful for Sunshine's consoling embraces.

It was during the first snowfall in early December when Rabbit knocked. He wanted me to get dressed and go to an urgent meeting.

'You won't like this,' Rabbit said, as we squelched through the mud and the snow. 'But I shall wait for Dara to tell you.' Dara and his Peshmerga were waiting for us. 'Mery, I have good news and bad news,' Dara said, as we approached. 'Which do you want to hear first?'

'The bad news.'

'This I want all my Peshmerga to know,' Dara's voice boomed out. 'Ali, the bastard son of a bitch who was known as Arpa, has betrayed us. He has poisoned five brave Peshmerga in his platoon and fled back to Kirkuk. Arpa has joined Abu Ali and is now working for the Mukhabarat along with his traitor father.'

Shouts of shock and anger erupted from the Peshmerga.

'Sunshine warned you not to trust him,' I said, facing Dara. 'I wish I had killed the bastard.'

'I wish you had, Mery,' Rabbit said.

'When the time comes, Arpa will pay, and dearly,' Dara said, raising his gun.

'What is the good news?' Rabbit asked.

Dara nodded to Rabbit, Popcorn and myself, and ordered the others outside. Once alone with us, he gave us the news, 'We have our man in Kirkuk, a brave person, and we should soon start receiving valuable information about Shawes Dog.'

'What about Kojak?' I asked.

'He must be put down at the same time as his father,' Rabbit suggested.

'I agree,' Popcorn said.

'So be it,' Dara decided. 'What do you want to call your plan, Mery?'

'Operation Freedom for Life.'

'Good,' Dara said, nodding his head, and then he looked up at me. 'We have a request from headquarters. The leadership want to meet you about the threat of a gas attack.'

'Excellent,' Rabbit said, excited. 'I am going with Mery. I know the way.'

I turned to Popcorn. He had obviously sent my message to the leadership. 'Sorry, Mery,' Popcorn said. 'I won't be able to go with you, I have a dispatch to deliver to the Halabja platoon. But good luck, my friend. At last, you will have the chance to meet our leaders.'

Rabbit and I were on our way just a few hours later. Time was against us, though I had wanted to spend a little more time with Sunshine, and kiss my gorgeous wife before I ventured higher into the mountains. It became colder as we gradually gained altitude and the snow became ever deeper. At times, we must have looked like two dwarves, our legs buried in drifts up to our thighs. We had to be careful not to slip down a gorge, and had to keep an eye on Rabbit's false leg. By the time we had reached the summit, our skin had turned blue from the cold, and Rabbit's newly grown moustache had icicles hanging from it.

On the other side the landscape glowed like golden honey in the sunlight. Rabbit and I spent most of the time talking about films. At one point we held hands and ran, shouting, 'Butch Cassidy and The Sundance Kid,' and threw ourselves into the air high above a ravine, our voices echoing through the valleys. Of course, we could already tell that it was not so steep on the other side. Save for a few slow-moving wild goats and watchful eagles gliding in huge, graceful arcs high above us, we were the kings of the mountains. In the evenings we would light a fire, have tea and bread, and soon move on again, walking all night. On the third day, we arrived at the headquarters just after dawn. We were fortunate to arrive in time for a leadership meeting that very day, so after sleeping for a couple of hours we were asked to leave our weapons and were escorted to the meeting, which was taking place in the open.

Jalal Talabani was visiting Massud Barzani, the two leaders standing side by side on a small stage. Talabani, a slightly chubby figure, and Barzani, short and thin, faced a few hundred Peshmerga and gave speeches about our armed struggle. We sat in the crowd and listened, cheering and applauding with them. Once question time came, I immediately raised my hand. Mr Massud gave me permission to speak.

'Thank you sir,' I said as I got up. 'My name is Merywan Rashaba. I am the grandson of King Sherzad, a brave patriot from Kirkuk. My grandfather was hanged before my birth, but he was a true Kurd and a great admirer of your father, General Barzani. If I may take this opportunity, sir, I would like to ask a couple of questions.

'First: Is the leader of the Kurdistan region of Iraq Mr Massud or Mr Jalal? Because as we all know, sir, every successful country in the world is led by one, and not two, leaders.'

'Well,' Massud answered, in his characteristically gentle, quiet way, 'that is a decision for our people to make. When we win the war and establish a democratic society, our people will choose whom they want as a leader in a free election, and I will accept and respect their decision.'

At this, the crowd broke into enthusiastic applause.

'Thank you, sir. My next question is to Mr Jalal. Sir, could you assure us that the devastating infighting between you, as the leader of the Patriotic Union of Kurdistan, and Mr Massud Barzani, the leader of the Kurdistan Democratic Party, has come to an end? If so, and to prove it to us, could you take Mr Massud's hand in yours?'

'That is an easy one,' Jalal answered, with a smile and his usual easy humour. 'Not for nothing I am called Mam, Uncle. I consider myself Mr Massud's uncle and have no wish to fight my nephew ever again. And in answer to your second question, I will take his hand and will not let go – even if he fights me,' he added, with a twinkle.

He took Massud's hand in his, and they raised their arms together, causing a wave of cheers and applause from the assembled Peshmerga.

'My last question is directed to both of our leaders. I once had a chance to meet Saddam Hussein and only spoke two words to him: "Happy Nawroz". I did this because I wanted to remind him that our history, culture and traditions go back thousands of years before he was born, before he sent his troops to destroy our land. We all know that Nawroz also belongs to our fellow Kurds in Iran, Turkey and Syria and, like us, sir, they too have the right to fight for their Nawroz, for their freedom. I find it hard to accept that our Peshmerga, under your leadership, should try to deprive them of that right. Sending Kurds to kill or be killed by Kurds from the other regions of Kurdistan does not do justice to our cause. Turkey, Iraq, Iran and Syria are equally our enemies, and we would surely do better to die united rather than bow to the enemy's pressure and fight each other. This has been our undoing throughout history. Our Kurdish leaders have fought for so long amongst themselves that they have forgotten the plight of our people, and forsaken many golden opportunities to achieve our goals. For once, at least once in our history, we should show our enemies that they can no longer play with us. We should show them that we Kurds are united and are prepared to die equally for our cause. We are Peshmerga, sir. We don't carry our guns to kill other Kurds, but to defend them from our common enemies. When I met Saddam, I felt intense hatred and anger. I wanted to kill him, and I would have done so if I had had a gun. I would hate to think that I might have the same feeling about our Kurdish leadership. So, Mr Massud Barzani and Mam Jalal Talabani, will you accept that fighting each other, or fighting our Kurdish brothers from the other parts of Kurdistan, is a deadly mistake and an act of treason?'

Both leaders stood there silently looking at me. All the other Peshmerga did the same.

Have I gone too far? Will I be punished for speaking the truth? Are my leaders true believers in democracy, and will they allow me to speak from my heart, or are they no different from Saddam? Rabbit got hold of my hand, showing that he approved of what I had said, and it gave me great strength of conviction to feel my Brader's hand in mine. Suddenly Rabbit broke the silence. '*Bijhi*, long live Merywan Rashaba...' he called out, and started to clap his hands. Another Peshmerga followed him and there was a storm of applause. I held the gaze of our leaders and when I finally saw them both clapping their hands, I knew that I had made my point. I exchanged a smile of relief and satisfaction with Rabbit as I sat down.

After a few more questions and answers from the other Peshmerga the two leaders retreated to a hut in the camp, and I was invited in to meet them.

They praised my bravery in expressing my beliefs in such a forthright way, and were keen to know exactly how I had heard about a proposed gas attack. I recounted my prison experience and tried to repeat the Ugly Arab's message word for word, 'If you, our leaders, ally yourselves with Iran for the final assault, Saddam Hussein will attack Kurdistan with chemical gas.'

Though they seemed impressed by the details I gave them and

courteously thanked us both for crossing the mountains to keep them informed, I couldn't be sure that they were really convinced about the terrible intentions Saddam had towards our people, or if our leaders already knew about these plans. However they chose to deal with the information, I was glad to have fulfilled my duty by delivering it personally.

Religion talks of peace but creates war

'You return to sad news, Mery,' the first Peshmerga we came across said, as Rabbit and I approached the base camp. 'Mr Dara will tell you.'

'What happened?' I asked, as I hurried towards Dara.

'Popcorn took the dispatch to the Halabja area,' Dara answered, but the sadness in his voice brought tears to his eyes and ours too. 'He and his two Peshmerga companions were ambushed by religious fanatics.'

'Kurds?' I said, bitterly.

'Yes. A group of traitors that call themselves "Mujahid Muslim". They're trained by the Mujahidin in Afghanistan. The Halabja platoon wants to know if Popcorn has family amongst the resistance, or should they bury him there?'

'I am going to bring back Popcorn to us.'

'Thank you, Mery. That's the least we could do for him.'

'Can I leave in the morning?'

'Of course,' Dara answered, and took me aside. 'I know Popcorn meant a lot to you. I intend to personally replace him in the FFLO, the Freedom for Life Operation.'

I held back my tears until I could embrace Sunshine in the courtyard. 'I can never forgive Kurds, or anyone else, for killing someone as kind as Popcorn in the name of religion.' I told her, lost in her arms. I did not wish Sunshine to know the truth about my mission. I was not only going to bring back my friend's body but also to face his Islamist murderers and make them pay for their outrageous crime. I was becoming as bloodthirsty as I had accused Rabbit of being. I longed to spend a night with my wife in bed as a husband, but all we could do was talk about Popcorn.

Rabbit was already sitting on the top of the Land Rover's cab when I walked out. 'I am coming with you,' he said. I was grateful. With Rabbit by my side, I felt as if I could walk through the gates of Hell. We shook hands with Dara and the rest of our platoon. I looked at Sunshine and smiled at her. That was all I could do in the presence of the others. Before I left, Sunshine and I had kissed for a long time in our room. I jumped into the back of the Land Rover, and the Peshmerga driver started the engine.

'I will be back soon,' I said to my sweet Sunshine, holding her hand as she walked alongside us before we accelerated away. She stood there, waving in the distance.

We drove across the Jafati valley to the Iranian border. This was the front line and the heartland of the armed struggle where the Kurdistan Front's headquarters and several thousand Peshmerga were based. We gave lifts to Peshmerga groups, to farmers and their animals, to newly arrived displaced people and also to five dervishes. They reminded me of my Thursday nights in the Takya, but I was no longer one of them. I was relieved to have changed my fate, to have freed myself from all that useless worshipping, and was on my way to avenge Popcorn's death at the hands of religious fanatics. The dervishes kept chanting as we drove along, and began to dance even as we left them on the highway from Qaladiza to Sardasht in Iran. This was the only route controlled by the Peshmerga; it crossed the border, and was therefore vital for the deliveries of supplies to the resistance from the Iranian government.

We left the car at the last Peshmerga checkpoint. From there onwards, all the lowlands were in the control of the Iraqi army. Rabbit and I had no knowledge of the area, but Dara had arranged for us to be met and guided on foot by a Peshmerga. A week after leaving Sunshine, we made it to the Halabja platoon's small base camp in the foothills of the Hawraman Mountains, just outside the village of Zalm.

Zana Sharazuri, the Halabja platoon commander, gave us a warm welcome, but he had bad news. Popcorn had already been buried. 'We had to bury him within three days, according to Islamic ritual,' Zana said.

'But Popcorn was Yezidi,' I objected.

'For his sake we decided to go ahead. It is better that way. You would not have liked to have seen your friend. The savages were not satisfied with executing him, but also mutilated his body. They cut off his ears, his tongue, pulled out his eyes and opened his belly. But we will not let his blood and those of his two friends be shed in vain. We are preparing an attack on the Islamist group and you are welcome to take part if you wish.'

That is exactly what I was hoping for.

'Who are these Islamists?' Rabbit asked.

'A group of brainwashed Kurds who are sponsored by the Iranian government in order to create trouble in the Kurdistan region of Iraq. They are barbaric. We have heard of them throwing acid on young girls wearing skirts, or killing entire families, including children and the elderly, for having a television. They loathe our fight for freedom and they mutilate any Peshmerga who falls into their hands.'

'Kurds have done all this?' I said. Once again I was disgusted by some of my people, especially as they were in the pay of our enemies.

'Yes, Merywan, and you must remember that Iran is supposed to be on our side in the attack on Iraq.'

'Which attack?'

'The final assault on Saddam Hussein.'

'We should not rely on Iran,' I protested. 'We should never trust our enemies, and should not forget that Iran occupies Eastern Kurdistan and deprives more than eight million Kurds of their freedom.'

'Well, do you have a better ally to suggest?' Zana asked, alarming me even more. It seemed that my meeting with the leadership had achieved nothing. Maybe I was naïve to think political leaders would change their course of action because of one speech by a young Peshmerga, but to trust Iran in our fight against Saddam was surely not the best strategy. I hoped to be proved wrong.

'Are there many of these Mujahid?' Rabbit asked.

'No, not yet. But with the amount of money that the Iranians offer to poor, young, unemployed men, they could soon spread and become a serious threat. Many of the Mujahid are farmers whose villages were destroyed by the Iraqi army and who have been left with nothing, so they have nothing to lose.'

'When are we to attack them?' I asked.

'The minute we get permission from our superiors. You had better rest. Tough times are ahead.'

Kurdistan, December 1987

My sweetheart Sunshine,
I miss you, your generous smiles, your warmth. I miss talking to you about our future plans for our new life in America. I spend most of my time along the river writing my story, and look forward to the day when I can hug and kiss you again. Forgive me for staying away so long. This was never my wish. We are waiting for the go-ahead to face Popcorn's murderers, but there are constant delays. I am starting to have doubts that we may ever get permission to attack the Mujahid, because of our leadership's close relationship with Iran. I am well, and most grateful to have Rabbit at my side. He also sends his love to you and to your mother. In case I don't make it back for the New Year, I wish you the happiest 1988.

I love you,
Mery

P.S. Please let Dara know that I am anxiously awaiting news of the FFLO.

The New Year came and brought more snow. We spent most of the time waiting in frustration for permission to attack the Mujahid, and finally, in mid-January, Zana gathered his platoon together. He had very bad news.

'The Iraqi army has launched a major attack on our Headquarters,' Zana said. 'The enemy's forces consist of thousands of regular army infantry, the Special Forces and Jash, backed up by helicopters, jets and artillery. Their aim is to surround and strangle our forces, to cut off Qaladiza's supply route and ultimately to wipe out our armed struggle. Our leadership believe they can only resist for two or three months. Therefore, to distract the Iraqi army and reduce the huge strain on the headquarters, it is imperative that our platoon and the few others in Halabja area urgently launch an attack to create a new front line. headquarters cannot spare many Peshmerga and we immediately need men. Our long fight for freedom depends on opening a new front. Our future depends on us. I do not wish to force my men to make decisions, but I want you to know that I would much prefer to die fighting for my freedom than living in exile in Iran. Most of us have wives and children, and it is also for their sake that we fight. I will fight. We must win this war.'

This unexpected news took everyone by surprise. This wasn't just an escalation of an already life-or-death situation. A hubbub erupted amongst the Peshmerga. I turned to Rabbit. He read my thoughts and nodded. 'My friend and I are with you,' I called to Zana. 'We want to stay and fight the enemy.'

'Thank you, Mery and Hiwa. We could really do with brave

Peshmerga like yourselves. Who else?' Zana's men raised their hands one by one.

Kurdistan, February 1988

Mery, My love,

I believe you made the right decision to stay and take part in the forthcoming battle to defend our people, our freedom. I miss you too and would have made the journey through fire to see you, but I have important work to do here. We had to shut down the school because we are all involved with helping out the many injured Peshmerga and villagers arriving from the Jafati valley. We have set up a basic clinic in the caves. Our medical team is made up of one doctor and a few volunteers like myself. Those who need major operations are sent to Iran. Our Peshmerga are fighting the enemy to keep control of the only route to Iran. If they fail, it will spell disaster for us. You might have heard about the Iraqi army's gassing of several villages. These gas attacks kill everyone and everything, and are intensifying each day. Our Peshmerga are not equipped to face this monstrous weapon, and we are retreating, giving away more and more of the liberated areas to the Iraqi army.

My love, I am well and out of immediate danger, but I am worried that you and your friends may be attacked by chemical gas too. I pray and send you all the good energy I can to protect you all from such evil. I did not have you with me for the New Year, but am looking forward to having you back before your next birthday. I would like us to celebrate it together and hopefully celebrate our victory at the same time. My mother's situation isn't improving, but I do not want you or Rabbit to worry about her. I am looking after her as best as I can. Dara sends his regards and wants you to know that he is making good progress with the FFLO. Please look after yourselves. Give Rabbit a hug from me and kiss his eyes.

I love you,
Sunshine

It was almost the end of February when I received Sunshine's letter. I was not sure that it was realistic to expect that Rabbit and I would be back with her for my seventeenth birthday, but I wished for it with all my heart. Our commanders were meeting secretly with the Iranians to discuss the attack. The plan was to liberate the town of Halabja, and from there move south towards Kirkuk. In a recent meeting I had expressed my concerns to our superiors about Saddam's intention of retaliating with chemical gas, and they too had their worries. But they believed the assault would succeed because the Iranians had promised to provide several hundred gas masks to be used by the Peshmerga in case of such attacks. The Iranians had also promised to supply our forces with all kinds of weapons, ammunition, night-vision binoculars, walkie-talkies, and medical assistants, and to send a force of three hundred Iranian troops to back us up and cover our attack, both from the sky with jets and on the ground with artillery.

The inhabitants of Halabja town and the surrounding area were our biggest worry. Our commanders had requested many more thousands of gas masks and special outfits for the civilians, and had asked the Iranians to open the border, particularly the route between Halabja and Nasud, to allow the population to take refuge in Iran in case of gas attacks.

To this end, our platoon had taken part in coordinating the forces of Peshmerga and those of the Iranians. To keep the eventual attack a complete surprise, we had had to move secretly, only during the night. So far, with the help of the Iranian army in building a temporary bridge over the River Sirwan, we had received large amounts of supplies. The bridge was narrow and all the goods had to be carried by mules and men. The poor animals were frightened; they had to be blindfolded and dragged across, so it was arduous work and took seven nights. Unfortunately, in the process, we lost a couple of Iranian men and a mule in the fast-flowing, icy river.

During the day, we hid in the caves and spent most of the time keeping ourselves warm and cleaning our gear of the mud that we trudged through and slipped in during the night. With the help of two Iranian radio operators, Zana reported our progress, and received the latest news and orders from our regiment commanders. Once the orders were given, five hundred Peshmerga would start the attack from four fronts, one of which was inside the town of Halabja.

Our platoon had been given the task of blowing up the Zalm Bridge. This was to cut off the Iraqi army's only supply route to the area of Halabja. The riverbanks were covered with minefields. As a joke, Zana suggested that Rabbit and I have a swim in the icy river towards the bridge.

I looked forward to the attack and to performing my Peshmerga duties, and mostly to the day when I could return home safely to the arms of the woman I loved. Sunshine's love gave me strength to keep going with the tough life we faced daily on the new front line.

I missed her so much.

A strange person

I was not to spend my seventeenth birthday with Sunshine, but nevertheless 11 March 1988 remains one of the most important days of my life. It was the day I met Teresa Miller.

At the time, we were discussing the best way to blow up Zalm Bridge. A warning came from a guard standing high up on a boulder. 'Two Peshmerga and a strange person incoming,' he called. We were used to getting warnings about Peshmerga arriving, villagers approaching or Iraqi helicopters circling above, but we wondered what he meant by a 'strange person'.

Zana went over to the track leading to our camp. We were all curious, and stared in the direction of the new arrivals, waiting to catch a glimpse of this mysterious figure. When they drew near, we were no wiser as to whether this elusive presence was a man or a woman, but the moment she took off her hat to greet Zana, letting her long blonde hair fall onto her shoulders, our mouths fell open in surprise. She was as beautiful as a spring rose.

What is she doing here, in this dangerous, forgotten part of the world? My heart raced and, for some reason, I felt she was there for me. To my delight, Zana called out, 'Mery, I need your help.'

I was so struck by her presence that I hardly looked away from her as I walked towards them. Within that short distance I studied her in detail. A tall, elegant woman in her early twenties, she looked very much like the stunning Julie Christie in *Doctor Zhivago*, with indigo eyes that seemed to mirror the very colour of the sky. She wore a thick yellow jumper under a heavy winter jacket, a pair of knee-high leather mountain boots, a yellow woollen hat, a backpack and a couple of cameras, one over her right shoulder and one around her neck.

Looking directly into my eyes, as if she already knew me well, she removed her gloves and shook my hand, still smiling broadly.

'Hello Mery, my name is Teresa Miller,' she said.

I had only ever seen such elegant foreign women in films. I greeted her and smiled back as I shook her warm hand. 'Please, can you explain to your commander that I am a journalist,' she said. 'I have your leadership's consent to stay with the Halabja platoon for a few days. I hope your commander will accept me amongst you?' Teresa produced a letter from the leadership and handed it to me. I felt very privileged to translate her words.

'Ask her,' Zana said, 'where she comes from.'

'I'm from America. I live and work in New York. But since Americans are not allowed in Iran, the only country through which I could travel to reach you, I travelled on my Irish passport.'

Zana nodded in admiration. 'We have a couple of Iranians amongst us, and they should not be aware that you are from America.' I translated Zana's words and Teresa seemed to appreciate them.

'Ask her, Why are you here?'

'To write an article,' she said. 'We know that Saddam has been using chemical gas in his war against Iran, but rumours suggest he may now be attacking the Kurds with these weapons, which are banned internationally by a treaty to which Iraq is also a signatory.'

'These are not rumours,' Zana responded. 'The Iraqis have already gassed several of our villages.'

'I have read the reports and heard the same news from your leadership, but those villages are now in the hands of the Iraqi army. The international community and the United Nations must see evidence.'

'My wish is that we will not see any evidence of this kind on our front,' Zana said, 'but we undoubtedly fear Saddam's gas attacks, especially if we manage to free Halabja.'

'Despite my mission, I agree with you wholeheartedly, and I hope you are equipped for such attacks.'

'Mery, let Teresa know that she is most welcome and she can have you as her interpreter for as long as she stays with us. But on one condition; she must know that we can't guarantee her safety.'

'I am aware of the risks. I use my cameras to take the photos which support my written work, but I need to know from Captain Zana if I can have permission to take pictures, and if there are any restrictions that I need to know about?'

'I don't mind at all,' Zana grinned. 'To start with, she can take my picture, as I am the commander here.' He proudly posed for Teresa's first shot in our camp.

I turned to greet Dara. I had hardly noticed him at first, so intent had I been on this 'strange person', but it was clear that he had accompanied her here.

'Don't ask me why, Mery,' Dara said, looking at Teresa, 'but she arrived in Razga looking for you.'

'How is Sunshine?' I asked.

'She is very well. She is doing a wonderful job at the clinic. She misses you a lot, and assures you she will agree with whatever decision you make after speaking with Teresa.'

'What does that mean?'

'I have no idea. Teresa should tell you.'

'How is the progress of the FFLO?'

'Excellent. I now have accurate information about Shawes Dog's movements.'

'When can we go to Kirkuk?'

'As soon as the new front is opened and Halabja is liberated. Until then I have been commanded to stay with this campaign.'

'Teresa is vulnerable here,' I said, 'and we know what could happen to her if she ends up in the hands of the Iraqis, or the Mujahid Muslims. Could you please ask Zana to let Rabbit, you and I personally take charge of protecting her?'

'That's a good idea, Mery. I will.'

The news about Shawes Dog and the unexpected arrival of Teresa and Dara were a great way to celebrate my birthday. She did not give joy only to me; her presence among the men raised the morale of every Peshmerga.

In the afternoon, after Teresa had taken some photos of the camp, she asked if I would accompany her to the river to explore the surroundings. On our way, I pointed out the minefields along the path, but my mind was on the news that I suspected Teresa was about to reveal. Rabbit and Dara stayed at a distance.

'Happy birthday, Mery,' Teresa said, when finally we were on our own.

'Thank you. Are you really from America?'

'I was born in Northern Ireland, in Belfast. My family had to leave because of the religious hatred and the fighting between the

Protestants and the Catholics. I grew up in America and have dual nationality.'

'Life is not fair, is it?'

'Why is that?'

'You have two nationalities and I don't even have one. I am not blaming you, but it feels like I'm a nobody… being stateless.'

'I can't possibly imagine it.'

'Are you famous in America?'

'Oh no, not at all. I've only been a journalist for a year or so. I became interested in this part of the world after meeting a Kurd in New York.'

'I heard that you are not here to write an article about the Kurds, you are here for me. Can that really be true?'

'Mostly for you, but also to help your people by taking your story to the world.'

'How can you possibly know about me?'

'I met your leaders. They told me of their admiration for you, and about the speech you made at one of their recent meetings. You are more famous than I am.'

'How do you know today is my birthday?'

'I also know that you are from Kirkuk, you grew up in Qala, and all your life you wanted to go to America to meet Clint Eastwood. He is your favourite actor and you call him Gringo… I know a lot more about you, Mery. I don't want to shock you.'

'You won't. After what I have been through, nothing will shock me.'

'Do you have any photos from your time in Kirkuk?'

'Yes, a couple of them that I always keep with me.'

'Can I see them, please?'

The photos were the ones Sunshine had saved from the time of our photography business in Kirkuk. I handed Teresa a copy of the same photo the Ugly Arab found in one of my letters sent to Gringo. It was a picture of Sunshine and myself standing between Jam and Uncle Hitch.

'With your long hair and your smile,' she said, looking at the photo, 'you look just as I imagined you would, as you have been described to me many times over.'

'By whom?'

'The Kurd I met in America,' Teresa answered. 'Who was he?' she asked, indicating Jam's smiling face.

'Jam?' I asked. I was beginning to doubt her words, yet she seemed to know so much about me.

'Yes, Jam.'

'Jam, the stamp and coin dealer from Kirkuk?'

'Yes, Jam. Your friend is also my husband.'

'Jam never told me about you, or said that he was married. He only mentioned an English girlfriend he once had in London.'

'Jam met Kathryn more than six years ago. I am talking about last year. I've been married to Jam for seven months now, since August 1987, when he first got to America.'

'It can't be, Jam was taken away by the Mukhabarat, I saw it with my own eyes. He must have been killed...'

Teresa did not let me finish. 'Jam was not killed,' she said. He is alive and well, and living in New York.'

'What?'

'They did torture him, and intended to execute him. He was taken to the south of Iraq to be Anfal and buried in one of the mass graves in the desert not far from the Jordanian border. Along with fifty or so other civilians of all ages, he was lined up to be shot dead. Who knows why or how, but he got lucky. He was shot only in his left arm, and he survived by hiding under a couple of dead bodies, playing dead himself. The execution squad left, believing they had killed everyone, and as the bulldozers moved in to bury the bodies in the sand, Jam crawled away, hidden by the clouds of dust. He told me there were many more injured who were buried alive. Jam's determination gave him strength to escape death, and somehow he made his way across the desert all the way to the American Embassy in Jordan.'

Teresa was right to worry about shocking me. I started to laugh at the fact that Jam had managed to escape the Mukhabarat. I had never heard such a story before, but of course Jam was unique. I was still not sure whether I could believe it, though.

'Jam escaped the Iraqis and got to America?' I had to ask again.

'Yes.'

'And he lives with you in New York?'

'Yes, he is my husband.'

I could hardly contain myself at this incredible confirmation, and felt like emptying my magazine into the azure sky in celebration. Instead, I threw my head back and shouted to the winds,

'Jam, I love you. I love you!' My voice echoed through the mountains and away, bearing my message to Jam. I turned elatedly to Rabbit and Dara to reassure them that I was not insane, merely overwhelmed by excitement and happiness. 'Jam is alive,' I called to Rabbit, and his face showed all the shock I had felt moments earlier. I turned to Teresa.

'How did you meet Jam in America?'

'I met him in New York when he had just arrived. I was doing a story called 'Land Of The Free', about the way America treats people who arrive seeking refuge from wars and persecution. I went to interview him, and ended up inviting him for dinner. I fell in love with him and we were married soon after. We are very happy together, but of course he is also deeply attached to Kurdistan, and he constantly talks about you. He kept looking for news of you. He never gave up hope of finding you alive and, thanks to your speech to the leadership, one day he phoned me. "Teresa, my love," he said. He was so excited. "Get ready for this, I have just read an amazing article in one of the Kurdish resistance's newsletters. Mery is alive, he is in the mountains in Kurdistan and is a Peshmerga." After celebrating the news with friends, he took your case to the United Nations High Commission for Refugees and applied for a visa for you as a minor. I offered to go out to Kurdistan the day after he obtained your visa. He knew how much you wanted to go to America and called my visit "Mery's Surprise of a Lifetime." He really wanted to be here with me, but he does not hold a passport yet. However, he sends you his greetings with this message: Up Kissinger's bum!' She laughed at the phrase, and also at my joy and surprise in hearing it.

Jam was alive! Teresa brought out a few photos of herself and Jam, pictured walking across the Brooklyn Bridge and arm in arm on the Staten Island ferry. I looked at Jam's handsome smiling face, his face lit by hope, having escaped the horrors of the Mukhabarat... and married this beautiful woman.

'See how happily I am smiling in this photo?' I said. 'Jam taught me how to smile.'

'You have the same smile right now, Mery,' Teresa answered, and after a pause, she came to the point. 'I have come to take you away with me to America.'

I had to look away from her before I could respond. 'Thanks, Teresa, I will have to think about it,' I said quietly, finding it difficult to sound convincing, as I had dreamt of going to America so much and for so long. 'Perhaps it is too late now. Things have changed. I must stay and fight this war, and I am married.'

'I have met Sunshine, she told me where to find you. She also asked me to give you some important news, as she could not tell you herself. She is pregnant.'

'Pregnant?' I had never dreamt that this could happen.

'Yes, she is. It's three months now. She wanted to tell you herself, hoping you might be back for your birthday. She is a lovely woman, and you are a lucky man. You are soon to become a father, Mery.'

A father! Me? Merywan Rashaba, the boygirl, soon to have a child! This was what I had desired so much but had hardly allowed myself to dream of. *Seventeen and already a father! I am truly a man now,* I thought, laughing and crying at once, both elated and almost sick with the shock of it. What an extraordinary feeling... one that could change your entire being so instantly. But the idea of bringing up a child in the same world that I had grown up in was too fearful even to contemplate.

As the days passed, Teresa settled into life in the mountains. She ate lightly, slept in a bed that she could fold within seconds, and then early in the morning would go jogging in the hills and, after building up a good sweat, would take a dip in the icy river.

I accompanied her on these early morning runs, and Rabbit and Dara tagged along behind, struggling to keep up. I too, with my sharwal, my gun and bullet belt, found it difficult running alongside Teresa. She often asked me to stop, but I insisted that I also wanted to keep fit. One morning, I jumped in the river too; as I said to Rabbit, it couldn't be so bad if an American woman could do it. But I shrieked from the icy water, which felt like swimming in a sea of needles. Rabbit and Dara, watching from the riverbank, nearly fell in, they were laughing so much.

During the day, she would interview Peshmerga and make notes, and visit Zalm village to talk to the farmers and take photos. In the evening, before going to sleep under the millions of stars, she talked to me about Jam, and their life together, her work and her office in New York.

Teresa had learned to play Kalamuste very well, an ancient game in which two teams take turns hiding and searching for a ring amongst nine hats. On our last night, Zana proposed that she lead the game. Teresa, Dara, Rabbit and myself teamed up against Zana and three more Peshmerga. We set the nine hats down on a blanket and started. Teresa was no less than ingenious when hiding the ring. To make it more exciting, Zana suggested a prize for the winner. 'If I lose, I will go for a swim in the river,' he said. The Peshmerga laughed and cheered in appreciation of his bet.

'What if you win?' Teresa asked, holding up the ring. Zana took it from her and slid the ring onto her finger. 'If I win, you marry me,' Zana answered, and more cheers followed. 'Sorry, it's too late. I have a husband.' Teresa said, and smiled. We all laughed, but although Zana's proposal of marriage was only a joke, I was glad that our team won. When she retreated and slipped inside her sleeping bag next to the campfire, I sat beside her. 'Teresa, your presence here means a lot to our Peshmerga,' I said. 'They feel you represent the world's support for our fight for freedom. Thank you for staying with us.'

'Mery, you are still too young to carry a gun,' she said, lifting her head. 'You could have a future in America. Jam is waiting for you, and finally, you could go to meet your Gringo.'

'I don't know if I could ever thank you and Jam enough for doing all this for me, but I can't go. I am married to Sunshine and to Kurdistan.'

'Jam doesn't like you becoming a Peshmerga. He believes you are not made for guns and killing, and that your talent and your life will be wasted in these wild mountains. He is convinced the armed struggle will bring nothing but more disaster to your people. He wants you to go to America to pursue your love of acting and filmmaking. He is so looking forward to seeing you that he even contacted Gringo and spoke to him about you.'

'Jam spoke to Gringo?'

'Yes, he did. I have a signed photo of your Gringo for you.' Teresa opened her backpack and handed over an envelope. I carefully opened it. My whole body shivered. 'From Gringo?' I had to ask again.

'Yes, Mery. From your Gringo, Mr Clint Eastwood.'

I pulled out the photo, one of Gringo in his latest film with a dedication written on the back. 'Do you mind reading it to me?' I asked. 'I would like to hear it in an American accent.'

'To Mery Rashaba. I look forward to meeting you. Come and see me when you get to America. Clint Eastwood, (Gringo).'

Teresa finished reading and gave me the photo. I placed it over my eyes and kissed it several times, before safely tucking it into the pocket close to my heart. 'A photo from Gringo! I have waited so many years for this. Thank you Teresa, thank you very much for coming, and for giving me news of my wife and my child, who I am sure will be as beautiful as her mother. Thank you for Jam's wonderful news, and for bringing me Gringo's photo, for offering me hope. Please forgive me for not being able to fulfil my promise. I can't go to America: I am no longer the same Mery Rashaba.'

Teresa could not hide her disappointment, but accepted my wishes. 'Good night, Mery,' she said.

'Good night, Teresa.'

I took out Gringo's photo, kissed it and read the message again. I would read those few precious words many times over the next few days, and each time would ask myself: *Should I take up Teresa's offer and leave with her for America?*

The poisonous clouds

The next morning, 14 March, Zana gathered us together. He stood next to several boxes of Iranian supplies. He displayed one complete chemical warfare protection suit, the mask, the filter, the anti-gas injections and the tablets. He demonstrated how to put on the outfit, and explained when and how to use the medicine. 'If you run out of gas mask filters, which last five to seven hours,' Zana said, 'you should keep your faces wet.'

A radio communication arrived, and Zana held the receiver, listening and nodding. When he had finished, he turned to us and called out, 'The time has come. We are to open the new front line and liberate our country from Saddam and his monstrous regime. Please remember, what makes us different from the Iraqi army is that we respect the rules of war: we don't harm or kill prisoners. That goes for all the enemy's forces, including the Kurdish traitors. I wish you all good luck and hope to see you soon celebrating our victory. I really could do with a bit of music and dancing.' The Peshmerga cheered. Zana picked up a complete anti-gas outfit and handed it to Teresa. 'You will need this over your bullet proof vest if you want to visit Halabja.'

'Thank you,' Teresa said.

'Mery and Hiwa, do you remember all the details of our plan?' Zana asked.

'Yes, sir,' we answered.

'OK,' Zana called, turning to his men, 'you brave sons of Kurdistan, lions of the mountains, Peshmerga who face death, this is the time and the day we have waited for. Let's prove ourselves.'

We made our way down along the riverbank, and by the late afternoon we were a couple of kilometres to the east of Zalm Bridge. The Iraqi army post on Goyan hill was clearly visible, and we hunkered down to hide until nightfall. When the darkness enveloped us, Zana signalled to Rabbit and me. We slung our guns around our necks and picked up the box of explosives and the detonator. I turned to Teresa. She smiled encouragingly. 'Good luck,' she mouthed, silently. I looked at Dara and he understood.

'Don't worry,' he said. 'I will protect Teresa with my life.'

We left our platoon and, moving silently, closed in on the bridge. From that point on, there were minefields on both sides of the riverbank. We found a hiding place and waited. 'You remember when we went to see *The Bridge on the River Kwai?*' I whispered. 'Yes,' Rabbit said, 'but this also reminds me of *The Alamo,* as they had to go through the river to take away the food supplies from the Generalissimo's forces.'

I laughed. Rabbit wanted to know why. I told him I was thinking about Gringo, when, in *The Good, the Bad and the Ugly,* he and Ugly carried the box of dynamite on the stretcher all the way to the bridge, and the funny way Ugly's bum pointed upwards as he hid his head, while debris rained around them from the explosion.

At one o'clock, as planned, the attack started from several fronts. The shooting was intense, bolts of light leaping through the sky. The Iraqis opened fire too, and the whole Halabja area became a battlefield. Shortly after, our platoon opened fire on the army post on Goyan hill and the two bunkers on either side of the bridge. I nodded to Rabbit, picked up the box and slowly immersed myself in the icy water. The river was not that deep, but to make sure I was not seen, I had to crouch down, and at times the water came up to my chest. The shooting above intensified with every step I took. From under the bridge I could see a few of the Peshmerga advancing towards the bunkers, lit by the night flares the Iraqis were constantly launching from the surroundings to help their helicopters spray our forces with machine-gun fire. Our platoon was tasked with taking out the machine gun on the hill, which was shooting in all directions. Under the bridge, I opened the box and began to fix blocks of TNT to its eight concrete pillars. I made sure each chunk of TNT was connected properly, and carefully ran the main cable away from the bridge. A spotlight moved across the river's surface, and almost immediately bullets struck the water beside me. Rabbit sprang into action, shooting the soldier dead, and he kept firing to provide some cover for me. I made it out of the river and handed him the cable, which he connected to the detonator. 'Put your hand on mine, Brader,' he said. 'Let's do this together.' 'Up Kissinger's bum,' we said in unison, and we pushed down the handle and turned it. Within an instant, Zalm Bridge was collapsing majestically into the river, and the main route for the Iraqi army to send land supplies to the Halabja area was no more.

We returned in jubilation, to be reunited with our forces and congratulated by our friends. Peshmerga were now attacking the army posts from the other side of the river and by dawn the whole area around the highway was under our control. Zana handed over responsibilities to another platoon commander. We had not finished yet; now we walked south, towards Halabja town, the heart of the battlefield. Teresa photographed the entire operation. She was as brave as a Peshmerga, though we stayed close by her, more concerned for her safety than our own.

The Iraqis were trapped and must have been surprised by the magnitude of our attacks. Despite their machine guns, rocket launchers, artillery, tanks and helicopters, they were powerless to halt our advance. Then the radio communicator gave us the great news: Halabja town was under siege. The main Iraqi military base in the area was now in the hands of our forces, and their artillery had ceased firing. By the late afternoon of 15 March, we entered Halabja town, attacking the central police station, the Mukhabarat headquarters, the militia and the governor's buildings.

The inhabitants of the town, men and women, took to the streets. The situation now descended into chaos, as the people who had suffered so brutally at the hands of Saddam's men ran ahead of the Peshmerga to get to the enemy. People were desperate to inflict their own justice, knowing they would not be allowed to kill or harm the monster's men if the Iraqi forces surrendered to the Peshmerga. I knew that we were winning when I saw the many portraits of Saddam on the main street covered in dirt, shot at and burned. I could not help but shed a few tears when I saw the Iraqi flag replaced by our beloved flag of Kurdistan on the governor's building.

The inhabitants' joy and lust for freedom erupted like a volcano, and it was impossible to resist joining in. Our platoon had one last army post to clear: the Kurdish traitors were the enemy's toughest bulwark of resistance in the town. A machine gun strategically placed on the rooftop made it difficult for our forces to approach them. Dara, brave as he was, asked for us to cover him, and the whole platoon fired as he took an RPG, positioned it on his right shoulder, aimed at the Jash and fired, blowing up the machine gunner who was proving such a threat.

The Iranian artillery, despite the many radio communications from our commanders, kept shelling right into Halabja, destroying several houses and killing a dozen civilians. They had difficulty accepting that such a small number of Peshmerga could free the town from the huge Iraqi army in such a short time. There were six dead among our forces and no more than twenty injured in the whole operation, but we had captured hundreds of Iraqi prisoners, as well as an incredible amount of ammunition and materiel, including tanks, armoured vehicles, anti-aircraft guns, rocket launchers and artillery.

The Peshmerga dispersed among the civilians, explaining how important it was to leave the town for the mountains towards the border, perhaps only for a short period of time, until the Iranian supplies arrived. Our commanders kept asking for the Iranian army to move in, to send supplies and, above all, gas equipment for the population. But their requests were not granted, despite the Iranian promises. Many thousands started to pack up and, in cars, tractors, trucks, Jeeps, carts, mules and on foot, they made their way out. Yet the majority remained, waiting for further news. Dara, Rabbit and I were with Teresa the entire time. She must have taken hundreds of photos by then.

That night, the town hardly slept as people celebrated. Zana's wish had come true. He took Teresa's hand and led her to join the many men, women and Peshmerga dancing. I also danced, although my mind was with Sunshine and our child. *Oh, how much I wish Sunshine were here with me.* The celebration lasted until dawn, and as it came to an end, we were met by some of the inhabitants who had fled earlier. They complained that the Iranian army was blocking their way across the border, about thirty kilometres away. This news spread rapidly across the town, and most of the people decided it would be better to stay than to risk such a journey.

Then came the horrendous noise of Iraqi jets, bombing the Sara district to the south-west, only a few streets away from us. The inhabitants panicked. The Peshmerga did not have much experience with the anti-aircraft guns, but nevertheless, a few did their best to fire back at the jet fighters. Other Peshmerga forces tried to help some of the people out of town as quickly as possible. Zana ordered his platoon to prepare for the worst and to make sure they were all wearing the anti-chemical-gas outfits.

At around 5 p.m. on 16 March 1988, as thousands made their way to the mountains, and thousands more were still leaving Halabja, the rest of the population hid in the basements of their houses, as the screams of the Iraqi jets rose over the town once again. When the bombs rained down, we heard the flat dull booms, like the sound of a broken drum, and realised that these were no ordinary bombs. Huge yellow-white clouds rose up, formed into massive mushroom shapes, and then quickly sank down, engulfing the town.

'*Kimiyawi*, Chemicals!' people shouted.

The air smelled rotten, sulphurous. I gave Teresa one last look before I put on my mask. She did the same, and we followed Zana to help more people out of town. The jets made another pass, gassing the population escaping across the plains, the hills, the highways and dirt tracks leading towards the border. In the confusion, our forces lost each other, but Rabbit, Dara, Teresa and I kept together.

The monster had decided to wipe us all out. The ultimate order had been given that no one should remain alive, not the animals, the birds, the trees, not even the insects. For three days we worked non-stop to help the terrified and disorientated civilians. We administered injections and anti-gas tablets to the injured, until we exhausted our supplies. We came across extraordinary, terrible scenes. A baby desperately trying to drink milk from a dead mother's breasts, mothers crying over the bodies of entire families, refusing to abandon them. Some were blinded by the gas, while others laughed hysterically.

Men, women and children of all ages had died in their hundreds, perhaps in their thousands. It was impossible to count them all at the time, but everywhere we turned, everywhere we looked and everywhere we went we found the contorted bodies of humans and animals. Many thousands fled to save their lives, most on foot towards the border. Some could barely walk, but crossing fields littered with dead and abandoned bodies they battled on, aware of their fate if they stopped. The air was filled with the screaming of children, people crying or shouting in panic, calling for help. For three long days Iraqi jets returned time and again, mercilessly cloaking the town and its surroundings in the suffocating clouds of death.

On 19 March, the Iranian forces moved in to the Halabja area, to announce that people should go to the border, where they had set up clinics. They provided a few helicopters to transport the most serious cases to hospitals in Iran, and sent several ambulances to pick up others along the roads.

Rabbit, Dara, Teresa and myself had one last chance to drive around Halabja, by then a ghost town littered with dead bodies. We came across a bridal couple, still in their wedding clothes, the bride clutching a bunch of red roses. Both had been poisoned, and Rabbit had just one injection left. The groom insisted that the bride should have it, while she protested that he needed it more. At last, we persuaded the man to accept it, since he had been more affected by the gas. We helped them onto their feet and they headed towards the mountains. Teresa took one last photo of a man holding his baby boy to his chest, lying by the door of their house, and then put her camera away, unable to bring herself to document any more of the horror surrounding us.

On our way out of town, I saw an Iranian cameraman filming the surreal scenes on the streets. It was then that I realised we did not have a single professional Kurdish filmmaker among the entire Peshmerga forces, or even the whole resistance, to document these extraordinary events. The destruction of the villages, the Anfaled people, the many battles and now this most horrifying act of genocide: none of this, absolutely nothing, had been recorded by Kurds. *How little our leadership know about the power of images. How little they respect the power of film, Gringo. They have been fighting for decades in the mountains and it has never occurred to them to send some young Kurds abroad to receive professional training in filming. They truly only know how to use guns.* This reminded me of Master Shamal's words, with regard to the importance of art and the role that film plays in society. *Master Shamal would have made a great leader.*

409

We got in the back of an open Peshmerga truck, but the road was blocked with dead people and their cars, so most of the time we had to drive on dirt tracks. We had used up all of our gas filters and badly needed to reach the mountains for some clean air.

'I am leaving, Mery,' Teresa said, as we took off our anti-gas gear.

'I am going across the border as soon as we get there. I need to get back to America, to report the news about Halabja.' I nodded, and stared back at Teresa blankly.

Near the border, we came across a checkpoint set up by Iranian soldiers. The commander ordered everyone off the truck. 'Who are you?' the Iranian asked, aiming his gun at Teresa.

'I am a journalist. I am Irish.'

'Passport?' he demanded. Teresa produced her passport for him to study. 'Irish?' he said. Teresa nodded. 'Not American?' He stared at Teresa suspiciously.

'No,' I answered. 'She is Irish, as she said, and we are in a hurry.'

'Welcome,' he said to Teresa, as he gave back her passport. 'Iran is in charge of the Halabja area now!' he shouted. 'We order you to put down your guns and retreat to Iran.'

'We take no orders from an Iranian,' I said. 'We are Peshmerga, and this is Kurdistan.'

'Peshmerga finished,' he answered. 'You leave your guns and go to exile in Iran.'

We refused, and pulled out our guns, standing face to face. I stood in front of Teresa to protect her. 'Perhaps you should listen and leave your guns,' Teresa said, calmly. 'He might be right to say it is finished for the Peshmerga.'

As we considered our next move, Zana and a group of his men arrived. The stand-off was broken, and the tension eased once Zana told us what he knew. The Iranian was correct in his orders, and we had to accept this if we wanted to cross the border. This was also the wish of our leadership. They wanted the surviving Peshmerga to be safe by retreating to Iran.

'We have freed our land from one enemy and now we're leaving it to another?' I demanded, angrily.

'Yes, Mery. We have no alternative,' Zana answered.

At this, the other Peshmerga put down their guns, but Dara,

Rabbit and myself held firm. 'Mery?' Zana entreated, trying to remove my gun.

'We are not going to Iran,' I answered, holding on to my weapon. 'We are only going to accompany Teresa to the border.'

'And then?' Zana insisted.

'We will return to our lines in Razga.'

Zana talked to the Iranian commander and they let us through. He got back into his jeep and left with his men. I sat on the truck floor and put my head in my hands, feeling the anger boiling the blood in my veins. Teresa put a hand on my shoulder. The truck stopped, picking up a couple along the road: it was the bride and groom who we had saved. They huddled together in a corner like a pair of frightened animals, unable to recognise us without our gas masks. I could not take my eyes off them, dressed in their wedding clothes, the bride still holding on to the wilted roses. We stopped to pick up more injured people along the way, some of whom clung desperately to the side of the truck as we bounced through difficult terrain to make it to the border. At last, we stopped by a spring to allow everyone to drink, wash and gulp in some much-needed fresh air.

I sat aside on my own. I was devastated by this turn of events. Saddam's brutality, Iran's betrayal, our leadership's miscalculation and their naive trust in Iran, all amounted to yet another catastrophic day in the history of my people. It was another blow to the armed struggle for our freedom, just as in 1975, when my uncles and thousands of other Peshmerga had been forced to put down their guns. This was all too much. Rabbit, Dara and Teresa joined me. 'Mery,' Teresa said, 'your visa is still good for America. Come with me. Jam is waiting for you, and he would love to see you in the land of your dreams.'

Such an important decision to make at such a difficult moment. I was frozen to the spot, numb, no more able to answer Teresa than I could look her in the face.

'Mery, what is going on?' Rabbit asked.

'Rabbit, this is all fucking wrong. We have lost, we should accept it, we have lost badly. It's finished.'

'What about your personal war?'

'I want to forget about the damn savage.'

'You won't be able to.'

I did not want Rabbit to see the truth in my eyes. I turned to Teresa for support.

'The Freedom for Life plan is complete,' Dara said, placing his hand on my arm. 'They are waiting for us in Kirkuk. Mery, it is now or never.'

I was buckling under their pressure. I hated to disappoint my friends so badly, to break the promises I had made to my wife and myself. Teresa gently moved Dara's hand aside. 'You will be fine, Mery,' she said. 'You come with me.'

'Rabbit, I have waited all my life for this chance. Please, Brader? As soon as I am established in America, I will come back for you, and for Jwana and Sunshine.'

'You can send for your wife, but I belong here, and will have peace nowhere else,' Rabbit said, taking hold of the gun I still clutched. 'But you, Mery, you never really belonged to this land, not in your heart. You were born to be a free soul, but were caged by fate in this godforsaken country. Now you have your angel to take you away to your so-called happiness in America.'

I let go of my gun, and watched disconsolately as Rabbit, then Dara, walked away from us. I was hurt to see my Brader so upset. *I know Sunshine will agree with my decision and will forgive me for breaking my promise, but can I forgive myself if I leave now?* I took out the photo of Sunshine and myself standing between Jam and Uncle Hitch. *Rabbit is right. How can I ever forget Shawes Dog?*

'Teresa, what will I do in America?' I said, keeping my eyes on the photo.

'You will start a new life in New York. You could go to the film academy, if that is what you want. You could make films about your people, about the many stories that you have, which hardly anyone is aware of. More than half the world do not even know that Kurds exist, let alone who they are, where they live, and in what tragic circumstances. You could become your people's ambassador. That is what Jam is doing, not through films, but by writing articles for the newspapers.'

'Does Jam ever talk about someone called Abu Ali?'

'Yes. It was Abu Ali who handed him to the Iraqis.'

'Teresa, I can't go to America.'

'Why?'

'I will never be happy if I leave now.'

'What about all your dreams, what about meeting your hero?'

'Listen, this is the most difficult decision I have ever had to make. I ask you to understand, please?'

'Does it have anything to do with Abu Ali?'

'Can we not talk about him ever again, not even if I come to America?'

'I won't, as long as you come.'

'I will, I mean I will do my best, I promise on my heart,' I said, solemnly placing my hand on my chest. 'I want to come, I have dreamt so many times of walking down the street to meet my Gringo. I have not changed my mind, but I can't leave yet. I have one last obligation to fulfil.'

Teresa looked me in the eyes. I did not want her to press me. I took out my notebook. 'I have almost finished writing my story. Please, will you take it with you to America?' Teresa nodded.

'Thank you. I have written it for Gringo, but you should only give it to him if I don't make it.'

Rabbit sat atop the driver's cabin, as usual, reminding me of the time when we had our first argument about religion. I climbed up alongside him and poked a finger into the side of his belly. Rabbit jerked, yelling spontaneously, 'Hey, motherfucker,' and did everything he could not to laugh. 'Brader, I am not going to America,' I said. 'Not until we put down the Dog.'

Rabbit beamed with pleasure, and handed back my gun. He stood up on the cabin and stretched out his arms, and starting to flap them as if flying. 'Spread your wings, Mery,' he called, 'and fly, fly far away with me to the land of peace and freedom.'

Just as on the day when we returned from the desert, we flapped our arms like wings, performing for Teresa, who raised her camera and captured our fleeting liberation to freeze it forever.

Farewell my Angel

This morning, Teresa Miller is leaving us. She is going back to the United States of America, taking with her all that I possess: my story. I call it 'The Good, the Bad, and the Gringo'. We are travelling slowly, a couple of kilometres from the Iranian border. I still have the colourful scarf around my neck, the one I bought from Aida. I am sitting on the floor of the truck, the AK-47 in my lap, and on top of it, my notebook. I am writing you the final few pages of my story. Teresa, not far from me, is taking pictures of the exhausted people walking, and of the many dead left on both sides of the track. Many more are crowding in and hanging on to the sides of our vehicle, and among the crowd in the back of the truck are a family of four lying huddled together, badly injured by the gas.

We round a sharp bend and the driver slams on the brakes. The road through the hills, which is little more than a track, is blocked by other cars and tractors. There are carts pulled by mules and donkeys too, carrying survivors and victims, heading in the same direction. As we jump off, Teresa takes one last shot of a dying family's children. Their innocent faces are now covered with inflamed yellow blisters, their eyes deeply sunken under swollen eyelids. They are crying for their lifeless mother and father lying next to them.

A boy trips and lets go of his blind grandmother's hand, screaming after her as she slides down the hill. No one has any energy left to help. It is a disaster beyond belief.

We push our way through. From the top of the hill I can see two giant posters of the Mullahs with their long white beards marking the border. One must be the Iranian president and the other, Imam Khomeini, both men who promised that they would never cease fighting before they saw Saddam Hussein crushed. I look around me. Instead of spring flowers, all I can see is a sea of people moving forwards. I watch the Iranian border guards on the other side ruthlessly pushing back the masses, as if they were pushing back helpless herds of sick animals.

I shut my notebook.

'Jam gave me this,' I said, as I held up my notebook to Teresa. '"Write your story as if it were a film, Mery",' he told me at the time.'

She took a photo of me, my notebook still in my hand.

'Jam! I laughed when he first told me his name,' I said, with a smile.

'I did the same when I first heard it.' But now Teresa didn't smile. *Jam is going to be disappointed to have his love coming home without me.*

'He is a true friend to me...' I faltered, unable to complete the sentence. 'If I make it to America, the first thing I will do is to give him a big hug, the biggest.'

'I wish you could come with me to New York, now.' As if she knew it was her last attempt to change my mind, she stood, looking deep into my eyes, but I shook my head. She hung her camera over her shoulder and held my face in her kind hands. 'Do you absolutely have to do this?'

'Yes,' I answered, without hesitation. I didn't feel so certain inside, but I didn't want her to see that I had doubts.

'Be careful. You are still very young, and I want you to come to America. I am sure Gringo will be very happy to meet you, too.'

'Sorry, Teresa,' Dara said, gently. 'Time to go.'

I folded Aida's scarf around the Super 8 film and my notebook. I held it up to my face like a sacred book and kissed it, closing my eyes. Then I handed my story over to Teresa.

'Do you mind if I read it first?' she said.

I wished that she had not asked. When I started to write my story I promised myself that Gringo would be the first to read it, so I was reluctant to agree, but I knew I owed her that much. She put her arms around me. For a brief moment I was lost once again in a film world and, for once, I was the hero in the arms of someone who genuinely cared for me. No longer was I Mery, used and abused by the Iraqi Mukhabarat, by Abu Ali, and tormented by the brutal realities of gas attacks and our leadership's misplaced trust in our Iranian enemies.

It all seemed so surreal, surrounded as we were by desperate people pushing past us, shoving us from side to side, crying and screaming. Here I was, embracing this woman, having known her for less than a couple of weeks. Yet she had given me hope, like no one ever had before. I drew my arms more tightly around her, breathing in deeply to fill my lungs and heart with all her trust and care. 'Thank you Teresa,' I said, still hugging her. 'My story is the most precious thing I possess.'

Now Teresa was battling her own tears. 'I will get it to him. I promise,' and she put my hand on her heart.

I barely registered her parting from me, and she had neared the border post, almost lost in the sea of people, when I called out,

'Teresa! Wait.' I ran to her and took the folder out of her backpack. 'I need to write a few more words,' I said.

Dear Mr Clint Eastwood,

Please forgive me for not taking the opportunity to leave for America, which I have dreamt of for so many years. Recently I told myself that this time nothing would stop me from leaving, nothing would deter me from my path and hold me back from going to you. I would have loved to fly out with Teresa, but I hope you can understand. I do not wish to keep Teresa any longer. I have to stop writing now. Please wish me luck, my dear Gringo, for my last task, because soon I want to be on my way to you. Thank you, with all my heart.

Your friend,
Mery Rashaba

P.S. The last chapter of my life I hope you will hear from me personally – if I live and make it to see you in America, that is. Or from my dear friend, Teresa, if I die.

The war is mine

Kirkuk, April 1988

A black four-wheel drive, with two fake Jash riding in it to guard us, followed closely as we drove down the highway to Kirkuk. We were clean-shaven, wearing new Kurdish clothes, sunglasses and turbans, and Dara was at the wheel of a brand-new black Toyota Super. Rabbit was alongside him and I was in the back seat. Dara had a pistol on his belt and an AK-47 hanging on the back of his seat. Rabbit had an AK-47 in his lap and I was holding an RPG. I also had a pistol and a couple of grenades on my belt, which was part of the disguise, as this was perfectly normal for Jash fighters, the traitorous dogs.

'Remember my name?' Dara asked. 'I am Mustashar Harzani, one of the most respected Kurdish Jash leaders, and you are my personal guards. Yes?'

'Yes,' Rabbit and I answered, nodding. Dara burst out laughing.

'I can't wait to get to the Kirkuk checkpoint,' he said, as he accelerated, indicating for the 'guards' behind us to do the same.

The Iraqis at the checkpoints were in a mood of celebration. They believed they had crushed the Kurdish armed resistance once and for all, and with our fake identities we went through without any problems. Kirkuk was never beautiful, but as the place where I had grown up and met Sunshine, with so many of my memories trapped in its streets, I could not help but feel emotional as we entered the city.

'Put on your sunglasses, Mery,' Dara said, watching me in the rear-view mirror. 'A Jash is a real man, and real men don't cry.'

The four-wheel drive overtook us and we followed them. They stopped outside an elegant detached house in the Azadi district, on the outskirts of Kirkuk, and immediately took up a position by the side of the main door to guard the surroundings. Rabbit and I kept watch, while Dara, gun in hand, pressed the buzzer twice. Dara's man in Kirkuk, the organiser of the Freedom for Life Operation, opened the metal door, as expected. He had covered his face with a turban.

'I must know everyone involved,' I said, as I walked in. 'So please show yourself.'

The man turned to Dara, then to Rabbit, and they both nodded. This puzzled me. He began to unfold his turban, but before he had exposed his face, my mouth fell open in shock. 'Kojak?' I asked, astonished.

'Yes, Kojak,' Dara said. 'Excuse me for not calling you Arpa,' Dara embraced him. 'Kojak has always been the one I could trust most in the mountains. But of course, Mery, we owe you an explanation.'

'After you came up with the Freedom for Life Operation,' Rabbit took over, 'I suggested Kojak for the job and invented the story of his poisoning five Peshmerga. Dara accepted it as the best disguise for Kojak, to give him credit with the Mukhabarat and his father.'

'Shawes Dog's old trick,' Rabbit clarified. 'He used a similar story to change his own identity in his transition from murderer to Abu Ali.'

'Kojak returned to Kirkuk on my orders and since then he has worked for the Mukhabarat and, of course, for us, preparing your plan,' Dara said. 'Thanks to him, we are back in Kirkuk.'

'Why did you hide it from me?' I asked.

'Your reaction to Kojak's story of poisoning Peshmerga was the best way of spreading the rumour, and it was necessary for the Mukhabarat to get the news from different sources, as we know there are spies even amongst our Peshmerga. If Merywan Rashaba believed it was a true story, so did everyone else.'

'I am so glad that you are still one of us,' I said, and shook Kojak's hand.

'If we succeed,' Kojak explained. 'We will be remembered for having accomplished one of the most important operations ever to take place in Kirkuk by Kurdish Peshmerga.'

'And if we fail?' Rabbit asked.

'The Dog will not kill us on the spot. He would rather take us alive, to publicly slice us open bit by bit. As you're well aware, we need to be prepared for all possible outcomes. Are you with me?' We could only nod. 'But I have one request,' Kojak said, looking into my eyes. 'I want to put down the Dog myself.'

I was taken aback for a moment, and my face must have registered my surprise, but Kojak waited patiently for my response. *I had refused to go away with Teresa to America, and had come to Kirkuk because I want to kill Shawes myself.* However, I soon found it in myself to grant his wish. 'You are his son. I will leave him for you.' I told him.

We spent that night in the house, running over the details of our mission until we were sure we were ready. While the others slept, I wrote about our journey from the border and how we made it to this place. Reading Gringo's words on the back of his photo, I was inspired to have another heart-to-heart.

'Dear Gringo, you should know that after leaving Teresa on the border and before heading for Kirkuk to accomplish our mission, I first wanted to see Sunshine. I really did not want to leave my wife alone at such a difficult time. I was anxious about her and wanted to make sure she was safe. We had to delay our journey to Kirkuk because Dara was trying to make contact with our lines in Razga. When he finally succeeded, Dara did not have good news. After the fall of the headquarters, all the surviving villagers in the area were evacuated to Iran, to refugee camps. Sunshine and her mother were amongst them. I wish I had had a chance to see my wife. I love her dearly and I miss her very much. My Gringo, I ask you and Teresa to please help Sunshine get to America just in case things don't go to plan. My ardent wish is for our child to be born in a free country.' I pulled out Sunshine's pendant and kissed it.

Rabbit, Dara, Kojak and I were the only people who knew the name of our target. I chose the morning of 28 April 1988, because on that day we knew Shawes Dog would drive down Republic Street on his way to the Mukhabarat. I also wanted to make the attack a special present for Saddam Hussein's birthday.

In the dark, I could only hear the sound of Kojak's heavy breathing and the noise of the traffic. Kojak and I were hidden in the boot of a taxi driven by Dara. *White and orange taxis were common in town; we would blend in and would not arouse suspicion when we followed Shawes Dog's car.* Once we were done with Shawes, we were to leave the taxi burning at the entrance of Ahmad Agha market and get into our Jash Toyota Super, guarded by our two fake Jash men. We had gone through the plan so many times that I could tell even from the dark boot when we were driving towards Qala, across the old bridge, turning onto Kornish Street and cutting left towards the one-way Republic Street, our final destination. Before we got to the Salahadin Cinema, I pushed out the back seat and could hear the loudspeakers along the street playing nationalist songs for Saddam's birthday.

'Rabbit, what are they showing in the Salahadin Cinema?'

'*Where Eagles Dare*,' Rabbit yelled, sitting in the passenger's seat.

'Great film,' I said.

Dara parked the car outside the famous Fakhri Pharmacy, following my plan to the letter.

'What are you going to buy, Rabbit?' Dara asked.

'Condoms,' he said.

Despite the tension, we laughed. Rabbit got out to buy some headache tablets; an excuse to park and wait.

Dara beeped once and immediately followed this by beeping twice more – the signal that he could see the target coming out of Doctor's Road and driving onto Republic Street. Rabbit quickly got back in and Dara drove away.

'Approaching the target,' Dara said. 'Get into position.'

'Good luck Dara, good luck Kojak, good luck Rabbit,' I said.

'And up Kissinger's bum!'

'Up Kissinger's bum!' everyone answered together.

We had a last laugh together. I charged my AK-47 in the dark. One shorter beep indicated that we were following the target. I felt the car accelerate, and I knew this was it: we must be overtaking the four-wheel drive. *I wish I could see Shawes Dog's irritated face, for nobody is allowed to pass him.* At one longer beep, I opened the boot's cover and flung a sack of nails onto the road behind us. The four-wheel drive swerved to avoid them, but the nails went home, puncturing the tyres. Behind them, a beetroot-juice seller's three-wheeled cart was moving into the middle of the road, blocking the traffic. Dara pressed on the brakes, and the taxi's tyres screeched. We were on target just outside Jam's shop, exactly as we had planned.

Everything happened at once. I pushed up and pulled off the boot's cover. Kojak lifted the RPG and positioned the heavy gun on his shoulder. Rabbit leapt from the car, and we both opened fire on Shawes Dog's men, with Dara providing cover. Bystanders, panicking, ran for their lives. This was a scene I never thought I would witness in the centre of Kirkuk, on the street where I had lived my most treasured moments with Uncle Hitch, Jam, Aida and Sunshine.

A blast from behind the four-wheel drive rocked Republic Street. We knew it was a fairly small explosion, but nobody else did. Pieces of the beetroot-juice seller's cart flew in all directions, but the man himself was safe. He had already repositioned himself and was opening fire on our target from behind. Shawes Dog was trapped in his bullet-proof car. Rabbit and I had his guards under control, because if they risked leaving the car we would finish them off. It was all going to plan and we had an easy target. But Kojak hesitated.

'Shoot, Kojak, we don't have time,' I called, as I sprayed bullets near the doors of the vehicle again.

'I can't, he is my father, my hands are frozen. I just can't...' Shawes Dog leant out of the window with his pistol, shooting desperately, barely aiming. I felt I could have safely stood still all day if he had been the only danger. I returned fire and he swiftly ducked back inside, while two of his guards leapt out of the back doors, firing in wide sweeps as passers-by dived for cover, or huddled behind their shopping bags, as if tomatoes and rice would protect them.

Iraqi police fired at us from the street side, and a couple from behind us. The whole street echoed with gunshots. 'Shoot, damn it,' I called again. 'Shoot, you are right on target!' I heard Dara and Rabbit shouting for Kojak, as they fired their guns. I turned to Kojak. 'Shoot the bastard traitor, now! Shoot!'

'OK,' Kojak stammered unconvincingly, before stumbling backwards as a bullet struck him. Shock registered on his face, but he had only been hit on his left arm, and I could see that he would be alright.

I grabbed the RPG from him, put the launcher on my shoulder and took aim, only to feel a bullet tearing into my stomach. I glanced down to assess the damage, and saw that the bullet had merely skimmed through my top rather than ripping open my guts, puncturing and searing my skin as it passed.

For a split second I saw a vision of Jam outside his shop watching me, Uncle Hitch taking stills, and Aida, my Christian princess, and Sunshine smiling at me. My focus snapped back, aimed the RPG and pulled the trigger. The rocket flew straight to the target, but Shawes Dog scrambled out of the car just in time. The car's reinforced steel doors blew off with deadly force, but they landed well clear of his cowering form.

He hid behind a lamp post as the four-wheel drive exploded around us. Rabbit helped Kojak into the taxi. As Shawes Dog got up to run, I shot him in the leg and he slumped to the ground. His driver and two guards were dead, but two others were still firing from the roadside. Dara, Rabbit and Kojak, despite his injury, kept firing at them until there was just one left, hidden behind the wreckage of the car.

More Iraqi army men were joining the skirmish, but they too were under fire, as Freedom for Life underground members that Kojak had planted opened up from the rooftops of nearby shops and buildings. Republic Street had become a war zone.

Shawes Dog had lost his pistol but was crawling towards one of his dead guards' guns. I ran and kicked the gun away, just as he reached his hand towards it. I grabbed him by his neck and dragged him to the middle of the road, right opposite Jam's shop and under a large poster of Saddam Hussein. I clutched his hair and bent back his head so that his face was looking up towards me.

'Don't shoot, please! Don't kill me...'

The Dog is crying and pleading at my feet.

'I will get you, Shawes Dog,' I moved my lips in the same way he used to say 'I will get you, Mery', and I pointed my pistol at his forehead.

'Mery!' Shawes Dog gasped. 'Mery Rashaba! Mery, please...' he said, doing his dying best to soften my heart.

'Mery, shoot the Dog and get back in the car,' Rabbit called.

I wanted to shoot him slowly, painfully, a bullet in his arms or legs for every person I so loved that he had taken away from me, but I could not risk our lives any longer. 'For my family, my friends and for my wife Sunshine!' I shot him in the head and put down the Dog once and for all.

I looked up at the poster of Saddam Hussein. 'Happy birthday, Mr President,' I called out, taking aim at Saddam's face.

Not a bad shot for an amateur of seventeen-year-old, eh, Gringo? I got him right between the eyes.

I was hit again, and this time I knew it was bad. The bullet ripped into my chest, piercing Gringo's photo in my pocket.

'Mery!' was the last thing I heard Rabbit shouting.

This could be the end, Gringo! Not such a sad end, my friend. The people of Kirkuk can now live with more hope.

'Mery, my love, you did it!'

Is that you, Sunshine? I opened my eyes. I was in my private viewing room, where my friends and I could be safe, and the best place I could have wished to be in that moment, in my magic world, in my beloved cinema.

I was on the floor, in Rabbit's arms, waiting for Norman to arrive with the doctor. Norman's projector was running, showing *The Good, the Bad and the Ugly*. I could hear that the soundtrack had reached the final scene where Gringo, my hero, the Good one nicknamed 'Blondie', shoots the Bad one and says to Ugly, 'You see, in this world there are two kinds of people, my friend: those with loaded guns and those who dig. You dig.' I knew the film so well, and mouthed the words along with my hero.

My dear Gringo, I am ready. Let's ride on, there are so many places I need to see, so many people to meet, cultures to explore, stories to tell. And so many films to make...

To the thousands of young girls and boys tortured to death,
The thousands of innocents killed by napalm bombs and chemical gas,
To the one hundred and eighty thousand civilians killed by Anfal,
All murdered by Saddam Hussein and his regime
And to the many Mery Rashabas who fought for their freedom but were not allowed to live life as they wished.